Herald Square

Herald Square
A novel of the Cold War

Jefferson Flanders

Munroe Hill Press

Excerpt from *Here is New York*, Copyright © 1949, 1976 by E.B. White.
Reprinted by permission.

Cover design by Mick Wieland Design
Cover photo © Louie Psihoyos/Science Faction/Corbis

ISBN: 0-6156-4368-X
ISBN-13: 9780615643687
LCCN: 2012940866
Munroe Hill Press
Lexington, MA

Printed in the United States of America

For my parents

"What makes a good newspaperman? The answer is easy. He knows everything. He is aware not only of what goes on in the world today, but his brain is a repository of the accumulated wisdom of the ages. He is not only handsome, but he has the physical strength which enables him to perform great feats of energy. He can go for nights on end without sleep. He dresses well and talks with charm. Men admire him; women adore him; tycoons and statesmen are willing to share their secrets with him. He hates lies and meanness and sham, but he keeps his temper. He is loyal to his paper and to what he looks upon as the profession; whether it is a profession, or merely a craft, he resents attempts to debate it. When he dies, a lot of people are sorry, and some of them remember him for several days."

- Stanley Walker, city editor, *New York Herald Tribune*

Part One

Friday, September 23, 1949

She had dreaded this day. They had left her alone for more than a year, but in the back of her mind she had known that the time would come when they would want to make use of her. Now, without any warning, she had been summoned.

The phone call came at nine o'clock that morning, just after she had finished her second cup of tea. When she answered, a man's voice, muffled, asked whether she was expecting a special delivery. She realized at once that it was the recognition code. She collected herself and responded as she had been instructed: "Not today, I believe that it's scheduled for tomorrow."

The voice—calm, deliberate, emotionless—slowly recited the time and place for a meeting. Then the phone line clicked dead, breaking the connection. She could feel her heart racing, and she tried to calm herself and focus on what she had to do next.

She got up from her desk, slightly dazed, and found her coat and umbrella. She made her way through the lobby to the women's room. She was lucky: it was empty. She felt a choking wave of nausea and she reached the stall in time to vomit her breakfast into the toilet.

She went to the sink and washed her hands and face with luke-warm water. When she looked in the mirror, she was startled by her sudden paleness. She pinched her cheeks roughly until they showed some color. She did not want to draw any attention when she left the Center. She gathered her coat and umbrella. Her watch showed 9:15, which gave her thirty minutes to reach the meeting place, Straus Park, three city blocks north.

On her way through the lobby, she greeted an older couple from Budapest with a quick nod and a forced smile, not trusting herself to stop and talk. She glanced over at the large wall map of the United States, dotted with colored pushpins marking every community where the Center had relocated a displaced person. She had helped many of the refugees find homes in their new homeland and she envied them for the safe harbor they had reached. That same outcome awaited the latest batch of DPs now crowded into the Hotel Marseilles, the shabby Upper West Side way station that had become a temporary home for the Center and its seemingly endless stream of refugees. It would not be true for her.

For a moment, she thought of running. She could stop at her apartment, collect her clothing and her $300 in cash savings, take a taxi to Grand Central, and catch the first train west. She could find some obscure place, perhaps one of the pushpins on the map, and hide as best she could. Yet it was not time to panic, she told herself. Once she learned what they wanted from her, she could decide whether to stay or to flee. When she accepted their help she had known that there would be a price. Now it appeared that the bill had come due and she needed to know what it might cost.

Outside, it was cool and gray, the air heavy with the threat of rain. At the 103rd Street subway station, she took the Broadway local one stop south, to 96th Street. She quickly stepped off the train a moment before the doors closed. She crossed up and over to the platform on the other side of the station and took the next local train back uptown to the Cathedral Parkway stop. As she left the train, she looked for any familiar faces from the downtown local and found none. She was confident she had not been followed. Once on the street, she walked east, along the north side of 110th Street, stopping at Amsterdam Avenue.

She waited for the traffic light to change, carefully scanning both sides of the street, alert for anyone watching. Once heading south on Amsterdam, she stopped twice on her way—first briefly to admire the roses in the window of a florist shop and then to duck into an apartment building doorway and fiddle with her umbrella—that let her again check to make sure that she had no followers.

She turned west, picking up the pace as she moved toward her destination, an island of green at the intersection of Broadway, West

End Avenue, and 106th Street that was named Straus Park. It was a well-chosen spot for their meeting. There were numerous benches in the park partially screened by a canopy of trees that still had their leaves. Anyone approaching could be easily spotted, and there were multiple exit points from the park.

Once she crossed to the park entrance, she spotted a man sitting on a nearby bench, a rolled-up umbrella in his right hand, the all-clear signal. The other benches were empty. When she got closer, she came to a dead stop—it was Morris Rose, her friend, her former lover, the man who had helped bring her to the United States, who had arranged for her job at the Center with the United Service for New Americans.

He glanced over and smiled when he recognized her. He motioned for her to join him on the bench.

"You look quite lovely, Karina," he said. "New York has agreed with you."

"I did not expect it would be you," she said.

"I'm sorry that I couldn't identify myself on the phone earlier."

"You gave me a fright. I thought it was one of them and—"

"No," he said, raising his hand slightly to stop her from continuing. "It doesn't have to do with them. Just me. I apologize. I couldn't meet you at the Marseilles and risk being recognized. But we have privacy here, and we can talk, as long as the rain holds off."

"Are you in some sort of trouble?"

"Afraid so. It looks like I've been compromised. I think I may have been tailed on the train from Washington, but I've lost them. That is, if they were there, and I didn't imagine them. Under the circumstances, it's hard not to be a bit paranoid."

She remained silent. Whatever he needed from her, he would tell her, but in his own good time. She knew how Morris thought. They had first met in Warsaw in late February 1946 when Sasha had introduced her to "the *Amerikanski*," as he called Morris, over a leisurely vodka-fueled lunch at the Polonia Palace Hotel's restaurant. The hotel was one of the few buildings in the city that hadn't been destroyed by the Germans after the Uprising. Foreign embassies and their diplomats had taken up quarters there.

She had surprised Sasha by conversing with Morris in English. Later, Sasha made her promise never to speak English in public again when he was around, for fear that word would reach the *zampolit*, the deputy commander for political work, and that Sasha's loyalty might be questioned.

Morris Rose had not impressed her at that first lunch. He had seemed soft, bookish, a weakling compared to the hard-bitten veteran Red Army officers in Sasha's circle, but her initial impression proved wrong. Morris was much tougher than he looked. He was decisive, not afraid to wield his influence, a clout she thought stemmed from his diplomatic status but later learned derived from a different place, from connections that Sasha and the other Russians respected and feared.

Now she studied his face as they sat together on a park bench thousands of miles from their initial meeting. Morris had aged noticeably since she had last seen him more than a year earlier. He looked tired, slightly gaunt. Streaks of gray now appeared in his once-glossy black hair. He fumbled with a package of Lucky Strikes and offered her one. She shook her head and waited as he lighted up and enjoyed a long drag.

"I've been careless," he said. "Stupidly so. Now I must try to fix this by myself, without involving our Russian friends. I haven't told Bob. No one knows that we are meeting. So this chat is unofficial, off the books."

"What do you need from me?"

"A simple favor. I must leave something of value with a friend here in the city. For safekeeping. Then I'll be away for a few days to give me time to assess the damage. Next week I may need you to pass a message to this friend. He will be holding my property. After tonight I won't be able to risk contacting him directly. Certainly not by telephone. So I need a go-between and you're the one person I can trust." He paused. "Will you help me, Karina?"

She nodded without hesitating. How could she refuse him? She owed Morris her life, after all. He had sheltered her after Sasha was recalled to Moscow in 1947, hiring her as his personal interpreter. Somehow he finagled a Polish passport for her, despite her Latvian nationality, and then arranged for her to leave Poland with him, to travel first to Vienna, and then, miraculously to the United States.

She had become his lover within weeks of Sasha's departure from Warsaw. They found mutual comfort in his narrow hotel bed, if not a deeper connection, but there were clear and silent boundaries to their relationship. She knew that he was married to an American wife who he never mentioned. He must have known something about her past, before Sasha, but he never asked her about Piotr and she never volunteered.

Months into their relationship, when he trusted her, he told her about his other life, his double life. He called it his small contribution toward fashioning a better world out of the ruins of the past. He was puzzled that she couldn't share his fervor for that transformation, but she had seen too much by then. She detested the slogans and the hard men mouthing them. Their affair ended when they left Austria. There was no emotional crisis, no angry break, just the mutual recognition that they were not well suited for each other.

Morris touched her arm and she realized he had asked her a question. She had been lost in her memories. "Can you go out tonight?" he asked. "To meet with my friend?"

She nodded. She would miss the Rosh Hashanah services at the Center, but she could make some excuse, perhaps that she wasn't feeling well. Morris explained that he had arranged for her to be casually introduced to his friend, through another man, Lonnie Marks, a press agent.

Marks would take her to a nightclub where Morris' friend, a newspaperman named Dennis Collins, liked to go on Fridays. If Collins turned up, Marks would try to pitch a story about the Center to him and would offer Karina for an interview, establishing a pretext for her to see Collins again.

"It's best if you meet by what appears to be chance," Morris said. "No mention of me. Should things fall apart, the less Collins knows, the better. The same for you. Only when you pass the message to him, later in the week, should he know of your and my connection."

"What is he like?"

"Denny? We've been friends since we were five years old. We haven't seen each other as much, lately, being in different cities. The war changed things for him. He had a hard time adjusting when he first got back. I guess it changed things for all of us, didn't it?"

"It did."

Morris rose to his feet. He looked up at the sky for a moment, gauging the weather. He cinched the belt tighter on his trench coat. She stood up as well.

"Do you ever come to this park?" he asked. He didn't wait for her answer. "Quite a strange place. A memorial for a rich couple, Isidor and Ida Straus, who drowned on the Titanic." She followed his glance over to the centerpiece of the park, a bronze statue of a young woman reclining above a small fountain, one leg dangling gracefully toward the water.

"No mention of the working men and women trapped in steerage below decks," he said bitterly. "They aren't remembered, but the heirs to Macy's, their oppressors, get their own public park." He shook his head, his mouth forming the tight smile that Karina knew signaled his anger. "Someday that will change, mark my words."

Then he turned back to her and, his mood changing, smiled with genuine warmth. "Thank you for helping, Karina," he said. "I will be in touch."

She watched him leave the park, bouncing slightly on his toes as he walked, a confident, boyish lope that she had come to think of as distinctly American.

She shivered. For the second time that morning, she felt the urge to flee. She wanted to run from the park, to leave New York, and find someplace to hide. Her hands began to tremble and she fought against the feeling of being trapped.

But she stayed, reseated on the bench. She waited patiently for ten minutes, following the rules she had been taught, even though the park remained deserted. Then she slowly rose to her feet and began the walk back to the Center.

One

Virginia Allen Bradford didn't belong at the Garden on fight night, with or without him.

It was hardly the place for an elegant girl like Penny, Collins told himself ruefully. The noisy building would be crammed with thousands of beery New Yorkers cheering, or cursing, the cut-rate gladiators frantically exchanging punches in the arena's square, canvas-floored ring. The stale smoke from countless cigars and cigarettes would fill the air with a bluish-gray haze, and there would be no escaping the sour-sweet smell of spilled Rheingold beer. You'd never bring a nice girl there on a Friday night date, Collins thought, but Penny put the lie to that, because there they were, and she was unquestionably a nice girl.

In fact, she had insisted on coming. It was her idea to watch Collins at work, even if that meant sitting through the undercard fights before drinks and dinner, so he had reluctantly called the Garden front office and had them hold two seats fifteen rows back from the ring. He didn't want Penny situated too near the brutality of a prize fight. Some sportswriters might call it the sweet science, but when you got up close there was nothing sweet about blood splattering onto the canvas, or a battered fighter's legs folding under him when, punched into insensibility, he crashed to the floor. No, better to have some distance from the ring.

"I've never been to a boxing match," Penny told him after they reached their seats. "I'm looking forward to this."

"I didn't ever think the fights would appeal to you," Collins said. They were still a little tentative with each other, wary, a tacit acknowledgment of the awkwardness of their shared past. "It's not the opera."

Penny wrinkled her nose. "I've never liked the opera."

"So then it's not Broadway. The Friday night fights can get a bit crude. They don't exactly draw the high society set."

"You learn something new every day," she said, playfully.

Then the bell rang, signaling the start of the evening's first bout. Collins reluctantly turned away from Penny, a stylish vision of loveliness in her tailored light-blue jacket with cinched waist and matching wide skirt, a strand of pearls circling her neck. With rationing over the fashion designers could use more material, and the new style accentuated Penny's slim figure and long legs. Her blonde hair was pulled back the way he had always been crazy about, highlighting her throat and the graceful nape of her neck. It had been too long since she had been at his side. While he knew he shouldn't stare at her, he wanted to, desperately. Who could blame him?

The opening fight was a six-round preliminary between lightweights, a warm-up for the later bouts. The fighters wasted no time after the bell rang, rushing at each other and swinging away for dear life. Collins glanced at the fight program, curious about the young boxer in dark green shorts who kept throwing a sneaky left jab. He was a Jersey City fighter named Frankie Marino with a listed weight of 131 pounds, a pound more than his opponent, a skinny Cuban named Velez.

Marino apparently didn't accept the conventional boxing wisdom that lightweights didn't have power, Collins thought, because he pinned Velez in a corner and started pounding away. The crowd urged him on, blood lust up, yelling for an early knockout, and Velez was lucky to stay upright until the bell rang, ending the round.

"He is quite cocky, isn't he?" Penny asked, nodding toward Marino's corner.

"The kid? A real show boat."

"Will he win?"

"Can't say."

"That's strange, Dennis. No predictions? I remember that you were always ready to make a prediction."

Collins shrugged. "Not anymore. I've lost my touch, I guess. Take tonight, for example. I never would have predicted that you would be here with me."

"I guess that makes me unpredictable," she said, lightly.

"I'm not complaining. It's great to see you again."

"Yes, it's great, isn't it?" She must have seen something she didn't like in his face because she glanced back at the ring, breaking off eye contact. Collins felt himself flushing, embarrassed. He was determined not to come on too strong, not to rush things with her. He wondered, not for the first time, whether she was having second thoughts about their date.

When Collins had telephoned Penny and asked her out, he told her that he wasn't calling just as an old friend. She had laughed and responded that since he had just turned thirty-two, he couldn't possibly be an old friend. Collins would have understood if she had turned him down: why bother with the complications of their past, with the bad memories? So when, in the end, she said yes, he had been caught by surprise. When they settled on Friday night for their date, he was even more surprised that Penny wanted to accompany him to the Garden rather than simply meeting him at a nightclub.

"I never quite understood your world," she said. "Before, I mean. Perhaps I can understand it this time."

"I'm flattered by the attention," he told her, and Collins had loved that she said "this time," with all that phrase seemed to promise.

As he had explained to her, his visit to the Garden was solely to watch the second fight on the card, which featured Gentleman Jack O'Reilly, an up-and-coming heavyweight from Brooklyn. O'Reilly's manager, Phil Santry, had been pushing Collins to come see his new fighter. With Joe Louis retiring, Santry hoped that Gentleman Jack could become one of the contenders in the now wide open heavyweight division. While Collins knew, and disliked, Santry from the old days, he agreed to watch O'Reilly fight because of the Brooklyn angle. Collins was always looking for stories that would appeal to readers in Flatbush and Greenpoint and Bensonhurst where the *Sentinel* sold well.

As the lightweights stood up in their respective corners, ready for the second round, Collins felt Penny gently tugging at his sleeve. She pointed to one of the ushers in the aisle, a boy in his late teens, who was beckoning to them. Collins rose from his seat and reluctantly made his way to the aisle, pushing past resentful fans as he momentarily blocked their view of the ring.

"Are you Dennis Collins?" the boy asked when he reached the aisle. "The newspaper guy?"

"That's me."

He gestured for Collins to follow him. Collins turned and waved to Penny, pointing to let her know where he was headed. She smiled and waved back. The bell for the second round was sounding as Collins trailed the usher out of the arena into the relative quiet of the entrance hallway.

"What's this all about?" Collins got right to the point. He didn't like leaving Penny alone.

"I dunno," the usher said. "A guy tipped me a dollar to pass this note to you and to make sure that you read it."

He handed Collins a plain, unaddressed envelope, sealed. Collins ripped it open to find a piece of expensive cream-colored stationary inside, folded in half; he nodded to the boy. "Don't worry. I'll read it. You can go."

Collins was sure to read it. Writing a column for the *Sentinel* six days a week, roughly half of the time on sports, half on politics and city life, meant he was always on the lookout for good material, especially since he couldn't afford stringers or assistants like Winchell and Cannon and Conniff and the other big name columnists. Story ideas and tips came from the strangest places. After the usher had left, Collins scanned the note:

Denny,
Meet me by the box office. Alone. It's important.
Morris

It had to be Morris Rose, his closest friend from childhood. Collins hadn't seen him for more than a year. Morris rarely made it back to New York from Washington, where he worked for the State Department. Collins wondered, annoyed, why his friend hadn't come down to ringside if whatever he wanted to talk about was so important.

Collins made his way back to his seats to explain to Penny what was happening. "I have to step away for a few minutes," he told her. "A friend with some sort of problem needs to see me. He's here at the Garden. I'll make it as fast as humanly possible."

She gave him a forced smile. "Of course, attend to your friend."

"I'll make it fast," he said. "I promise."

He hurried through the labyrinth of the Garden's ground floor corridors. Some fight-goers were milling around in the corridors, not interested in the preliminaries, and a fair number of fans were still arriving, so it took Collins several minutes to work his way through the crowded hallway to the lobby.

He was impatient and irritated by the time he located Morris Rose by the box office windows. Morris was impeccably dressed in a russet-colored suit, his white handkerchief making a neat triangle in his front pocket. He had a trench coat under his arm. Morris shook Collins' hand eagerly, flashing a wide grin. Collins found himself grinning back, his irritation evaporating.

"Too long," Morris said. "It's been too long, Denny boy."

"You're the big Washington insider, now. Too busy to see the plain folks back home."

"And you're the famous columnist-about-town. Was that Penny Allen with you?"

Collins nodded. Morris must have spotted them in their seats before he sent the usher with the message.

"She looks lovely." He arched his eyebrows. "Thought she was ancient history. Considering how it worked out for you two the last time."

Collins ignored the comment. "How did you track me down here?"

"Friday night? Big fight at the Garden? Where else would you be?"

That made sense, and Morris had always been a precise, logical thinker. He would have made a perfect Jesuit, Collins had always maintained, if his parents, dedicated Socialists, hadn't raised him as a freethinker.

"And I tried calling you at the *Sentinel*," Morris said. "You weren't in, but I told them that I was your long lost cousin from Dublin and one of the editors thought that you might be here. You were, except I didn't expect Penny to be here slumming along with you."

"We're only here for the O'Reilly fight, then to dinner."

"Reservations at the Stork, I'd imagine."

Collins nodded. "Am I that predictable?"

"Nothing wrong with being predictable."

Collins was becoming impatient. He made a show of checking his watch and saw it had been ten minutes since he left Penny. Morris ignored the hint.

"So what do you think?" Morris asked. "Are we going to take the pennant?"

"Only half a game out," Collins responded, wondering, with more than a touch of irritation, why his friend didn't drop the small talk and get straight to the point.

"Hasn't it been great watching Jackie Robinson make them eat their words? Remember Jimmy Cannon saying Robinson was a thousand-to-one shot to succeed in the majors? Now Robinson is leading the league in hitting. And what about Newcombe? A hell of a pitcher. So much for the racists and their color bar." Morris' eyes gleamed with emotion, moved by the thought.

"Newcombe pitches tomorrow night against the Phillies. Can you stay over? It'd be just like old times."

Morris shook his head. "Afraid not." He lowered his voice and Collins had to lean in closer to hear him. "It's the reason I'm here. I need your help. I'm in a bit of a jam."

Morris paused to pull a stylish silver cigarette case out of his coat pocket. He took a cigarette out—Lucky Strikes, his favorite brand, Collins remembered—and tapped it gently a few times on the case. Morris' hands trembled slightly as he thumbed his stylish silver lighter and lit his cigarette, an uncharacteristic display of nerves. He took a quick first puff.

"Let's step over here," he said, taking Collins by the jacket sleeve and gently pulling him to a spot closer to the corridor and farther from the line of people at the box office. Collins wondered why Morris thought they needed more privacy.

"Not to be rude, but can we get to the point?" Collins asked. "I don't like leaving Penny alone this long."

"Sure, Denny, sure." Morris took another quick puff of his cigarette and exhaled before he spoke again. "Apparently I've come under suspicion."

"Under suspicion? What the hell are you talking about?"

"The internal security people at State seem to have questions about my loyalty. It's because of the Hiss mess. Anyone who doesn't think like Karl Mundt or the other reactionaries in Congress is suspect. They've been sniffing around me for a few months now. I'm afraid we're at the start of another Red Scare in Washington, just like what happened in 1919."

Collins understood immediately. It made sense that Morris might be a target of a loyalty probe. His parents had been committed radicals, and when Morris was a boy they had brought him to leftist rallies to protest the lynching of Negroes in the South or to show solidarity for striking workers. Collins always figured that the experience had the exact opposite impact of what the Roses had hoped and had inoculated Morris against their radicalism. Once Morris left home, his politics had become conventionally liberal. But for a nervous security officer, the file on Morris might raise questions—raised a Red, always a Red.

"I'd be happy to vouch for your loyalty," Collins said. "Tell me who to call. I'll tell them that Morris Rose is as loyal as they come."

His friend laughed. "Thanks for the offer. If the security officers were talking to me, I'd give them your name. That's the strange thing. I've been getting the silent treatment. I'm in some sort of limbo. But friends in the Department are warning me that I'm a target."

"That's tough," Collins said.

"So you see, I need a different sort of favor."

He reached into his front coat pocket, fished around for a moment, and then produced a small aluminum film canister. He held it out to Collins, wordlessly. Collins hesitated and then accepted it, reluctantly, wondering why Morris was walking around with a film canister in his pocket, and what it had to do with any favors.

"Can you hold this for me?" Morris asked. His tone was apologetic. "Just for a week? I have to go away for a while, but I promise that I'll retrieve it from you bright and early Friday."

Collins held the canister in the palm of his hand. "What's in it?" he asked.

"A few office memos on film that back me up, that prove I'm not a subversive. I know what you're thinking. You can relax. There's nothing classified on the film, just the pathetic back-and-forth of government bureaucrats. I just don't think it's wise to carry it around with me right now."

Collins gave him a hard stare. He didn't like the situation at all. After the stories about Whittaker Chambers and Alger Hiss and the famous (or infamous, depending on your point of view) microfilm of State Department documents Chambers had hidden in a Maryland pumpkin patch, being handed a film canister from a government employee of liberal political views was the equivalent of being handed a live grenade with the pin pulled.

Collins had covered parts of the trials of both Alger Hiss and Judith Coplon in New York federal court and stolen government documents had been at the center of both cases. The jury had deadlocked over whether Hiss had committed perjury by denying he'd given secret documents to Chambers, then a self-professed Soviet agent. Coplon, a Barnard College graduate, had been convicted of stealing documents from the Justice Department and passing them to her Russian lover, a Soviet operative named Valentin Gubitchev. It wasn't that Collins believed that Morris would be mixed up in anything like that, but he knew a clever prosecutor could make any situation seem sinister in the current climate.

"What are these memos doing on film in the first place?" Collins asked.

"It's my insurance policy. It's complicated, Denny. I think I'm suspected of passing some information to a Russian diplomat or two that I shouldn't have. The memos prove that I had proper authorization to talk to them when I was last in Poland. They show that I acted under the direction of my superiors at State. I couldn't very well walk out of the State Department building with the originals, and I couldn't be sure that one of the crypto-Nazis there wouldn't destroy them as a way of screwing me. So now I have my own independent proof of what happened."

"So why have me keep them? Shouldn't you keep them close?"

Morris shook his head. "Denny, I'm looking over my shoulder every ten seconds. I'm paranoid as hell. I feel like the guy in *Casablanca* with the letters of transit and the Germans after him. I half expect an FBI agent to show up with a warrant for my arrest any minute, and I'm sunk if they find me with the film now. It'd make me look guilty when the truth is the exact opposite—I just have it to protect myself if someone decides to tamper with the evidence or destroy it. This week will tell. A friend of mine, an Under Secretary, has promised to straighten things out. He's sympathetic, thinks I've been singled out because of my politics, not because I represent a real security risk. He's going to talk to Dean Acheson himself if he has to. By the end of the week he thinks it can all be resolved. Then I can return to Washington and get back to work. So if the investigation gets called off, I'll never need to use the documents. Hell, I haven't even developed the film. But it's best if it's not in my possession until I can get things squared away."

Collins felt the canister in his palm. Testifying to his friend's loyalty was one thing, getting tangled up in possessing illicit copies of government documents was another thing. He wanted no part of it. He covered the canister with his hand to hide it from passers-by.

"It all seems a bit convoluted."

"I know. I wish it weren't so complicated. But some of these Washington security types are ruthless. I'm sure the ones who are anti-Semitic know my grandfather was Jewish. The bastards wouldn't hesitate for a moment to frame me. Read the newspapers, Denny, they imagine there's a Red under every bed."

Collins closed his hand over the film canister. He knew that if the situation was reversed, and Collins had been falsely accused, Morris wouldn't hesitate to help him. There would be some risk in holding the film for Morris, but not much. But he couldn't shake a sense of uneasiness over the situation.

Morris had finished his cigarette; he dropped it on the floor, grinding it with his right foot. He exhaled. "You ought to put that in a pocket," he said. "Out of sight."

Collins slipped the canister into his suit pocket. No need to leave it out in open view where it could be seen, he told himself, even if he decided not to keep it.

"Should I find someone else?" Morris asked.

"Why me?" Collins asked in return. "We haven't seen each other in at least a year. You show up out of the blue with this. Why did I draw the short straw?"

Morris fidgeted with his expensive silk tie before he spoke. "I can trust you. You don't have any connection to the government, so holding it doesn't compromise you the way it would any of my friends in the Department."

"What does Ruth say about this?"

Ruth, the practical one in the Rose marriage, had always been a bit of a schemer when it came to Morris' career. Collins would have bet that it was her idea to enlist the Under Secretary to make the case for her husband.

"She's with me on this, Denny. She wants me to fight the bastards. I could have resigned a while ago, been done with it, practiced law in D.C. or back here. One of the big New York firms made me an offer last spring. But I stayed because I haven't done anything wrong."

Morris fiddled with a fresh cigarette for a moment before lighting up. He took a slow puff, and then exhaled the smoke with a long half-sigh. "Did you hear Truman's announcement today?"

"I haven't been near a radio."

"They have the bomb." His voice grew tight with suppressed excitement. "Truman announced that the Russians exploded a nuclear weapon within the last few weeks. It's going to put everyone on edge, especially the security types. It's another good reason for laying low, so I've decided to head to Vermont. A friend has a summer cottage near Burlington. No phone, no electricity. I can let things cool down. I left a letter for my superior at the Department explaining that I had a family emergency and would take some vacation time." He turned to face Collins, his handsome face intense with feeling. "It's just one week. That's all. I'm confident it will get fixed and the dogs will be called off. I promise that it won't be any longer."

"If for any reason I can't come collect it myself, then I'll send you the address of my attorney. You can mail it to his office in Georgetown. Look, it's simple. Only two people in the world know about the film. You and me. So there shouldn't be any risk in this for you at all."

Collins nodded reluctantly. His answer was what it had to be, because he was Morris Rose's friend, perhaps his oldest friend, and that obligated him. They had known each other since grade school. He trusted Morris. Loyalty counted, Collins told himself, and he was loyal to his friends, loyal to a fault—wasn't that the saying?

"One week," Collins said. "I can hold the film for one week."

Inside the Garden, there was a sudden burst of noise as the crowd suddenly came to life, roaring and cheering. Either there had been a knockdown, or the fight between the lightweights had ended. Collins checked his watch again. It had been fifteen minutes since he had left Penny's side. Morris dipped his head towards the arena, acknowledging Collins' need to return. "Give my best to Penny, then," he said. "With any luck I'll see you next Friday."

They shook hands and then Morris scanned the lobby, as if he was searching for someone. He seemed anxious again, harried, but Collins couldn't blame him for being tense—his friend's life had been turned upside down.

"Hey," Collins said. "You're a smart guy. You'll figure a way to fix this. I'm sure of it."

"I hope so," Morris said. "Just hold on until you hear from me." He smiled, wanly, and tapped Collins a few times on his right arm in a gesture of reassurance. Then he turned and moved into the stream of fight-goers passing by. In a moment, it seemed, he was out of sight, swallowed up by the crowd—gone, Collins thought, without a trace.

Two

Back inside the arena, Collins found that the first fight had finished and the ring was empty of boxers. He hurried down the aisle, impatient to get back to Penny.

When Collins reached his row and spotted her, he felt a sudden wave of tenderness and longing. She couldn't be too comfortable, left alone in the middle of a prize fight, perhaps wondering if she had made a mistake in agreeing to see him again.

Penny accepted his apology with a nod of her head.

"I hope you were left in peace while I was away," he said as he took his seat.

"No Fight Night Lotharios, if that's what you mean."

"Who won the fight?"

"The feisty one," she said. "Marino. The Cuban boxer went down in the final round and the referee counted to five but then he got back up. That's when I almost got a beer bath from the man in the row behind me." Her soft, cultured voice sounded out-of-place at ringside.

"I'm sorry. I shouldn't have left you alone. It was someone with a tip for a column. A talkative type." He wasn't going to tell her about his strange meeting with Morris Rose. It had nothing to do with her, and he would never involve her, even tangentially, in something that could get messy.

Their conversation was interrupted by cheering from the crowd as the ring announcer began introducing the next pair of boxers, beginning with Gentleman Jack O'Reilly of Brooklyn, New York, "wearing green trunks with shamrocks and tipping the scales at 225 pounds." O'Reilly had an impossibly boyish freckled face for a man of his size. His opponent, an older journeyman from Paterson, N.J. named Vincent Brown, had a receding hairline and a fleshy paunch that suggested he hadn't been training seriously. Brown's record had more losses than wins. It figured, Collins thought, because Santry had never been one to take chances. He liked to match his fighters with butchers or bartenders who fought part-time.

"I'm afraid we won't be able to talk once this starts," Collins told her.

"We'll have time at dinner. I am enjoying this, don't worry."

"You are?"

She smiled at the disbelief in his voice. "It's so different. I like it. It's so alive here. I've been watching the fans as much as the boxers. They're so passionate."

"They all have money down," Collins said. "Bettors aren't sentimental. They're passionate about their bets paying off."

The bell rang for the first round. Collins leaned forward, eager to see whether Santry's Gentleman Jack could fight. Unlike the lighter weight classes, there was always the possibility of a knock down, or a knockout, with the heavyweights. He had watched Joe Louis and Jersey Joe Walcott fight in this same ring two years earlier, when Walcott dropped Louis twice but then was robbed by the judges when they awarded the aging Louis a split-decision victory.

Gentleman Jack seemed confident enough, advancing quickly towards his shorter opponent, but after a minute of throwing tentative jabs Collins could see that he didn't move well.

"Too slow," he said out loud.

"He's no Marino?" It was Penny. Collins glanced over at her, struck again by her beauty of her profile, and her quick sense of humor when she grasped something.

"No Marino," he said. "Not even close."

When he had invited Collins to the fight, Santry had told him that his new fighter had been training at Stillman's Gym with Whitey Bimstein, so it wasn't that O'Reilly lacked professional attention. He was just ungainly. Sometimes big fighters could compensate for their awkwardness with power, with an ability to punish their opponents and, Collins thought, perhaps that was the case with Gentleman Jack.

O'Reilly quickly cornered Brown. He began throwing combinations and then followed a left jab with a sweeping right, which Brown managed to block. When O'Reilly dropped his left hand, Brown instinctively responded with his own straight right, catching O'Reilly's suddenly unprotected chin. Gentleman Jack staggered back, his legs wobbled and buckled, and then the bigger fighter went down, collapsing onto the canvas. The referee jumped in and began the count, directing the surprised Brown to a neutral corner. Clearly Brown had never imagined he'd knock down the crowd favorite, let alone in the first round. He stood in the corner, nervously shifting his weight from leg to leg, looking over at his handlers.

O'Reilly sprawled on the canvas, stunned and disoriented. As the referee reached the count of four, the downed boxer rolled over and pulled himself onto one shaky knee. He had staggered to his feet by seven. The referee motioned both boxers to the middle of the ring and they touched gloves. The crowd was yelling for blood, but Brown failed to finish off O'Reilly. Instead, he threw a few tentative jabs and when O'Reilly parried them with his left, Brown backed away.

They exchanged a few weak punches and then warily circled each other until the bell rang to end the first round. Gentleman Jack moved unsteadily back to his corner and dropped onto the stool. His corner man doused him with a small bucket of water and began talking to him earnestly as he applied smelling salts. Strangely, Brown's corner was silent. The journeyman sat on his stool, breathing heavily, sweat pouring down his face and chest, eyes fixed on the floor.

"I thought the big boxer, the Irishman, was supposed to win," Penny said.

"He is. But he lowers his left when he throws that right hook combination and it leaves him open for a counterpunch. That's what just happened when Brown knocked him down."

Collins turned back to the ring. When the second-round bell rang, O'Reilly came out of his corner as confidently as he had at the start of the fight. He threw several left jabs and Brown backed up, content to smother the punches. In a moment the older fighter was against the ropes, covering up, and O'Reilly followed a left with a telegraphed right hook that glanced off Brown's gloves. O'Reilly again dropped his left when he threw his hook, leaving himself vulnerable for a moment, but Brown didn't capitalize on the opening. The crowd was behind O'Reilly now, happy to see him rally and take the initiative. A large angry pink blotch appeared on Brown's belly where O'Reilly now focused his punches. Even fifteen rows back they could hear the sound of his gloves slamming into Brown's body.

In response to the hard pounding, Brown again tied up O'Reilly. The referee inserted himself between the boxers and slapped at Brown's arms so O'Reilly could break free. Brown looked to clinch again, grabbing and holding the younger fighter. There were catcalls from the crowd at Brown's clutching tactics. That's when O'Reilly took control. Frustrated by the clinches, he pushed Brown away and immediately threw a left-right sequence. When Brown moved forward to clinch, he walked into a sudden right uppercut that snapped his head back. He bounced off the ropes and then slowly slid to the floor.

It didn't look to Collins like Brown was hurt that badly, but the boxer sat there on the floor, unwilling or unable to move. The crowd roared in approval; they loved knockdowns. The referee shooed O'Reilly to the neutral corner and began the ten-count. It was clear that Brown had no plans of getting back up. He spit out his mouthpiece, and Gentleman Jack raised his gloves over his head in triumph, his corner man rushing out into the ring to congratulate him.

"So have you changed your mind?" Penny asked, turning to Collins. "Do you have a better opinion of Gentleman Jack now?"

"Afraid not. He couldn't handle a real heavyweight."

Collins heard some scattered boos, most likely from men who understood boxing and weren't impressed. From what he had seen, Gentleman Jack wouldn't last two rounds against an authentic heavyweight, one who would counter with a hard right whenever O'Reilly dropped his guard. But he recorded a KO against Brown, and for tonight that made him a crowd-pleaser.

"Let's get out of here," he told Penny. They weren't going to stay for the main attraction, two name lightweights, Terry Young and Enrique Bolanos. "Time for dinner. How about the Stork?"

Penny tilted her beautiful face towards him and Collins longed to kiss her slightly parted lips, but he fought against the urge. "The Stork would be lovely," she said, "but can we get in? It is a Friday."

"We can get in," Collins said. At that moment he would have handed Gregory, the maitre d' at the Stork, his week's paycheck to make sure they did—even though Collins knew that a reserved table awaited them—because he wouldn't disappoint Penny for the world. Even if he knew the odds were that she was going to disappoint him in the end.

He had lost her once before. He was in the Pacific in the spring of 1944 when she had fallen for a rich diplomat named Taylor Hill Bradford and after a whirlwind romance had promptly married him. Bradford had been in New York on a brief leave from his job with the American embassy in London when they met. After the war, the couple had moved to Washington, where Bradford went to work at the State Department.

Collins saw Penny twice after he returned from the Pacific. The first time, on a bitterly cold day in January 1946, he had bumped into her by chance near St. Patrick's Cathedral on Fifth Avenue. They had an awkward conversation on the street. She apologized for breaking the news of her engagement to him by a letter, and Collins lied and said that it didn't matter how he learned, and then he wished her and her husband well. There wasn't anything else to say.

A year later they saw each other again, under vastly different circumstances, this time at a memorial service for her husband at Grace Church in Greenwich Village. Taylor Bradford had been a casualty of the civil war in Greece. He had disappeared in early 1947 while visiting American military advisors north of Thessaloniki. Bradford had gone missing while en route to a remote outpost; two weeks later his bullet-ridden body had turned up by the side of a mountain road, a victim of the Communist partisans.

When Collins approached Penny after the service, he had stumbled through a few words of condolence and then, after she had thanked him for coming, he had quickly retreated. Penny had moved west, to San Francisco, where she stayed with her older sister for ten months before returning to Washington. Then, nearly two years since the memorial service, she had surfaced in New York. When Collins heard from friends that she had returned, it took him a few weeks to find the courage to ask her out.

He remembered what his father used to say, "Fool me once, shame on you. Fool me twice, shame on me." Collins was probably going to end up the fool, but he didn't care. As long as he had an outside chance with Penny he would keep trying. That was love, wasn't it? He couldn't help himself. Fatalism didn't mean you stopped trying, he told himself, it just meant that you expected the worst would happen and when it came it was no surprise.

Collins pushed his way through the crowded aisle, shielding Penny who trailed behind him. When they reached the main lobby, Collins heard his name being called. It was Phil Santry, the fight promoter.

"I'm sorry," Collins said to Penny. "I should talk to this fellow. Why don't you wait for me by the box office window? This won't take but a moment."

He didn't want Penny next to him when he talked with Santry because he knew he would lose his temper if and when Santry began leering at her.

Collins walked over and reluctantly shook Santry's flabby hand. Santry had gone to seed over the past few years—the promoter had moved up a few weight classes himself, and his face had a puffy, sweaty look.

"Leaving early?" Santry asked. "Not staying for the main go?"

Collins nodded, hoping that he could cut the conversation short.

"My guy at least got the win," Santry said. "I'm afraid Jackie wasn't sharp tonight. He got caught by surprise in that first round, but he recovered well enough. He's better than he looked, trust me."

"The proof's in the pudding. Isn't that what they say?"

They never had cared much for each other when they worked together in the city room of the *Sun*. Santry had left the paper to shill for Mike Jacobs and the Garden's fights, and then to managing boxers himself. Collins had stayed, escaping the police beat and thriving in the sports department and eventually landing his own column at the *Sentinel*. That alone was enough to make Santry jealous, Collins knew, because an Irishman will forgive you for anything but rising above him and Santry was dark Irish to his very core.

Santry shrugged. "Good undercard, though. Like the light-weight from Jersey?"

"Feisty. Is he yours?"

Santry smiled proudly, as if he was somehow responsible for Marino's victory. Promoters and managers always wanted to take credit when their boxer won. Collins couldn't resist a final jab at Santry. "Brown went down like he'd been rehearsing all week. Maybe you should have matched him with Marino."

Santry gave him a pained look. "You know better. The fight was on the up-and-up."

"Sure, Phil," Collins said.

"Come to his next fight. We're prepping Jackie for bigger and better things. He'll show better."

Collins shook his head, and told Santry that he had to go.

"Who's the broad with you?" Santry asked as Collins turned away from him. Collins ignored him. He wasn't about to introduce Penny to Phil Santry.

He walked over and took Penny's arm, steering her toward the exit. "Sorry for all these interruptions."

"Not at all. I enjoy watching you at work."

"I've had to desert you a couple of times tonight. I'm sorry. I didn't think I would have to leave your side."

"I understand," she said. "You're working. That's what I wanted to see. I've always wondered what it is that you actually did, covering the news."

"When I figure it out, I'll let you know."

"I'm glad I came," she said. "The atmosphere is fascinating. It's so alive, here."

Collins smiled. "That's what happens when they serve beer in paper cups. Booze livens things up. Ask any Marine MP."

"We've never talked about that," she said. "About you and your time with the Marines."

"We haven't. Although there are so many other topics—most of them a lot happier—to talk about, and now I'm free and clear to do so for the rest of the evening."

"Is that a promise?"

"A promise?" Collins hesitated for a moment. "That I'll be free and clear? I'll do my best."

She laughed. "Just your best? Can't you do better than that? Vow your unwavering and undying devotion to me?"

As he heard the affection and happiness in her voice it made Collins feel good in a way he hadn't for a long time. She was enjoying herself and simple as that might be, Collins didn't want her to lose that feeling. He would take it slowly, he told himself.

"Undying devotion?" Collins stopped and gave her a mock bow. "You have that already," he said. "You always have."

Three

Penny Bradford might have been out-of-place at the Garden fights, but with her well-tailored clothes, classic features, and natural grace, she clearly belonged at the Stork Club. Collins was the one who didn't fit in. He had more in common with the waiters and bouncers and cooks than the Stork's regulars, or the patrons of the other exclusive Manhattan places like "21," El Morocco, and Sardi's. That didn't stop him from going to the nightclubs, though, and Collins liked being able to walk right past the gawkers and tourists as if he truly belonged inside. That Friday night when their taxicab deposited them in front of the Stork Club at 53rd Street, the beefy guardian of the front door, Al, happily ushered them past the gold chain barrier and into the restaurant.

After checking Penny's coat and his hat, they made their way through the lobby and past the glittering long polished bar on the left, Penny slightly ahead of Collins but with his hand gently touching her elbow, guiding her, letting everyone know that she was with him. She attracted more than her fair share of glances from the men at the bar. When they reached the glass doors to the main dining room, Collins looked around. Sherm Billingsley, the owner, apparently wasn't there, but Gregory, the nightclub's distinguished-looking maitre d', came over to greet them with a broad smile.

"Could be a Subway Series again, Mr. Collins," Gregory said. "Just like two seasons ago. You think the Dodgers can do it?"

"They're only half a game back," Collins said, "and I like their chances tomorrow when Newcombe is pitching."

"I know Shotton managed them to the Series in '47, but I miss Durocher. Does Shotton really know what he's doing with the pitching staff?"

"Ask me again at the end of the week," Collins said and Gregory laughed. It was rumored that Branch Rickey, the general manager of the Dodgers, and his assistant and son, Branch Jr. (nicknamed "The Twig" by one of the sportswriters), would be looking for a replacement for Burt Shotton when the season ended.

"You remember my friend, Mrs. Bradford?" Collins asked as a way of reintroducing Penny to Gregory.

"Of course, I remember," he said. "It has been some time, but welcome back to the Stork, Mrs. Bradford."

"Thank you," she said. "It's nice to be back. It doesn't look like anything has changed from the last time."

"As it should be," Gregory said. "The Stork is supposed to stay the same. We'd have a revolt on our hands if we changed anything."

As Gregory showed them to one of the better tables, near the dance floor, Collins glanced over at the mirrors on the opposite wall of the room and caught his reflection: a thin, dark-haired man with a slightly anxious look on his face. Collins wondered whether he and Penny looked like they belonged together as a couple. If they didn't, he was the reason.

It was a typical Friday night at the Stork: attractive women in fashionable evening wear, their men in dark suits, the Cigarette Girl and Photo Girl circulating from table to table, the band playing dance numbers. There were lots of out-of-towners, wide-eyed, drinking in the atmosphere. The tourists whispered to each other, slightly awed by their surroundings, hoping to catch sight of a celebrity, a Hollywood or Broadway star, a famous athlete, politician or socialite. There seemed to be more tourists than usual; Collins figured some of the Stork regulars were observing Rosh Hashanah.

Billingsley knew what he was doing, Collins thought. The Stork's owner had realized that people would spend money if they believed the Stork Club offered them an entrée to café society—illusory or not—and he did all he could to deliver that to them. Newspaper columnists were warmly welcomed, for they helped burnish the legend. The signature Stork Club ashtrays, the souvenir storks, the phones that could be brought to your table, the attentive waiters, the preferential treatment for celebrities and good-looking girls, the famous New Year's Eve parties, all of it was designed to make the Stork Club appear glamorous and cosmopolitan.

The truth, Collins thought, was that if you took the words "Stork Club" off the front canopy you'd be left with overpriced drinks and so-so food. The band wasn't bad, but that alone wouldn't draw enough customers to cover the monthly rent on an East 53rd Street location.

Collins noticed there weren't any ballplayers in the Stork when he glanced around the room. All three New York baseball clubs had been out on the road. The Giants were in Cincinnati. The Dodgers had the day off, but the club had only returned from St. Louis to LaGuardia by DC-6 in the mid-afternoon. The Yankees had split a doubleheader in Washington and were playing in Boston over the weekend, with Joe DiMaggio, the Yanks' best player, in the hospital with viral pneumonia.

Collins ordered champagne—it had always been Penny's favorite—and when it came they raised their glasses to each other in a silent toast. Collins studied her for a moment. There were delicate lines around Penny's eyes and mouth that hadn't been there five years ago, but she remained a remarkably beautiful woman. He was careful not to gaze at her too long. They watched the crowd for a while, which was the reason everyone came to the Stork in the first place, and listened to the house band.

"This is simply marvelous," she said. "Isn't it?"

"When you put it that way, it's hard to disagree. Do you mean that it's marvelous compared to the Friday night fights?"

"In addition to the fights," she said.

"I was worried that it might be a bit too crass."

"I always liked seeing you in your milieu. It was entertaining."

"I've broadened my milieu," he said. "I write about the truly respectable crowd now, too. The bankers and lawyers and country club types who are smooth enough that no one notices their hands in the cookie jar."

"Ouch," she said. "Don't be cross. It wasn't meant to be a criticism."

"I even cover theater these days," he said and smiled so she could see that he wasn't offended. "Legitimate theater."

"I know. I read your column faithfully whenever I am in New York."

"You do?" He tried not to let his pleasure show too much. "Good. The *Sentinel* can use as many readers as it can get."

"I always feel as if I can hear your voice whenever I read your column. Do you hear that from other people?"

"Once in a while," he said. "And then I'm not sure it's meant as a compliment. What does that voice sound like to Virginia Allen Bradford?"

"A bit of a wise guy. Sure of what he likes and dislikes."

"I plead guilty. That sounds like me. So we agree on my voice. What sort of voices have you been hearing in Washington?"

He watched her carefully as she shifted in her seat.

"Older voices," she said. "My mother. Taylor's mother. You know, the whole Georgetown set."

"I don't know."

"You're fortunate, then. It gets stifling. That's why I am back in New York. I figured a change of scenery might do me good. All of my memories here are happy. Relatively happy, that is."

"I like the memories here, too."

They were silent for a moment and he remembered how it had been when they first started seeing each other. From the start, he had treated it as a fling, because he knew a girl like her could date any man she cared to, and he couldn't believe it would ever get serious. So they had fun together, and he didn't make any demands on her. Collins figured he represented a passing curiosity for her, someone entirely different from the men in her social circle, the corporate lawyers and Wall Street bankers who planned on moving to Connecticut and Westchester and commuting to the city after they got married.

Collins liked to think that she kept on seeing him because he became more to her than a diversionary fling. At least he hoped she felt that way. There was definitely a spark between them. When they had been dating, the simple things felt right—their kisses, the way they danced together, their shared sense of humor, and their passion in bed. It had not been perfect, of course. She hadn't liked his quick temper or his sharp tongue. Collins hadn't cared for the way she flirted with other men and she was infuriatingly careless about money in the way only rich people are. Yet, together, they had something.

When he decided to go overseas in 1944 to cover the war, they had their worst fight. Collins couldn't bear staying in New York when virtually all the men his age had gone into the service. He was tired of the questioning looks and the sly comments about why he was not wearing a uniform. Penny argued that he was being stupidly heroic and that whether or not he went off as a war correspondent would make no difference in what she called the Big Picture, but would affect the two of them. Collins figured that whatever they had together, it would last until he returned. It didn't. Her Dear John letter to him arrived when he was covering the Marine assault on Saipan.

Penny's soft voice brought him back to the Stork Club and the here and now. The band was taking a short break.

"You said you've been covering theater. Have you been to many plays recently?"

"I try to make opening night when I can. If there isn't a big game or fight scheduled that night. And how about you?"

"I haven't been out much," she said. "I'm taking my return entry to Manhattan night life somewhat slowly."

"Slow and steady wins the race."

"Which race is that, Dennis?" she asked and he laughed.

The band had returned and began to play again; a few couples left their tables and drifted to the dance floor.

"Shall we dance?" he asked, and she nodded.

"I haven't danced in ages. I'll be horribly clumsy."

"I doubt that."

So they danced. The band was playing "Some Enchanted Evening" and Penny sang along softly to the melody as they moved across the floor. She had a pleasant, gentle soprano voice and she knew all of the lyrics. Collins had admired the song the first time he heard Ezio Pinza sing it, when "South Pacific" had opened at the Majestic in April, but he had grown tired of Perry Como's lazy, sentimental version on the radio. Hearing Penny sing it made him appreciate the song again.

Collins breathed in her perfume and marveled at having her in his arms again. He had been convinced that she had been lost to him, irrevocably.

"You haven't forgotten how to dance," he said.

"Isn't it like riding a bicycle? You can pick it up again quickly?"

"You're too modest."

"No, I'm not. I'm very vain and you know it."

"If you are, you have some reason to be." He leaned in towards her left ear so he couldn't be overheard. "Have I ever told you how swell you are?"

"Swell?" She giggled. "Yes, I believe you've told me how swell I am, Mr. Collins."

"Well it deserves to be repeated. Thanks for coming along with me tonight. It's been too long."

She was silent, leaving Collins to wonder what she might be thinking. Their bodies and hands touching brought back memories for him and, he was sure, for Penny, as well. With his hand resting on the small of her back, he remembered the last time they had slept together, her narrow waist and long legs, the look on her face in the throes of passion. He tried not to think about it, afraid that he would become aroused right there on the dance floor. He hadn't been a monk since she left him, but he hadn't found another woman who compared to her, in or out of bed.

He was saved when the band swung into a faster number, "Rum and Coca Cola," and Penny quickly pulled him off the dance floor. Collins noticed that one of the tourists, whose crimson necktie almost matched his florid face, was eyeing Penny from across the room.

"Please excuse me for a moment, Dennis," she said. "I should fix my war paint."

"I'll walk you as far as the Cub Room," he said. "I need to check out the competition."

He escorted her as far as the entrance to the Cub Room; the stairs to the ladies rooms were located at the other end. He glanced over at Table 50 to see if Walter Winchell was there, holding court. He wasn't. When he turned back, he gave the ruddy-faced stranger who had been staring at Penny a long, measuring look. The man averted his eyes. Then, from the far side of the room, near the glass doors, Collins saw Lonnie Marks, a Broadway press agent, waving to get his attention. He kept waving so Collins detoured over to his table.

The management at the Stork frowned on table-hopping, but they looked the other way for newspapermen. Lonnie was sitting with an attractive young woman with dark hair and dark eyes. Her looks reminded Collins a bit of Dorretta Morrow, the Broadway singer, a Brooklyn girl who answered to the name of Dorreta Marrano at home.

Lonnie Marks represented a few Broadway shows and did occasional publicity work for some of the movie studios. Lonnie had fervently backed Henry Wallace when he ran for President on the Progressive Party ticket in 1948 and he was known for his support of left-wing causes. Collins was a bit surprised to find a girl at his table, because Lonnie's reputation was for preferring friendships with handsome, well-dressed younger men, usually of slight build.

"You're not writing as many columns on the important issues, Dennis," Lonnie said, giving him a mock scowl. "It makes me cross. Too much baseball and boxing these days."

"Think so?" Collins mixed things up with some columns on politics now and then, but he knew better than to stray too far from what he did best.

"I really, really admired your columns on the Hiss trial this summer and the one on how government loyalty oaths are, what did you call them, a contradiction in terms? Great to see someone go after the bastards."

Collins gave him a vague smile and didn't respond. He had learned to steer clear of discussions about what he had written. Collins was about to return to his table when Lonnie quickly turned to the young woman. "Forgive my rudeness," Lonnie said. "I'd like you to meet my friend, Miss Karina Lazda."

"My pleasure," Collins said.

"Miss Lazda works for the United Service for New Americans. There's a column there for you, I think. She's part of the group handling the displaced persons coming to New York from Europe. She's been telling me the most amazing stories about them."

"Is that so?" Collins turned to her and realized, now that he was closer, how her skin was lighter in color than it had appeared from across the room. The girl knew he was studying her and she blushed slightly, smoothing the front of her dress.

"We have sixty DPs arriving tonight at Idlewild," she said. Her accent struck him as more English than Eastern European, as if she'd learned from a Brit or had lived in England. She had a nice voice. "They flew in from Munich. Twenty-four Jewish and the rest Poles and Lithuanians. Many of them were in the camps. Almost half of them are children."

Collins knew there had been slightly more displaced persons accepted into the U.S. the year before, but he figured that the pace had slowed, and he said so.

"There are many more waiting," she said. She fastened her dark eyes on him. "Waiting in camps in Germany and Eastern Europe."

"How long have you been doing this?" he asked. "Working for the United Service?"

"Since I arrived in this country," she said. She didn't continue and say exactly when she had arrived, and where from, but he let it go.

"Your English is quite good."

"Thank you," she said. "I studied it for many years as a child."

"Is the Stork your first stop tonight?" Lonnie asked Collins.

"I was over at the Garden earlier," Collins said. "Went to see this new heavyweight from Brooklyn in action."

"Boxing seems so barbaric to me," the girl said quietly. "I cannot understand the appeal. Why it is allowed in civilized society."

"It appeals to our basic instincts," Collins said. "For men, that is. The warrior instinct."

"Not mine," Lonnie said and giggled.

"Don't you think we should evolve beyond this?" she asked, speaking to Collins directly. Collins liked the sound of her accented English. The more he listened to her, the more he could hear the Slavic influence. "Should we not endeavor to civilize that instinct?

"It's deep in us," he said. "Better to find ways to let it come out. There are pictures of Egyptians boxing with leather wrapped around their fists from five thousand years ago. Matches attended by the Pharaohs. It gives men a chance to test themselves. Very elemental."

"An appeal to our baser instincts," Lonnie said. "The vicarious thrill of watching men beat up other men and perhaps wishing we could do the same to our boss, or our annoying neighbor, or to anyone who crosses us."

"Speak for yourself," Collins said. He couldn't help but smile at the thought of Lonnie throwing a punch.

"What of the men who box?" It was Karina, her eyes still fixed on him and Collins could see that he hadn't convinced her of anything. "Does it not brutalize the boxers as much as it does the audience?"

"It's a job for them," he said. "Most of them think that it beats pounding nails or pumping gas. They make pretty good money. In a way they're entertainers, just like the Broadway actors that Lonnie promotes."

"The actors have talent," the girl said. "I don't know that I would say that about your prizefighters."

She took a cigarette pack, Camels, out of her purse, and Collins quickly produced his silver-colored Zippo, a gift from a young Marine captain, Charlie Adair, who had become his friend on Okinawa. Collins lit her cigarette and she thanked him with a brief nod and a polite smile.

"Did you know that we have more than a thousand Jewish DPs in our Center at the Hotel Marseilles celebrating Rosh Hashanah tonight?" she asked.

"Wouldn't that would make a good column?" Lonnie asked.

"It would help if you could write about us, Mr. Collins," she said. "If their story is in the papers, perhaps it can stir the government to action. This Senator McCarran continues to block the Displaced Persons bill. It is wrong to let them wait in those camps a day longer than necessary."

Collins was impressed by her passion on the subject. He was partial to that quality, and even more so when it came from a pretty girl. It could change your perspective on someone, he thought, when they cared so strongly.

"It's worth a look-see," Collins said.

"A look-see?" She seemed confused by the phrase.

Lonnie patted her hand. "It means Dennis is interested, Karina."

"How about Monday or Tuesday?" Collins asked. "Perhaps I can talk to some of these people at your Center. Hear their stories. That's what the readers want—the stories of real people, not the bureaucratic stuff about legislation."

"I think I understand, Mr. Collins," she said. "I shall call you on Monday to arrange a time."

"I have a tip for you as well, Dennis," Lonnie said. "They've cast Ethel Waters in that new Carson McCullers' play 'The Member of the Wedding.' It's opening just after New Year's at the Empire. She'll sing that gospel song 'His Eye is on the Sparrow.' A guaranteed show stopper."

Collins nodded. It would make a good item to include in one of his Tuesday columns where he asked and answered questions about sports, show business, and politics. Ethel Waters had gotten positive reviews for her performance in the movie *Pinky*, which was still showing in the Times Square movie houses. He pulled his reporter's note-book out of his inner coat pocket and penciled a few notes. He told Lonnie he would see what he could do and the press agent beamed at him.

Collins made his farewells, shaking Lonnie's hand and nodding to the girl. When Collins glanced over at his table, he noticed that Penny hadn't returned yet. He was crossing the dance floor when he saw that Red Face, the man who had been staring at Penny, was now talking to her by the exit to the Cub Room, blocking her way back to the table. He must have intercepted her on her way back from the ladies' room, Collins thought. Penny made eye contact with him over the man's shoulder and Collins could see she was annoyed. She might be too polite to do anything about it, but Collins wasn't.

Collins could feel his temper rising as he walked across the floor. He tapped the man on the shoulder; when Red Face turned around. Collins could smell the booze on him.

"Disappear," Collins said. "Scram."

"I'm talking to the lady."

"The lady is with me. So get lost."

Red Face cursed under his breath and Collins could feel his heart pounding much faster and a slight roaring in his ears. He clenched his fists, struggling to stay under control.

"Why don't you back away now?" Collins asked. "Don't make a scene."

"You're the one making the scene, buddy."

Collins began to push past the man to interpose himself, but Red Face grabbed at the lapels of his suit. Then he made the mistake of shoving Collins and swinging at him. That gave Collins more room for an effective punch and he caught Red Face with a straight right, flush on the chin, just the way he had been taught by Digger Callahan at the Hibernian club back in his Golden Gloves days.

The man collapsed onto the polished dance floor in a heap. Collins had a moment of regret, because he knew Penny would be upset at the public scene. Still, Red Face didn't crash into a table and the dance floor was relatively empty so he didn't collide with any of the couples who had been dancing. If you hadn't seen the punch, you would have thought that he had slipped and fallen by accident onto the floor.

One of the Stork waiters had reached Red Face before he got up from the floor, a look of dazed surprise on his face. A large man in evening clothes, one of the nightclub's bouncers, was quickly at Collins' side and made sure that he was positioned between Collins and Red Face.

"Excuse me, Mr. Collins," he said, placing a restraining hand on his arm. "This isn't acceptable. We all need to calm down."

Collins noticed one of the nearby middle-aged female tourists was staring at him wide-eyed—she'd gotten her money's worth. She'd have a story to tell in Steubenville or Springfield when she got back home. Punches thrown at the Stork Club! Collins remembered that Hemingway had told Sherm Billingsley that a good fistfight every six months would help promote the Stork Club.

Red Face was holding his jaw as the waiter helped him to his feet. Gregory arrived and began trying to smooth things over. Penny stood next to Collins, frozen in place, and Collins didn't dare look at her face. Gregory invited Red Face to move to the Cub Room where he could enjoy his dinner and drinks compliments of the Stork Club, and the man nodded, still dazed. Another one of the bouncers and Gregory escorted him towards the Cub Room, but not before Gregory shot Collins a disapproving look.

Collins followed Penny back to their table in silence. The band was playing "Stardust" and people were dancing again. Collins' right hand was beginning to hurt and he wondered if he had broken a knuckle. He kept his hand out of sight, below the tabletop, so he wouldn't draw Penny's attention to it.

"You didn't need to hit him," she said, her voice low and intense. "He was a harmless pest. You could have just escorted me back to the table. There was no call for a fight."

"I'm sorry." Collins didn't try to defend himself, even though Red Face had swung at him first. Penny was right. He could have let one of the bouncers handle it if he hadn't lost his temper.

"What got into you? Why ruin our evening?"

"I'm sorry," he said and Collins hoped she could see his genuine remorse.

"I thought you might have changed."

It hurt him hearing her say that. "I have," he said. "My temper just got the better of me."

"Can we go?" she asked.

"What about dinner?"

"I'm not hungry. And I don't want to sit here all evening being stared at."

Collins didn't think that anyone was staring at them, but he knew better than to argue. He pulled the chair out for her and Penny stood up, shoulders stiff from anger. He threw two ten-dollar bills on the table for the waiter and took her elbow, gently guiding her out through the main room. Collins made sure to move at a comfortable pace. He wasn't going to skulk out of the Stork.

On their way out, they passed Lonnie Marks and Karina Lazda and it seemed to Collins that the girl evaded his glance. She must have watched the fracas with Red Face and had her worst suspicions about him confirmed, that he was not only a defender of the violence of boxing but also a practitioner of its brutality. Collins waved at Lonnie and he waved back with a silly grin. Lonnie had enjoyed the show.

They waited in silence while the coat check girl found Penny's coat and Collins' hat. He slipped a dollar into the slotted box they had for tips. At the door of the nightclub, Al nodded and patted Collins on the back a few times, as if to signal his silent support. Word of the scuffle had already circulated among the club's staff. Once they were on the street, away from the cluster of people waiting to get into the Stork, Collins stopped and faced Penny.

"I'm sorry, I should have kept my temper," he said. "Can we take a walk so that I can cool down? Up to the Park?"

She hesitated for a long moment and then nodded silently. Collins was relieved. He had expected her to ask for a taxicab to take her home.

The first two knuckles of his right hand, where he had caught Red Face's chin, were throbbing with pain. Collins jammed the hand back into his pocket. He knew he had made a hash of things, but Penny was still with him. He certainly was going to try his best, he told himself, and perhaps he could somehow salvage what was left of their night on the town.

Four

They walked west from the Stork Club along East 53rd Street, then up Sixth Avenue until they reached Central Park South. It was a cool evening, with a hint of rain in the air, so the sidewalks weren't as crowded as might be expected for a Friday night at the close of September. Collins didn't try to start a conversation, calculating that silence was the best course, at least for the moment. They strolled towards the entrance to the park at the Artist's Gate, pausing at the statue of Simón Bolívar on horseback, an impressive sculpture that rose above them on a grayish granite platform.

"He looks sad," Penny said softly. "Does he look sad to you?"

Collins gazed up at Bolívar's impassive bronze face, trying to see him through Penny's eyes. He didn't want to say the wrong thing, so he played it safe, with a little humor. "For a statue, I guess so."

"I wonder why?"

"Disappointed in love, perhaps?" Collins immediately regretted making the comment. Would Penny think that it was a reference to their past?

"Maybe not. Perhaps he's just saddle-sore and it's pain, not sadness, in his face."

Collins laughed. Penny hadn't lost her quick wit.

Once in the park proper, they walked together to the edge of the Pond and stood there, gazing over at its surface. The reflected lights of the apartment buildings and the Fifth Avenue hotels, the Pierre and the Sherry-Netherland, gleamed brightly on the water.

Despite the chill, there were other couples strolling along the park's paths. When Collins peered into the autumn sky above them, it was difficult to make out the stars. Now, with no fear of U-boats or Luftwaffe bombers, the incandescent glow of New York had returned after dark and they said it could be seen a good twenty miles out in the

Atlantic. Collins thought of that Vaughn Monroe song, "When the Lights Go On Again All Over the World," that had been so popular during the war. The lights were back on, but with the news about the Russians and the bomb it made him wonder how long they would stay that way.

They stopped to sit down together on a vacant park bench. Collins tucked his bruised right hand into his coat pocket and in doing so, brushed against the canister of film, a sudden, unwelcome reminder of Morris and the favor he had requested. It was a favor granted, Collins thought, which he hoped he wouldn't regret.

"Do you remember Morris Rose?" he asked Penny.

"Vaguely," she said. "One of your best friends from childhood, wasn't he?"

"He was. Then we drifted apart a bit. He went to Columbia, and then law school and then into the government."

"I remember him as a very intense person."

Collins knew that meant Penny had not cared for Morris. The people in Penny's world were never intense. They didn't have to be.

"He was always much smarter than the rest of us," he said. "I figured Morris would end up on the Supreme Court. He was always reading, always debating, always wondering why we couldn't change things for the better."

"Quite political, wasn't he?"

"Less so today. Always an idealist. I think he joined one of those Socialist groups at Columbia, but now he's a conventional New Dealer."

"What made you think of him?"

"I saw him recently," he said. "Sort of a chance meeting. It brought back a lot of memories."

"Memories and Morris Rose. It's poetic. 'God gave us memories that we might have roses in December.' Isn't that the saying?"

"Is it? I hadn't heard that before."

"You haven't? Isn't it lyrical? It seems very Irish."

Collins turned towards her. "It's way too optimistic for my tribe. We tend to dwell on the dark side of life."

She rewarded him with a laugh.

"So what is Morris Rose doing now?" she asked.

"He's in the Office of European Affairs in the State Department, focusing on Eastern Europe. He's one of their top experts on the region. One of his grandfathers came from Warsaw, and Morris is a quick study and he's picked up some Russian and Polish."

"Then I would imagine that he keeps very busy these days."

"Morris is only happy when he's busy. He hasn't changed from when he was a kid."

"Have I changed much? From before?"

"You are as lovely as ever on the outside, but you don't need me to tell you that." Collins paused. "How have you changed otherwise? I couldn't say. I'd need to spend a lot more time with you to know."

She smiled. "You're still very obvious, Dennis, but I'm flattered."

"I plead guilty, again. Can't blame a guy for trying."

"And how have you changed?" she asked. "Other than the temper?"

Collins was grateful to her for the opening. Maybe he did have a chance, he told himself, and maybe she was looking for him to prove he wasn't the same old Denny. "When I went overseas I saw some things I wish I hadn't. You think you know what it will be like, but you really don't have a clue. I didn't. It does one thing, though. It gives you a real appreciation for how marvelous life is. How fragile and how precious it is. So I hope I'm a little bit wiser than before. No question that I'm older. I look it, don't I?"

"The gray hair at your temples makes you more distinguished. That's better than 'older.' You're still as easy to talk to as ever, and we haven't talked in ages. Not since that dreadful afternoon we ran into each other on Fifth Avenue."

"It was dreadful," Collins said. It was a struggle for him not to say something bitter. "Being out of touch certainly wasn't my choice."

"Let's not dwell on it. It won't change anything, will it?" She paused. "I shouldn't be so tough on you. It's just that I was so looking forward to tonight."

"Were you?"

"I've been cooped up for so long," she said. "It's been dreadful, feeling that I am supposed to act a certain way, behave a certain way. I don't feel that at all. I'm not ready always to do the proper, considered thing. I am twenty-eight years old—that's not completely ancient, is it? I've been drifting from day to day, doing the same things, seeing the same people, saying the same things. Is that living? I'm at the point where I could scream."

She rose to her feet and Collins followed suit.

"Scream away," he said.

She smiled and he gently pulled her close to him and kissed her lightly on the lips. She didn't resist. He kissed her again, a little harder, and she eased away from him.

"The first kiss was nice," she said.

"Still need to scream?"

"No, that feeling has passed. Thank you."

"So maybe I could be good for you? What the doctor ordered?"

She reached out and ran her fingers through his hair. "You could be, Dennis. I'd forgotten how much I like being around you, how I missed talking with you. But it's been a while. I wouldn't want to rush anything. Do you understand?"

"I think so."

They walked back out of the park, past Saint-Gaudens' gilded statue of General Sherman and into Grand Army Plaza. The drivers of the horse-drawn carriages were calling out to passers-by, looking for fares, and weekend tourists ringed the Pulitzer Fountain. Across from them, the Plaza Hotel was ablaze with lights and activity. Collins asked Penny if she wanted to stop off at the Oak Room for a drink, but she told him that she was tired and was ready to go home.

Collins hailed a Checker cab and climbed in after her, telling the cabbie to take them to Penny's apartment, on West End Avenue.

They didn't talk on the way. She let him hold her hand in the cab—he used his left hand, because his right was still hurting—and he was content to sit next to her, her head resting gently on his shoulder. He didn't speak until they were into the lobby of her building.

"Can I come up?" he asked. "A night cap? Maybe listen to some music and talk?"

"No, Dennis, I don't think so."

Collins didn't say anything in return. The doorman, an older man in an ill-fitting uniform, was staring at him and Collins gave him a hard look in return. The man glanced away.

"I'm sorry," she said. "Not now. Things are too complicated."

"I'm not complicated."

"No, you're not complicated. But…things are."

"I'm sorry about what happened, tonight," he said. "I truly am. I can keep my temper under control. I promise. I'd like to take you out again. Another chance. If that's not too complicated."

"That's not too complicated. Perhaps in a week or two. I have to go to Washington for a brief visit starting on Monday."

"Can I call? Just to talk?"

"If you like," she said.

"Tomorrow?"

She hesitated.

"Too soon? Tell me."

"No, not too soon," she said. "But we have to go slow."

She kissed him demurely on the cheek. She got into the waiting elevator and gave him a slight wave as the shiny bronze doors closed. Collins was left looking at his own distorted reflection, an awkward smile frozen on his face.

Five

When Collins arrived at his apartment building, he found his older brother Frank waiting for him in the front lobby. Frank was stationed in a comfortable armchair, a copy of the *Daily News* opened to the sports section across his lap. He nodded and gave Collins a crooked smile, the same smile he'd given him after an eight-year-old Dennis had hit the baseball through Mrs. Galvin's first floor plate glass window.

"Figured you might eventually turn up," he said. "Let's go for a drink."

They walked over to Mallory's bar, a few blocks away from Collins' apartment and settled into a corner booth. Collins glanced around. The three regulars at the long, dark mahogany appeared totally entranced by a comedy on the flickering screen of a new Philco television set. The bartender brought Collins a beer and his brother ordered a boilermaker.

Frank carefully placed his well-made fedora on the tabletop. He had graduated to plainclothes after ten years wearing a dark blue policeman's uniform and Collins figured the sharp clothing was his way of making up for lost sartorial time. His fedora must have set him back at least $40 at a store like Rogers Peet, Collins thought, four times what Gimbel's charged for a hat.

"So I just missed you at the Stork Club," his brother said. "I figured I'd find you there on a Friday night. Al told me that you clocked some tourist who was bothering your date."

"It's true. I was there with Penny."

"Al mentioned that as well."

"We could use Al on the city desk. He's on top of all the news. I guess I lost my temper when this guy started bothering Penny. He took a swing and I knocked him down. She gave me hell for it afterwards."

"Didn't know Penny was back in town. Or back in the picture."

"Just a night out. I took her to the Garden for the undercard. Santry's heavyweight, Gentleman Jack."

"Sounds like old home night, with Penny Bradford and Phil Santry." His brother took a sip of whiskey and followed it with a gulp of his beer. "I'm a little surprised about Penny. You do know what you are doing? I mean, you took it pretty hard last time."

"Once burned, twice shy. I'm taking it slowly."

"I wish I could believe that."

"Believe it." Collins raised his glass and drank some of his beer. "So why was my big brother following me around tonight?"

Frank grinned sheepishly. "I haven't seen you in a month. Figured we'd get caught up. I'm hearing that after the election we're going to be looking closely at the fights. Thought that'd be of some interest to you."

His brother cupped one hand over his cigarette as he lit up. He exhaled, leaned back, placing the package of Chesterfields on the table. He noticed Collins looking at them. "Want one?"

"I quit," Collins said. "Remember?"

"That's right. I forgot."

Collins took another sip of his beer, enjoying the taste. "So New York's Finest will be investigating the fight game?"

"And our friends in the District Attorney's office."

"Why wait until after the election?"

Frank shrugged. "I don't know, Denny. Politics. Maybe they want to make sure the Mayor gets back in, first."

"O'Dwyer's got no worries. He's a cinch."

"They must have their reasons. When we start the investigation, I hear your buddy Santry is on the list for a thorough look-over. I wanted you to know that."

"My buddy? Not quite." Collins glanced over at his brother, who had finished his initial shot and beer and had signaled the bartender for another. Collins had half of his beer yet to drink. He wondered how much Frank knew about his past dealings with Santry.

"I wanted to give you a heads up, especially because of Santry," his brother said. "But you're telling me that's not a factor, right?"

"Right. As far as I'm concerned, Santry's just another shady fight promoter. So how soon should I put an item about this investigation into the paper?"

"Patience, Denny. There's nothing official yet."

"You like being patient about it?"

"Not a bit." His brother slapped his palm on the table. "I even wish the Feds would help in the investigation. Never thought I'd say that. They're too preoccupied with chasing Reds. The FBI spends all their time in Flushing Meadow, trailing the Russian delegates to the United Nations. The lazy bastards can't wait for that new UN building to finish up over at Turtle Bay so they won't have to leave Manhattan to do their surveillance."

"So there's time for hunting Reds and fellow travelers, but no time to investigate the criminals in boxing? What about Frankie Carbo and International Boxing Club? Why aren't they looking into that?"

"Carbo don't have the A-bomb, Denny."

"If that's the new threshold for investigation, then you might want to turn in your badge. None of the criminals in this city have the A-bomb. At least not yet."

"Real funny. But wait until we're ready on this. There are lots of jumpy people in the fight game right now. They won't want a lot of attention. Nothing premature in the paper. I don't want to be worrying about your health."

"You're kidding me, right?"

"It could get rough," he said. "They're not afraid to hurt people." Something in Collins' face made him pause, and Frank cleared his throat. "I know you've seen rough, during the war and all. I wasn't questioning that."

Collins looked over at the white package of Chesterfields his brother had left on the tabletop, his eye drawn to the gold and red crown over the "Ch" in script.

"I'll try one of those, Frank," he said. "One can't hurt."

"Your call." His brother grinned. "What is that they say? 'Always buy Chesterfields'."

He pushed the package across the table. Collins found his Zippo and lit up a cigarette, his first in two months. He took a few puffs, enjoying the taste. Arthur Godfrey might tout Chesterfields' mildness in the magazine ads, but Collins thought they actually had one of the stronger tastes, which he liked.

"Frank, have you ever heard the saying 'God gave us memories that we might have roses in December?'"

"Can't say that I have. It sounds like something grandma would have said."

"I've been thinking about memories," Collins said. "What with seeing Penny again. And I bumped into someone from the old neighborhood today. Morris."

"Morris." His brother repeated the name without any enthusiasm. "So what's his story these days?"

"He's still in Washington, working for the State Department."

"Still a Red?"

"Not quite. He's getting more reasonable as he gets older. Probably voted for Truman."

Frank grunted. "Doubt that. I figure him for Wallace, along with his wife. She's even more of a lefty than Morris."

"Who'd Maureen vote for?"

"Truman. She would vote for the Devil himself if he ran as a friggin' Democrat. I almost canceled her out. I was tempted to vote for Dewey—he was damn tough when he went after the rackets. But at the end I came to my senses and went for Truman."

"Will you give Maureen my best?"

"I will, Denny. She keeps buggin' me about why my younger brother doesn't come over for dinner. You haven't seen Brendan in four months."

"After baseball is over," Collins said. "Ask Maureen what night is best and I'll be there."

Collins finished his cigarette, and after Frank downed the last of his beer, they split the bar tab. His brother promised to call if he heard any more about the fight game investigation. Frank carefully adjusted his fedora and headed off towards the subway station.

Collins checked his watch: it was just past one o'clock. He stopped at a newsstand near his apartment to purchase the Saturday morning papers. He went through them once he was back in his apartment. They were filled with the President's announcement about the Russian atomic bomb. The *Times* went for a three-deck headline:

ATOM BLAST IN RUSSIA DISCLOSED;
TRUMAN AGAIN ASKS U.N. CONTROL
VISHINSKY PROPOSES A PEACE PACT

According to the *Times*, Soviet scientists had exceeded earlier American predictions by three years about when they were expected to develop a nuclear device. Collins turned to the sports pages. There was only a brief mention of the Friday night fights at the Garden because they had finished too close to deadline.

He decided it was time for bed. With two columns to write, it'd help to get some sleep before he started banging out copy in the morning. Collins hoped he could stay busy all day so he wouldn't have time to brood about his stupid behavior at the Stork Club.

He thought about how strange it was to have seen Penny and Morris in the same evening. He fished the film canister out of the pocket of his suit jacket and put it on his night table, next to the bed. He would be happy when Friday rolled around and Morris retrieved it.

Collins remembered the first time the two of them had walked alone across the Brooklyn Bridge, when they were twelve years old.

They had been awed by Roebling's masterpiece, the way it hung gracefully suspended in air across the East River, the curve of the bridge, the battleship gray steel cables. When they had reached the Manhattan side, Morris had looked north at midtown's skyscrapers, the Chrysler and the Empire State buildings, and told Collins that when he grew up he was leaving Brooklyn and moving there, to the city, to go to school and then to work.

"I'm never coming back, Denny," he said. "I belong here, not back there."

Today whenever Collins made that trip across the bridge and looked north to the Chrysler Building's steel spire flashing in the sun, like some modern-age cathedral, he remembered Morris' vow. He glanced over at the canister of film sitting on his night table. Old neighborhood friend or not, it would have been better if Morris hadn't involved him. He wouldn't rest easy until it was out of his hands.

"No problem, Morris," he said out loud, wasting the sarcasm on the empty room. "Glad to help out."

Saturday, September 24

She woke from a nightmare, gasping for air, her heart racing. She turned on the small shaded light on the bedside table and tried to calm herself, breathing slowly and deeply, until she felt the pounding in her chest subside.

Her dream had been incredibly vivid.

She and Morris had been walking through the shattered ruins of the Old City. Concrete, bricks, and masonry were piled high on either side of the street where buildings had once stood. They passed scores of poorly dressed pedestrians, many with their heads bowed in resignation as they wandered, dazed, through the blasted landscape. When they came to Theater Square, Morris told her solemnly that he could go no further; she had to push on alone and find what he had lost. If she failed, he explained, he would be punished.

To her surprise the Great Theatre was standing intact and when she passed through its doors she found herself suddenly, magically, standing on the stage. A huge, silent audience filled the seats in front of her. The balconies with their tiers of boxes and open galleries were jammed with well-dressed opera-goers as well. Musicians stirred in the orchestra pit. Hundreds of feet above them, the giant chandelier glittered.

She could see Piotr and Sasha sitting together in the front row, and standing in the wings backstage to her right there were three other figures. She peered over into the dimly-lit backstage and realized that it was Morris and two other men, who she could not recognize at first, and then she saw that they were Dennis Collins, the newspaperman, and Lonnie Marks.

She knew they were all waiting for her to sing, but when the orchestra began to play and she opened her mouth, try as she might she could produce no sound. Her throat felt constricted, as if she was beginning to choke. She could mouth the words but she couldn't make any sounds. Tears of frustration came to her eyes. Somehow her singing was connected to saving Morris and Sasha and even Piotr.

Again she tried to sing, but she could tell from the angry faces of the audience that they could not hear her. They began to whistle and when she stopped to tell them that she was trying her best, they began booing. She tried to flee from center stage but found her feet stuck to the floor. Then there came the sound of an air raid siren and the audience rose and began streaming toward the exits of the theater.

She could not move, not matter how hard she tried to lift her feet. The warning siren grew louder and louder and she could hear the high whistle of a bomb falling toward her. She was frightened, sure that she was about to die. There was a thunderous noise and then a blinding light.

That was when she woke. Still groggy, she found her cigarettes and fumbled with her matches until she could get one to light. A few long drags made her feel better.

Even now, with the lights on, she felt a sense of dread. She glanced over at the clock—it was just past four o'clock. The nightmare made no sense, she told herself, a jumble of her Warsaw memories mixed in with the stage fright no performer ever completely forgot and the repressed emotions stirred up by the sudden reappearance of Morris.

She opened the small drawer on her bedside table and looked at the small Colt revolver nestled there on top of several handkerchiefs. She had purchased it from one of the maintenance men at the Hotel Marseilles, Ivory Johnson, telling him that she lived alone and needed a gun for self-protection. Ivory had shown her how to load the pistol and had given her some tips on how to use it; she didn't tell him that Piotr had taught her how to fire a Luger when the first reports had circulated in Warsaw of advancing Red Army soldiers raping and killing Polish women.

She left the drawer open but didn't touch the weapon, its boxy shape shining an ugly blue in the lamplight. She wondered if she could use it, when and if that time ever came. Could she point it at another human being and squeeze the trigger? She told herself that she could if she had to, although she prayed that she would never confront that choice.

She closed the drawer and fished another Camel out of the package. It was still hours until dawn, but she didn't think she would be able to go back to sleep. She had a long day ahead of her. She would be helping the new arrivals settle in at the Marseilles. It would be their first day in New York and they would be disoriented after the long flight from Europe. Part of her job was to reassure them that they had reached a place of safety, where they could forget the past and start over.

The refugees responded differently to arriving in America. Some quickly took to their new surroundings, eager to begin life anew. Others, after years of living at Landsberg and Zeilsheim and Feldafing and the other camps, seemed numbed and confused by the change. Then there were those who withdrew completely. Often it was because they realized that they would not be returning to their homeland, to their ancestral villages and towns, that they had been, indeed, displaced—permanently. The staff at the Center kept a close watch for signs of severe emotional distress by recent arrivals; they were to refer the most troubled to a Columbia University psychiatrist who donated his services.

She rose from bed, and found her way into the living room. She loaded her phonograph with four 78 discs of the Russian violinist Mischa Elman playing Bach's Suite No. 3. She sat in the overstuffed chair in the corner with the lights off and listened to Elman's plaintive performance of Air on the G String.

She cleared her mind of the dream and of the day's routine ahead and thought about the beauty of the coming sunrise over her adopted city. She found herself moved by the exquisite interplay between violin and piano and, unbidden, tears began slowly trickling down her cheeks, as she lost herself in the music and waited for the dawn.

Six

His right hand began hurting as soon as Collins woke. His first two knuckles were swollen and tender to the touch and he found it hard to make a fist without considerable pain. He cursed aloud. Collins would be lucky if he had avoided breaking his knuckles on Red Face's hard, bony jaw.

He placed the round rubber plug into the bathroom sink drain and filled the basin with cold water and ice and then soaked his hand for five minutes. It seemed to help. He was able to flex his hand afterwards and managed to shave without nicking or cutting himself. Dressing wasn't as awkward as he had feared, although knotting his tie did make his hand start to throb with a dull pain.

Collins found himself thinking about Penny, and how surreal—in the light of day—their night seemed. Had he really danced with her, kissed her again? She had seemed to accept his apologies for the Stork blowup, but a day later, would she reconsider? Would she believe that he hadn't changed, that he was still a hothead?

He knew that he shouldn't come on too strong. No bouquets of roses delivered to Penny's apartment, no appearances in her front lobby asking to see her, no overly aggressive phone calls. He had to wait, to be patient, to show her that he had matured.

He decided that he would have breakfast first and then call Penny before he left for work. He would make it a casual call, just to tell her how much he had enjoyed the evening and he wouldn't prolong it if she didn't want to talk. When he grabbed his wallet and keys from the night table, he decided to take Morris' film canister, dropping it in his coat pocket. The phone rang as he was reaching for the doorknob. He walked back over and picked up the receiver.

"Hello, Denny," a female voice said. Whoever it was, she sounded far away. It wasn't Penny, he realized with a sharp sense of disappointment.

"Hello," he said. "Who's this?"

"A friend from the old days," she said and then Collins recognized the voice. It was Ruth Rose, Morris' wife, on the other end of the line.

"I see," he said. "How are you?"

They had never warmed up to each other, perhaps because she saw Collins—still a carefree bachelor—as a bad influence on Morris. In turn, Collins didn't care for her overbearing personality or for her politics, either, which were a lot further to the left than Morris. They had declared a wary truce, of sorts, and treated each other with politeness. It helped that they didn't see much of each other.

"I'm fine. I'm calling because I have a message from Morris. It's hard for him to get to a phone. He wanted you to know that one of his other friends will be in touch."

"How soon will that be?"

"Not until the end of the week," she said.

"This is stupid," he said. "Why is Morris playing cat-and-mouse? I'd be more than happy to go to whoever is handling the investigation and vouch for Morris."

There was a long silence. Ruth knew how to convey her displeasure, even over a long-distance line. Collins didn't envy Morris. She had to be difficult to live with during the best of times, and no doubt she had made the last few weeks a living hell for Morris.

"That would be a big mistake. Don't do that. Please don't. We really believe that everything can be cleared up this week. We have some very influential people helping behind the scenes. I can't talk about it on the phone now. I'm sure you understand."

Collins didn't really want to understand and thought about telling her that, but he didn't want to quarrel with her, so he swallowed his objections. If Collins had a few anxious days until Thursday or Friday so be it—he owed Morris that.

Ruth spoke again. "We have to be careful. That's why I am calling you from a pay phone."

Collins was taken aback for a moment. She obviously was concerned about a wiretap on her home phone, which could mean the FBI was working with the State Department security officers.

"This will be over soon," she said. "Please be patient. Morris appreciates your loyalty and so do I. Neither of us will forget. It's so unfair that anyone with any progressive politics in their past has to face this sort of inquisition. But it will be over soon. I promise." She had spoken quickly, trying to be persuasive, but Collins didn't feel reassured.

"Okay," Collins said. "But you should know that this whole thing makes me nervous."

"Just be patient and it will work out."

She hung up the phone without saying goodbye. Collins heard a number of clicks and hisses after she broke the connection at her end but he couldn't say for sure that they were abnormal. Could it be the sounds of a wiretap? He doubted it. How could they know which pay phone she was using? He put the receiver back into its cradle slowly.

He pictured Ruth's narrow, intense face, her bobbed dark hair, the nervous habit she had of biting her fingernails. She was pretty in a gamine way, but she struck Collins as overly nervous, high-strung. Morris didn't mind, apparently. Who could truly tell what went on between a specific man and a specific woman? Collins couldn't, nor had he been particularly successful himself at figuring out the opposite sex. Morris and Ruth had been married for ten years, so there had to be some continuing chemistry there, something binding them together.

Collins left his apartment and walked over to the All-American Diner on 75th Street between Columbus and Amsterdam. He checked his watch when he slid into one of the open booths—it was 9:15. He arranged the morning papers in a pile on the Formica tabletop and took the time to read them more carefully while he waited for his order of scrambled eggs, toast, bacon, potatoes, and a small stack of pancakes. He liked big breakfasts. There were a couple of customers smoking nearby and the aroma made him yearn for a cigarette.

He hadn't looked too closely at the *Daily News* the night before. It took the same tack on the Russian nuclear weapon story as the *Sentinel* had. The editors at the *News* had fronted two photos: one of Secretary of Defense Louis Johnson being questioned by the White House press corps in Washington and appearing quite harried as he strode away, and the other of Soviet foreign minister Vishinsky over in Flushing Meadows at the United Nations. The Russian official looked unruffled, but then again, Collins thought, unlike Johnson, he didn't have any explaining to do to his bosses.

Collins flipped to the sports section. After he and Penny had left the Garden, Terry Young had upset the favorite, Enrique Bolanos, in the main event. The fight had gone the distance, ten rounds, and Young had apparently cut up the Mexican pretty badly. There was no mention of the undercard fights, nothing about the shaky victory of Gentleman Jack O'Reilly or the show put on by Frankie Marino, the kid from New Jersey.

He turned to the *Times*. On an inside page, near the bottom, an Associated Press story was entitled: "Key Reds in Capital." It quoted claims by officials at the House Un-American Activities Committee that Communists in Washington, D.C. had suddenly gone into hiding. Collins couldn't help himself; he found his hand straying to his coat pocket, touching the film canister nervously. He muttered to himself how ridiculous he was being; there was no connection to Morris and a day earlier he wouldn't have thought twice about the story. Then again, a day earlier he hadn't seen the anxiety and tension in Morris.

Nicky Demetrios, the diner's owner, emerged from the kitchen and waved when he saw Collins. He came over to the table. They had been friends long enough that Nicky felt free to interrupt Collins' newspaper-reading routine to talk sports—in fact, his interruption had become part of Collins' weekend morning routine.

"We're goin' to win again, Mr. Collins," he began. "Can't stop us. Not with our line-up and Mr. Allie Reynolds. And Mr. Tommy Henrich. And when he gets better, Mr. DiMaggio."

"Is that so?" Collins asked. He had asked Nicky to call him Dennis several times but Nicky believed in honorifics, even for newspapermen and baseball players, two groups Collins thought were particularly undeserving of the honor.

"You don't think so, Mr. Collins? Why is that, please?"

Nicky didn't really want him to agree. He loved to debate, which gave him a chance to display his baseball knowledge, all the facts he had culled from his relentless study of the newspapers and from watching his beloved Yankees on television. Nicky attended only one game at Yankee Stadium a season—his annual pilgrimage to the Mecca, the shrine, of the Bronx Bombers—but he'd purchased a television set as soon as they began televising Yankee home games.

"What about the Red Sox and Mr. Ted Williams?" Collins asked. "If they win this weekend in Boston, then the race will be tied."

"That will not happen," Nicky said. He never lacked confidence in his adopted team. When the Yanks occupied first place, God was in His heaven and all was right in the world. He fully expected that the Yankees would appear in the World Series every fall. Nicky had gone into mourning the prior season when Cleveland usurped the Yankees' proper role as American League pennant winners. "Mr. Casey Stengel knows how to manage this team."

"We'll see," Collins said. "Just a week to go. Next Sunday ends the regular season."

"We will win the pennant," Nicky said. He rose from the table, triumphant. "We are consistent. Very consistent. Mel Allen says that is the sign of a great team."

Collins found the baseball talk a welcome diversion. He hadn't thought about atomic bombs or Soviet spies or whether Penny would agree to see him again. He finished what was left of his breakfast, collected his newspapers, and paid the cashier at the front.

Collins had been thinking about smoking a cigarette all morning and once outside he stopped at the closest newsstand and bought a pack of Chesterfields. He stripped the cellophane from the package and opened the top and took out a cigarette and lit it up. He took a long, deeply satisfying puff. The tobacco's strong, almost abrasive taste made him remember why he had liked smoking. If he was going to start again, he figured that he might as well get his money's worth. It would only be for the week, he told himself. Once Morris took his film back and the pennant race was over he would quit.

By the time he got back to his apartment, it was already ten o'clock and his phone was ringing. It rang three or four times when he was fumbling with the key and lock, and to his surprise it kept ringing, long enough for him to reach the receiver before the caller hung up. He answered and knew immediately it was a long-distance call from the hissing background noise.

"Hey, Denny." It was Morris. "Sorry to bother you."

"No bother."

"I wanted to say thanks. Ruth tells me that you're willing to be patient. I really appreciate it."

"There's a choice?" Collins assumed that a worried Ruth had phoned Morris and that Morris was calling to make sure that his friend wasn't wavering in his commitment.

Morris ignored his question. "Like she told you, a friend will contact you about the meeting."

"A friend?"

"Believe it or not, I have other friends. Some even are willing to do favors for me."

"Where are you, Morris?"

"Where I need to be right now. See you at the end of the week."

The line went dead.

Collins figured it was as good a time as ever to phone Penny; she was a late riser. He went to his desk drawer to get his address book. When he opened the front cover, he glanced at the first photo tucked inside: a snapshot of Penny and himself taken at a skating party at

Rockefeller Center. It must have been in 1943, he decided, and he studied her face for a moment, struck by her radiance, and the elegance of her classic features.

He had carried his best photo of Penny with him to the Pacific, one she had given to him before he left. It had been taken on Nantucket: she peered at the camera with a relaxed half-smile, her hair windblown, her beauty and grace captured for posterity the moment the shutter clicked. But Collins didn't have it anymore. When he got her Dear Denny letter, he gave into anger and disappointment and ripped up the photo. He regretted his impulsiveness later.

There was another photo in his address book: a group shot at Ebbets Field taken before the third game of the 1947 World Series. One of the *Sentinel* photographers had spied Collins, his father, and Morris in the stands and had snapped it as a favor for Collins.

Collins glanced at their pleased faces. While the Dodgers beat the Yankees that day, 9-8, with Eddie Stanky and Carl Furillo each hitting two-run doubles, they ended up losing the Series in seven games. Collins didn't care. He had been happy to be back in New York in one piece to enjoy the simple things like watching baseball on a sunny fall afternoon with his father and best childhood friend. After Saipan and Okinawa the simplest pleasures seemed more than enough.

In fact, when he first came back he couldn't get enough of the small things: strolling down the glistening sidewalks of the city on a rainy day, dodging to avoid the umbrellas of the oncoming pedestrians; visiting his old Brooklyn haunts; enjoying that first cup of morning coffee and watching the rush hour crowd head for work, heads down, oblivious to the damn miracle that was life itself.

That was the New York he had lost for a time, the city etched in his mind whenever he had escaped into his memories, determined to block out the grim deadliness of the Pacific slaughterhouse. Of course that imagined city was better than the real one, but who didn't cling to fantasy at some level?

When Collins next checked his watch it was already 10:30. He stared at Penny's phone number in his address book. It was ridiculous, he told himself, to be so anxious, but he knew he felt that way because it mattered. So he dialed her number and sat waiting for her to pick up, but the phone kept ringing. He hung up after fifteen rings. He found himself lighting up another Chesterfield. He would need to buy another pack soon at the rate he was smoking them.

He picked up the photo of Morris, his father, and himself again. It had been two months later that his father had died, at 64 years of age. Frank had called Collins that morning at the *Sentinel* to tell him. His father, a stickler for promptness, proud that he had never been late for a day's work in his life, had not shown up at the Con Ed office. They found him in his bed. His heart had just stopped working.

Collins knew that his father had been disappointed that his second son had not gone to college and become an accountant or a lawyer. That Collins had passed the age of twenty-five without marrying a conventionally sweet girl with a County Cork ancestry and starting a family had been a source of unhappiness for both of his parents. He knew they had disapproved of his pursuit of Penny. She was out of his reach, from an alien world of money and privilege.

His parents only met Penny once, in Manhattan, when they suffered through a strained dinner together at El Morocco. It was a bad choice on Collins' part. His parents, uncomfortable in a nightclub, hardly spoke and Penny treated them with a distant, condescending politeness that hurt Collins more than if she'd snubbed them outright. This was in early 1941, a year before Collins' mother died from liver cancer.

"A very pretty girl," his father said later. "She must have her pick."

"Maybe so," Collins said. "For now, I'm it."

His father said nothing further but Collins knew what he was thinking, that in the end Penny would never settle on him, that he couldn't compete with the Social Register types, the sleek stockbrokers with summer homes and private incomes. Collins didn't make the mistake of bringing them together again.

Collins looked over at the clock. He had let half an hour slip by. He picked up the phone and tried Penny's apartment again. He only waited five rings before he hung up. He cursed his own impatience. He was acting like a teenager mooning over his first crush.

Penny had said that he could call her today, but that didn't mean she would be waiting by the telephone. If he was smart, he wouldn't get his hopes up. Hadn't he resolved to be patient? That would be smart, too, he told himself, but since when was a man blindly in love particularly smart? He was willing to risk being disappointed again, or being played for a fool. He had tried living without her, and without hope, and that was worse.

Seven

Collins was running late and while he hated the thought of being trapped underground on a bright, fair autumn day, he fished a dime out of his trouser pocket and took the subway to work. Twenty minutes later, he emerged into the midday sunlight of Herald Square.

It had turned out to be a beautiful fall day, the air crisp and the sunlight glancing off the stone and glass of the buildings, casting a warm, amber glow over the open space of Herald Square. They had done right in tearing down the El in 1938; the overhead train tracks had been a looming and noisy distraction, disrupting whatever symmetry the square had.

Now the blocks around Macy's and Gimbel's were crowded with animated Saturday shoppers, many with parcels and bags in their hands, keen to enjoy their weekend freedom. The aroma of roasting chestnuts wafted from nearby vendor carts. Collins had to slow his pace at times because of the jam-packed sidewalks.

He glanced over at the statues of Athena and the bell ringers at the Herald Square Park, at the intersection of Sixth Avenue and Broadway. The sculpture had once been on the roof of the old Herald headquarters building, at Sixth Avenue and 35th Street, and the bell rang on the hour, keeping time for the workers in the area before the advent of cheap wristwatches.

Traffic clogged the streets as well. The city's economy was booming again: few vacancy signs in the apartment buildings, construction all over, from the boxy United Nations building being erected at Turtle Bay to new housing in Brooklyn and the Bronx. Peace had brought prosperity, and New York seemed awash in money. They might be rationing meat in England, and much of the rest of Europe might go to bed hungry, but times were good again in America.

Collins envied the people around him. He regretted having to spend any time indoors that afternoon, but that was the reality of newspaper work, and he knew that he had to write his Sunday column. Then, after a quick supper, he had the game ahead of him and at least he could look forward to that.

When Collins reached the *Sentinel* building on West 39th Street, before he entered he glanced up at the sign over the front door:

The New York Sentinel
Conscience of the City

The slogan had been a favorite of the paper's founder, John Watt Longworth, and had appeared on the front page until his death. Neither his son, nor grandson, Frederick Longworth, the current publisher, cared for it and so while it stayed on the sign out front, the slogan had disappeared from the pages of the newspaper. And it remained on the sign, the newsroom wags said, only because Fred Longworth was too cheap to spring for a new one.

The newsroom was located on the fifth floor and when the elevator broke down (which was quite often, actually) it was quite a hike up the stairs. Inside the *Sentinel* newsroom Collins found the usual Saturday afternoon crew, diligently working away on the Sunday edition. For some reason they couldn't get the temperature right in the newsroom: it was too hot in the summer and freezing cold in the winter and no matter the complaints it seemed beyond the capabilities of the maintenance staff to adjust the temperature. Yet for all its dinginess, it still felt like home to Collins.

Fred Longworth didn't share his grandfather's zeal for political reform; he seemed more interested in the *Sentinel*'s turning a profit than in crusading for better government, and he left his editors more or less alone. The paper had supported FDR throughout the New Deal and had endorsed Truman for re-election, although Collins heard that Longworth preferred the "little man on the top of the wedding cake" to the "little piano player in the White House." Most of the paper's working class readers favored Truman, not Governor Dewey, so Longworth left well enough alone.

Collins always felt that he could write what he wanted in his column as long as he sold papers. He enjoyed the freedom; he couldn't ask for a better situation. There were always worries in the newsroom over the *Sentinel*'s shaky financial position, and occasional speculation that Longworth might sell the paper to Hearst or Scripps-Howard, but Collins didn't give those rumors much credence. If Fred Longworth sold the paper he wouldn't get invited to the best cocktail parties and have his phone calls returned with the same alacrity. That counted for something; there were other currencies that mattered, even to the very rich.

Collins acknowledged the weekend regulars with a nod as he made his way over to his desk. He had decided to write his Sunday column that afternoon, but would wait a day to write Monday's. Depending on what happened with the Dodgers, he would have a relatively easy Monday column to write. If they lost to the Phillies he could offer up their eulogy, if they won, then he could focus on what the Brooks needed to do in their last few games to steal the pennant.

He knew what he wanted to write about for Sunday, but he had a hard time getting started. Once he got past the opening, the lead, the rest of the column would write itself. Collins fumbled in his pocket and found the Chesterfields. He lit one up and took a long drag. He promised himself a reward: once he had his opening, he would take a break and phone Penny again.

One of the night side copy editors, Hal Diderick, glanced over at him. "Smoking again?"

Collins nodded. Diderick not only worried about his own health, but also that of everyone else in the newsroom. It seemed he was visiting a new doctor every other week, entranced by vitamin therapy one week and homeopathy the next.

"Sorry to see that. Bad for your wind."

"I'm not a miler, Diderick," Collins said. "I hadn't planned on entering the Milrose Games anytime soon, so I'm not worried about my wind."

Diderick pursed his lips, disappointed. "It's an expensive habit," he said.

"Don't worry about me. It's just for the rest of the pennant race. I'm going to quit again once the season is over."

"Sure. If you say so."

"Cold turkey. I've done it before." Collins looked at him closely. "Your eyes look a little bloodshot, Diderick. Are you coming down with something?"

"I don't think so," he said. Collins had hit the target, though, because Diderick immediately looked uneasy.

"You look a little peaked," Collins said. "Gray in the face."

"Is that so?"

Collins nodded solemnly. Diderick excused himself and Collins saw him headed to the men's room, where there was a mirror. With any luck, he'd leave Collins alone for the rest of the day.

Collins didn't want to deal with Diderick or any other distractions. He had too much on his mind. He kept returning to the events of the night before. The war had changed a lot of things: young widows weren't expected to mourn for too long. The idea was to get on with life, and who could argue with that? So maybe Penny was ready to do so—it had been some two years since she lost her husband.

Collins never did meet the other guy, Taylor Hill Bradford. He had studied the clips on Bradford when he got back to New York after the war. There hadn't been much: the marriage announcement, with a grainy photo of Penny, and then one brief story about a speech Bradford had given to a local women's group on foreign policy accompanied by a small headshot photo. He had wavy blond hair and a prominent chin. It looked like an expensive photo, a Fabian Bachrach portrait.

Collins got up from his desk, suddenly restless. He wandered over to the office of Peter Vandercamp, the paper's managing editor. Vandercamp was an intriguing figure; it was said his Old New York family had disowned him when he converted to Catholicism as a young man and that he had entered the seminary only to decide he wasn't called to the priesthood.

Van had ended up in newspapers. He had been best friends with John O'Hara, the novelist, when they were both working at the *Trib*. If the *Sentinel* could be said to have a resident intellectual, it would have to be Vandercamp. He didn't swear (curses represented an imprecise, and unimaginative, use of the King's English, he claimed) and he rarely drank. City desk regulars claimed that Van went out for a drink on V-E Day, but since Collins wasn't there to witness it, he remained skeptical.

This Saturday Vandercamp was dressed in an unfashionable dark gray suit, white shirt, and dark blue tie. Collins always thought that with his shock of white hair and bushy eyebrows Van would have a made a great prince of the Church, perhaps a bishop or maybe even a cardinal.

"How's the column coming?" he asked Collins.

"You'll like it, Van," Collins told him. "It's an O. Henry story. What was the one with the wife cutting her long hair and selling it to buy the husband the watch fob, and then he sells the watch to buy her combs?"

Vandercamp peered at him over the top of his reading glasses. "'The Gift of the Magi.' So what's your story about?"

"A woman named Angelica Anders is working on a machine press down on 27th Street and her arm gets caught, almost torn off. Her fellow workers don't know what to do. She's bleeding badly and they call for the ambulance, but she'll be dead by the time it gets there. What saves her is this former Army medic who's in the building delivering a package. He puts a tourniquet on the arm and that keeps her alive until they can get her to the hospital for a transfusion."

"So where's the O. Henry angle?"

"The medic, a guy named Joey Gallegos, can't wait to get away from the scene. Doesn't want any thanks. He's hightailing it out of the building when one of the cops responding to the accident recognizes him. There's a warrant out for Gallegos. Armed robbery. He's arrested on the spot. Think about the irony of it. If Gallegos doesn't stop and save her, he remains in the clear. But he stays and he buys himself maybe fifteen years upstate."

Vandercamp nodded once, in encouragement. "That's a story. Who did you talk to?"

"I interviewed the Anders woman at the hospital. She lost the arm, but she's going to live. And I talked to one of Gallegos' Army buddies from the Lower East Side who says he was fearless as a medic. Gallegos was in Patton's Third, saw some of the heaviest action in the Battle of the Bulge. When he came back to New York, he just couldn't adjust to civilian life. Jumped every time a car backfired."

"And the armed robbery?"

"Fell in with the wrong crowd and went along for the ride."

Vandercamp nodded again, satisfied. "Let's see what you can do with it."

"What else is going on?" Collins asked.

"Not much. We have today's New Year sermon of Rabbi Goldstein of Temple B'nai Jeshurun well in advance. A hand-delivered copy. The good Rabbi will make some interesting comments. I quote: 'We in the United States are going through an anti-Communist hysteria such as one does not find in Western Europe, which is much closer to the problem than America.' He also says, and again I quote: 'The Red witch-hunting which is bedeviling artistic, academic and scientific circles is a spiritual retrogression in American life.'"

"A spiritual retrogression? Will that make it into the *Sentinel?*"

"And crowd out the crossword puzzle? We don't have the space of the *Times* or the *Trib*. Of course you could interview Rabbi Goldstein, get him to amplify on his remarks for your Monday column. Contrast his old-fashioned common sense with the ridiculous panic in Washington."

Collins looked at Vandercamp doubtfully. He didn't want to write about the Red Scare until the situation with Morris was cleared up. Why draw unwanted attention? Besides, the new young editor over at the *Post*, Jimmy Wechsler, was doing a great job of hammering the witch hunters. Wechsler, a Young Communist who'd seen the light, had been fearless in going after J. Edgar Hoover and HUAC.

"Waste a column on that during the best pennant race in both leagues in years and years? With the Yankees and the Dodgers in the thick of it?"

Vandercamp frowned. Collins knew that he disappointed Van at times, but he wasn't the first editor to be disappointed by Dennis Collins, nor would he be the last.

Collins decided to change the topic. "Van, who said 'God gave us memories that we might have roses in December?'"

Vandercamp reflected on the question for a moment. "J.M. Barrie," he said. "That's J.M. Barrie. It's from the opening of *Courage*."

"The Peter Pan J.M. Barrie?"

"The very same."

"He wasn't Irish was he?"

"Lord no. Scots. Barrie was a Scot."

Collins was duly impressed that Vandercamp had dredged up the origins of the saying from somewhere in the recesses of his memory. They were interrupted by Hal Diderick. He held a sheaf of UPI wire copy, ripped directly from the teletype machine, and he was bursting with self-importance.

"Did you hear the latest about Lowell Thomas?"

Diderick relished being the exclusive source of the most up-to-date news. Vandercamp gazed over at him with mild but undisguised distaste and Collins thought, not for the first time, that Diderick was lucky that he compensated for his abrasiveness with competent editing skills. Collins was curious what news there could be about Thomas, Columbia's roving radio reporter.

"Thomas's in the middle of nowhere, climbing in the Himalayas, near Tibet and he breaks his hip. Fell off a horse near some place called the Karo Pass. He was carried by litter to a little village with a name I can't pronounce. They're saying it may take weeks to get him back to civilization."

"If he's in the middle of nowhere, how do you know this?" Vandercamp asked.

"His son is with him, Lowell Thomas, Jr., and he sent a cable back to Columbia Broadcasting. Looks like the old man is out of commission for a while."

Vandercamp nodded. "We'll find some space for it inside, first ten pages."

Collins walked back to his desk, sat down at his typewriter and started his column. He was a fast writer and once he had figured out the first line, the rest of the 600 words would flow. It took two tries, both rolled out of his typewriter and ripped into little pieces, before he got it:

Monday started like any other day for Angelica Anders. After all, how do you know that this is the day your life changes forever? There is no prior announcement, no swell of the violins like in the movies, nothing to hint at what lies ahead.

For Angelica trouble was waiting just around the corner, unexpected, unwelcome—the thief in the night of the Gospels—except it came during the day, not the night, a glorious luminous September day.

Monday started like any other day for Joey Gallegos. How do you know that this is the day your life changes forever? That you'll do the right thing but pay for it with the most valuable coin any of us have—our time and our freedom?

Then it only took twenty-five minutes to finish. After Collins delivered the four typewritten pages to Vandercamp, he decided he deserved a break. Van would read the column slowly, editing it carefully. He wouldn't be ready to discuss any changes or rewrites with Collins for at least half an hour.

Collins decided to call Penny again in the meantime. He found an empty office where he would have some privacy and dialed her number. It rang ten times and no one answered. He cursed. Collins promised himself that he wouldn't call her again that day.

When he reentered the newsroom, Diderick was at his desk, holding the phone to his ear, and he waved him over.

"Phone," he said. "For you."

Collins hoped, irrationally, for a moment, that it was Penny, but when he answered it he heard the voice of Phil Santry.

"Denny," Santry started. "We didn't finish our conversation last night at the Garden."

"We didn't?"

"I was wondering if we could have lunch sometime soon. On me. I want to talk to you about a few things."

"Sorry, Phil, I'm pretty much tied up with baseball for the next few weeks."

Collins didn't want to go to lunch with Santry. In fact, he wanted to spend as little time with him as possible.

"How about a cup of coffee?"

"What's this about, Phil?"

"He's a lot better than he showed."

"I don't know about that. That rent-a-bum you had in the ring last night knocked O'Reilly down pretty quickly."

"Give him a break, will you? Everybody has a bad night. O'Reilly can punch, I promise you that. I hope you'll keep an open mind on this."

"I've got an open mind. Punching power isn't going to do him much good if he keeps dropping his guard. He'll be flat on his ass. A real heavyweight is going to hurt him badly. You shouldn't put the kid's health at risk with a mismatch."

"That's your opinion."

"I'll tell you what. I'm getting tired of this racket. You should hope I don't write about O'Reilly, or about the rest of the fight game. It's rotten and you know it."

"You wouldn't want to do that," Santry said, his voice suddenly tight and wary.

"Why not?"

"I think we both know why. Lots of us have good memories."

"Is that a threat?"

They both knew what he was talking about. Collins had made a few mistakes back early in his career when he first covered the fights, before the war, before coming to the *Sentinel*. He wasn't worried about being embarrassed because he knew Santry really didn't want to dredge up the past. He had just as much to lose as Collins did.

"Call it what you like," Santry said. "You're forgetting where you came from. I don't think that you want to disappoint people. That'd make them unhappy."

"I seem to be good at that, Phil. Disappointing and making people unhappy."

"I don't need your wise mouth. I'm telling you this for your own good. You have a sweet thing going now. Don't ruin it."

"I'm glad to hear that you have my best interests at heart," Collins said. "I'll sleep better tonight knowing that."

That's when Santry told him to fornicate himself, but in less elegant terms, and slammed down the phone. When Collins hung up, he saw Vandercamp motioning to him through the glass window of his office. Collins went over to his desk.

"Nice job," he said. "We may sell some papers with your column. I'm starting it on page one and jumping it inside."

He handed Collins the copy and Collins looked through it quickly. There weren't a lot of pencil marks, but Vandercamp's few changes had improved the flow of the column. Van understood that Collins wanted to be known for his writing. Let Walter Winchell have his catch phrases and his table at the Stork and his radio program; let Jimmy Cannon build his New York tough-guy reputation and scrape for one-liners; Collins wanted to be different, respected for the way he chose his words, for using them with precision and care.

Collins could have guessed beforehand that Van was going to like Angelica Anders' story. It appealed to his Catholic sensibilities. Joey Gallegos had sacrificed himself to save Angelica. The makeshift tourniquet on her arm kept her alive, but doomed him to prison. "What else could I do?" Gallegos asked the police, but the truth is that he had a choice. He could have walked. Did he redeem himself with that sacrifice? Or was Gallegos kicking himself for being a fool while he sat in a Rikers Island cell waiting for his court appearance?

Vandercamp had already written in the typesetting instructions for the linotypers, so he was done with Collins. Collins turned to leave.

"A strong column," Van said. "Like I said, I'm putting it out front. Back to bread and circuses for Monday?"

"Back to baseball, America's favorite pastime."

Vandercamp shrugged. He would have preferred more columns like the one Collins had just written, that touched on larger issues. Of course, Van would see some grand design in Gallegos showing up to save the day and what it meant for his eternal soul. Van could have his theology, Collins told himself. Collins just hoped his column might buy Gallegos a little leniency when he faced sentencing before a tough criminal court judge.

Collins saw what happened with Anders and Gallegos as a matter of chance, a series of coincidences: no divine plan, no Supreme Power playing chess. He figured Angelica Anders was lucky that a former Army medic was making a delivery to her building. Lucky, not blessed.

He wished it wasn't that way. He wished God paid more attention to the human comedy. But Collins didn't believe that He predestined Lowell Thomas to fall off a horse in Tibet and break his hip, or that He willed Gentleman Jack's win at the Garden, or that He directed Morris Rose and his problems to Collins' doorstep. Or that He kept Penny Bradford from answering the telephone. In short, Collins didn't think He cared about every leaf falling. More than a year in the Pacific Theater had disabused him of that notion for good, although Collins might concede that there really was nothing good about it.

Eight

Collins didn't get overly sentimental about ballparks.

They were a place of work for him just as they were for the players and who got particularly sentimental about the office? But Collins understood why the fans might grow attached to what they saw as *their* park, to Yankee Stadium or Fenway or Shibe Field or the Polo Grounds.

Collins didn't pay much attention to the grandeur of the architecture or the history of the place, like the fans, but graded the ballparks based on how clear a view he had of the infield from the press box, and how far he would have to walk to the men's room.

All that being said, he felt differently about Ebbets Field. Collins was fond of Brooklyn's ballpark; there was something very familiar and comforting about the place, even if it had grown a bit shabby.

He had watched his first professional baseball game at Ebbets, when he was eleven years old. Even now he could remember his excitement and wonder at walking through the marble rotunda, marveling at the grand chandelier towering above him with its baseball-bat arms, and being delighted by the beauty of the green field when he reached his seats. His father took him to see the Dodgers play the Giants as a birthday gift on August 26, 1928. They held on to win the game, 4-3. More than twenty years later Collins remembered the friendly crowd in the stands around them, smiling and joking, enjoying all aspects of the game.

When Collins got upstairs, the press room was far from full. It was missing the big name sportswriters and columnists. Red Smith of the *Trib*, Jimmy Cannon from the *Post*, and Arthur Dailey of the *Times* had traveled to Boston for the Yankees-Red Sox series. It made sense. The real story was in Boston, not Brooklyn. The Yankees were trying to regain the World Championship and the Red Sox stood in their way. The Dodgers weren't seen as real contenders.

Collins got along fairly well with the Dodgers beat writers. Most of them understood that was paid to write columns that got people talking and that sometimes meant challenging the decisions of the manager in print or questioning the play of the team's stars. It also meant that at times Collins wasn't as welcome in the clubhouse, and some of the beat guys disliked him for stirring up resentment from the players and making their job harder. Collins couldn't worry about it.

He checked his watch. He had about fifteen minutes until the game started, and he figured he could call Penny and still head over to the press box in time to see the first pitch. He used the pay phone in the hallway.

Her number rang unanswered for ten rings before Collins ended the call. Maybe she had gone away for the day, he rationalized. He figured he could call her after the game, and she would be back in her apartment by then. Collins could play it very casual then—"Hey, the Dodgers game just finished and I had a moment and I thought I'd give you a call." There would be nothing desperate about it, he told himself.

He turned to walk down the hall to the press box when he noticed a tall man in a drab brown suit, a fedora in his hands, moving quickly to intercept him. The man was clean-cut, athletic, with the muscular build of a halfback.

"Dennis Collins?" he asked.

Collins nodded in response.

"I'm Agent Andrew Caldwell of the FBI." The man flipped open his leather wallet to display his badge. "They told me at the newspaper I could find you here."

Collins nodded again.

"Sorry to bother you," Caldwell said. "I have a few brief questions, and then I'll be on my way."

"Sure," Collins said. "But you ought to stick around. Should be a pretty good game tonight. Don Newcombe is pitching."

Caldwell smiled and shook his head. "Afraid I can't," he said. He produced a small notepad and a pencil, opening it. "I understand that you are friends with Morris Rose." He waited for Collins to respond, his pencil poised at the ready.

"We are friends. Are you working on his security clearance? Is Morris up for a promotion at the State Department?"

"Something like that. When did you last see him, Mr. Collins?"

"Friday."

"Yesterday? The occasion?"

"He's my friend. We've known each other since we were seven, eight years old. Do I need an occasion?"

"Fair enough. Where did you see him?"

"At the Garden. Fight night."

"What did you talk about?"

"Mainly about the Dodgers. I asked him if he could stay over in New York and catch a game with me. He said he couldn't stay." Collins stopped and glanced at his watch. "Look, I don't mean to be rude, but the game is starting in five minutes. What is this all about?"

"We've been asked to help locate Mr. Rose. It's a matter of some urgency involving his work at the State Department. We've been told that he's been in New York and we thought he might have contacted you."

"Morris has gone missing?" Collins asked, stalling for time. He wanted to know more before he answered any questions.

"He has been out of touch since Thursday. His wife doesn't know where he is and Mr. Rose didn't tell anyone in the Department where he was going. As far as we know you're the only one who has seen him since. Did he tell you where he was going?"

Collins shook his head. He wasn't about to tell the FBI where Morris was. He owed him that, at least.

"Did he mention anything about trouble at work?"

"Trouble? What sort of trouble?" Collins had been interviewing people long enough to know that answering a question with a question bought time to think.

"Any kind of trouble."

"Not that he mentioned to me."

"Any trouble in the marriage? Girl trouble?" Caldwell was fishing, Collins thought, hoping to connect with one of his questions.

"Like I said before, we talked about the Dodgers. That's it."

"And you watched the fights together?"

Collins hesitated slightly. "He couldn't stick around long. I was just there for the undercard myself. Checking out a heavyweight from Brooklyn named Gentleman Jack."

"I see. Did he say why he had to leave early?"

"I figured that he was traveling back to Washington on a late train. He said he couldn't stay overnight so I assumed the reason was that he was headed home."

Caldwell closed his notebook. "Thank you for your help, Mr. Collins," he said. "Should you hear from him in the next few days, I'd appreciate you letting us know." He handed Collins a business card.

Collins pocketed the card. He watched as the FBI agent made his way down the hallway, weaving through the incoming fans. Collins wondered if Morris knew that the FBI was looking for him. Had his plan of laying low in Vermont backfired? It appeared that Morris was in deeper trouble with his superiors at the State Department than he realized. It was serious enough that the FBI had gone to the trouble of sending an agent out to Ebbets Field to interview Collins.

In the press box, he found Pete Marquis, the *Sentinel*'s Dodgers beat writer, scribbling on his scorecard. Marquis was chewing gum, his jaw working furiously. During the course of a game he would chew several packages worth of Wrigley's Spearmint gum.

"The Yanks lost," Marquis said without looking up. "Kinder was sharp for the Red Sox."

"They still have the lead. Up one, right? The Yanks won't keep losing."

Marquis sighed. "I suppose so. It'd be grand if they lost, though, wouldn't it?"

Down below, on the field, there was a sudden burst of activity. It was "Don Newcombe Night," a special promotional event, and the tall Negro pitcher was being escorted to home plate. Collins noticed they had a shiny new Buick parked by the on-deck circle. Newcombe and his wife were presented with the car keys in a ceremony at home plate. The crowd applauded warmly. Marquis gave Collins a wry look; they both knew how fickle the Dodgers faithful could be and how quickly cheers could turn to boos. Then, after the national anthem was played over the public address system, the Phillies' young centerfielder Richie Ashburn stepped into the batter's box and the game began.

Newcombe looked great in the first inning. He was keeping the ball down and it looked from where Collins was sitting that he had great control of his pitches. The Phils sent out a rookie pitcher, Jocko Thompson, and the Brooks got to him quickly for a run in the second and then in the third inning Pee Wee Reese slapped a shot off Gran Hamner's glove at shortstop for a single, followed by hits by Carl Furillo and Gil Hodges. Olmo, the Dodgers' left fielder, singled in Furillo and Hodges to make it 4-0 in favor of the home team and the Phils reliever Russ Meyer gave up a single to Roy Campanella to make it 5-0. It was great to get an early lead, Collins thought, especially with Newcombe pitching under the lights.

Newcombe wasn't just good, he was nearly unhittable, so there was little suspense the rest of the way. He had some help in the field—in the fourth inning Snider made a long run in center field to catch a short fly by Ennis—but he kept pitching effortlessly into the ninth inning. That was when he gave up a long home run to the Phillies catcher, a stumpy guy named Andy Seminick who had once been a coal miner. Seminick pulled the ball into the lower left-field stands.

"He hit that one hard," Marquis said. "For an old guy."

"Just because he's balding doesn't make him that an old man," Collins said. He checked the program. Seminick was born in 1920. "He's not even thirty years old."

"That's an old twenty-nine. Hell, he looks older than you, Denny."

Collins ignored the jibe and glanced down at the Dodger's dugout. No sign that Shotton was looking to remove Newcombe. After walking Bill Nicholson, the big right-hander settled down and got the final two outs, and the Brooks had themselves a very satisfying win, 8-1. It had been a good night. Jackie Robinson had kept his National League batting lead, hitting a clean single. Ralph Branca was pitching the next game and he'd been effective. The prospects for the Dodgers, with five games to go, had improved.

"The Cards have a 3-0 lead over the Cubs," Marquis announced. "Seventh inning. Looks like they're going to stay a half game ahead. The Dodgers can catch them tomorrow. And if they can play like the way they did tonight the rest of the way..." Marquis didn't finish his sentence; he didn't need to. Collins knew how to complete it...*if they don't screw up at the very end and disappoint us, the way we fear they will, the way we expect they will.*

Dodgers fans were eternally wary; their hopes had been dashed too many times in the past to give them any authentic confidence, but they hoped against hope anyway. His father once told Collins that rooting for the Brooklyn Dodgers was fitting for an Irishman: the Irish understood that beauty didn't last long and that sorrow always waited just around the corner.

Collins said goodbye to Marquis and headed back into the hallway. He decided against calling Penny again. He walked down into the stands, negotiating his way through the happy fans leaving the ballpark. When his father was still alive, he would have walked over to where he and Uncle Hugh had their seats, season tickets, near the right field foul line. They would be waiting for Collins, standing near the aisle, beers in hand. Uncle Hugh would have handed Collins a beer in a waxed paper cup, cold and sharp to the taste, and they would have stood there with their thirty-cent Schaefer beers and talked for a few minutes, about the season, about how well the Dodgers had been playing. It would have been one of those times when you want to linger, to savor the moment, to stop time for a moment or two.

On the way home, he thought about the wonderful absurdity of getting paid to watch grown-up men playing a kid's game and then writing about it. In the Pacific the soldiers and Marines never wanted to talk about the political news from back home, the front-page stuff, when they learned Collins was a newspaper correspondent. They could have cared less about Congress or FDR's latest pronouncement, but talk to them about who was the better ball player, Ted Williams or DiMaggio, and you could count on a spirited discussion. No doubt baseball represented an escape, but wasn't that a good thing? Who could begrudge the escape of Ebbets Field?

He arrived back in his apartment about 11:30. He felt drowsy and was ready to go to bed. When he switched on the overhead lights in the apartment, he saw that there was something wrong. The desk drawer had been left open and the one of the cupboard doors in the kitchen was ajar as well. Someone had been in his apartment. Collins looked around, turning on the light in his bedroom where he spotted more signs of an intruder, or intruders. His slippers had been on the floor near the bed; now one was near the door and the other, a few feet away.

He quickly went to the bedroom to check the top drawer of his dresser, where he kept $100 in emergency cash in a small billfold. To his surprise it was still in the right hand corner, where he had left it, undisturbed. When he counted the bills, it was all there. But his small leather-covered box of cufflinks had been moved to the right side of the drawer, when he kept it on the left. He opened it: all of the jewelry was still there. He sat down in his most comfortable chair in his living room and tried to think. If there had been burglars in his apartment why hadn't they taken the cash?

Collins got up from the chair. Maybe the doorman could help. He rode the elevator down to the lobby and found Jimmy sitting there. He looked pleased at the interruption.

"Good one for the Dodgers tonight, huh? You see the game, Mr. Collins?"

"I did. Newcombe was sharp." He paused. "I had a question, Jimmy. Anyone stop by looking for me when I was at the game?"

"Can't say that they did. Expecting a guest?"

"No, I'm not expecting anyone. Anyone else around?"

"What's wrong, Mr. Collins? Everything okay?"

"It looked like somebody was in my place. Nothing was missing, but I wondered if maybe there were repairs or something going on in the building I didn't know about."

Jimmy thought for a moment. "Only new people in the building were the telephone guys. Right after I came on. Just after five."

"Telephone guys?"

"Repairmen. Said there was a problem with the telephone line on your floor. They said they wouldn't have to go into any of the apartments but they borrowed a passkey just in case."

"That probably was it."

"First time I've ever seen the Bell guys working on Saturday."

"First time for everything. Isn't that what they say?"

Collins went back up to his apartment, troubled by the situation. The telephone repairmen, if that was what they were, had clearly been in his apartment. He decided to call his brother. When he went to find Frank's home number in his address book, the photos weren't inside the front cover. He turned the address book over and shook it but nothing fluttered out. He checked the inside of the drawer and then the rest of the desk. No photos. He was sure that he hadn't moved them from the address book.

Whoever had entered his apartment had taken the photos. Apparently that was all the intruders had taken. He was immediately suspicious. Why would the only thing missing be a photograph that included Morris? Whoever took the snapshot was curious about Dennis Collins and his friends. Could they have known about his meeting with Morris at the Garden?

Collins recognized that he was jumping to conclusions, but what else explained the search of his place? Who was it? He figured it had something to do with Morris' security clearance. State Department security officers? The FBI? Why didn't they just obtain a search warrant and comb through his apartment in broad daylight? In any event, it had been a clumsy fishing expedition. If they had been looking for something that would connect him to Morris, other than the photo, they would have come up empty. Collins reached into his pocket to touch the canister, thankful that he had taken it with him.

He decided against phoning his brother. It could wait for the morning. It would give him some time to think the situation through before he involved Frank. Or at least that's how he rationalized it.

Sunday, September 25

When she woke she rolled over to look at the well-worn alarm clock on her night table the clock hands showed that it was just minutes before six o'clock. Then, with a start, she remembered that it was Sunday, her day off, her day to sleep in if she liked.

She lay in bed, still groggy and tired, yet certain that she wouldn't be able to get back to sleep. She turned on the light and found the book that she had been started days before, E.B. White's *Here is New York*. Rebecca Friedman at the Center had recommended it and Karina had purchased it as a way to learn about her adopted city.

She sat in the wingback chair in the living room and opened the book to the slip of paper she had employed as a bookmark. She had been reading for five minutes when she came across a passage that made her gasp in dismay.

The city, for the first time in its long history, is destructible. A single flight of planes no bigger than a wedge of geese can quickly end this island fantasy, burn the towers, crumble the bridges, turn the underground passages into lethal chambers, cremate the millions. The intimation of mortality is part of New York now; in the sounds of jets overhead, in the black headlines of the latest editions.

She thought of the shocking news on Friday, that the Soviets now had the atomic bomb, and the nausea she had felt when Morris had first called her on the phone at the Center made a sudden return. She fought it back, taking long slow breaths, and when she felt better she went over to her small desk so that she could copy the passage onto a piece of stationary. She took her time, checking her version against the book to make sure she had the words correctly.

"I can't," she said out loud, expressing what she had been thinking. She would help Morris if she could, out of loyalty and friendship, but she could not work for the Russians, no matter the consequences. She could not have that on her conscience. She had no illusions about what that could mean and it frightened her to think about what she might have to do, but she had reached a point of no return.

She would not be able to stay in New York. Once she had finished with Morris, she would tell Rebecca that she needed to take a few days off from work. She would leave as quickly as possible. She had spent the last year arranging new lives for the refugees who came to the Hotel Marseilles, so she had a clear idea of how she could disappear. She would avoid cities where Poles and Latvians and Lithuanians had been resettled, places where Yatov and his men might search for her.

Instead, she would find a town where she could make a living by teaching piano and voice, perhaps a college town. She would keep to herself, and avoid émigré circles if there were any. It would be critical that she not draw attention to herself. She had to disappear for a time, become invisible. And if, despite her precautions, the hard men found her like they had other defectors, she would have the revolver.

She regretted having to leave the Center and the ordinary life she had fashioned since arriving in New York. It was something she never imagined could happen during the last years of the war when she thought she would not survive to enjoy a normal life again.

She decided that she would spend her Sunday walking around her adopted city, saying farewell. She pictured her route. From her apartment, she would walk east to Central Park and then south through the park, enjoying the autumn leaves, until she left the park at the Merchants' Gate at 59th Street. She would stop by the Russian Tea Room for tea and a cherry blintz and chat with the stocky owner, Sasha Maeef, who reminded her of her uncle, Raimonds, with his subversive sense of humor. Then on to the frenetic activity of Times

Square, and perhaps a subway ride to Greenwich Village, before returning to the Upper West Side later in the afternoon.

She could not complain about having to leave. Her stay in the city had been an unexpected gift, a time to rediscover what it was like to exist without fear and deprivation, the way she had lived before 1939. It had restored her in some deep way. She would miss all of it, the sense of being at the center of things again, but she couldn't change what she now had to do. It was necessary, and now that she had decided on her course, there was no turning back.

Nine

His hand felt much better in the morning and Collins was able to shave and brush his teeth without wincing. As long as he didn't punch anyone else, he figured the swelling of his knuckles should be gone by the following weekend. There was some ugly bruising, but it looked worse than it felt.

When Collins called his brother and told him about his apartment being rifled and that the only strange people in the building had been telephone repairmen, Frank didn't say anything in response at first.

Collins thought for a moment that their connection had been broken. "Frank?"

"I'm here. You're sure there were telephone repairmen in the building?"

"I'm sure."

Collins could picture the frown on his brother's face. "I'll come by in an hour to look around. Leave the apartment the way you found it."

Collins walked over to the All-American for breakfast. He ordered coffee, scrambled eggs, and toast and leafed through the Sunday papers.

He turned to the *Sentinel* first, and found Van had given his column a catchy headline: "No Good Deed Unpunished?" Collins reread his column, wondering if it would do any good for Joey Gallegos. It would be a shame if the kid ended up doing hard time.

The other Sunday papers were filled with stories about the Russians and the atomic bomb, and Collins turned to the sports sections. They all headlined Don Newcombe's victory and the Yankees' loss to the Red Sox. The Yanks naturally got more play. The editors saw the once and future champs, the top dogs, as the biggest story in New

York sports, even when they were stumbling and the underdog Dodgers were winning.

There was also an intriguing boxing story. Jake LaMotta's handlers announced that he had injured his shoulder so badly in training that he had to pull out of his upcoming middleweight title fight with Marcel Cerdan, the Frenchman, originally set for Thursday. Because the group managing LaMotta, the International Boxing Club, was an unsavory outfit, there would always be questions when there was a late cancelation of a fight or when a favored fighter lost to an underdog. Two years before, in 1947, the Boxing Commission had suspended LaMotta for tanking a fight in the Garden.

Collins wondered about the real story behind the LaMotta withdrawal. Were they trying to delay the match in the hopes that Cerdan might retire (which he was said to be considering) before LaMotta had to fight him again? Collins wouldn't be surprised if there was something fishy behind the injury. He couldn't take the time during the biggest week of the baseball season to try to nail it down, but he was sure there was something more involved.

After breakfast, Collins waited impatiently for Frank in the lobby of his building, guiltily chain-smoking his Chesterfields.

He knew that he had to be careful around his brother. He couldn't tell him about his promise to Morris. Collins would have to be cautious, because for all of his tough-guy bluster, Frank had always been a keen observer of people, remarkably sensitive to changes in mood. It was a quality that had made him a good street cop and a better detective.

Collins also knew that if he told the complete truth, his brother would want him to call the FBI, to give them the film in the canister. Collins couldn't do that. Perhaps it was a foolish schoolboy loyalty, but he wasn't about to contribute to the railroading of Morris Rose. What was going on was a mockery of justice and he wouldn't be part of it.

Frank showed up at 10:30, still in his Sunday best.

"Don't have a lot of time," he told Collins. "Due over at the in-laws for Sunday dinner and you know how cranky Maureen can get when we're late."

They rode the elevator to the fourth floor in silence. When they entered the apartment Frank walked around from room to room, stopping to check closets and drawers. He spent the most time inspecting Collins' desk. When he was finished, his brother gave Collins his crooked smile. "Denny, this looks like a Bureau job."

"The FBI?"

"It has all the earmarks. They like to use the workman ploy, New York Tel or Con Ed, to get inside the building. Whoever went through this apartment knew what they were doing. Professionals. They kept their gloves on. We could dust the place from top to bottom and never find a print."

"It doesn't make any sense. Why would the FBI do this? It's got to be someone else. I had an argument with Phil Santry on the phone yesterday about whether boxing is on the up-and-up, and about his latest fighter, Gentleman Jack. He was pretty angry with me. You think it could have been Santry sending a message?"

His brother shook his head, unpersuaded. "This is a bit too subtle for the people who run with Santry. Their way would be to give you a good beating to make sure that you got the message."

"But Santry has a motive. Here's how I see it: I get in an argument with him in the early afternoon. Maybe he thinks I'm writing a column on boxing being under the thumb of the mob, or I'm going after his new stiff in the paper. He gets his friends to search my apartment, looking to see if I have any documents or incriminating evidence."

"Not likely. It just doesn't fit."

"Maybe they think I'm about to blow the whistle. Did you see in today's papers about LaMotta? Canceling his fight with Cerdan? There's something going on. Maybe they think I've got something on LaMotta and they went through my desk to see if I have any documents or incriminating evidence."

"Do you?"

"No. But they don't know that. And Santry might be encouraging them to think that I do."

"Maybe. But this doesn't fit this boxing angle the way I see it. I have to tell you that."

His brother wandered into the bedroom. He looked at the telephone on the bed-table and hesitated. Then he went over and picked it up. He took a penknife out of his trouser pocket and worked on the phone receiver, whistling an off-key version of the song "Personality." He suddenly stopped and grunted.

Collins started to say something but his brother pantomimed zipping his lips. He had removed one of the caps off the phone mouthpiece and he pointed to a small wire inside the receiver. He carefully replaced the cap and then he motioned for them to leave the bedroom. He didn't say anything until they were in the hallway.

"We can talk in the lobby," he said.

They rode down to the lobby, again in silence. Once they had stepped off the elevator, his brother pulled Collins to one side.

"What the hell is going on?" he asked.

"I don't know what you're talking about"

"Why would the Feds plant a microphone in your phone? I recognize their work. Someone in the Bureau wants to listen in to your calls. With the set-up they've put in, every phone call you make can be recorded."

Collins immediately thought about the calls with Ruth and Morris. How would their conversations sound if they were replayed before a federal jury? He was fortunate that the calls had come before Saturday night, before the visit of the "telephone repairmen." Collins didn't think he would be able to bluff his brother much longer, so he decided to tell him about Morris.

"Well," he said slowly. "If it's the FBI, like you say." He stopped. He figured that he needed to think out loud for his brother's benefit. Wasn't that the way it would go if he wasn't hiding anything? "I'm not working on anything right now that'd cause them to do this. No mob stories. Nothing across state lines."

"Think, Denny. There's got to be something. You're not getting tips from someone on a grand jury, are you?"

"Nothing like that." Collins paused. "I've been writing about sports a lot. I'm not running into too many government types…" He let his voice trail off, then, as if he was thinking, trying to recall something. "Except one, I guess. Morris Rose. If he counts. I told you I saw him recently."

His brother's expression immediately changed. The look on his face was that of a man who had been struggling with a complicated problem and suddenly found the answer.

"Morris? When was this?" His brother had always disliked Morris and his politics. Frank had asked Collins more than once over the years why Morris insisted on lecturing everyone on the need to change the world. What was so wrong with the world, anyway?

"Friday night. At the Garden."

"You saw him at the fights?"

"He was passing through. We talked for ten minutes or so. I wouldn't have thought twice about it, Frank. He told me that he wasn't happy about his situation at work. Something about a loyalty investigation. He thought that it would blow over."

Had Collins caught the right tone? He looked over at his brother, who nodded his head and whistled. "Jesus. That makes this—" he motioned towards the ceiling, as though the gesture took in the tossed dresser drawers and bedside phone bug four stories above them, "— more understandable."

"There's more," Collins said. "They had an agent come out to Ebbets last night, before the game, to ask me about Morris. Whether I knew where he was. Apparently he's gone missing."

Collins could see the sudden wariness on his brother's face. Collins knew that he had to show some anger. That's how someone who didn't have a canister of microfilm with State Department documents on it nestled in his pocket would react, and so that's what he did. "Are we turning into a police state?" he asked, surprising himself with his own sudden emotion. "What gives them that right? To bother me at work? To tap my phone?"

"They're just doing their job," his brother said. "Hell, they could have a grand jury empanelled. Or they've got a judge directing this."

"Or they don't."

"It wouldn't be the first time they played Lone Ranger. But if Rose is in trouble of some sort, you're the logical person to watch in New York." Frank paused, squinting as he pondered the situation. "Let me talk to someone at the Bureau that I know. Find out what I can, in an unofficial way."

Collins nodded. It had gone as well as he could have expected. He hadn't told his brother everything, but it was for the better.

"So what now?"

His brother gave Collins a look of concern. "You're not mixed up in Rose's crap in any way are you?"

"No, I'm not even a fellow traveler."

"Real funny. People lose their jobs over this shit. They end up on lists. Not-to-be-trusted lists, blacklists. If it turns out that Rose is really bad news, you could end up in serious trouble."

"Can you hear yourself, Frank? If Morris is bad news?"

His brother shrugged. "One thing I've learned as a cop is that people don't walk around with signs on their foreheads telling you that they're an embezzler or a second-story guy. No different with this. Rose wouldn't be eager to tell you if there was anything to this loyalty investigation."

"There isn't. Trust me."

"Have it your way," he said. "Morris is clean as the driven snow. But I'll have that chat with the guy I know at the FBI just in case that somebody's been peeing in the snow bank."

"What about the bug in the phone?"

"What about it?"

"Should I take it out?"

"Suit yourself. But don't think if you take it out that your apartment is clean. They usually plant more than one microphone. They always want a back-up."

After Collins had thanked him for coming over, Frank tipped his fedora, and left. Collins went back upstairs to his apartment and found a pair of scissors. He unscrewed the phone in his bedroom and snipped the wire to the microphone. He left the device in the phone, figuring that if they came back to check, they might think that it was sloppy work the first time. Then he checked the phone on his desk—and was relieved to find the mouthpiece was clear of bugs.

He took a deep breath. Of his unfinished business, that only left Penny. Collins picked up the phone, figuring he would give it one more try for the day. To his surprise the phone was answered on the first ring.

Penny immediately recognized his voice. "Oh, Dennis, it's you."

He didn't like what sounded like disappointment in her voice. "Did I interrupt something?" he asked.

"I am expecting a call from Washington."

"Should I get off the line?"

"We can talk for a little while."

"I'm pleased that I caught you at home. I tried yesterday, but no luck." Collins was thankful there was no way she could have known how many times he had called. He couldn't very well ask her where she had been, but she took pity on him.

"No, I wasn't in. I went to visit a girlfriend in Connecticut. Sarah Roberts. I don't think you ever met her. We were in school together. She has a little baby boy, whom I met for the first time. Quite adorable."

"I wanted to thank you for Friday night. I had a great time. And I'm sorry for embarrassing you. My fault completely. I should know better."

"How is your hand?"

"It's a bit swollen. I won't be playing the violin for a while."

She laughed. "A man of hidden talents."

"Except I'd need lessons first before I played."

"Truthfully, you didn't strike me as the violin type."

"I hope I didn't ruin the entire evening for you."

"I had a nice time, Dennis. Most of the time. The dancing and the walk through Central Park were lovely. And I realized again how easy it is to talk to you. Just like old times."

"That's great to hear. I was hoping we could go out again sometime soon."

"That would be nice," she said. "But I have to go to Washington and I don't know for how long I'll be away. A few matters I want to resolve."

"It sounds quite serious," he said. "A bit mysterious." He was hoping he could encourage her to talk more, prolong their call.

"More complicated than mysterious. I need to make my life simpler. Cleaner. Perhaps someday I can explain it all to you."

"I'd like that." It wasn't much, Collins knew, but at least she was talking about seeing him in the future.

"I read your column today," she said. "Very lyrical and very sad at the same time. I liked it. I hope that the judge takes into account that this Gallegos fellow saved a woman's life. It wouldn't seem quite fair to put him in prison for twenty-five years."

"That's what I am hoping. I'm going to try to be there when he comes into court. I'll write another column right before the hearing, to remind the judge."

"You are a good man, Dennis Collins."

It wasn't what Collins wanted to hear.

"When can I call you?" he asked.

She paused. "I won't be back for a while," she said. "We really shouldn't make any plans. Not until I have a better idea of when I'll return. So it would be best if I call you."

"When do you think that will be?"

This time she didn't pause. "I don't know. I just told you that."

"I'm sorry," he said. "I'll be here."

"I wish this was simpler," she said. "But it isn't."

Then she said goodbye and after Collins followed suit he heard the click of the phone being hung up on her end. He reluctantly put his receiver in the cradle. He didn't like the way the call had ended. For that matter, he didn't like the way it had started.

He sat staring at the phone, the instrument of his unhappiness, and wondered if this was the end for them. Penny was going back to Washington and she didn't know, or wouldn't say, when she would be back.

Collins remembered a wartime joke about "Dear John" letters. Fred, the soldier in the platoon who loved to read aloud his letters from his girl back home, starts in on his latest letter. "Dear John," he reads, and then stops. His buddies urge him to go on reading. "That's all she wrote," he says and holds up the sheet of paper—blank except for the salutation. "Must be a mistake. My name isn't John."

Was he misreading Penny in the same way? She had said some things that gave him hope—that she had missed talking with him, that she had enjoyed dancing with him—but that wasn't much to go on. He didn't want to admit that it was over, but it didn't look good.

He would not call her again. It wasn't just a matter of pride. He would have called Penny every ten minutes—pride be damned—if he thought that was the way to her heart. But it was clear that she didn't care to hear from him. It was best to move on, to admit that he had been mistaken. They weren't going to recapture what they had the first time around. It was foolish to think otherwise. He didn't regret having tried, but now, he told himself, it was time to call it quits before he began caring too much again.

Ten

Back in the Ebbets Field press box, Collins welcomed the diversion of covering another baseball game. It would at least help keep his mind off phone taps and ex-girlfriends. As the first few innings rolled by, the Phillies couldn't hit the starter for the Dodgers, Ralph Branca, but Collins wondered whether Branca could last the entire game.

For their part, the Dodgers got to the Phillies pitcher Ken Heintzelman for two runs in the fourth inning on a single by Roy Campanella, and then a solo home run by Gil Hodges in the sixth. Between the sixth and seventh innings, Pete Marquis tugged at Collins' sleeve. He was obviously nervous about the game and wanted to make small talk.

"I hear the entire Giants brass went over to Yankee Stadium last night. Horace Stoneham, Feeney, Carl Hubbell, Mel Ott, even Durocher."

"What for?" Collins didn't have to contribute much; Marquis was happy to carry the conversation by himself. Collins didn't feel like talking. He kept trying to banish Penny from his thoughts, and he kept failing.

"Maybe because they wanted to see what a pennant race is like?" Marquis laughed at his own joke. "Who knows? It can't be easy when you're the only club in town that's out of it. Twenty-three games out of it. So who do you think they want to win the National League? A dollar to a doughnut that it's not the Dodgers."

"Think so?"

"I know so. Who likes getting shown up? I know that I don't. You think I'm happy when friggin' Dick Young gets a scoop? Why should the Giants be any different? They look bad when they're the only New York team out of pennant contention. Hell, they were out of it before the All Star break."

"I guess you're right," Collins said. "But don't get ahead of yourself. The Dodgers haven't won anything yet."

"But it's looking good, isn't it?" Marquis asked, waving towards the field. "Figure Branca keeps pitching like this and they're right on top of the Cards. They'll close to within a half game."

"If wishes were kings, we'd all have cakes and ale for Christmas."

"Forget Christmas, how about first place in the National League by October?"

Collins gave him a doubtful look. It was natural for Marquis and the beat writers to pull for the team they were covering. If the Dodgers made it to the Series, then it would be Pete Marquis writing the lead story for the sports section, the story everyone read first. The Series meant more people would be reading your best stuff: other sportswriters, editors, publishers. Careers and reputations could be made.

By the top half of the eighth inning Collins figured that most of the Ebbets crowd had begun anxiously counting outs. Six to go. The Dodgers had a 3-1 lead, Branca had struck out nine. But the first sign of possible trouble came at the start of the eighth, when Branca didn't come out to the mound. Instead, it was Jack Banta, a young right-hander, warming up.

That was when Tex Rickards came on the public address system to make an announcement that quieted the crowd. "The reason Branca is leaving the game—he has a blister on his hand and it broke." Marquis and Collins looked at each other in disbelief. Collins had never heard management provide an explanatory announcement quite like that before. There was something eerie about it.

"If you can't pitch, you can't pitch," Marquis said out loud. He was chewing his gum rapidly. "Maybe Banta can hold 'em. Six outs. All we need from him is six lousy outs." His tone of voice didn't convey much confidence. He chewed his gum furiously.

It went poorly from the start for Banta. The first Phillies hitter, Richie Ashburn, laid down a bunt and when Banta came off the mound to field the ball, he collided with the third baseman, Eddie Miskis. No throw and Ashburn was safe at first.

"Great start," Marquis said. "They look like Little Leaguers."

The next batter, Gran Hamner, hit a line drive to left center field. Until the very last moment Collins thought Duke Snider was going to reach it with a sudden burst of speed, but the ball tipped off his glove. Hamner ended up on second and Ashburn at third.

"Where's our luck gone?" Marquis asked.

Banta's confidence had to be shaken. It was one of the worst situations for a reliever—to put runners on without retiring anyone. No outs. The Phillies first baseman, Dick Sisler, a left-handed hitter, was next up to bat and Banta's bad luck continued. Sisler hit a bouncer up the middle that neither Pee Wee Reese nor Jackie Robinson could make a play on, and both runners, Ashburn and Hamner scored. Tie score, 3-3 and no outs. When the next batter, Del Ennis, tried to bunt to advance Sisler to second, he popped out to Roy Campanella.

"Finally," Marquis said. "Finally we get an out."

Then Marquis groaned—the Phils' burly catcher, Andy Seminick, dropped the second bat he was using to warm up and left the on-deck circle. He sauntered up to the batter's box. Collins knew Marquis was remembering the long home run Seminick had hit the night before.

They were not held in suspense for very long. Seminick swung at the first pitch and from the sound of contact it was clear he had hit the ball a long way. It landed in the left center field stands, driving in Sisler and putting the Phils ahead 5-3.

Ebbets Field fell quiet, deathly still, as Seminick rounded the bases. Sisler waited at home plate to congratulate him.

Marquis cursed. "I told you, Denny. I told you that Seminick was going to hurt us again."

"It's not over," Collins told him, but it turned out that it was. The Phillies had inserted Russ Meyers in at pitcher in the seventh and he only gave up one hit and one walk in his three innings. After the last out, the disappointed fans began to quickly file out of Ebbets.

Marquis put his head in his hands. "They blew the pennant tonight. I could see it coming and there was nothing that could be done. If Branca stays in, they win. Damn it, Denny, why do they always screw up? I know why they call them the Bums, because they are bums."

"Don't count them out. Winning four games in a row isn't impossible. As long as Shotton can go with Newk and Branca in two of the last four games, there's hope."

"With our luck Branca's blister will keep him from pitching the rest of the way. And all of the games are on the road."

"I'm glad you're looking at the bright side of things, Pete."

Marquis had been filing copy continuously during the game. He called in a lead to the *Sentinel* sports desk and then headed down to the dressing room to try to get a quote from Shotton about the pitching change. Collins had to finish off his Monday column; he was now on deadline as much as Marquis.

He banged out a new lead on the portable typewriter. At least it was original, he thought. He would be the only newspaperman in New York arguing that the Dodgers still had a solid chance to win the National League pennant. They had to play the last four games on the road: two in Boston and then the final two in Philadelphia. The Brooks had not played well against either the Braves or Phillies, and the Cardinals had an easier schedule, but Collins would argue that the Dodgers had the better pitching. They could sweep the last four and hope that the Cards faltered. They just needed a few breaks.

After he had handed his column to the *Sentinel* messenger, he packed up and left, taking a cab back to Manhattan. When Collins reached the door to his apartment he tensed up, wondering about uninvited guests. A quick walk through all of the rooms convinced him that his things were untouched. He had been so wrapped up in his call from Penny and then the Dodgers game that he hadn't thought much about Morris and the canister of film in his coat pocket.

He found a bottle of Rheingold in the refrigerator and poured himself a glass. He went into the living room and put one of his Billie Holliday records on the player. He didn't bother to turn any lights on. Collins didn't generally drink by himself and not at night and not on an empty stomach. He had a healthy respect for how the Irish curse could ruin a man and he hated waking up in the morning with a hangover.

He sat there and drank the first beer, savoring the taste, enjoying the sound of Holliday's smoky voice. He hadn't listened to the Lady in a while; she was singing the song "I'll be Seeing You," and it brought back a lot of memories, dancing with Penny, making love with her, watching her breathe softly as she slept. He lit up a Chesterfield and closed his eyes. He knew the lyrics to the song by heart. It was a shame that Holliday wasn't performing any more in the jazz clubs on 52nd Street; she'd lost her cabaret license after her last brush with the law. The record came to an end. Collins went back into the kitchen and took another beer. He started the disc again.

Collins walked over to his desk and picked up the phone and dialed Penny's number. He counted eight unanswered rings before he placed the receiver gently in the cradle of the phone. He cursed himself, loathing himself for his own weakness.

What would he have said if she had been home and picked up the phone? "This is Denny, and if you haven't figured it out already, I'm hopelessly in love with you." Or if Penny had answered, would he have hung up the phone in embarrassment, unable to say a word? Collins guessed he was lucky that he wasn't forced to make that awkward choice. He couldn't honestly say what he would have done.

Part Two

Monday, September 26

She slept fitfully for the third night in a row, abandoning the warm comfort of her bed well before sunrise.

She sat in her small kitchen with a cup of hot tea, one overhead light on, her phonograph playing Mozart's Symphony No. 40 at a low volume, and thought about what she must do that day.

She would keep her promise to Morris and contact the newspaperman, Dennis Collins, and make an initial connection by arranging his visit to the Center. Then, when the time came, she would communicate whatever message Morris had for him and afterward, she had resolved, she would leave the city.

Her help for Morris would discharge any of her past debts to him, she told herself. Then she would be free to leave. There was no telling how Anatoli Yatov would react when he found out that Morris had recruited her into an impromptu adventure of his own design. She had no intention of staying to find out. At some point Yatov would realize that she had left New York and she could only hope that her trail would have grown cold by then. She didn't worry about Morris; she figured that he would have planned for all eventualities. He was too clever not to have devised an escape plan of some sort.

Outside, it had begun to grow light.

She had met with Yatov—or Bob, as he insisted being called—twice since coming to New York. Her brief but intense interviews with him had left her exhausted and shaken. She had been surprised by Yatov's nondescript appearance, his thinning hair, watery eyes, and pasty complexion. He wasn't much taller than her. If she had passed him on the street, she would have guessed that he was a shop clerk or a down-on-his-luck bookkeeper. There was nothing about him that even remotely hinted at who he was or how dangerous a man he was.

In their interviews, he had politely but relentlessly questioned her about her work at the Center, about her routine, about her friends, about whether she had taken a lover. He spoke in a heavily accented but grammatically-correct English. Occasionally he stopped to scribble notes in a small, black notebook. He wrote with a thick pencil. His face had never betrayed what he was thinking, but his eyes were flint hard and she was sure that behind the impassive mask he despised her as a collaborator, a woman of loose morals, a spoiled and degenerate bourgeois artist.

Yatov had made it clear that she would be expected to follow his orders without question. He had been direct about the power he held over her—she had entered the country under false pretenses and the American Immigration authorities would not hesitate to deport her back to Poland if they ever saw her true dossier. He did not need to tell her what her reception in Warsaw would be like upon her return.

When he realized that she had fled the city, she knew that he would try to find her. He could not allow her to escape. He would want to make an example of her, to show others what happened to those who betrayed the organization. Her relative insignificance as an agent didn't matter. He would send men after her, she was sure of that.

She resolved not to panic. She had survived harder times, she told herself. After the partisans killed Piotr in 1944, assassinating him in a broad daylight ambush on Kanonia Street, she did not think she could go on, but she did. She found shelter with Elzbieta Jasinski and her husband, fellow opera singers, on their small farm twenty miles outside of Warsaw. She used the cache of gold coins Piotr had left her to buy their food. She stayed there through the Uprising and its horrific aftermath in October when the Nazis began the deliberate destruction of the city. She had been grateful for safe harbor, conscious of what her friends risked by sheltering the wife of a man despised as collaborator.

When the Russians arrived in January 1945, her instincts for self-preservation took over. She needed protection not only from the drunken Red Army soldiers now at large in the city, but also from the likelihood that she would be denounced, because of Piotr, to the authorities. On her second trip to Warsaw, she had spotted Colonel Alexander Ivanov drinking alone in a small café. There was something sensitive about his eyes and mouth and she did not hesitate when he invited her to join him at his table. She never regretted her decision to become his mistress—Sasha proved to be generous and kind. In truth, she had no other options.

In comparison, what Morris had asked her to do was easy. The difficulties would come later, after she had left New York. She had only to meet with Collins twice: once to arrange and translate his interviews at the Center, and then once to deliver whatever message Morris might have for him.

She wondered what story Morris had spun to enlist Collins' help. It couldn't have been the truth, of course, but knowing Morris, it would have been persuasive. Lonnie Marks had told her that Collins often championed the underdog in his newspaper column. Morris no doubt would have played the part of the persecuted diplomat, hounded by reactionaries.

Dennis Collins did not strike her as a complicated man. She understood why Morris would choose him as a friend. Collins wore his heart on his sleeve—she had always loved that phrase in English— and Morris would have been attracted by that openness, so different from his own cautious and calculating nature.

She had watched Collins on the Stork Club dance floor with his date, Penny Bradford. According to Lonnie, she had spurned him years before. When Karina saw the way Collins looked at his glamorous companion, she had ached for him. His need and vulnerability was written so plainly on his face. She found herself instinctively disliking the Bradford woman; it was irrational, she knew, but the feeling was there.

She found herself thinking about the pain men and women caused each other. When she was a child, living in Riga, she had been frightened by the fights between her parents, her mother's icy complaints and her father's vodka-inspired rages. He had left when

Karina was nine. Her mother died of cancer three years later, and her father, a wealthy importer of farm machinery, had sent her to Warsaw to live with her aunt, Jana, where she could take singing lessons with the voice coach who had taught Elisabeth Schumann, the German soprano.

She saw her father only once more, when he visited Warsaw in the spring of 1939 and had tried, in his own awkward way, to apologize. He had come to one of her performances, at the opera, and when they met afterward had praised her singing so effusively that he embarrassed her in front of Piotr and her friends.

He had returned to Latvia and they had lost touch. Her uncle Raimonds surfaced in Warsaw in August 1941, after the Germans drove the Soviets out of Latvia, to tell her that her father, his brother, had not survived the *Baigais Gads*, the Year of Horror. It was a foretaste of what was to come. Morris had been right when he had said that the war had changed things. It brought random death and destruction, hunger and despair, leaving its survivors with memories they wished they could forget but could not.

According to Lonnie, Dennis Collins had been a war correspondent in the Pacific and she imagined that he had seen some terrible things. Lonnie said that Collins hadn't been as happy-go-lucky when he returned and she understood immediately. When she had first come to New York she had struggled with the contrast between the shattered world she had left behind and the carefree existence of the Americans around her.

Like the veterans she had met, Collins had witnessed the reality of war. It wasn't something easily forgotten. There was something in his face that she liked, a gentleness hiding behind the wise-guy exterior. If she had met him under other circumstances, she could easily have fallen for him.

She found herself hoping that Morris wouldn't ask his friend to do anything that would compromise him later, if things went badly. Of course Collins could be given no idea of what Morris was actually up to—even Morris would not be rash enough to risk revealing his connection with Yatov. He had to keep Collins in the dark, to make use of him without revealing the true nature of his dealings. She recognized that there was no other way, but at the same time it was profoundly wrong—a betrayal of sorts—and Morris had to know that.

Eleven

Collins woke up to a slight headache behind his eyes. It was still dark outside, thanks to that weekend's switch-over to Daylight Savings Time. He got out of bed and found his way in the dark to the bathroom. Once he was on his feet he felt a little better. Collins took a brief warm bath and then shaved.

The swelling and discoloration on his hand wasn't as pronounced as before, and he figured it would be fine in a few days. He shook two Bayer aspirin out of the bottle and took them with a glass of water. They would help with the headache and the hand.

By the time Collins reached the street the sun was up. It promised to be one of those sunlit, cool autumn days in New York where the light made everything seem golden. You might wish that it could stay that way forever, but you knew it couldn't. You had to savor the day for what it was. It wasn't the perfect weather for his mood because he had nothing to savor.

When he got the papers at the newsstand, he checked the *Sentinel* first. They'd put his column on the front page with the headline: "Collins: Brooksies Ain't Done!" He was alone in that belief, it seemed. When he returned to his apartment to drink a cup of coffee he discovered that the other papers were all counting the Dodgers out, with Jimmy Cannon proclaiming that the season was over for both the Yanks and the Dodgers.

Collins' prediction didn't look so good in light of some of the post-game quotes from the Dodgers locker room. Ralph Branca had told the beat reporters that there was nothing wrong with his hand, that his blister wasn't bad enough to pull him from the game. Shotton was sticking with the story that he removed Branca as a precautionary move. Roy Campanella, the catcher handling Branca, ducked the question. Collins had always believed that harmony in the clubhouse was overrated. Baseball teams won all the time when the players didn't get along. But a squabble between one of your best pitchers and the manager in the last week of the season wasn't a promising sign.

After he finished his coffee he went back outside into the golden light to hail a cab for his commute downtown. He reached the *Sentinel* thirty minutes later than usual. Before Collins reached the elevator bank, Rudy, the front lobby attendant, stopped him to deliver a message. The publisher had asked that Collins stop by his office first thing. Collins was surprised. He saw Fred Longworth only a few times a year, at the office Christmas party, at whatever rare social event Collins might be covering that Longworth attended, but hardly ever at the *Sentinel*.

"He give a reason?" Collins asked. He wondered, for a moment, if the FBI had contacted Longworth.

Rudy shrugged. "It was Miss Musgrove that called down. She didn't say what for, Mr. Collins, just to let you know when you came in."

Collins took the elevator to the top floor, the twelfth, where Longworth had his elegantly decorated offices and a private dining room, all with stunning views of city's skyscrapers and, to the west, a glimpse of the Hudson River and the gentle hills of New Jersey.

Collins paused at the huge windows and looked down at Herald Square, hundreds of feet below him. The surrounding buildings glistened, their walls bleached by the sunlight. Pedestrians crowded the sidewalks of Broadway and Seventh Avenue, and on the streets a steady stream of trucks, Checker cabs, city buses, and an occasional sedan flowed by, horns blaring, gears shifting.

He could never work on the twelfth floor, Collins decided, because he wouldn't have been able to tear himself away from the view. There was something mesmerizing about the activity below, the human ant hill of a big city seen from a God's eye view.

It made him wonder where Penny was. Had she left for Washington? Was she sitting in Penn Station a few city blocks away waiting for her train? Did she think of him, at all, or was he already yesterday's awkward romantic problem, dealt with, disposed of, an afterthought at best?

Collins stopped at the desk outside Longworth's main office and checked with his elderly secretary, Miss Musgrove. She disappeared into the inner office and Collins didn't have to wait very long before she ushered him into the publisher's office, gently closing the door behind him. Longworth came out from behind his desk and advanced across the room with his hand outstretched.

"Dennis," he said, pumping Collins' hand like a politician. "Great to see you."

"Good to see you, sir," Collins said, surprised by Longworth's sudden friendliness.

"Are you heading over to the Stadium for the Yankees game?"

"I'm going to pass on that," Collins said. "Working on my column."

"Any plans for lunch?"

Collins shook his head.

"Splendid. Then if you would be so kind as to accompany me to the Yale Club, I'll buy you lunch. I have a friend in town who is a fan of your column and who would very much like to meet you. He'll join us there."

The *Sentinel*'s publisher called Miss Musgrove on his intercom and asked her to make reservations for three at the Yale Club.

"I think you will like my friend, Matthew Steele," Longworth said. "We'll take a car over. Why don't we meet in the lobby? At noon?"

"Sure," Collins said. "At noon."

Collins took the elevator back down to the newsroom, wondering about the invitation. Longworth's friend was probably an out-of-towner who wanted to grill Collins about his baseball heroes. He could imagine the questions: "What was Joe DiMaggio really like? Were Babe Ruth's appetites as prodigious as rumored? How was Jackie Robinson getting along with the white players?" If that was the case, he didn't mind spending the time with Longworth's rich friend—he'd

124

make his publisher happy and at least get a free lunch out of it. And, best of all, Longworth's summons had nothing to do with the FBI and Morris Rose. Collins could breathe easy on that front.

When Collins arrived at his desk he found a scrawled message placed on top of his typewriter: Karina Lazda requested that he call her at MO9-5525. He realized it was the girl from the Stork Club, Lonnie's friend, the one working for the United Service for New Americans. He was surprised. After the incident at the Stork Club he figured that she wouldn't want to have anything to do with him. When he reached her on the phone, she got right to the point.

"The other night you said you could provide us some publicity, Mr. Collins," she said.

"I wouldn't call it publicity," Collins said. "I thought there might be a column in what you are doing, what's going on with the DPs. I'd hoped to come by your Center and see what it's like for them."

"I read your column yesterday," she said. "About the medic who saved that woman. It was quite moving. I see now why Lonnie thought you could help. It is so very important that your readers understand that there are still many others in refugee camps in Germany and Poland hoping to come to America. We must get that message out to them."

They quickly agreed that Collins would visit the Hotel Marseilles later in the day, at 3:30, and Karina Lazda would arrange interviews with some of the recently arrived refugees. She would translate for those whose English wasn't adequate.

After Collins finished the call with her, he took a few minutes to look through his reporter's notebooks for the notes he habitually scribbled during the week for his "Ten Questions" column. He looked over at his phone several times, not that he expected it to ring with a call from the person he most wanted to hear from.

At five minutes before noon, he took the elevator down to the lobby. Longworth was already there, waiting for him. On the ride over to the Yale Club, Longworth wanted Collins' opinion on which was the best college football team in the country, and he seemed pleased when Collins told him that it had to be Army again.

Longworth's friend was waiting for them in the wood-paneled bar of the Yale Club. Matthew Steele was a slim, handsome man in a well-tailored two-button gray Brooks Brothers suit. His wire-rimmed glasses and thatch of brown hair gave him a slightly professorial air. Collins figured he was somewhere between forty and forty-five years old.

Steele apparently did want to talk about baseball. Once they were seated at a large table, glistening silverware and porcelain arranged on a starched white tablecloth, and had ordered drinks (bourbon and water for Longworth, a Manhattan for Steele, and a glass of beer for Collins) he asked about the Dodgers.

"I see you stand alone today, Mr. Collins. The other New York papers all officially pronounced your team dead. The Cardinals are now hands-down favorites to win the pennant. And yet you won't give up the ghost?"

"It's the stubborn Mick in me, I guess," Collins said. "We're drawn to lost causes and underdogs."

"There's an unfortunate truth in that. The Irish favor the underdog in most fights. Although Mr. de Valera's flirtation with the Nazis came when they looked like they would be the winning side."

Collins decided to ignore the comment. If Collins had deeply Republican sentiments he might have been offended, but he didn't, so he wasn't. And he certainly wasn't about to start defending Eamon de Valera or any other politician, domestic or foreign.

He responded with his own question. "So what do you do for a living, Mr. Steele, if I might ask?"

Longworth coughed in distress and shifted in his seat. "You have to expect some direct questions from Dennis," he said to his friend. "Don't say that I didn't warn you in advance. He's a newspaperman, after all."

Steele waved his hand. "Quite all right." He fixed his blue eyes on Collins. "I'm in the government, Mr. Collins. Based in Washington, although I make occasional jaunts to New York and to places near and far."

"That takes in a lot of territory," Collins said. "Any specific part of the government?"

Longworth shifted in his chair again. It was clear he didn't like the line of questioning.

"Security, for the moment," Steele said. "In a way. More informal than anything official."

Collins looked at him closely. Steele was too Ivy League to work for the FBI. J. Edgar Hoover recruited his agents from Fordham and Notre Dame, selecting eager young men who had been raised to respect authority and could be trusted to follow orders. Steele didn't fit the profile. So who did he work for? The State Department? Or the Central Intelligence Agency, the successor organization to the Office of Strategic Services, the band of dashing bluebloods who had engineered the U.S. espionage effort against the Germans?

"By the way, this lunch is off the record, Dennis," Longworth said. "I should have mentioned that earlier. It allows us the luxury of candor."

Collins looked over at his publisher. "Quite frankly, I didn't quite expect a front-page scoop, Mr. Longworth. I'd gladly settle for a stock tip or two, considering the surroundings."

Steele laughed. Collins sensed that Steele didn't take Fred Longworth too seriously; he could see the *Sentinel*'s publisher's cheeks had flushed red. Apparently it wasn't lost on him either.

The waiter returned and took their lunch orders. Steele and Collins both chose club sandwiches; Longworth had a Salisbury steak and potatoes. Collins turned back to Steele.

"I imagine that you're quite busy these days," he said. "Security. It appears as though that's the largest worry in Washington today."

"I imagine so. Someone has to worry about it."

"And subversion."

Steele took a sip of his cocktail. Collins sensed that Steele was taking his measure as they sat there, facing each other.

"Subversion," he repeated. "That's not on my dance card, per se. I am tied up with somewhat more prosaic duties. Cleaning the Augean stables in a way."

"Mixed metaphors," Collins said. "Dance cards and stables."

"My apologies," he said. "Poorly mixed metaphors. I regret I don't have your way with words. And what exactly are your politics, Mr. Collins?"

Collins shrugged. "It's no mystery. I tend to side with the little guy, the underdog." He looked over at Longworth. "Our readers."

"Underdogs like the Dodgers?"

"Sure, they qualify."

"And political underdogs? I've read some of your past columns. Most recently on the Hiss and Coplon trials."

"Then you know I don't play favorites. I didn't think the government had much of a case against Hiss and I said so. I thought Coplon was guilty as hell and I said so."

"I did read them." Steele seemed amused, as if he knew something that Collins didn't. His air of superiority was beginning to annoy Collins. "I appreciated your case-by-case approach. It's what I would expect from an independent sort of chap like yourself."

"Hell will freeze over before I turn into Westbrook Pegler and start foaming at the mouth about the Red Menace."

"Now who is mixing metaphors? I wouldn't imagine that you would ever Red bait. I take you for a loyal chap. Loyal to your friends, to the old neighborhood, to the Dodgers. It's written all over your face, if not in your column."

"I thought loyalty was quite fashionable these days. Loyalty oaths. Loyalty programs."

"You might be surprised to find that I agree with you on the question of loyalty oaths. They are the last refuge of the Neanderthals in Congress. All of it would be a lamentable waste of time, if it didn't keep the amateurs from poking their noses into truly important matters. So I say, let them have their loyalty programs."

"I'm not sure I follow you," Collins said.

Before Steele could answer, their waiter returned. Conversation stopped while he served their lunches. Collins had managed a few bites of his sandwich when Steele resumed the conversation.

"Did you hear about the press conference Congressman Velde held yesterday in Washington? He's a former FBI agent, now a member of the Un-American Activities Committee. Quite an excitable chap. Velde announced that there are 150 American Communists and Soviet agents trying to pry away our atomic secrets. Thinks we need a Congressional inquiry into our disgraceful security set-up." Steele paused, considering his words. "He represents a growing number of people in Washington, I'm afraid."

"You are afraid?"

Steele closed his eyes briefly, and then when he opened them he looked directly at Collins. It was a strange mannerism, Collins decided, but it somehow humanized Steele. "I dislike the amateurism," he said. "The lurid stories in the newspapers. Discretion is the better part of valor in these matters. We must be patient. We must recognize that our adversaries are patient people. They believe that they have the force of history on their side. We must match their patience."

"Well, then, I'd say your approach is losing ground, Mr. Steele. I don't see any patience on display in Washington. Just a lot of wild accusations against innocent people with progressive politics."

"You sound as if it's personal."

"Actually it is. A friend in the State Department has told me about the loyalty program there."

"That would be Morris Rose?" Steele asked. "You're his oldest friend, I understand."

"I don't hide our friendship," Collins said, immediately on guard. How did Steele know about his relationship with Morris? Was Steele with the State Department security office? Collins wondered whether his invitation to lunch had been solely because of his connection to Morris.

"Have you seen him recently?" Steele asked, keeping his tone casual.

"Is that an official question?"

"So the answer is yes, you have seen him."

"I had a clean-cut G-man ask me the same question last night at Ebbets Field," Collins said. "I have no idea where Morris is, and I told him that."

Somehow it wouldn't have surprised Collins if Steele already knew Morris had been in New York, and that Collins had met him. But he wouldn't tell Steele anything useful. He didn't trust the man. Steele could go to hell as far as Collins was concerned. He was not going to say or do anything that would hurt Morris.

"I know that Dennis will be cooperative in this matter," Longworth said. "All of us take these security questions seriously, Matthew. Very seriously."

"What are your friend's politics?" Steele asked Collins. He leaned forward slightly, his earlier casual air gone.

"Do you mean is he a subversive? Absolutely not. Unless rooting for Joe Louis over Max Schmeling and hoping that Franco would lose in Spain makes you a subversive."

"I rooted for Louis and against Franco," Steele said. "I guess then that I should be suspect as well."

"Count me in," Longworth said. "I'm a Joe Louis fan."

The waiter interrupted them to remove their lunch plates and bring coffee. They sat there in an awkward silence until he had finished, and then Longworth spoke up.

"You know what President Seymour is saying in New Haven?" he asked. "He claims that there will be no witch hunts at Yale, because there are no witches there."

"Well, that will be a swell trick if he can pull it off," Steele said.

"I don't believe there are any witches," Collins said. "Not at Yale, not here in New York and certainly not in Washington. Just as there weren't any in Salem. What is it that song in 'South Pacific' says: 'You've got to be taught to hate and fear, it's got to be drummed in your dear little ear?' The problem starts with ambitious and unscrupulous politicians trying to drum this absurd notion of Red subversives into our ears."

"It has been my experience that hate and fear doesn't have to be carefully taught," Steele said. He had lost none of his good humor. "*Homo sapiens* need little instruction. Take your average American teenager in 1944, from, say, a small town in Iowa or Indiana. An innocent. Give him basic training, teach him how to kill, and then ship him to a place like Okinawa. Let him experience Kamikaze attacks, banzai charges, the mutilation of his dead buddies. He'll grow to hate and fear quite quickly, I would wager. You should know, since you witnessed Saipan and Okinawa, didn't you, Mr. Collins?"

Collins nodded. He knew then with certainty that if there was a file on him anywhere in Washington, whether in the War Department or the FBI archives, Steele had read it from cover to cover.

"Then you at least know what a man is capable of, under the circumstances. As to the spies, I can assure you that they do exist, although certainly not in the numbers Velde and others are claiming."

"Where were you during the war?" Collins asked. "Based in Washington, then, too?"

"Oh, no," Steele said. "I operated from Switzerland for the OSS. Neutral territory you might think but one thing I learned in Berne and Zurich and other points of the compass is that there is no real neutrality. It is an illusion. There comes the day when you have to choose a side. In or out. Home team or visitors."

"And you would choose the Yankees, no doubt," Collins said, hoping to irritate him. He didn't succeed, for Steele responded with a slight smile.

"Mr. Collins, will you be disappointed to learn that I'm not a Yankee fan?"

He had Collins there.

"I assumed that you were," Collins told him.

"Then you would be wrong," he said. "I am one of those rare birds, a native of the District of Columbia. Consequently my team is the Senators. Sadly we are firmly in last place, which shouldn't be too surprising when you consider that Ray Scarborough represents the ace of our pitching staff. So you see, at least in baseball I find myself on the side of the underdogs."

Steele reached across the table and handed Collins his business card. It was on thick, expensive stock and bore only his name, an address on East 67th, and a phone number.

"A favor, Mr. Collins. Should Morris Rose contact you during the next few days, I'd appreciate it if you would let him know that I am quite interested in chatting with him."

Collins knew that he should have resisted the urge to make the smart comment, but something in his nature always carried him over the top. "Why on earth would Morris want to chat with you?" he asked. "No offense intended."

"None taken. I think you can relay to Mr. Rose that it would be to his great advantage to have this discussion with me. I think he will find me immensely more—" Steele paused for dramatic effect "—*sympathetic* than some of the other people who are looking for him. They don't share my appreciation of the grays in life."

"Did you answer my question?" Collins asked.

"Your friend will understand," he said. "I'm sure of that."

"I'm beginning to regret that this lunch is off the record," Collins said. "Seems like there might be a story here. Anatomy of a witch hunt."

"That would be a shame. It would be in no one's best interest if any of this found its way into the newspaper."

"It won't," Longworth said quickly. He looked at Steele, ignoring Collins. "You have my word, Matt."

"I'm sure I do, Fred," Steele said languidly.

They had finished their coffee and Longworth signaled the waiter, who returned to the table and handed Longworth a slip. The *Sentinel*'s publisher scribbled his initials on it and the waiter gave him a slight nod. No money openly exchanged hands for their lunch and yet the absence of cash made you think of it, Collins thought. Ironic that the very thing meant to take the crassness out of the transaction did nothing but accentuate the power of money. After all, only the wealthy signed club chits. They walked out of the Yale Club together and Steele and Longworth both shook Collins' hand when they reached the street. Collins excused himself from the car ride back and headed downtown to walk back to Herald Square and the *Sentinel* building.

Collins fumbled in his coat pocket and found the package of Chesterfields. He lit one up and thought about what Steele had said. He hadn't been fooled by Steele's good manners and soft-spoken charm. There was a calculated hardness to Steele. Collins had met men like Steele before. They filled the officer corps and the executive suites. They knew how to lead, how to get things done. Steele, an OSS veteran and now a trusted part of the national security apparatus, clearly understood power and how to wield it.

It couldn't possibly be a good thing for Morris Rose that Steele had such a clear interest in his whereabouts, Collins thought, or that Steele had traveled from Washington and arranged an interview with Morris' childhood buddy on such short notice. It couldn't possibly be a good thing for Dennis Collins, either.

Twelve

Collins considered the disturbing aspects of his lunch with Longworth and Steele on his walk back to the *Sentinel* building. The more Collins thought about it, the more he realized that Morris' decision to wait out the week in Vermont had raised even more suspicion. It was obvious how the security types—like Matthew Steele—interpreted his disappearance as an admission of something, if not of his outright guilt.

In a way, Collins thought, you could understand the paranoia. By now, it had become second nature to them: the security operatives had adopted the Napoleonic Code toward subversion. They assumed guilt. If the innocent got treated roughly it didn't seem to matter, so long as the investigators could cover themselves, could avoid blame if any real subversives did turn up. There were always men like Congressman Velde to find fault. Steele and his colleagues in Washington had to assume the worst and act on it; that way they had cover if things went wrong.

Morris was clearly in deep trouble. His career at the State Department had to be over. Who would promote a suspected security risk or keep him in sensitive positions? Why bother? Morris would be lucky to land a position at one of the white shoe New York firms after this episode.

Collins knew that some of this applied to him, as well. He was walking around with a roll of undeveloped film of State Department documents, film handed to him by a government official under suspicion. Collins could be putting his own job at risk if he got entangled too deeply. At least, he told himself, there were only two other people in the world who knew for certain that he had the film, and he could trust both of them.

Collins didn't go directly to the newsroom when he got back to West 39th Street. Instead he stopped off at the newspaper's library. He figured there might be something in the *Sentinel*'s archives of news clippings that could shed some light on the situation.

He filled out a request form, asking for whatever the morgue had on Matthew Steele, Congressman Velde, and then, impulsively, he added Karina Lazda. The young woman behind the counter looked unhappy at having her reading interrupted, reluctantly abandoning her book, Mika Waltari's *The Egyptian*, when he handed her his request slip. When the young librarian returned from the stacks she handed him two books, "Who's Who" and the Social Register, and three manila folders.

"There are entries for Matthew Steele earmarked in both books," she said. "And these are the clippings on Steele, Velde and Lazda."

Collins thanked her and took the books and folders and sat down at one of the library's worn wooden desks. He turned to the material about Steele first. According to "Who's Who," Matthew Steele had been born in Washington, D.C., in 1905. He followed his undergraduate education at Yale with a doctorate in Russian history from Cambridge University. Steele left the faculty of Johns Hopkins in 1940 to serve in the Army, starting as a captain and ending as a major. He was a member of the Army/Navy Club in Washington and in New York, the Union League Club, the New York Athletic Club and the Yale Club.

The *Sentinel*'s three clips on Steele were all very brief. One of them, from 1939, was an announcement that Steele would be a luncheon speaker at a meeting of the New York Cipher Society with the topic of "Reflections on Vigenère's *Traicté des Chiffres*." Collins had no idea who Vigenère was, but he wrote his name down in his reporter's notebook. Collins consulted "Who's Who" again and saw that Steele was not only a member of the New York Cipher Society but also of the American Cryptogram Association. The other two *Sentinel* stories had brief mentions of Steele; he had been in attendance at a New Year's

American Red Cross ball in 1939, and was listed among donors to a Yale Club capital campaign.

The librarian had also marked the page in the *Social Register* with Steele's listing: his New York address was given as East 26th Street and Madison, which Collins knew was the location of the Union League Club. That was the extent of the morgue's information on the man. Nothing to hint that Steele was with the CIA or that he was a former OSS agent. His biography, at face value, suggested only that he was an eccentric professor, a socially-connected bachelor with interests in Russian history and cryptology.

Harold H. Velde's life was an open book in comparison. The "H" stood for "Himmel," and after looking through the clips, Collins wondered if anxiety about his German roots had turned Velde into a Red-baiter. Velde had been elected to Congress from Illinois, and he had taken to his role as a HUAC member with a special zeal. Collins could see why Steele didn't think much of him. Velde would have been an enthusiastic Brownshirt in Germany, closely following the reactionary party line, just as he was in Congress.

The slim folder on Karina Lazda contained only one clipping, and it was from the *New York Times*, not the *Sentinel*. The librarians did that occasionally, especially for background on the arts and culture, where the *Sentinel*'s coverage was spotty. The headline, dated September 19, 1939, read, "Miss Lazda Concert Canceled," and the story went on to report that the October 20 Carnegie Hall concert by Miss Karina Lazda, mezzo-soprano, formerly of Riga but now of Warsaw, had been canceled. The promoters were not sure when it would be re-scheduled: *Miss Lazda was to sing selections from Bach, Mahler and Bizet's Carmen, and opera lovers in New York are disappointed that this highly-praised singer's American debut has been delayed.*

It had to be the same woman, Collins thought. The name was too distinctive. He wondered what had caused the cancelation of her concert and then remembered the events of mid-September 1939. The Wermacht had rolled across the border into Poland early in the month, followed by the Russian invasion from the west. Warsaw had been occupied by German troops by the end of September. Not an easy time to travel to New York.

Collins collected the folders and the books and returned them to the front desk. The young woman didn't look up from her novel.

Back in the newsroom, Hal Diderick stopped Collins before he could reach his desk.

"Nothing new on Lowell Thomas," he reported. "He's apparently still somewhere in the mountains of Tibet, being carried in a litter or sedan chair to India. The hot story today is about Tokyo Rose. The jury gets the charge against her and I'm expecting a verdict and a conviction later tonight. Should make the front page, don't you think?"

"It's been almost four years since the war ended," Collins said. "The story's getting old, don't you think?"

"Treason doesn't have a statute of limitations. Not that I know of."

"The Japanese are supposed to be our friends now, aren't they?"

"Friends? After what they did? You were there. You saw the atrocities. We should have sent their damn Emperor to the gallows. Tokyo Rose deserves the noose, too, as far as I'm concerned."

His anger brought Collins up short. Collins remembered then that Diderick had lost his older brother at Guadalcanal. There were people all over the city, all over the country, in the same position: a brother, a son, a father, a friend killed by the Japanese somewhere in the Pacific. There had been healing in the years since V-J Day, but the wounds were still raw for some. Tokyo Rose's trial in San Francisco must have surfaced some of that pent-up emotion in Diderick.

"We had the war crimes trials," Collins said. "Last year we hung a bunch of them—Tojo, Hirota, a few others. I figure it's time to put it behind us. Not to forget, ever, but you can go crazy living in the past."

Diderick's face hardened and he muttered something before he walked away. Collins really didn't know what else to say to him. Why dwell on what you couldn't change? The past was lost time, done and over.

Collins had a light day ahead: his Tuesday column was the easiest of the week to write. He titled it "Ten New York Questions" and in the two years since he had started writing it, he had never struggled for material. In the column he would ask ten questions, making them provocative and funny and sometimes sarcastic, and then he would answer them. Once he outlined the questions, it was a breeze to write. He could usually knock out the entire column, from start to finish, in about an hour.

He decided to start with Lonnie's tip about Ethel Waters starring in "Member of the Wedding." He had three or four baseball questions he could ask (*Who would be managing the Yankees and Dodgers in 1950, considering the questions raised about Stengel and Shotton? What did the Giants need to do to become contenders?*) and he could finish with a political question, maybe something about the growing bitterness of the Senate race between John Foster Dulles and Herbert Lehman.

He typed the first question: *Who will stop the show in the upcoming Broadway play based on Carson McCullers' best-selling "Member of the Wedding"?* Sometimes he wrote all ten questions first and filled in the rest of the column. Other times he completed it question by question: it depended on how much time he had. Collins was close to finishing the column when his phone rang. He answered with his name, but the caller didn't identify himself in return.

"Saw you at the Garden Friday night," the caller said. He had a husky voice.

"Is that so? Who is this?"

"That don't matter. I'm calling with a question. How come there's nothing in the paper about that Gentleman Jack fight? What's going on with that?"

"What do you mean?"

"Come on, you were there. Brown lay down for him. Brown's a stiff but he could have knocked O'Reilly out. Anyone could see that. He takes a damn swan dive."

"Did you have money on Brown?" Collins asked.

"Not that stupid. I just like to see clean fights."

"Do you have any proof that it wasn't clean?"

"Proof that your buddy Santry had it rigged? That's not the sort of thing where they put it in writing. But you were there. I saw you talking with Santry afterwards."

"Sorry, but all I saw were two clumsy fighters. There's no news in that."

"Ask Santry what he's got lined up for O'Reilly. Two more fights and they're going to have him fight for the title. I hear it will be with Walcott. It's all been arranged."

Collins snorted in disbelief. "You must be kidding. There's no way he's ready for Walcott. Where did you get your information?"

"Ask Santry." The man was insistent. "See what he says."

"Where did you get your information?" Collins asked again.

"What difference does that make? I'm giving you a story. Are you going to do something with it?"

"That depends if it checks out."

"It will check out," the man said. "You just gotta show some guts." Then he hung up on Collins before he could ask any more questions.

The call got Collins thinking. Why not add a question in his column that gave the boxing establishment, and Phil Santry, a jab or two? The way Santry reacted toward the column would tell as much as any interview ever would.

He quickly typed out his final question: *Will New York boxing clean up its act before it ends up like the waterfront unions, answering tough questions about fraud, corruption and organized crime involvement in front of a Congressional hearing? Or will the District Attorney move first?* Then he finished his column with: *Here's how bad it has gotten in the New York fight game. There are rumors that Gentleman Jack O'Reilly, one of Phil Santry's fighters, is being prepped for a title fight. That would be a travesty. Better put Dodgers shortstop Pee Wee Reese in with Jersey Joe Walcott than O'Reilly. In fact, Pee Wee probably has a better chin and a better right.* Collins smiled to himself. That last line would certainly get Santry's attention.

Since Van had Sundays and Mondays off, Collins typically asked Diderick to read his column before it was copy edited. Diderick didn't have much of an ear for prose but he was a passable editor and he generally caught any obvious mistakes. Collins gave him his column and waited by his desk while he read it. Diderick was a fast worker; he didn't agonize over every word. He whistled out loud when he reached the end of the second typed page.

"An investigation into New York boxing?" he asked. "You have some insider tipping you about this?"

"I hear things," Collins said. "There's talk that the Mayor will have the District Attorney take a look-see. After the election."

"And what about Santry's boy? You knocked him pretty hard."

"I saw the fight," Collins said. "It didn't smell right. O'Reilly is no heavyweight contender."

"When you were at the *Sun*, weren't you and Santry buddies?"

"Nope," Collins said. "You've got the wrong guy. We worked together over there for a bit. That's all."

"Funny. I thought you two were close."

Collins cleared his throat. "Even if we were, I couldn't look the other way on something like this. His new fighter is a stiff.

"You know the way this reads people are going to see the words 'organized crime' and 'Santry' in the same paragraph and figure that he's dirty. Santry won't be too happy with you."

Collins shrugged. He wasn't going to worry about Phil Santry's feelings. He would write what he wanted to about boxing. Santry would keep his mouth shut about what went on in the old days. Collins wasn't going to be blackmailed about their shared past and Santry would realize that the moment he read the column.

When the copy desk was finished, Collins decided to head up to the Hotel Marseilles early. He glanced over at the television set in the sports department; it was showing the Yankees-Red Sox game. In the fourth inning the Red Sox held a 3-0 lead. He regretted that he hadn't gone out to the Stadium. There might be a good column there

140

about how Casey Stengel and the Yankees were in genuine danger of becoming the baseball equivalent of "Dewey Beats Truman."

Maybe Jimmy Cannon had it right after all; both the Yanks and the Dodgers were finished. That would mean Collins would have to eat some crow a week from now—at least about the Dodgers. It wouldn't be the first time he had guessed wrong publicly, nor would it be the last.

Thirteen

The Hotel Marseilles, an aging Beaux Arts building at Broadway and 103rd Street, had little to recommend itself to travelers other than its vaguely romantic name. When Collins arrived, he found the hotel lobby filled with refugees of all ages, primarily German and Polish Jews who had survived Nazi persecution and then had been accepted as immigrants into the U.S.

They sat on shabby couches and well-worn chairs, some clustered in small groups, talking quietly. Piles of luggage from recent arrivals had been stacked against the far wall. As he looked around, Collins heard snatches of different languages—he recognized French, German and what he took to be Polish.

Someone had placed a vase of fresh flowers at the front desk counter. Collins thought it was a nice touch considering the hotel's general shabbiness. A stooped-over, white-haired woman behind the front counter blinked several times when he asked for Miss Lazda. She mumbled something to herself and came out from behind the counter and disappeared down the hall. A few moments later Karina Lazda emerged.

At first Collins almost didn't recognize her. She seemed older than the woman he had met at the Stork Club. Her hair was pulled back, and her face without makeup was paler than he remembered. Her slate gray dress and an off-white cardigan sweater accentuated her plainness.

She extended her hand and they shook, formally. She motioned him to follow her into a side room. On the wall Collins saw a prominent sign: "SO SIEHT AMERICA AUS!" and a large colored map of the United States studded with pins. Photos of city street scenes were posted around the map, with ribbons leading back to the pins of specific places: a photo of a jazz band led back to New Orleans, one of a cable car had a string to San Francisco.

"It is too loud in our lobby to talk," she said. "It is because of all of the new people who arrived on Friday. They are still settling in."

They sat down across from each other at a battered wooden table. She fished out a pack of cigarettes from the pocket of her sweater and retrieved a cigarette.

She held the pack of Camels out to him. "Would you like one, Mr. Collins?"

"I shouldn't. Trying to quit."

"But do you want one?"

Collins nodded and took a cigarette from the package. He lit both of their cigarettes with his Zippo. He took a long drag, thoroughly enjoying the sensation. He caught her looking at him curiously.

"Do you often deny yourself such simple pleasures, Mr. Collins?" she asked. "Why, may I ask?"

"They're not good for me. I'm told they'll kill my wind."

"Kill your wind?" She was puzzled by the phrase.

"That's slang. It means it will hurt my lungs. I won't breathe as well when I smoke."

"I see. I find that they are calming for me. I would be most reluctant to forgo them."

Collins took out his reporter's notebook and placed it on the table. He had learned it was easier to get people to talk if he waited until they were comfortable with the conversation before he started scribbling. Then, once the talk was flowing, it seemed entirely natural for him to casually open the notebook and begin jotting down notes.

"I read your newspaper this morning," she said. "To prepare for your visit. What you wrote about the Dodgers. Do you think they can accomplish this pennant?"

"I do. And we would say 'win the pennant.'"

She shrugged gracefully at the correction. There were holes in her English, or at least in her American English. "The other newspapers do not agree," she said. "Did you play this baseball?

"A little, when I was a kid. I spent more time boxing. Golden Gloves."

"Golden Gloves? What is that?"

"It is a competition, for amateurs, younger boxers. The finalists get to fight in the Garden before a big crowd."

"So did you get to the Garden?"

"I'm afraid not. That's why I cover sports. Not all that good at them. I do like boxing, though."

"I will tell you further why I do *not* like boxing," she said and he recalled her negative comments at the Stork Club. "I had an older friend from Prague. An actress, Anny Ondra. She married a famous German boxer, this man Max Schmeling. Do you know of him?"

"Yes. I know of him." Collins smiled. Max Schmeling, one of Hitler's darlings, was famous in New York. Schmeling had defeated Joe Louis in 1936, and the Nazis had made a big deal out of their vaunted Aryan warrior defeating the American champion. Then Louis had knocked out Schmeling in the first round of their rematch two years later at Yankee Stadium. Collins had covered the fight and had been delighted by Schmeling's crushing defeat.

"Max was Hitler's favorite," Karina said. "Did you know that Hitler loved boxing? In fact, he wrote about it in *Mein Kampf*. That is another reason I detest it."

"Even a stopped clock is right twice a day," Collins said.

"I do not understand."

"It's an old saying. Even a broken clock tells the time correctly twice a day. It means that even Hitler wasn't always wrong."

She folded her arms across her chest and frowned at him. "When the war came, they forced Max to become a paratrooper. He was almost killed in the invasion of Crete. Anny told me the story of what happened next. They tried to make him say that the British were responsible for atrocities. He would not. Anny was worried that he would be arrested by the Gestapo."

"Max Schmeling arrested?" Collins couldn't help but show his skepticism, and Karina frowned again.

"Anyone could be arrested," she said. "Fame was no protection. The Gestapo didn't care. They made their own laws."

Collins found the mention of the Gestapo jarring. It had been four years since the end of the war in the Pacific, and slightly longer since the Allies had ended Hitler's twisted experiment in Europe. Not long enough for anyone to forget completely what they had seen. But then again, Collins thought, Karina was confronted with the unfinished business of the war every day, a human reminder, so it had to be near impossible to forget. And for all of the people in the Center there could be no forgetting.

Karina explained that she had found a few of the DPs who spoke English fairly well. "When they don't, I will translate."

"You speak German and Polish?"

"And Latvian. I was born in Riga. And I have learned some Italian and French."

She stood up, excused herself, and went to find his interview subjects. Collins wondered what had brought her to the United Service and the Center—it seemed a long way from singing opera. She was too remote, too wary, to volunteer the reason.

Collins sat there quietly until Karina shepherded the first couple in to see him. Collins figured Mordechai and Rifka Lewin were in their late sixties. They spoke fluent, if accented English and as they talked for a few minutes Collins kept his notebook closed. The Lewins had lost all of their immediate family during the war. They thought immigrating to America from Poland might let them start over, if it was possible to really start over. Collins could understand their fatalism.

"We are going to Cincinnati," Mordechai Lewin said. "Have you been to Cincinnati, Mr. Collins?"

"I have. I've been there to watch the Dodgers play the Reds. Crosley Field. Stayed downtown at the Cincinnatian hotel on Vine Street, I'm afraid Cincinnati doesn't have much of a team this year. It's a nice city, right on the river. Friendly people."

Collins didn't know what else to say. The truth was that if it weren't for baseball, he never would have visited Cincinnati. He couldn't imagine a good reason to return, other than to cover another sporting event.

"We would prefer to stay here," Rifka Lewin said. "Here in New York."

"Many of our guests would prefer that," Karina said quickly. "But we cannot absorb so many people in New York. We would not be able to find them sponsoring families and congregations."

"We understand," Mordechai Lewin said mildly.

"We are not complaining," his wife said. "It is just that there are so many of our own people here. We feel safe here."

"You will find that you feel safe in Cincinnati as well," Karina said. "Several of our families have settled there and are quite happy."

"Are there many Germans there?" Mrs. Lewin directed her question to Collins.

"German-Americans? They're all over the country. Here in New York, too. But they're Americans. The vast majority had no more use for the Nazis than any of us did."

"What about the Bund?" Mordechai Lewin asked.

"A small group," Collins said. "Discredited completely by the war."

"And this man Lindbergh?"

"Also discredited. There is no argument now about the danger of the Nazis. You won't find many German sympathizers in Cincinnati or elsewhere, for that matter."

"If we were younger we would be going to Israel," Lewin said. "But it is a country that needs the young, not the old."

The next two couples told similar stories. Years in a DP camp, the sudden wonder of coming to America, the desire to leave the sadness of the war years behind them, to try to forget, even when, like the Lewins, it didn't look like that could ever really happen. During the interviews, Collins could tell Karina was watching him closely. He wondered what she was thinking. Did she feel any attraction toward him?

He had enough material for a decent column when Karina told him that she had one more interview left to do. She returned with two small children, a boy and a girl, two scrawny little kids with big brown eyes. They looked so lost, so scared, that it was impossible not to have your heart go out to them, Collins thought. Karina introduced them as Josef and Hannah, brother and sister.

"Hello," Collins said. "Pleased to meet you both."

"Hello," the boy said. Collins estimated that he was twelve. His sister remained silent, gripping her brother's hand firmly. She had to be seven or eight. Karina said something to them both in Polish and the boy smiled. The girl just looked at her brother.

"Hannah is shy," Karina said. Hannah looked up when she heard her name, quickly glancing over at Collins and then averting her eyes.

"That's quite all right," Collins said. "I was shy at Hannah's age. Please tell her that."

Karina translated. Hannah buried her face in her brother's side, embarrassed at the attention.

"How did they get to America?"

Karina drew the story out from Josef as Collins scribbled down the key facts in his notebook. Josef and Hannah had been living with their aunt, who was married to a Catholic, in a village thirty miles south of Warsaw, sent there by their parents for safekeeping. Their parents had either died in one of the concentration camps or in the Warsaw Ghetto uprising in 1944. Either way, the children had been orphaned, and when their aunt died a year later, just after the war ended, they ended up in a DP camp. There in the camp an elderly Polish woman, a widow named Hella Berliner, had become attached to them and had fought to bring them to America with her. They had arrived at the Hotel Marseilles two months ago and had slowly been acclimating to their new life.

"What are the plans for them now?" Collins asked Karina.

"We did not place them in an orphanage because they did not want to leave their friend, Mrs. Berliner. She tells us now that she cannot take responsibility for them. She feels that she is too old. So we are arranging for a new family to take them in."

"Do they know this?"

"Not yet. We will take it very slowly with them."

"I like Yankees," the boy, Josef, said suddenly, in English. "Joe DiMaggio."

"Have you been to a game?"

The boy looked over at Karina. She translated the question and then gave Collins his answer. "He has seen the games only on television. We have a television here in the hotel."

"Please tell him that I can take care of that," Collins said. "I can arrange tickets for Josef and his sister for one of the Yankee games this coming weekend."

"You do not need to do that."

"It's my hook for the column. It's how I can best write about your work. A young boy, a refugee, who roots for Joe DiMaggio. On the path to becoming an American and what better way than to become a baseball fan? I will have a ticket for you, or for whoever from the United Service wishes to accompany them. It will be great publicity. Call Lonnie Marks and ask him about it if you don't believe me."

"What about Mrs. Berliner?"

"She can go as well. The three of them and someone from your Center. A photographer from the *Sentinel* can take some pictures."

Collins could see that Karina wasn't enthusiastic about the idea, but there was a great column to be written about Josef and Hannah, a column that would bring home to *Sentinel* readers what it was like to be a displaced person, adrift in a strange new country.

"I will ask them," she said, reluctantly. She bit her lip gently before translating Collins' offer to the children. Josef rewarded Collins with a grateful smile and when she saw her brother's face, Hannah imitated him. It was her first smile of the day, a small victory, Collins thought.

With their interview complete, Karina took the children back to their room. While she was gone Collins finished up with his notes, trying to capture as many of the details as he could: the way Josef tilted his head when he spoke, Hannah's sweet shyness, Karina's protectiveness.

When Karina returned she offered him another cigarette from her pack without asking. He again lit their cigarettes and they took their first puffs at the same time. There was something intimate about it, he thought, like the cigarettes smoked after making love. He wondered if she sensed that at all and he wondered again about her as a lover, what her body was like under that drab dress, what she would be like in bed. He felt guilty for a moment. He had been pursuing Penny Bradford with the same intent only a day before. Except, he reminded himself, it was clear that pursuit had hit a dead end.

"So why aren't you singing?" he asked. "Shouldn't you be appearing at Carnegie Hall? They invited you once, why not again?"

She stiffened noticeably, drawing back from him. "How did you know about that?" she asked, her tone suddenly cold. "Who told you? Lonnie? Did he tell you? He had no right."

"Wait a minute. Don't blame Lonnie. I checked the newspaper's library. I stumbled across your canceled concert appearance back in 1939. Because of the war?"

She nodded her head, somewhat placated. "Yes, it was the war."

"Selections from Bizet's Carmen? I can't say I've ever heard it sung."

"It has been a long time. It has been ten years since I have sung Bizet."

"Do you have plans to sing here?"

"Some day, perhaps," she said. "But I am not sure. It seems so frivolous after all that has happened. Rich people dressing up to go to the opera house so they can be seen and show off their clothes and their jewelry." She frowned at the thought. "Do you know a singer I truly admire?"

Collins shook his head.

"Vera Lynn. During the war, so many people listened to her on the radio. The 'White Cliffs of Dover' and 'When the Lights Go on Again.' She kept our hopes alive. She made you believe there would be a life after the war, a better life."

"I prefer jazz singers," Collins said. "Like Billie Holliday. Have you heard any of her records?"

"Of course I have," she said. "A beautiful voice, but such very sad songs."

She took a long drag on her cigarette and exhaled, letting the smoke drift out into the room. "Why do you stare at me, Mr. Collins?" she asked. Collins flushed. He didn't realize that he had been that obvious.

"Was I staring?" he asked. "My apologies. It is because I find you intriguing."

"No need to apologize for that."

"I don't mean to be rude. I don't mean to embarrass you. I imagine a good-looking girl like you has to brush off strangers all the time."

"I am not embarrassed. And I do not consider you a stranger."

"May I take you to dinner, then?" Collins asked. "Tomorrow night?"

"This is for your column?"

He met her gaze without flinching. "Not completely. I ask because I would like to get to know you better."

"That is your interest, then?"

"You aren't spoken for or engaged, already are you?"

"I am not. And you, Mr. Collins?"

"Afraid not."

"Then, I will go to dinner with you, Mr. Collins." She said it matter-of-factly, almost off-handedly. Collins wondered suddenly if she was truly interested in him, or in the prospects of a night out and a nice dinner, a break in her routine.

"Then call me Dennis or Denny."

"Dennis. Please, then you may call me Karina. You should know I am occupied here with my work until late in the day, and so I will not be available until seven o'clock."

"I'll come here to pick you up? Any place that you'd like to go?"

"There is an Italian restaurant nearby," she said. "It is called Trattoria Il Riccio, and the food is excellent."

"And you do not deny yourself that simple pleasure?"

"Why would I deny myself that?" she said with a smile.

He suddenly pictured her features transformed by passion and he flushed, looking down at the table so she couldn't see his face and guess what he was thinking.

"Very well," he said. "I will be back here tomorrow night at seven o'clock sharp."

"Sharp?"

"Exactly at seven."

"I think I have learned more slang from you, today, than I have in a month. Seven o'clock sharp. The stopped clock. Kill my wind."

"I'm always available for lessons," he said. "I'm sure I can teach you some more slang at dinner."

"I am sure that you can," she said, now openly flirting.

Collins left the Hotel Marseilles feeling pretty damn good. He knew he had the material for a great column on the New Americans, and the prospect of dinner with a pretty girl. When Collins got into the cab, he asked the driver about the Yankees-Red Sox score. The cabbie cursed.

"I should know better than to bet on baseball," he said. "The Red Sox won, 7-6. Yanks blew a three-run lead. Fell apart in the eighth inning. Big play at the plate. This catcher for the Yanks I never heard of missed tagging Johnny Pesky. I don't know what's wrong with the Yanks this season. It might be that damn Stengel. Why isn't Berra behind the plate? Important game and Stengel isn't playing Yogi Berra? I don't think that he knows what he's doing."

"That could be," Collins said. He didn't want to argue with the driver. Berra had an injured hand, which would explain why he wasn't catching, but there were few things Collins was certain about and one of them was that you weren't going to win a sports argument with a New York cabbie.

He had the cabbie let him off at Mallory's. He planned on a few beers and a light supper. Once inside Collins found that the regulars were talking about how the Yankees should have won, how the umpire had missed the call at the plate, and what a lousy job Casey Stengel was doing managing the team.

It was Monday night so "Arthur Godfrey and His Talent Scouts" were on the television, on Columbia. Collins ordered a steak sandwich and a few beers and sat in a booth and watched the television for a while. He caught a bit of "Candid Camera" and decided to head home when it finished at 9:30. When he got back to his apartment he was ready for bed. It had been a strange day. The lunch with Steele, the phone call about Santry and Gentleman Jack, the visit to the Hotel Marseilles and then the unexpected connection with the enigmatic Karina Lazda.

It would be good for him to find someone new, he told himself, a welcome diversion, a way to put Penny behind him, to start over, with no history, no bitterness. Taking Karina out quickly would keep him from brooding. And he couldn't have picked someone more different from Penny. There was nothing about Karina to remind him of what had been and what would never be.

Tuesday, September 27

The phone on her desk rang as Karina was reviewing a thin file of documentation on a newly arrived family from Lithuania. She flinched, startled by the sound. She picked it up on the second ring and heard a male voice greeting her. It was Morris, and he didn't bother with the recognition phrase this time.

"Can you talk now?" he asked.

"I can."

"Did you meet Denny Collins at the Stork?"

"I did. He was there with his date."

"Penny Bradford. I know, I saw them together earlier at the Garden. Denny is asking to have his heart broken again. But that's neither here nor there. More importantly, can you see him again in person without raising any suspicion?"

"Yes. Lonnie convinced him that he should write a column about the Center. He came to the hotel yesterday and interviewed me and some of the refugees. Now that I have made the connection, it will be easy for me to pass him your message. What should I tell him?"

"We're not ready for that yet, I'm afraid. I'm not sure when I can return to New York. There have been some unforeseen complications in Washington." He hesitated for a long moment. "Although I don't want to, I may have to involve Bob in my affairs and that will take me down a road that I'm not sure I am ready to go."

She didn't reply at first. Things had to have gone horribly awry if Morris was considering turning to Anatoli Yatov for help. Once he involved Yatov, Morris would have to cede control of the situation. The Russian would make the decisions and Morris would lose all freedom of action.

"Surely you can find a way to resolve this without him," she said. "He won't have your best interests at heart, Morris. You must know that. He will only want to protect himself and his network here, not you."

"I am aware of that," he said, annoyed with her. "Trust me, I have no intention of becoming expendable. I still have some leverage and some of it is tied up in what Dennis Collins is holding for me. So we have to handle him carefully. Can I count on you, Karina?"

"You know you can," she said. She thought about telling Morris that she had accepted a dinner invitation from Collins but she decided not to. It would only complicate matters, and she didn't want Morris to start asking her questions.

She could rationalize that seeing Collins would help further establish their connection, but that was a half-truth. She had been flattered by his attention and she was attracted to him. She didn't want Morris to know that, for she knew it would complicate matters.

She would have to be careful with Dennis. He liked to ask questions, and he was persistent. She couldn't afford to let her guard down when she was dealing with him.

"Thanks," Morris said. "I won't ever forget this."

"It is nothing," she said.

"Expect my next call on Thursday," Morris said. "In the morning." Then he hung up without saying goodbye.

She replaced the phone receiver in its cradle. Her options were narrowing. Despite what she had said to Morris, she wasn't sure that she could follow through now and help him if Yatov had entered the picture. She considered, for a moment, leaving that very morning, returning to her apartment to pack her suitcase, and then taking a westbound afternoon train.

She rejected the idea. She couldn't do that yet. She had to wait, to see what Morris would ask her to do, what message he would ask her to carry to Dennis Collins. That was when she could weigh the right and wrong of it with her eyes wide open and make her decision.

Fourteen

In the morning, the golden weather of the day before had vanished. The sky was overcast and threatening when Collins went out for breakfast. He had placed Morris' film canister securely in his left suit coat pocket before he left his apartment.

At the All-American, Collins sat in his favorite booth and ate his scrambled eggs and toast while he read the papers. He started by looking for any news out of Washington about the HUAC investigations. Nothing.

He would have paid to see Phil Santry's face that morning when the boxing promoter opened up the *Sentinel* and reached the last question in Collins' column. Santry should have known better than to threaten Collins; it almost guaranteed an unfavorable reference in the paper about Gentleman Jack. There was some irony in it, Collins thought. He constantly rebuffed the people, like Lonnie Marks and his fellow press agents, who desperately wanted to place an item in his columns. Those who wanted to stay out of the paper, like Santry, were the very ones who ended up in it, often to their dismay.

The sports pages highlighted the Yankees' loss to the Red Sox and the disputed squeeze play at home plate. It looked like the league might fine the club's third-string catcher Ralph Houk, Casey Stengel, and Cliff Mapes, the Yanks outfielder, for their outbursts over the play at the plate. Mapes had to be pulled away from the umpire, and he hadn't even played in the game.

When Collins returned to his apartment, he could hear the phone ringing as he unlocked his door. He expected it would be Diderick or another editor from the *Sentinel*, or perhaps even Santry calling to curse him out for the column so he took his time in reaching the phone. When he picked it up, he was surprised by Penny's distinctive soft voice on the other end of the line.

"Dennis," she said. "I'm glad I caught you before you left for work."

"I'm here," Collins said.

He didn't know what to expect. He had assumed that weeks of silence would follow before he heard from her again. He fought back hope. Perhaps she was calling to let him down, to say she wouldn't be back in New York, or that she didn't think they should see each other again.

"That you are," she said. "I'm in luck today."

"Are you in Washington?"

"No, I'm still in New York. A change in plans. As it happens, I didn't have to go to Washington after all."

"Did you resolve whatever it was that you had to? The complications?"

"In a way," she said.

"In a way that you like?"

She paused, and he wondered what was bothering her. She didn't seem very sure of herself, which wasn't like Penny.

"I told you, Dennis, that it is complicated. I guess that I am dealing with it in stages. This is one of those stages."

"So I'll be blunt, Penny. Where do I fit in?" Collins figured that he had nothing to lose. Better to know where he stood, he told himself, than living in romantic limbo.

"I am trying to figure that out," she said. "That's one of those stages, I guess. Forgive me for not having a better answer."

"Does that mean I may fit in your life? There's a chance of that?"

"I think so. But I'm not sure. I'm confused, I guess."

"They tell me I'm a good listener. So maybe you can talk to me about it. Are you free for dinner some night this week?"

"I am free. And I would love to see you, Dennis. I think it would help."

Collins was surprised at the warmth in her voice. It was certainly a change from their call on Sunday, the last time they had talked.

Maybe she had reconsidered. He didn't care, he was just happy that she wanted to see him.

"How about tomorrow night for dinner and a show? Can I come by your apartment and pick you up? Say, six o'clock?"

"Not dinner for tonight? I'm surprised at you, Dennis, for letting the grass grow under your feet."

A second surprise. She was eager to see him. But Collins hadn't forgotten his date with Karina. He thought for a moment about calling Karina and canceling their dinner, but decided against it. He wasn't going to drop everything for Penny and be disappointed if she changed her mind again.

"Sorry," he said. "I'm tied up with something that involves the newspaper. Can't get out of it."

"I won't feel slighted then," she said. "If it's work and not a date with another girl."

"I'm hardly the Don Juan type. Not even close."

"I know women find you very attractive. I think it's your boyish charm."

"I'll take that as a compliment, despite the boyish part."

"It is a compliment."

"Any place you would like to go?" he asked.

"Surprise me," she said. "I'm sure that has worked wonders with the other girls you take out. We don't need to see a show. I'd rather get caught up."

Collins wondered about her references to his dating other women. Penny had never paid much attention to the competition, not that there ever had been any serious rivals for his affections. Could Karina have said something to Lonnie Marks about their date and could word have somehow reached Penny? He realized how unlikely that was.

"I'll surprise you, then. I'll call tomorrow and let you know where we should meet."

"Tomorrow then," she said. "It will be wonderful to see you again."

After they hung up, Collins sat there for a long moment, puzzled. The call had been so unexpected, and so different in tone, that he wasn't sure what to think. It was almost as if he and Penny had switched places in the space of twenty-four hours. Now Penny was the one eager to see him, and Collins was feeling ambivalent. Was he just setting himself up for more pain and loneliness when Penny changed her mind again? And then there was his dinner with Karina. He wasn't going to change his plans, even if seeing her now somehow seemed awkward.

A few moments later the phone rang again. It was his brother, and he greeted Collins with an expletive.

"I thought we agreed that you would wait on this boxing thing," Frank said. "I didn't expect you would jump the gun and put it in the paper."

"You thought I should wait," Collins said, slightly flustered. "I didn't agree to anything. You didn't say I couldn't use it now. Not directly. At least that's the way I remember it."

"Everyone is stirred up over here. I'm getting the evil eye. They all think the story came from me."

"They're always going to think that. Even so, what I put in the column should make it easier for the Mayor to call for an investigation. The District Attorney and the brass at Centre Street should be happy."

"They're not. They want the investigation *after* the election. I told you that."

"I'm sorry, if you're taking heat for me," Collins said. "Give it a couple of days. It will blow over."

"That's easy for you to say. You can print whatever the hell you want and you don't have to deal with the consequences."

"I said I was sorry."

"Great," Frank said. "I'll be sure to tell the guys here that my younger brother is sorry. That will work wonders for me."

He hung up before Collins could say anything more.

On the way to work, Collins had the taxi driver drop him off a few blocks from the *Sentinel*, east of Herald Square. He knew there was a small record shop on 38th Street where he hoped to find a gift for Karina. The shop-keeper, a middle-aged woman with a broad, expressive face, brightened when Collins asked if they carried any of Vera Lynn's records.

"The new one?" she asked, with a trace of an English accent. "The Decca?"

"Actually, I wanted some of her older songs, from the war."

"Ah," she said, "one of the albums from Rex Records. That should fill the bill." She went to the far corner of the store and returned with a record album.

"Let me put it on the player," she said. "This one has 'The White Cliffs of Dover.' " She carefully placed the needle on the record and they stood there and listened to the song.

There'll be bluebirds over the white cliffs of Dover
Tomorrow, just you wait and see
There'll be love and laughter and peace ever after
Tomorrow when the world is free

When the song had finished and Collins turned to the woman, he saw that tears were rolling down her face. She dabbed at her cheeks with a small lace handkerchief.

The woman carefully lifted the needle from the record and looked over at Collins, not yet completely composed, but trying to brave her way through it. Collins decided to act as if nothing had happened, and he told her that he would buy the record. She took his $3.95 and rang up the purchase, and then put the record in a brown paper bag. She kept her eyes on him when she handed him the bag.

"I don't sell too many of her records from the war," she said. She seemed to want to talk. Collins guessed it could get fairly lonely in the shop; it didn't look like she was doing too much business. "Everyone seems to want the latest songs," she said. "Perry Como. Frankie Laine. The new singers. I guess the older songs can bring back difficult memories."

"That they can."

"Were you in England during the war by any chance?"

"No," he said. "I was not. This is for a friend who likes Vera Lynn."

"I was in London for the Blitz and then for the rockets, the buzz bombs and the V-2s. When I hear that song it brings it all back. I don't mind telling you that this has been a bad time for me, the past few days. I don't like reading in the papers about atomic bombs. I thought we were all done with that. Haven't enough people died?"

"You won't get an argument from me on that."

"Where did you serve?" she asked, assuming from his age that Collins was a veteran.

"The Pacific," he said. "I covered the end of the war as a correspondent."

"Then you know."

"I guess I do." He paused, wondering whether he should say more. "Thank you for playing the song for me. I'm sure my friend will love it."

"I hope it brings back only the best of memories."

"I hope so, too," he told her.

Fifteen

After Collins finished at the record shop, he walked directly to the *Sentinel*. When he exited the elevator on the fifth floor, he found two square-jawed young men in dark suits and identical starched white shirts sitting in the rickety chairs at the newsroom entrance. He immediately recognized the man closest to the elevator as the FBI agent, Andrew Caldwell, who had questioned him at Ebbets Field.

Caldwell rose to his feet as Collins approached and Collins fought the sudden urge to jam his free hand into his left suit coat pocket, where the film canister resided. He clutched the paper bag with the Vera Lynn record in it and kept his left hand by his side.

"Do you have a moment, Mr. Collins?" Caldwell began, positioning himself so that he blocked entry to the newsroom. "Agent Leary and I have a few additional questions."

"Why don't we step into the conference room, then?" Collins asked, gesturing with his free hand toward the conference room door, which was adjacent to the newsroom. It was cramped but they would at least have some privacy. Collins saw no need to advertise that the FBI wanted to grill him.

Once in the conference room they all sat down at the small circular table. All of the walls featured framed historic front pages from the *Sentinel*. The most recent was from September 2, 1945 and it had an oversized headline:

JAPS SURRENDER!

The two FBI men faced Collins, and Leary produced a small notebook. Collins figured that he would take the notes and Caldwell would lead the questioning. Caldwell glanced over at the paper bag.

"Been shopping?" he asked.

"As a matter of fact I have," Collins said.

He knew that Caldwell wanted to ease into the interview, to try to establish common ground. Collins used the same technique. He decided he would play along. "Found what I was looking for. A record by Vera Lynn. Know her music?"

"A bit. 'White Cliffs of Dover?'" Caldwell said. "I'm more of a Glenn Miller man, myself."

"And Agent Leary," Collins said, including him in the conversation. "Who is your favorite? Paul Robeson?"

Leary flushed but didn't respond to the dig. J. Edgar Hoover had made it clear that he considered the great Negro singer and actor to be a Communist stooge. Robeson had been in the news a few weeks before when thugs from the American Legion and other veterans' groups had stoned the cars of concert goers after one of Robeson's outdoor performances in Peekskill.

"So what can I do for you gentlemen?" Collins asked, turning to Caldwell. Collins had a pretty good sense of what was coming next, but he figured it was best to feign ignorance. He hoped to get a quick sense of how far their investigation had progressed.

"We're still looking for your friend," Caldwell said. "When you met with Morris Rose Friday night you're sure that he didn't mention any trouble at work?" Caldwell was cool, patient. He wasn't going to let Collins wander off on a tangent.

"Like I told you, we talked about the Dodgers."

"You sure about that?" Leary's question had a nasty tone. Maybe he was still angry over the Paul Robeson crack, Collins thought.

Collins nodded. "I'm sure."

"Was he alone when you saw him?" It was Caldwell, picking up the stray threads of the interview, keeping it professional, neutral.

"He was."

"Did he ask you for any assistance? Money, a place to stay, anything of that sort?"

"My problem with this interview is that you keep asking me questions that wouldn't make sense unless Morris was in some kind of trouble. Is it connected to you not being able to locate him? Is that what you are concerned about?"

They looked at each other. Caldwell nodded slightly, signaling Leary, giving him the go-ahead to answer. Leary had been designated the bearer of bad news, the tough guy, the one to apply pressure.

"He has some urgent questions he needs to answer," Leary said. "In connection with a loyalty investigation. Urgent questions."

Caldwell cleared his throat deliberately. "Can I be frank with you, Mr. Collins?"

"Sure. Go ahead."

"I'm a little disturbed that you don't seem surprised by this line of questioning about your friend. Almost like you knew it was coming. That doesn't give me the best feeling."

"Why should I be surprised? Morris works in the State Department. It's not a secret that there are witch hunts in Washington these days. Now you show up and start asking the questions you'd expect if such an investigation was underway."

"What do you think about that? That we're investigating your friend."

"I think that it's lousy. I don't think it accomplishes a damn thing."

"But you wouldn't impede such an investigation."

"Is that a question?" Collins asked.

"We have some photographs we'd like you to look at," Leary said.

The FBI agent didn't wait for a response; he pulled out a small manila envelope from his shiny leather valise. He opened the string clasp on the envelope and produced two small photos, headshots of young women. He held up the first photograph, a smiling woman with a face that would have been pretty if not for her too-prominent nose. Collins guessed that she was in her mid- to late-twenties.

"Ever seen her?" Leary asked.

"No. Never." Collins didn't see any harm in answering. He didn't know her.

"Are you sure? You haven't seen her in Morris Rose's company?"

"I'm sure of that," Collins said. "Not only have I never seen her before, but I surely haven't seen her with Morris."

"Okay," he said. "How about this one?" He handed Collins the second photo, this one of a somber, dark-haired woman. She was better-looking than the first, with more symmetrical features and high cheekbones. There was something about her that struck Collins as being familiar, but he couldn't place her. He stared at the photo for a long moment before he realized it was a photo of a much younger Karina Lazda. He tried not to show his surprise.

"She looks familiar," Collins said. "I feel like I know her. Do you have a name for her?"

"We thought you might help us with that," Leary said. "That's the point of this exercise. We show, you tell."

"Sorry," he said.

If they didn't know her name, Collins wasn't about to identify her. He needed to talk to Karina first and find out what her connection to Morris might be, and why the FBI had her photo. "Like I said, she looks familiar. But I haven't ever seen her with Morris, either."

"I didn't say anything about her and Rose," Leary said.

"I guess I was anticipating your next question," Collins said.

"Well, you were wrong."

"You don't know this woman, then," Caldwell said. "No idea who she might be?"

"I'm being careful," Collins said. "I wouldn't want to steer you wrong."

"I'll bet," Leary said.

"Hell of a job you boys have," Collins said. "Questioning the loyalty of a guy whose only offense is that he hated the Nazis before the rest of us and that he was a fan of the New Deal. I feel much safer about the Red Menace already."

"We aren't paid to assume things," Caldwell said. "I used to think you'd be able to tell who was willing to sell out his country, and who wouldn't. Now we know better."

"What about the reputations and lives of the people you're investigating? They can be ruined, you know. It's nigh impossible to find a decent job once you've been labeled a subversive."

"We don't make mistakes like that," Caldwell said. "Trust me, when we say someone is a subversive, they are."

"Forgive me if I'm skeptical about that," Collins said. "I've covered the cops for too long. They're human and they make mistakes. You can make them, as well."

Caldwell shrugged at Collins' naiveté and rose to his feet. Leary followed suit, reluctantly; he looked like he would have welcomed the opportunity to work Collins over a bit.

"Call us immediately if you are contacted by Morris Rose," Caldwell said.

"Before you go, can I ask you a question or two?"

"What do you want to know?"

"I was wondering how effective wiretapping has been for the Bureau. Planting microphones, listening in on people's phone conversations." Collins watched the FBI man closely, hoping to gauge Caldwell's reaction to the question.

"I can answer that," Caldwell said, smoothly, unruffled by the question. "It's a tool. Just like our little chat today. It can help us piece the puzzle together."

"I had one more question," Collins said. "Are you coordinating your investigation of Morris with Mr. Steele?"

"Steele?" It was Leary. It was phrased as a question, but Collins could tell that he recognized the name by the quick glance he exchanged with Caldwell.

"Matthew Steele. He seemed to know about you. Said he was from the government. I figured that he was from the State Department or CIA."

"When did you see him?" Caldwell asked.

"The other day. We had lunch at the Yale Club. He asked some of the same questions about Morris Rose that you have. I figure that you could save yourself some time and cut down on the overlap if you coordinated your investigations."

"You'll be hearing from us," Caldwell said, his tone suddenly preemptory. "Like I said before, if you hear from Rose we want to know." Collins wanted to ask Caldwell if he should call him before or after he phoned Steele, but he decided to leave well enough alone.

"Good luck, boys," Collins said and was rewarded with a dirty look from Leary.

After they left, Collins waited a few minutes and then went to the men's room at the other end of the hallway. He dashed cold water on his face. He dried his face and confronted his image in the mirror: did he look guilty? Collins thought about the canister in his pocket and wondered what he had gotten himself into. He didn't have any regrets about having been evasive with the FBI. With any luck he would never see Caldwell or Leary again, or Steele, for that matter.

Collins had to trust that Morris would have the situation cleared up by the end of the week, his security clearance affirmed, his loyalty to the United States validated. When they next met, Collins had a fair number of pointed questions that he'd want Morris to answer. He had no idea where Karina might fit in the picture, but he was sure over the next few days he would figure it out, one way or the other.

Sixteen

Collins thought about his brief FBI interview on his cab ride uptown to the Hotel Marseilles. It was disturbing, to say the least, that the agents had Karina's photo. Collins didn't think they would have shown him her photo if there wasn't some direct connection to their investigation of Morris. It made him wonder about Karina's sudden appearance in his life. The odds were against it being coincidental, so Collins decided to bring Morris up casually over dinner and see what sort of reaction he got from Karina.

At 103rd Street and Broadway Collins told the driver to pull over and let him out. He paid the cabbie and then hopped out of the taxi. He was startled when another cab jammed on its brakes and stopped ten feet from him. One of the two men who got out of the other cab, a young man with slicked-back hair, gave Collins a hard, challenging stare. Collins ignored him. That was New York, he thought, always some young kid walking around trying to prove he was a tough guy, ready to take on the world.

Karina was waiting for him in the lobby of the Hotel Marseilles. She had dressed up for the occasion, wearing an indigo-colored dress in a rayon crepe with a v-neck and long, slim sleeves. It was belted at the waist, accentuating Karina's slim figure, and Collins noticed that she was wearing lipstick and makeup, transforming from the plain woman of the day before into a polished, and beautiful, young woman.

She seemed out-of-place in the shabby, drab world of the United Service for New Americans, as if she had accidentally wandered into the lobby by mistake on her way to an elegant dinner party. Collins stopped and made a show out of admiring her appearance and she smiled broadly—what girl didn't like to be flattered?

"You look smashing," he said. He handed her the paper bag with the Vera Lynn record in it. "A gift," he said, and encouraged her to open it. She smiled when she saw the record's title.

"I thought you might like it," Collins said. "You do have a record player?"

"I do," she said. "Thank you. I do not have any records of my own."

"None? But you have a record player?"

"It is borrowed." She hesitated. "The records I listen to are borrowed, as well. A friend has loaned me the apartment where I am staying. Everything I must borrow, but friends are generous."

Collins helped her into her fitted coat. She didn't say much on the walk to the restaurant. Trattoria Il Riccio matched Collins' expectations for a New York Italian restaurant: red tablecloths, a poster of Naples on the wall, a simple menu. He ordered a bottle of Chianti and they had a salad followed by linguine with marinara sauce. The waiter brought them a loaf of Italian bread and Collins broke it into pieces. For a thin girl, Karina could eat. She didn't pick at her food, she attacked it. He watched, fascinated by the contrast between her polite reserve and her now near-ravenous appetite.

She caught him watching her. "I am sorry," she said. "I forget my manners. It is just that I remember when I had very little to eat. It is something that you cannot forget easily."

"No big deal," he said.

"It is not very lady-like," she said. "I'm embarrassed."

"Don't be. And don't stop or slow down on my behalf. I eat fast myself."

"When you are truly hungry, when there is very little food, it becomes quite simple. How to find that food. The stomach does not care for all of the civilized veneer. Veneer, that is the correct word?"

"Yes, it is. A fifty-cent word. You don't hear it too often."

"I like the sound of it," she said. "Veneer."

"Now that you mention it, it does have a pretty sound. We must have stolen it from the French."

"Lonnie says that you do not write about politics very often in your newspaper, but about the sports a lot. About baseball. In Warsaw, in the days before the war, all they wrote about in the newspapers was politics."

"I think my readers would be bored by it. With everything else going on in the city—the shows on Broadway, the nightclub scene, the sports, the stories that might get missed otherwise, like Joey Gallegos." Collins watched her face. "You do not approve?"

"It is not whether I approve or not. Lonnie says that you are a fine writer and that it's a waste..."

"A waste to write about baseball games?"

She nodded.

"Instead, I should be on my soapbox proclaiming to the world—what? That Congress should pass some bill that will cure all of our problems? That if we had voted for Henry Wallace the Russians wouldn't have built an A-bomb?"

"That is perhaps what Lonnie would want," she said.

"And you? What do you think?"

"It's only one part of life," she said. "It should never become so all consuming. I have seen too much to believe in one noble cause or the other. It is just words, words that are twisted to allow some men to gain power over others. The hard men. I don't care to hear those words anymore."

"That's why I like writing about baseball. There's something clean about what happens on the baseball diamond. There's nothing false. I'm sure it's that way when you sing, there's got to be something clean and right about singing a piece of music the way it was meant to be sung."

"Yes, there is."

"Don't you miss singing?"

"There are other ways to find what is clean and right."

"Such as what you do at work? Helping the refugees, the displaced?"

She nodded. "They have suffered a great deal. It is natural to want to help. I wish I could do more. Even during the war people would help each other, share what little they had. You must know this. Lonnie said you were in the war."

"I was an observer. Like most newspapermen, I was there to watch and report what I saw. I was in the Pacific Theater the last couple of years of the war."

"Then you know," she said in a quiet voice. "You know there is no glamour or romance to it. That it is an ugly, horrible thing but that there can be moments of great kindness."

"Not everyone here understands that," Collins said. "Back home they had blackouts and food rationing. The fighting took place far away from America. I think people thought they were making sacrifices for the war effort by buying war bonds."

"I wish I had come here to this city before the war," she said. "In 1939 I was so disappointed when my concert had to be canceled. I was very cross about it. That is petty, isn't it? The Germans and the Russians are invading Poland and I am upset about a concert. Dante reserved a place in hell for the uncommitted. In the vestibule. Perhaps that is where I will end up."

"Let's hope not," he said. "But save a place for me."

She looked down at the table, and then slowly raised her eyes to his face. "You have not been married, then, Dennis? "

"No. It turned out differently than I planned. Someone made a better offer to the girl when I was away during the war."

"I'm sorry."

Collins shrugged. "I'm not the only one who discovered that absence doesn't necessarily make the heart grow fonder. So how often do you get invited to dinner by men, once married or not?"

"Not often," she said. "But it has happened."

"And what do you do?"

"I haven't accepted any invitations to dinner from men, once married or not," she said. "Not until tonight. Unless you count Lonnie, but I do not think that he really counts."

"I see." Collins looked at her directly, weighing his next comment. "So why did you agree to come to dinner with me?"

"I don't know," she said. "You are so different. You are no boy. Lonnie thinks very highly of you, and I thought you might be interesting to talk to."

"And have I lived up to advance billing?"

Karina smiled at him, but she didn't respond directly. "So it is fair for me to know, then, why you asked me to dinner, is it not?"

"Other than the obvious?

"The obvious?"

"I don't need to flatter you, Karina," Collins said. "You must be aware of the effect you have on men, and I am obviously not immune. And I thought you might be interesting to talk to. So here we are. "

She remained silent, and it was then that Collins decided to bring up the subject of Morris. He didn't want the conversation, or the relationship, to go much further until he knew more. "My old friend Morris Rose tells me that I am too much of a romantic. That my problem is that I put women on a pedestal."

"That is remarkable," she said quickly. "I know Morris Rose. If it is the same Morris Rose, that is. We have dealt with him in arranging for some of our DPs to come to America. He has been one of our few allies at the State Department. It is wonderful what he has done."

"A small world," Collins said. "My friend Morris works at the State Department. There can't be two of them."

So there it was, he thought, she readily admitted to knowing Morris, and their connection seemed a natural one. Morris handled Eastern Europe and refugees for State, so it was logical that they would encounter each other. It could very well be coincidence that they had met, just as Morris was running into trouble. But why did the FBI have an interest in her? Was it just vetting anyone—known or unknown—who came into contact with Morris? Or was it more?

"Speaking of coincidences, I ran into Morris on Friday. Just before I met you and Lonnie at the Stork Club."

"We have not seen him at the Center in many months. How is he?"

He was about to respond when he glanced up and saw two men in ill-fitting suits standing by the front of the restaurant. Collins recognized one of them. It was the young tough with the slicked-back hair who had given him the challenging stare on the street earlier. Collins didn't like seeing them there. He sensed it meant trouble.

The men walked through the restaurant, brushing past the owner; he backed away, giving them a wide berth, wanting to have nothing to do with them. They stopped directly in front of Collins' table.

"We need to talk to you, Collins," the older of the two men said. He had an angry-looking scar on his face, near his left eye.

"I don't know that we've been introduced," Collins said and stood up and moved into the aisle. He wanted to keep Karina completely removed from the discussion.

"We're friends with Phil Santry," the scarred man said. "Good friends."

"Have you been following me?" Collins asked, and realized that he knew the answer: the men had been in a cab right behind him, probably all the way from Herald Square and Collins had been too preoccupied to notice.

"We need to talk," the leader said.

"Not in here," Collins said. "I'll come outside and we can talk there."

"Suit yourself," the younger tough said in a mocking tone. He had been silent up to that point.

"Please excuse me," Collins said to Karina. "This will only take a moment."

She looked up anxiously at him but remained silent. Collins realized that she was terrified.

"Don't worry," he said, with what he hoped was a reassuring smile. "This won't take long."

"It won't take long," the man repeated, again mocking Collins.

Collins realized the dining room had also gone silent. As they left the restaurant the other patrons in the Trattoria Il Riccio averted their eyes. He glanced back and saw that Karina had stayed at the table. That meant Collins didn't have to worry about her—just about himself. When they reached the sidewalk, he looked up and down the street hoping to find a cop walking his beat. There were no blue uniforms in sight, so he was going to have to talk his way out of trouble, if he could.

"So what can I do for you gentlemen?" he asked.

"It's what you can do for yourself," the scarred one said.

"What's that?" Collins kept his tone polite.

"Keep your fuckin' mouth shut in that fuckin' column of yours."

"Shut about what?"

"You know," he said, and then without warning punched Collins hard in the stomach with his balled fist. Collins doubled over from the pain. The punch had come so quickly that he didn't have time to evade it or block it.

Collins straightened up slowly, gasping. "Isn't there another way to handle this?" he managed.

"Maybe he doesn't listen good," the younger tough said. "It's possible that he is just stupid." He pushed Collins back against the storefront wall of the restaurant and Collins felt the bricks at his back.

"Did Santry send you?" Collins asked. He brought his hands up, ready to protect himself. If they weren't carrying guns he might have a fighting chance.

"You ask too many fuckin' questions," the leader said. "That's your problem."

"Your problem," the younger tough repeated. Then he stepped in and swung at Collins' head. This time Collins had more warning so he blocked the punch and countered with a quick right hand, clipping his adversary's chin with his fist. Collins hand stung—the knuckle hadn't completely healed from Friday—but the man staggered backwards. Unfortunately that meant Collins had to ignore the scarred man for the moment, and his punch caught Collins just under the right eye. Collins bounced off the brick wall and collapsed onto the sidewalk.

While Collins was still stunned, the scarred man pulled him up and held him by his arms so the younger tough could take a few swings at Collins. They weren't out to kill Collins, he knew, because they could have, if they wanted to. It was mainly body blows, smashes to the solar plexus. One of the punches caught Collins in the ribs and he gasped again in pain. The leader let him go, then.

"There's plenty more of that if need be," he said. "Remember that when you're thinkin' of getting wise again."

He pushed Collins into the wall and Collins fell down again, onto the sidewalk. Collins didn't move. No heroics. He figured that he would stay down and protect his head by covering up. Collins heard them muttering to each other, and then their voices faded. When he slowly pulled his head out from under his arms, he could see that they were gone. He got up slowly, feeling the pain from where he had hit the wall. Then he vomited onto the pavement, losing everything he had eaten.

Collins knew that adrenaline would block a lot of the immediate pain so he staggered back into the Trattoria Il Riccio, past the shocked customers and a mute Karina—he waved her away—until he reached the men's room in the back. He locked the door behind him. Collins took a deep breath and felt an immediate shooting pain in his right rib case. He spit into the sink and was glad to see there wasn't any blood. He managed to get the cold water running, and dashed it over his face. Then he cleaned up his suit coat.

When Collins looked in the mirror to comb his hair, he could see there was a large red mark under his eye, where the scarred man had caught him with the first punch. It was swelling rapidly but it didn't look like the eye was going to close up; the punch had glanced off the side of his face.

Karina stood up when he returned to the table, a look of distress on her face.

"Are you all right?" she asked.

"I'll live," Collins said. "I don't feel like finishing dinner, if that's all right with you."

"I understand," she said.

Collins called the proprietor over and asked him for the bill.

"We don't want your money, sir," he said. "Please just leave. We don't want no trouble here."

Collins wasn't about to argue with him. He didn't feel like he should be blamed for making a disturbance, but he could see why he wouldn't be welcome. Fistfights weren't good for business, despite Hemingway's theory. Before they left, Collins draped his trench coat over his shoulders—he didn't want to risk putting his arms through the sleeves with his ribs feeling the way they did—and handed Karina her coat with an apologetic smile. Once they were on the street Karina took his arm and Collins realized that he was still a bit wobbly.

"Are you sure you are all right?" she asked.

"Bruised pride," Collins said.

"We must get some ice on your eye," she said. "I live nearby. A few blocks. We can go to my apartment."

"You don't live at the Hotel Marseilles?" Collins was confused. His cheekbone had really begun to ache. He hoped that if there was swelling it wouldn't block his vision. He knew he was going to end up with a shiner.

"I discovered that I can't stay there all the time. It is not healthy. Remember how I told you that I borrow? I have an apartment that I am borrowing."

"You must think I'm an animal," Collins said. "In fights all the time."

"I do not think that."

"They didn't give me a choice. They were angry about something I wrote in the newspaper today about boxing. Actually, a friend of theirs was angry. They were just delivering the message."

"Hah, boxing!" she said, in a triumphant tone, as if her views on the evils of the sport had been validated.

Later, Collins could not remember how they got to Karina's apartment. From the time they left the restaurant until they reached her second-floor room the trip was all a blur. Karina had him sit down in an overstuffed wingback chair and she put ice, wrapped in a cloth, on his cheekbone. It stung at first, but after a minute or so Collins could feel it go numb and stop throbbing.

"Would you like a drink?" she asked. "Something strong?"

Collins nodded and Karina disappeared into a small kitchen and returned with a glass of amber-colored liquid. He took a few gulps and felt the warmth in his throat.

"What is it?" he asked.

"Krupnik. Polish spirits made with honey." She smiled. "It can be used as a disinfectant, too."

He sat back in the chair and watched her as she took the Vera Lynn record out of the paper bag. She carefully placed the disc on her record player and started it playing. They listened for a while Collins finished his drink.

"Would you care to dance?" he asked.

"To dance? Are you crazy? You are hurt."

"Not that hurt, and I feel like dancing."

"Are you sure?"

"I'm sure."

She nodded her agreement and Collins stood up, wincing slightly at the pain.

"Are you sure?" she asked again.

"It will hurt a lot more tomorrow," he said. "Not so bad, now."

When Collins took her hand in his it was cool to the touch. He placed his other hand in the small of her back and she followed him as they began to dance, a slow fox-trot. Collins tightened his grip a bit, bringing her closer to him, smelling her perfume and her hair.

"You like to dance, don't you?" she asked, and he remembered that Karina had been at the Stork Club and must have seen him dancing with Penny.

"I do," he said. "And you dance quite well."

"Thank you."

"I'm the one who should be thanking you. I'm sure you didn't bargain on having your dinner ruined. I'm sorry."

She didn't say anything but then she leaned in and kissed Collins full on the mouth. He gently pulled her close and kissed her again. She moved her body next to his and Collins tried to suppress the gasp from the sudden pain in his ribs.

"I don't mean to hurt you."

"You're not hurting me," he said and kissed her again, this time gently cupping his free hand around her breast. She didn't pull away, but kissed him harder. They moved into her small bedroom, kissing each other hungrily. She broke away to go to the window and draw the curtains. Then she took Collins by the hand and led him to her narrow bed. In the other room Vera Lynn was still singing about the White Cliffs of Dover.

Karina didn't hesitate as she began unbuttoning Collins' shirt while he fumbled with his belt buckle. Then she took her own belt off, and unbuttoned the front of her dress. Collins began undressing quickly, when he looked over Karina had removed her dress and was in her slip. She pulled the bedspread down and climbed under the sheets. She never took her eyes off Collins as she reached over and switched off the lamp on her side table. Collins, now naked, joined her in the darkness, kissing her on the lips again, as he slipped under the sheets.

The record had come to its end and the sudden silence from the other room made him pause and then he felt the soft skin of her legs touching him. Collins made love to her then, slowly, enjoying the feel of her skin, her mouth on his mouth, her thin fingers on his back, trying to disregard the pain in his ribs and cheekbone. Neither of them spoke. Karina pulled him tighter at the moment of her climax, gasping hard for breath, her hands clutching him. In response he drove himself into her deeper, matching her hunger, and then suddenly he was climaxing himself.

They lay there for a long time afterwards, bodies still touching, her hand gently stroking his chest, her breath warm and sweet on the side of his cheek. Finally she stirred, and rose from the bed. Collins watched from the bed as she stood there for a moment, her body slim and pale in the dim light of the room, reflecting in the mirror. Then she found her slip and put it on, turning to look at him with a small smile.

He got up, wincing from the pain in his side, and pulled on his boxer shorts. He sat on the bed, watching her as she lit a cigarette and took a puff on it. Then she came over to the bed and put the cigarette between his lips. Collins took a long drag, enjoying the taste. What was it about smoking after you'd made love? No cigarette ever tasted better, he thought. She sat next to him in the dark and they took turns with the cigarette, passing it back-and-forth.

"Did you know that Max Schmeling saved the lives of two Jewish boys?" she asked in a low voice. "The night of Kristalnacht. His friend, who was Jewish, asked him to hide his sons, which Max did."

"Why do you tell me this?" Collins asked.

"Because it is never so simple," she said. "I am not Jewish, Dennis, unless having a distant aunt on my father's side who was counts."

"I figured you were," he said. "Working at the Center and all. Not that it makes any difference to me, one way or the other."

She took a long drag from the cigarette, lost in thought for a moment. "We like to think that we can say who is good and who is evil," she said, finally. "That one man or woman is a devil, and the other an angel. Sometimes we can only do what we can. And that is enough. Sometimes we cannot do anything. We are paralyzed. But who is to judge? Unless they have been there."

"Well, you certainly have most people beat in that department. Your work, I mean. What you are doing for the refugees at the Hotel Marseilles. That's more than most people do in a lifetime."

"It is nothing," she said. "I am not a particularly courageous person. I know this about myself."

"I don't think in those terms anymore."

"But you have courage," she said. "Look at yourself. You are not afraid to stand up to people. Even if it is dangerous."

"Getting beaten up isn't courageous. It's stupid."

"I do not have that. Physical courage. My legs get weak and I cannot think what to do. I felt that way in the restaurant tonight with those horrid men. I froze. I wanted to hide." She was whispering. "Do you recall what I said about politics earlier? I hate what it does to people. The ideology. To live by these mindless slogans. Always encouraged to sacrifice for the Party or for the Fatherland or Mother Russia. Two sides of the same coin. Why do they feel we need them to fashion a family for us?"

"But you are in America, now," he said, hoping to lighten the tone. "We're too busy trying to make money to worry too much about slogans."

"Morris Rose would disagree with you."

"No doubt," Collins said. "I've known Morris a long time, and he takes great pleasure in disagreeing with me."

"You are so different," she said. "You and Morris."

"That we are."

They had finished the cigarette. He left the bed and slowly got dressed. It was late and he was exhausted. He needed to get back to his apartment and get a good night's sleep.

"The girl I saw you with at the Stork Club," Karina said. "She is very beautiful."

"Penny Bradford. What did Lonnie tell you about her?"

"I'd rather not say."

"You won't hurt my feelings," Collins said. "You can tell me."

"He said that you had been a couple years ago, but that she married a different man when you were overseas, a man who was killed in Greece. Lonnie guessed that you were hoping to resume your life with her." She stopped, reluctant to continue. Collins knew there was more.

"What else did he say?"

She played with a lock of her hair, reluctant to continue, stalling for time.

"You can tell me," he said. "It won't be anything I haven't heard before."

"Lonnie said that you were a fool, that she would never marry you. That she is quite conventional and that you are not of her social class. He said you were wasting your time." Her brown eyes remained fixed on his. "I am sorry. This is a very strange conversation to have with a man who has just been in your bed."

"It is hard to hear such things said out loud," he said. "It's nothing I haven't thought myself. But when you're in love you don't calculate the odds, you tell yourself that there's hope. You grasp at straws."

"Grasp at straws?" She was puzzled by the phrase and Collins found himself smiling.

"That's what a drowning man does, grasps at straws, at anything floating by. I guess that's not a bad description of how I've been when it comes to Penny Bradford."

"It does not have to be so," she said.

"No, it does not," he said, surprising himself. "But I have to take it a step at a time. Tonight was a step."

"I am glad to hear that."

Collins didn't say anything. He found his trench coat and put it on over his shoulders. He didn't ache as much—the physical act of love, and the accompanying surge of adrenaline, had helped mask the pain. Karina, barefoot, came with him to the front door, still dressed only in her slip. They kissed again at the door.

"When will I see you again?" he asked.

"When do you want to?"

"Tomorrow," he said. "Would you like that?"

She nodded. "It has been very sudden, Dennis. I did not expect this. It is confusing. I must get things straight in my head."

For a moment Collins wondered whether he should ask her about Morris again, about her relationship with him, but he decided against it. Nor did he say anything about the FBI having her photo. How much candor did you owe a woman you have just slept with for the first time? Someone who is still a stranger? Collins wasn't sure but he figured that it could wait until tomorrow. Collins took her in his arms and she stood on her tiptoes to kiss him again on the lips. He promised to call her.

When he got to the street he stopped at a newsstand and bought the late papers and scanned the sports pages. The Yanks had won, 3-1, against the Athletics, but the Red Sox had kept their one game lead in the American League by beating the Washington Senators. There was promising news in the National League for the Dodgers; the Cards had lost to the Pirates, so that meant the Brooks had picked up half a game. They were still alive.

Collins walked over to Broadway and hailed a cab. He needed to get back to the apartment and quickly put some more ice on his eye to keep the swelling down. Thanks to Phil Santry's friends, he was not only going to be sore and bruised in the morning, but he was also going to look like hell.

Wednesday, September 28

The suddenness of it had surprised her. She had never thought that she would find herself in bed with him so quickly, even though there had been a sexual tension between them from the start, and the more she got to know him the greater her attraction grew. By the way he looked at her, she knew he found her desirable.

She had been shocked by the incident at the restaurant. The sudden violence had brought back unwelcome memories from the past. She had been impressed by his courage in confronting the two toughs by himself and by his brave front afterward when he was clearly hurting from the beating they had given him.

Once they were alone, in the apartment, she had found herself drawn to him, wanting to comfort him. She could tell he was in pain and yet he wouldn't admit it. It became something more when they began dancing and she felt him press his body against hers. She hadn't danced with a man in years, and she liked the feeling of moving in time to the music. When she kissed him, impulsively, for the first time and he responded she did not hold back.

She had no regrets. She had learned to act on her feelings, to grasp whatever happiness she could. Why not? She had learned how fleeting life could be. Why wait if it felt right in the moment? In fact, living like that meant there could be no regrets.

And she felt no shame. The irony was that no matter what he might think, she was no sleep-around, no wanton. She had only three lovers before Dennis; some of her girlfriends from the opera had boasted of three lovers a year. Since her arrival in New York, she had slept alone. Dennis Collins was the first man she had let into her bed since Morris.

Their sudden involvement complicated things. It made it harder for her to engineer a clean break with her past. She could not leave the city now without warning Dennis about Morris. Soon she would have to tell her new lover the truth, a truth that would have consequences for her, as well.

When he learned of her past she would most likely lose him. She had no illusions about how he would react. Accepting what she had done and what she had been was too much to ask of a man.

He would also discover that she had deceived him from the very start. How could he trust her? Worse, she would have to reveal her entanglement with the Russians. She hated the thought of telling him. She had finally found a man who promised her the deeper intimacy she had longed for, but now she would have to sacrifice that.

Later in the week, Morris would want to meet with Dennis and before that occurred she would have to reveal all of the ugliness to Dennis. He had to understand what helping Morris would mean. She couldn't imagine him cooperating once he knew who controlled his friend.

She had a day or two before things would come to a head. She told herself that she would have the courage to do what was necessary, that she would not shy away from what she now saw as her duty.

Seventeen

Collins didn't care for the look of his bruised face staring back at him from his bathroom mirror in the morning. He sported a large shiner under his right eye, and a slight cut near his right cheekbone. It hurt to take a really deep breath. He figured that he would be all right; he hadn't coughed up any blood and a couple of cracked ribs wouldn't kill him.

He thought about what had happened the night before, and it had a surreal quality in the light of day. The attack by Santry's thugs had come without warning and later he had certainly not expected to find himself in Karina Lazda's bed.

Would their sudden encounter lead to anything more substantial? What was she feeling now? She might be having second thoughts—they had begun their affair impulsively. Living through the war years he knew how quickly desire could hit when the future was uncertain.

There was Penny to consider, as well, but Collins didn't feel guilty about his night with Karina. He owed Penny nothing. He had known Karina only days—but she had met him more than halfway emotionally, something he couldn't say about Penny.

Collins went to his desk and found the number in the phone book for the local florist on West 72nd Street. He arranged for a dozen red roses to be delivered to Miss Karina Lazda at the Hotel Marseilles. He had the florist include a card that read: *To Karina, Thinking of you, Denny.* He thought about saying more in the message but decided against it. The roses would carry whatever meaning Karina cared to find in them.

There also was still the matter of Phil Santry. Collins wasn't sure about how to respond. He figured his brother should know about the attack by Santry's buddies, in the event there was further trouble, so he phoned him.

Frank had cooled down from the day before and sounded almost apologetic when they exchanged greetings and some small talk. Collins pictured his immaculately dressed brother surrounded by his fellow plainclothes detectives—living up to the adjective "plain" with their out-of-fashion suits and ties, many of them shiny and threadbare. Frank would stand out, an Irish peacock in the drab environment of a Manhattan police station.

"I had a visit from some tough guys last night," Collins told him. "Upset over the column."

"Upset over the stuff about the boxing investigation? What did they have to say?"

"They didn't want to have much of a discussion. Told me they were friends of Santry. They wanted me to stop writing about boxing. Made that very clear. They pushed me around a little."

"Are you okay?"

"A black eye. Sore ribs. That's all."

His brother whistled. "That's all? That's something. You know who these guys are? Do you want to file assault charges?"

"I don't know who they are. Let's keep this quiet for now, anyway. It'd be my word against theirs, in any case because there weren't any witnesses." Collins wasn't about to involve Karina in his troubles, and the owner of Trattoria Il Riccio would never be willing to testify.

"Santry was behind it?"

"No question. The thugs told me that. When I get the chance I'll make sure Santry knows how much I appreciate his involvement. I'll let him swing first, too, before I clobber him."

"There are other ways to handle this. If you can get the names of the guys involved, I'll see what I can do about sending them a message."

"Maybe later. For now I wanted you to know, officially, in the event there's more trouble."

"Speaking of trouble, I've been asking around about your friend. I'm grabbing coffee with my Bureau contact later today. He owes me a favor, so I should get something about the situation from him."

"Call me after you see him, would you?"

"Count on it," he said. "And Denny, do me a favor?"

"Sure."

"Stay clear of trouble between now and then. Stay away from Santry. Keep your head down. You can't afford to have anyone else pissed off at you."

Once on the street, Collins pulled his fedora brim down to try to hide his black eye. He had his customary breakfast at the All-American and skimmed through the papers. He started with his own column, which he had dashed off the day before about mayoral politics and O'Dwyer's prospects for re-election. It made him grimace because it wasn't one of his best. Then he turned to the sports pages. Other than Tuesday's games, one of the top stories was that Casey Stengel, Ralph Houk, and Cliff Mapes had been fined by the American League president for their part in the dispute over the call at home plate in the Yankees-Red Sox game.

Despite Monday's loss, the Yanks weren't out of it just yet. Their win over the Athletics on Tuesday put them a game behind the Red Sox and they played the A's, one of the weaker teams in the American League, again in the afternoon, with Tommy Byrne on the mound. There was some talk in the papers that Joe DiMaggio was hoping to play by the weekend.

The Dodgers had traveled by train to Boston for their two game series with the Braves. It was strange for Collins not to be there with them—he definitely would have gone if he hadn't felt obligated to stay in New York so he could return the film to Morris.

One other story caught his eye. In Washington the House Un-American Activities Committee had resumed its hearings into alleged Soviet efforts to steal atomic secrets in 1943. They were blaming a "Scientist X" at the University of California's Berkeley radiation laboratory of leaking vital information. One of the Berkeley atomic researchers, Irving David Fox, had taken the Fifth when the HUAC counsel asked him whether he'd been a Communist, or part of a Communist cell, while working on the atomic bomb. By itself that didn't mean anything, Collins told himself. Just because you've got lefty politics and that you were a Party member at some point doesn't make you a Red spy.

After Fox finished his testimony, committee aides made it clear to the reporters there that they knew all along that he wasn't a spy—the true Scientist X was someone else and HUAC was considering naming him later in the hearing. Collins wondered how guilty Morris might look if forced to testify under oath and asked lots of questions about his past. Collins was fairly certain that Morris had never joined the Party, but he couldn't swear to it.

Collins returned to his apartment building lobby to check his mailbox. There wasn't much of interest, just some bills, his copy of the latest *New Republic* and *The Sporting News*, and a letter from the New York Athletic Club informing him that he needed to pay his dues or have his privileges suspended. A small postcard, with a photo of the Ethan Allen Tower on its front, attracted his attention. Collins turned it over. It had been postmarked Sept. 26 in Burlington, Vermont and read:

> *Nor shall my sword sleep in my hand*
> *Till we have built Jerusalem*
> *In England's green and pleasant land.*

The card wasn't signed, but Collins immediately recognized the lines from one of William Blake's poems, a bitter critique of British capitalism. More than once, before the war, when they stayed up drinking and talking about the political situation Morris would recite the Blake poem by heart. This had been during the early years of the new Roosevelt Administration and Morris, about to graduate from Columbia Law, was eager to get to Washington.

"There's no way they can stand in the way of history," he said. "The money boys and the bankers. They can't stop us. The changes this country desperately needs will happen. It is just a matter of when."

"Looks like the President is off to a good start," Collins had said.

"He is only scratching the surface," Morris said. "That's why I want to get to Washington now. To help speed things up in my own small way."

"You can only go so fast. It takes people some time to adjust."

"That's exactly the reason that we need more sweeping changes. The reactionaries are knocked back on their heels for the moment. As soon as they regroup they will counterattack, to try to return us to a society where privilege and power decides. We can't let that happen."

"I'm sure FDR and his advisors have thought of that."

"It doesn't matter. We don't have to wait for the President. There will be enough of us who are willing to embrace the flow of history."

"Who would 'us' include?"

"All of the young progressives headed to Washington," he said, his eyes shining; Morris had been more than a bit drunk and consequently, overly melodramatic. "Think of it, Denny. Thousands of educated young people dedicated to progressive causes. We will serve in every branch of government, every department. Imagine how that commitment and energy will advance us, whether or not FDR wakes up."

"Building a new Jerusalem?" Collins asked, impressed with himself that for once he had mentioned the Blake poem before Morris did.

"Sure," he said. "You could say that. A new Jerusalem on the Potomac."

It didn't happen that way, of course, Collins knew. First, Roosevelt had to do something about the economy and there was the long, slow climb out of the Depression as the country got back to work. It did take time for people to accept the changes of the New Deal. Progress didn't come as fast as Morris and his friends would have wanted.

And then that flow of history shifted in unanticipated ways, with the rise of Fascism in Germany and Italy and the defeat of the Loyalists in Spain. Domestic reforms didn't seem as important all of a sudden. Morris transferred to the State Department from Commerce for that very reason. After Pearl Harbor there was no question, defeating the Japanese and the Nazis became the first and only job.

Collins held the postcard in his hand. He understood why Morris had sent it. He wanted Collins to remember their past. Collins looked around the lobby, making sure that he was alone before carefully ripping the postcard into small pieces and depositing them in a nearby wastebasket.

As he left the lobby and went back into the street, Collins reflexively glanced around. No sign of anyone watching. He would have felt foolish if it weren't for the microphone planted in his phone. If they were willing to bug him, he thought, why not shadow him?

When he reached the *Sentinel* he knew he would be ribbed about his black eye. His reputation for a short fuse and quick fists would guarantee that. As it happened, Hal Diderick was the first person Collins encountered.

"You're a hell of a sight," Diderick said. "What does the other guy look like?"

"Guys," Collins said. "Plural."

"That's not according to Marquis de Queensbury rules. It's supposed to be one at a time."

"That's what my father always said."

"How sore are you?"

"Sore enough. I'll live, though. It means I'll look like a pug for a couple of days, but there are worse things."

His first order of business was to call one of his friends in the Yankees front office, Ted Petersham, and arrange tickets for Josef and Hannah, Mrs. Berliner, and an escort from the Center. He explained the situation to Petersham and promised him that the *Sentinel* would send a photographer by the seats to take a picture of the group enjoying the game.

"The boy is a DiMaggio fan," Collins explained. "Great publicity for the club."

"Perfect," Petersham said. "Saturday happens to be DiMaggio Day."

"Is he going to play?" Collins asked.

"They say that he's feeling better and should be able to play by the weekend. He's taking batting practice today. The truth is that he lost a lot of weight in the hospital—almost twenty pounds. We'll see. On Saturday, I'll meet these children of yours, Denny, and welcome them on behalf of the ball-club and show them to their seats. Have your group come to the will-call window forty-five minutes before the game and ask for me."

When Collins thanked him for accommodating his request, Petersham laughed. "So can payback be that we're not going to see any more columns in the *Sentinel* about how the Yankees ought to have colored players in uniform like the Dodgers?" Like most baseball executives, Petersham had a long memory for negative press.

"Not quite" Collins said. "All that I keep saying is that you're only hurting yourself by not taking advantage of all that talent. Look at what Newcombe has done for the Dodgers this season."

"I can't disagree. It takes time. We may be buying some Negro players from Kansas City next year. Start 'em in the minors like Rickey did with Jackie Robinson."

"Can I quote you on that?"

"Not yet," Petersham said. "Seeing as how you're so keen on the Negro Leagues, I'll give you an exclusive when we're ready."

"Okay," Collins said, ignoring the sarcasm. "I'll hold you to that."

After Collins had finished his call with Petersham, he found an empty office and phoned Karina.

"They are beautiful," she said. "The roses. You have embarrassed me in front of the other women here. They want to know who my new admirer is."

"Did you tell them?"

"I told them that they were from a friend. Were they terribly expensive, Dennis? I don't wish you to think that you must make extravagant gestures."

"It was nothing. When can I see you again?"

"That's up to you," she said. "I would like to see you whenever you can. I know a woman is supposed to play coy, but that is the truth."

"Later tonight?"

"When?"

"I will call. I have to catch up on some work. I won't have time until much later." Collins gave her the information about the Yankees tickets. He promised her that he would phone later in the afternoon, and it was only after he hung up that he remembered he had promised to take Penny out for dinner. He would have to call Karina later and explain that something had come up and that he couldn't see her.

When he came back out to the main newsroom Diderick had more news.

"It's pouring in Boston," he said. "Marquis just called looking for you. Looks like the Dodgers game will be rained out."

"What are they going to do about a make-up?"

"Marquis said Shotton is stuck. Normally they would play it on Friday, the next open date. But if they get rained out Friday, they lose the game completely—no make-up because it's the end of the season. So Marquis thinks Shotton will ask for a doubleheader tomorrow."

"Tough to bank on winning both games of a doubleheader."

"You're the one who predicted they'd come back and win the pennant. Changing your mind?"

"Not yet. The Cards still look shaky."

Collins went back to his desk and sat down in front of his type-writer. Now that he had the Yankees committed to providing the tickets, writing the column about Josef and Hannah would be easy. He pulled out his reporter's notebook, quickly paged through his notes from Monday's interviews, and began.

Josef and Hannah will see their first American baseball game Saturday at Yankee Stadium, but they will be unlike any of the other children attending the Bombers' crucial showdown with the Boston Red Sox.

They are only weeks removed from the harsh reality of life in a Polish Displaced Persons camp. Orphaned by the war, they have come to America for a new life, where they have found a welcome refuge with the United Service for New Americans in the Hotel Marseilles, the gathering spot for recently arrived DPs.

"When they first arrived, Hannah would not speak," Karina Lazda, a United Service worker explains. "Not a word. Now she will say a few words in Polish to us. And she is smiling. That is a milestone for her, and it makes all of us so happy."

Josef, twelve years old, has learned some English—nearly all of it connected to his new favorite pastime, watching the New York Yankees and his hero, Joe DiMaggio, on television.

Saturday he may see the Yankee Clipper in person.

Collins didn't pause once when composing the first four paragraphs—the words flowed effortlessly. The column was writing itself. He was interrupted by Diderick, who stopped by his desk with a fistful of wire copy.

"Remember we talked about Tokyo Rose the other day? About the war being over?"

"I remember."

"This just came in from Australia," he said. "They captured nine Jap soldiers in Madang, in New Guinea. Holdouts. Guess the war isn't completely over."

"Maybe. But imagine what those soldiers are going to think when they learn they're our allies now. They'll realize that they wasted the last four years living in the past."

"It's not living in the past that's the problem," Diderick said. "It's forgetting the past. I just want to see all the accounts settled. All the unfinished business resolved. That's all. That's when I'll be at peace."

"Let's hope that's sometime soon," Collins said. "Because if you ask me, it's better to move on as quickly as possible."

"Only when you can," Diderick said. "When the accounts are settled. Not until then."

Eighteen

It was almost noon before Collins took a break. He thought about the postcard from Morris and decided that he would call Ruth Rose. He would encourage her to pass along the message to her husband that Collins was even more anxious to get rid of the film canister in his jacket pocket.

Collins left the newspaper and walked to a drugstore in Herald Square across from Macy's where he knew there was a phone booth. He closed the door tightly before he had the operator place a long-distance call to Morris' number in Washington. He quickly fed the coins into the phone until he had reached the required amount. The phone was picked up on the fifth ring.

"Hello." It was Ruth, breathing heavily, as though she had come up a flight of stairs.

Collins placed his handkerchief over the mouthpiece of the phone before he spoke. He felt foolish doing it, but he figured it would mask his voice if anyone was listening in. "This is a friend from New York," he began.

"Yes, I see."

"I'm getting slightly anxious, here. It's already Wednesday afternoon and I haven't heard from anyone at my end."

"Patience."

"I've been patient. I'd like to get this over with soon."

"We haven't forgotten. You should be contacted tomorrow. By then, everything should be in place."

"If you talk to our mutual friend let him know that I don't appreciate being put in this position. He wasn't completely square with me about the situation. I've had some visits from people who seem quite eager to talk to him. Official visits."

"We're doing the best we can," she said. "You'll hear tomorrow."

Then, before Collins could respond, she quickly said goodbye and disconnected at her end. Collins replaced the receiver, dissatisfied with the call. Ruth had not yielded an inch. Collins still had the film and he still had to wait. The call had been worth it, though, in one sense—he had been able to voice his frustration. Even if it was recorded, neither of them had said anything compromising. They had been on the phone no more than sixty seconds.

Collins walked back through Herald Square, envying the innocence of the throngs of shoppers and pedestrians he passed on his way, caught up in their workday routines, on the way to lunch or to run errands. They were not worried about FBI interrogations or thugs from the boxing world. They were blissfully focused on their own lives.

Once back at his desk, Collins sat around reading the other papers for a while. He was debating going back out for a sandwich when one of the copy boys stopped by his desk and told him he had a visitor. Collins glanced over to the newsroom entrance. Matthew Steele waved at him, clearly out-of-place in the shabby surroundings with his bow tie and expensive Brooks Brothers' suit. Collins got up from his desk and went over to greet him, properly wary. Steele smiled faintly when he saw Collins' black eye.

"Spat with the girlfriend?" he asked.

"Something like that."

"I heard you were in the Golden Gloves. Didn't they teach you to keep your guard up?"

"Let's say I didn't see it coming and leave it at that."

"Can you spare time for a spot of lunch?" Steele asked, glancing at his expensive wristwatch. "Promise to get you back here quickly. My treat."

"Is this a special occasion of some kind?"

"A chance for us to get caught up," he said. "About some of the matters we touched on at the Yale Club. I'm confident that it will be worth your time."

Collins shrugged. He didn't see why not; perhaps he could learn something from Steele about the status of Morris' loyalty investigation. Steele proposed that they lunch at a nearby restaurant, so they left the *Sentinel* and plunged into Herald Square's lunch hour pedestrian traffic. Steele moved effortlessly, gracefully—he was light on his feet—and Collins found himself lengthening his stride to keep up.

Steele steered them to a small lunch place, Bewley's Luncheonette, on West 36th Street, tucked in right off Broadway. Once inside, Collins looked around, surprised, for it wasn't what the sort of restaurant he expected Steele would choose. Bewley's was filled with working people, mainly from the garment industry, catching a hurried meal on their lunch break. There was a long lunch counter, some scattered tables and several booths. The menu ran to meatloaf and mashed potatoes, hamburgers, and open-faced sandwiches. Steele walked over to the one empty booth and slid into the seat facing the door; Collins followed him and took the seat across from him.

"Is this your idea of slumming?" Collins asked.

"Again you have made assumptions about me, Mr. Collins. Actually, my favorite lunch place in Washington is very similar to this. Hearty food. No pretension."

"You don't care for pretension?"

"Only when called for," he said, with a faint smile.

"Call me Denny, then."

"Matthew," he said, reaching over to shake Collins hand in a strange, awkward gesture. The harried waitress poured two cups of coffee without their asking and then took their orders. Collins asked for a bowl of minestrone soup and Steele for a club sandwich.

"So, about our chat," Steele said. "The reason for this lunch. I have a few items of interest that I thought we might cover."

He reached into his suit pocket and produced a manila envelope. Steele carefully opened it and slid out two glossy photographs, handing Collins the first of the photos. It was a slightly smaller headshot of the first female the FBI agents had shown Collins on Tuesday.

"I've seen this photo before," Collins said. "And I don't know her and I've never seen her. I told the FBI agents that when they showed it to me."

"I take it that Hoover's chaps have been by to see you again."

"They have. They seemed quite irritated that they haven't found Morris yet."

"There's no reason for you to know this woman," Steele said. He explained that she was a secretary by the name of Helen Shoemaker, employed by the FBI in the Counterintelligence Division in Washington. "She is no longer working there, by the way. She's in federal custody. You might be interested to learn that she has been having an affair with your friend Morris Rose."

Collins remained silent. Steele would be sorely disappointed if he thought Collins would be shocked at learning that Morris had a girl on the side.

"Miss Shoemaker was arrested last Thursday in Washington," Steele said. "Apparently she allowed your friend Rose to view several confidential Bureau documents of an extremely sensitive nature. Then Rose went missing the next day."

"Why are you telling me this?"

"Context. I want you to appreciate why we are so interested in your friend."

"This is a fairly fantastic story. It doesn't sound like anything Morris would do. Why should he care about FBI documents?"

It was hard for Collins to believe that Morris, the by-the-book lawyer, would consciously break the law. Even as a kid playing stickball in the street, Morris had always been a stickler for the ground rules. Collins was more willing to allow variations on the rules, but Morris would have nothing of it.

"Unfortunately I can't tell you the nature of the documents. They are top secret, and for once they actually do fit that classification."

They were interrupted by the waitress bringing them their food. Steele waited until she had left before he spoke again. Collins took his first spoonful of the minestrone soup. It was delicious, rich and savory with beans, onions, celery and carrots; he was hungrier than he had realized.

"Miss Shoemaker claims that Rose had asked her to obtain these documents to help clear him of false allegations. Not a very convincing story if you ask me, but she's a woman in love. She would have believed anything he told her. A romantic, it seems."

"What are you saying?" Collins asked, his voice growing louder.

"Please, Denny," Steele said. "Discretion is the better part of valor. Keep your voice down, please, and I will try to explain."

"I'm all ears."

"This is why I need to talk with your friend. You see, it is particularly unfortunate that it was Miss Shoemaker who borrowed the documents in question." Steele paused. "An FBI employee, one of their own. Hoover has been excessively proud of their security record and now we have Miss Shoemaker and this indiscretion. Hoover is frantic that this not be made public, especially in light of the Coplon matter. A second breach of security in the Bureau would be particularly embarrassing. Hoover can be quite vindictive and I don't envy your friend when the G-men catch up to him."

Collins shook his head. "If Morris asked to see the documents, and I don't know that he did, then there's an explanation, a logical one. I'd guess he wanted to be prepared for whatever charges were going to be leveled at him, so he could refute them. Have you thought of that?"

Steele raised his eyebrows. "That's one interpretation. I find it passing strange that a midlevel State Department bureaucrat would have such an interest in files from the FBI's Counterintelligence Division. Even stranger that he would need to keep the documents overnight before returning them to his lover."

Collins shook his head. "There's an explanation for that as well. He needed to review them, take notes."

Steele shrugged. "That may be. But you can see why I'm eager to talk to your friend."

Then Steele handed Collins the second photograph. Collins already knew that it would be Karina Lazda. It made sense—Steele and the FBI were using the same photos, following the same leads. Collins glanced at the photograph of Karina briefly and then handed it back to Steele.

"The FBI showed me this as well," he told him.

"I'm sure that they did. You recognize Karina Lazda, don't you?"

There was no point in denying it, Collins knew, and he felt himself tense up. "I know her, yes. You must be having me watched. What does Karina have to do with this, other than knowing Morris?"

"Not quite sure about that, yet," Steele said.

"What do you think? What does your file on her say? You have her photo for a reason, don't you?"

"It will not please you," he said.

"Maybe, maybe not. Try me."

"Very well, then." Steele paused, weighing his words. "Karina Lazda has a colorful history, you see."

"Don't we all?"

"Not like her, I am afraid. Her associations, past and present, are troubling. I say that not as a judgment, strictly as a fact. For example, we believe that she may have assisted Russian military intelligence in the past, in Poland. We don't know what exact role she plays now here in New York, but we believe she remains under the direction of the Soviets, as an operative with the code name Soprano."

"So you claim that she is—" Collins stopped. He didn't want to say the word "spying" out loud. "She is implicated in some sort of illegal activity?"

"It does have that appearance."

"What does this have to do with Morris?"

"We understand that they were lovers," Steele said. "We're not sure but again, there are signs pointing to such an entanglement. She was his interpreter in Poland and he brought her to Vienna. Then she lands a job in New York at this refugee center through his influence."

Collins was stunned into momentary silence. To hear Matthew Steele calmly talk about Karina as a possible Soviet agent and as Morris' lover went beyond the fantastic to the surreal. Yet while Collins might find it easy to reject the notion of Karina spying, that she might have slept with Morris seemed much more plausible. She had let him, a stranger, someone she hardly knew, into her bed and so why not Morris? Morris was certainly capable of it, married or not.

"Why should I believe any of this? You can't be certain of any of this."

"Her past is a quite vivid one, marked by a string of unfortunate entanglements. In Poland she became involved with a member of the elite, Piotr Malinowski, just as the war began. He had dabbled in producing opera before the war, which is how they met. Malinowski's family managed to keep their shoe factories open even after the Wermacht arrived and they began supplying the Germans. Elements of the Home Army in Warsaw assassinated Malinowski in '44 for collaborating with the Nazis. There are gaps in what we know, but apparently Miss Lazda moved in next with a Red Army officer, which I imagine saved her from retribution by the partisans." He paused to take a careful bite of his sandwich.

"The Red Army officer, Alexander Ivanov, leaves our tale when he is recalled to Moscow in '47 as part of a purge of the officer ranks. Karina Lazda somehow commences working for Morris Rose. Again, there are gaps. Did she seduce him at the direction of the Soviets? We don't know. Rose arranges for her to be brought to the United States through the DP program and he fixes the paperwork to elide over her Fascist ties. By then it appears their affair had ended. He's not one for long liaisons, apparently. That brings us to the here and now."

Collins didn't respond. Somehow he knew that Steele was telling the truth as he knew it—his confident recitation of Karina's background had been impressive in its detail, proof that Steele had spent time with her file.

Steele put his sandwich down. "Forgive me if this is a bit abrupt. There's no way you could have known about her past. Your role in all this appears to be quite tangential. Accidental. On the other hand, the sudden appearance of Karina Lazda in your life might not be a total coincidence. Why she has been brought into contact with you is an intriguing question. Can you provide any illumination?"

"Any illumination? I met her through Lonnie Marks, a press agent. I thought that her work with the DPs might make a good column. That's all."

"Quite a lovely woman."

"Do you think so?" If Steele was having him watched, Collins figured he knew about his evening with Karina. That might explain why Steele chose to tell him about Karina and Morris; perhaps he thought that as a jealous lover Collins might prove more tractable.

"Where did you first meet her?"

"At the Stork Club on Friday night. Like I said, she was with Lonnie Marks."

"How does she know Marks?"

"I'm not quite sure. What do you think? You're the one who likes solving ciphers."

"Ah, I see," Steele said. "You have researched my background, then, have you?"

"Just scratching the surface," Collins said. "There's not a lot in the public record. I haven't started making phone calls yet."

"You won't find much. Easier to just ask me whatever you want to know."

"Where do you fit in?" Collins asked. "Who do you work for, officially, and why are you investigating Morris?"

"Fair enough. I can tell you that. Officially, I work for the Central Intelligence Agency, although I imagine that doesn't come as any surprise to you. I have an interest in Morris because the FBI does, and I am their liaison on this sort of matter. CIA doesn't operate domestically, so I have to rely on my friends in the Bureau when we need help here in the States."

"This sort of matter? What sort of matter?"

"What sort of matter? A senior State Department official disappears the day after his paramour confesses to passing him top-secret documents. And then another of his girlfriends, one with close connections to the Soviets, suddenly surfaces in the company of his boyhood chum in New York. That would seem to warrant mild concern on our part, if not setting off outright alarm bells."

Steele leaned forward, displaying a sudden intensity. "We believe that Rose has gone to ground here in New York. If we are correct, it would be natural for him to turn to you for help."

"I haven't seen him since Friday," Collins said.

"He will contact you again, though. I feel confident that he will. Miss Lazda's sudden appearance on the scene has convinced me of that. And when he does, what should we do about it?"

"We? Don't include me in this."

"Would you hear me out on this? I have a few ideas about what you might do."

The waitress cleared their plates and refilled their coffee cups. After Steele had stirred two spoons of sugar into his coffee, he took a small sip and then leaned back against the back of his seat.

"I've had a discussion about this very matter with some friends of mine in Washington. Carter Clarke, head of the Armed Forces Agency and then my own boss, Admiral Hillenkoetter. While the course of action that I have proposed is unorthodox, they are in agreement with the general direction. All that is needed is your cooperation."

"My cooperation?"

"Your cooperation."

"Doing what?"

"Very simple. Just pass along our message to Morris and validate its sincerity. That's all."

"And why would I do that? I don't know what to believe, but I still think you have it wrong."

"Why would you do that?" Steele repeated Collins' question. "It's very simple. Assist us out of loyalty to your country."

"There's loyalty to a friend involved, as well. I don't believe that Morris has done anything wrong. All I have to say otherwise are your unsubstantiated allegations. So I don't see this as a matter of my patriotism. Isn't that always the last refuge of the scoundrel?"

"Fine," Steele said slowly. "We will give you a chance to help demonstrate your friend's innocence. All we need to know is where and when Rose plans to see you next. And we'd like you to carry a message to him. We are very eager to talk to him and it would be in his best interests to do so."

"What about Karina?"

"We don't know whether she is part of all this, acting on Morris' behalf, or under other direction. She may be Morris' idea of a human insurance policy. A way to keep an eye on you if he has plans for you, based on the old neighborhood loyalty. I would recommend that you play along with her and see what happens. I imagine that won't be too painful, will it?"

Collins didn't care for Steele's insinuation, but he bit back an angry response.

"Why are you telling me this?" he asked.

Steele took another deliberate sip of his coffee.

"I want to open a channel to Rose. I'm intrigued by him, to tell the truth."

Now it was Collins' turn to be amused. "By Morris?"

"His obvious intelligence. His broad range of friends. His ability to mesmerize young women. He is not your run-of-the-mill career diplomat. He's a man of many parts, isn't that the phrase? The very first time that I read his file, I asked myself: who is he? What is he like? What can you tell me?"

"What can I tell you about Morris? He's always a few moves ahead. Logical. He thought like a lawyer even as a young boy. He was the clever one."

"And the women?"

"He's good-looking and he's confident. That's the draw."

"What about when he's in a bind? What then?"

"He's not the type to panic. He'd think his way through."

"And you've seen him when times were good and times were bad?"

Steele's question made Collins think back to the only time he had ever seen Morris in tears. It had been on the March Saturday in 1939 when Madrid fell to Franco's Nationalist troops, the day they all knew the Spanish Republic was finished, the gallant struggle for democracy strangled by the Fascists. The strange thing, Collins remembered, was that in the weeks afterwards, Morris had not been as devastated by the defeat of the Republicans as he would have expected. He had rebounded quickly, announcing that he had decided to join the State Department—because he thought he could make a bigger difference on the inside than on the outside.

"I've seen him in good times and bad," he said. "The same Morris." He paused. "By the way," he said, looking to change the subject. "Who is Vigenère?"

"A Frenchman, expert in cryptology. He developed a twist on simple substitution ciphers. Simple but elegant. We've only known how to crack Vigenère ciphers for fifteen years." Steele gave Collins an amused look. "My talk in New York ten years ago? Did that turn up in your research?"

Collins nodded in acknowledgement.

"What else can I tell you?" Steele asked.

"How did you get into this particular line of work?" Collins had found that it was a question that often led to unexpected answers, and he hoped it would reveal more about Steele.

"The war," Steele said. "I found in the OSS that I could make a contribution with my work. Afterward, it dawned on me that our country would need men like me in its intelligence services. So the people sitting around us—" and Steele gestured with his right hand to take in the entire room "—can go about their lives not worrying about another shooting war. Think of me as one of their guardian angels."

"The devil being the Russians."

His comment produced a pained expression on Steele's angular face. "Not the Russians, per se. Only those infected by the collectivist thinking of that grubby little scholar, Marx, and his acolytes, Lenin and Stalin. The true believers. Those are the dangerous ones, and the sickness isn't confined to the Russians. They can be found in all of the great cities of the West—New York, London, Paris, Rome. We know that the First Directorate has agents in those cities to recruit them and control them. It is our role to resist this through whatever means necessary. All of the people sitting here enjoying lunch are oblivious to this struggle."

"Would they approve of the means you adopt, if they did know about it?"

"They do not wish to know about it. Ignorance being bliss, and all. I do believe it is better for all concerned that way. Those of us in the shadows must sometimes, by necessity, resort to some harsh tactics. Mind you, I do not apologize. What we do must be done. It lets the rest of you keep your hands clean."

"One other question," Collins said. "How long have you been following Morris?"

"A month. Until Thursday, when we lost him. He disappeared, without a trace, in the crowd at Penn Station after he arrived on the train from Washington. That alone should raise questions in your mind. It's not every day that our field people are fooled, certainly not by amateurs. He's evidently been trained on evading surveillance."

Collins shook his head. "Too fantastic to believe."

"I don't ask you to believe," Steele said. "Just inform Rose when he contacts you that I'm eager to talk with him and that I'm a reasonable man. He could do worse."

Steele rose to his feet, signaling the end of the conversation, and Collins followed him as Steele paid the bill at the cashier. Steele insisted on walking back to the *Sentinel* with Collins. When they reached the lobby he pulled Collins to the side and handed him another one of his business cards.

"Please don't forget what I said earlier about calling me," he said. "You can reach me any time, day or night, through the phone number on this card. The sooner I can talk with Rose, the better. Any delay now might have dire consequences for him, I'm afraid, so do call."

After Steele left, Collins stood in the lobby for a long moment. What he had learned had changed things; it was possible that some of the documents on the film came from the FBI. Collins recognized that he needed to get the film developed, to see what the documents said, to make sure they exonerated Morris. Then Collins could turn it over to Morris on Friday with a clear conscience. He couldn't risk taking the film to a commercial lab but he could ask Colm Higgins, one of the *Sentinel* photographers, to develop it for him.

He was lucky; Collins found Higgins alone in the cramped quarters of the third floor photo department.

"Does that hurt?" Higgins asked, looking at Collins' eye.

"My eye? It looks worse than it feels."

"How did it happen?"

"Some guys who disagreed with something I wrote and decided to register their complaint directly."

"You didn't suggest a letter to the editor instead?"

"They weren't in the mood."

"I'll hand it to you, Denny," Higgins said. "You're taking it well. Most guys wouldn't find much humor in it."

"I'm cursed, I guess, to see the humor in most everything."

"These days it's not a bad curse to have."

"Perhaps," Collins said. He explained that he needed some film developed, and Higgins proved happy to do a favor for him; Collins had wrangled Opening Day tickets at Ebbets Field for Colm and his brother.

"It's microfilm," Collins said. "So you'll need to enlarge it and make prints."

"No problem," Higgins said. "When I'm done, where do I send the prints? City room?"

"No, I need them as soon as possible," Collins said. "I'd appreciate it if you keep the prints and negatives here and call me when they're finished. I'll come pick them up. And don't be surprised when you see them. Just some photos of some boring government documents, memos, that sort of thing. They're for a story I'm working on."

"I can do that. But probably not until later tonight or first thing Thursday. Do you want a roll of replacement film now?" Before Collins could respond, Higgins disappeared into the darkroom. After a few minutes he reemerged, and handed Collins a new canister. "Here you go," he said. "I'll develop your originals later. There's a fresh roll in the canister."

Collins thanked Higgins and shook his hand, ready to leave. He figured he had done all that he could for the moment. The developed film would answer some of his questions, and Morris could answer the rest when they next met.

Nineteen

Collins skipped taking the elevator and walked up the two flights of back stairs to the newsroom. He pocketed the canister with the fresh, undeveloped roll of film. When Collins opened the stairwell door to the hallway, he found an unexpected visitor waiting there—his brother. Frank didn't look particularly happy; in fact, he looked downright grim. He grabbed Collins' elbow roughly, causing him to wince, and pulled him away from the newsroom entrance.

"What the hell is going on, Denny?" he asked. "What have you got yourself mixed up with?" Collins could see that his brother was trying, not too successfully, to control his temper.

"Just a minute," Collins said, worried that Frank's deep baritone could be heard even over the clatter of the typewriters in the newsroom. There was no need to broadcast his troubles. "Let's find some place private to talk this over."

Collins maneuvered him into the same side conference room that he had used with the FBI agents. They sat down facing each other.

"What's this all about?" Collins asked.

His brother brought his fist down on the conference table and pounded it hard enough to make it jump. "It's the FBI. I went to see my friend at the New York field office and got an unpleasant surprise. He introduced me to Special Agents Caldwell and Leary. It wasn't a friendly chat. They wanted chapter and verse on you, and on Morris Rose."

"Chapter and verse?"

"Some tough questions. Would you lie to protect Morris? Had I ever heard you and Rose talking about the Russians or about the international situation? What political groups did you belong to? Are any of your friends Socialists? Or Communists? I can't say I was happy getting the third degree from them. So tell me, Denny, because I don't like getting sandbagged—what the hell is going on? Why are they so stirred up?"

"I told you before that they're convinced that Morris is a security risk. They're working overtime to make him look like a subversive. Because I'm his friend they must think I know more about his life than I do."

"I'll say," he said. "They think you've been less than truthful. Evasive is what Leary said."

"Leary is an arrogant prick," Collins said.

"Tell me something I don't know. Are you covering for Morris? Is it loyalty, Denny? Warren Street doesn't mean there's any special obligation to him. Morris can fend for himself. You gotta understand that and take care of yourself."

Collins stood up, now angry himself. His brother didn't share his loyalty to Morris, but Collins couldn't believe that he would want him to inform on a friend, one they had known since childhood.

"There's a time and a place to rat?" Collins asked him. "Is that what you are saying? Is that what I should understand?"

"If Morris is so stinking clean and snow white pure, then it isn't ratting. But I got a bad feeling he ain't so clean."

"That's what you have wrong. It doesn't matter to Caldwell and Leary whether Morris is totally innocent or reporting atomic secrets by short wave directly to Uncle Joe in the Kremlin. They don't care about the truth of the matter. They have been told to find something, anything, that will make Morris look guilty. That's all this has ever been about."

By then, his brother had begun to calm down. That had always been his pattern, Collins thought. After an initial outburst, Frank's temper would cool and he would become relatively reasonable. He gave Collins a doubtful look.

"You can stay clammed up about Morris and that's your choice. The FBI can't make you talk. But for God's sake, Denny, I hope you aren't helping Morris in any way. No money for train tickets. No passing messages, or mailing letters for him."

"Nothing like that."

"I don't want to see you ruin your life for that little shit. He's not worth it. Just remember what they say: a dog with two homes is never any good. You better be sure that Morris doesn't have two homes, or you'll end up in the witness box at Foley Square."

"Do you really believe that Morris could be a subversive, whatever that is?"

His brother hesitated. "He's always been a bit too smooth an operator for my taste. I don't honestly know what to say. But that's not for me to figure out; it's not my jurisdiction. That's for the Feds."

"And I don't trust the people who are supposed to figure it out. I'm not willing to leave it to them."

Collins rose to his feet, finished with the conversation but his brother motioned for him to sit down again at the conference table. Collins reluctantly sat back down.

"What about the girl?"

"What girl?"

"They showed me her photo. Didn't give me a name. Dark hair, dark eyes. Pretty. Asked me whether I knew her or had seen her in your company. I told them no. Is there anything more I should know?"

Collins decided to evade his brother's questions for the moment. "I don't think you really want to get mixed up in this any further. You've done enough already, checking with your friend at the FBI. I'm sorry you're involved in any way. I promise I won't do anything stupid."

"I hope you know what the hell you are doing," Frank said. "Because I'll level with you, I think you're in way over your head. But I'll stay clear and from this point on I can't help you. Not with the FBI involved and not with my boss already pissed because of the column about the boxing investigation."

Collins stood up again and this time Frank followed suit. Collins didn't want to answer any more questions, mainly because he didn't want to lie to his brother.

"And the girl? You didn't answer my question."

"I'm having dinner tonight with Penny. Her idea. You know how I felt about her before and that hasn't changed."

His brother sighed in exasperation. "Remember that I can't help you now, Denny. Not in something like this. It ain't a parking ticket or even a high stakes poker game. No fixes. You'll be on your own. No older brother to the rescue."

"I've been warned, then. Believe me, I want this over more than anybody. And it should be. Soon, by the end of the week."

Collins moved towards the door but Frank stopped him by taking his arm. "If it goes bad, you know how to reach me," he said, his tone softening. "I would do whatever I could."

"Nothing's going to go bad," Collins said. "I'm just sorry I put you in a tough spot."

After his brother left, Collins ducked back into the conference room, not ready to return to the newsroom. He didn't really know what to think. The FBI appeared no closer to finding Morris than they had been the day before. Why were they so interested in Karina? Did they believe, like Matthew Steele, that she was working for the Russians? Collins didn't get the feeling that it was the sort of information Steele would share with the FBI. In fact, Collins would guess that Steele shared as little as possible with Caldwell and Leary.

The smart thing to do would be to end it with Karina, Collins told himself. With the FBI looking for her, she had become a liability. And Steele knew what he was doing when he broached Karina's history. He knew the sort of questions Collins would start asking himself. How could she have been involved with a Polish collaborator? And what of her affairs with a Soviet officer and with Morris? Had she been ordered to seduce Collins by the Russians?

Yet at the same time, Collins felt Steele's portrait of Karina didn't square with the woman he knew, a woman who abhorred violence and disliked politics, whose entire demeanor softened when she dealt with the displaced at the Hotel Marseilles. She just didn't seem like a Russian operative, even a reluctant one.

Collins wanted time to think. He closed the door to the conference room and phoned the Marseilles. He reached Karina immediately, and quickly explained that he had to cancel their plans for the evening.

"I've got to stay late here," he said. "I need to finish the column about Josef and Hannah, so I am afraid that I can't see you."

"I am disappointed, but I understand," she said.

"Rain check for tomorrow. Let's meet somewhere after you're done at work. Dinner and drinks?"

"I would like that," she said. "Very much."

Collins got off the phone with a hurried goodbye. He had bought himself some time. With any luck he would establish the Friday drop-off with Morris, and then he would break it off with Karina, face-to-face. That was the smart thing to do.

As Collins was crossing the newsroom to his desk, Hal Diderick stopped him to tell him that Marquis had called. "It's going to be a doubleheader for certain between the Dodgers and the Braves tomorrow in Boston. Are you taking the train up tonight?"

"Not sure," Collins said. "Something else has come up."

"You got to be kidding me. Something else? What's her name? That's the only thing I can think of that could make you skip maybe the two most important Dodgers games of the season."

"If it was a girl, I wouldn't be much of a gentleman if I started talking about her, would I?"

Diderick flushed. He had always struck Collins as one of those married men who envied what he perceived as a bachelor's freedom.

"Sure, Denny," he said. "No offense meant."

"None taken."

Collins waited until Diderick had retreated to his own desk, and then he called Penny and arranged to meet her at one of his favorite restaurants, Maison Henri, a French place on West 47th Street. He decided to walk there, he was restless and he wanted to clear his head.

Penny was waiting for him in the cramped front lounge of the restaurant when he arrived. She had a martini on the small table in front of her, which surprised him, because Penny had never been much of a drinker. She kissed him on the cheek in welcome and then dabbed at the lipstick she left behind with her napkin.

"What happened to you?" she asked. "Your eye?"

"I zigged when I should have zagged."

"It looks awful. Who hit you?"

"Someone who didn't like something I had written. We agreed to disagree." Collins shrugged, knowing that he was confirming Penny's worst fears about his lifestyle, even if the confrontation hadn't been his fault. The bartender reluctantly poured a beer for Collins (the French had never properly appreciated beer, he thought) and Collins brought it with him to their table. He found his cigarettes and lit one up, eager for the soothing taste of tobacco.

"I thought you had stopped smoking," she said.

"I had quit. But someone told me I shouldn't resist the small pleasures in life. So here I am. A beer and a cigarette."

Just then the front door opened and François, the proprietor of the Maison Henri, arrived. He gave them a warm welcome, kissing Penny's hand and giving Collins a Gallic hug (Collins winced from the embrace, and hoped Penny didn't notice). Collins patronized Maison Henri because of the excellent food and because, unlike many of the other French restaurants in Manhattan, it had a welcoming atmosphere. Collins liked the place, and he liked François and his family.

François led them to one of the better tables, set back in an alcove where it offered more privacy. He seated Penny across from Collins, his hand gently on her waist as he held her chair for her. His open admiration of Penny struck Collins as quite French. Instead of ordering from the menu, Collins asked François to choose the dishes for the meal. He beamed and gave them a small bow, promising that he would serve them Maison Henri's best. François waved to a waiter and gave instructions, and within minutes they were enjoying a bottle of Cabernet Sauvignon along with a green salad.

"Speaking of fights, what about the battle of El Morocco?" Penny asked.

Collins raised his eyebrows, not sure what she was talking about.

"You didn't hear? I'm surprised. Last Saturday night Humphrey Bogart and his playboy friend, Bill Seeman, got into an altercation in the wee hours of the morning at the El Morocco."

"What sort of an altercation?"

"It is a funny story, actually. They had purchased two large stuffed toy panda bears, for Bogart's little son, Steve, and they brought them to the club. They were there having a night cap at 4 AM, and they left the bears unattended for a moment. On a dare, a couple of the girls there tried to steal them. One was Robin Roberts, a model, and the other was Maureen Rabe, the banker's daughter. Bogart grabbed the panda from the model and she fell on her derriere."

"And the other girl?"

"Apparently she was pushed, too, and her boyfriend, Johnny Jelke, got angry. They say Jelke's a gangster of sorts. Supposedly Bogart threw a saucer at Jelke and Jelke smashed some plates on Seeman's shoulders. The bouncers broke it up and made Bogart and his friend leave. I hear the model is going to charge Bogart with assault. I think it may be a publicity stunt."

"Doesn't quite fit Bogart's tough-guy image," Collins said. "A toy panda? Roughing up a fashion model?"

Penny giggled. "It's just one of the eight million stories in the Naked City."

Collins thought back to the first time that he had met Penny, at a society party in a Fifth Avenue penthouse apartment. Collins was there only because a friend of his, Andrew King, had been dating one of the girls there and had invited him along.

Collins had felt distinctly out-of-place at the party and so he had been drinking freely and was pretty tight by the time he met Penny. He never would have approached her if he had been sober, he realized later—her icy beauty would have scared him right off. She thought Collins was funny and to his surprise she said yes when he asked her out, and before he knew it they were dating and before long they were lovers.

He had been sure that they wouldn't last more than a few weeks, that he would be Penny's romantic experiment for 1939. He was proved wrong. There was something there between them, more than just the physical attraction. Penny told Collins that she felt as if she could be herself around him, whatever that meant, and for a while Collins was convinced that he had found the woman of his dreams. The problems surfaced later, like they always did. But even when she broke it off twice, they ended patching it up and seeing each other again. Until Collins went off to the war and she met Taylor Bradford.

"A penny for your thoughts," Penny said, bringing Collins back to the present.

"Just thinking," Collins said. "About the good old days, and about us. Except that makes me a hypocrite, of sorts. Just this morning I was telling one of the editors that we should let the past be the past."

"He disagreed?"

"He thinks that first we have to resolve any unfinished business."

"I agree with him," Penny said.

"Doesn't it depend on whether the pain of resolving the past is worth the gain? Otherwise, I think it's best to forget."

Penny didn't reply. She picked at her salad and Collins couldn't help think of Karina's unabashed appetite. Penny ate very little because it helped her keep her slim figure but also because she didn't know what it was like to be truly hungry. Until you're deprived of something, Collins thought, you don't understand its value. More than two years eating Army and Marine rations had taught him that lesson; now he savored every well-prepared meal he encountered.

Penny might not have been eating, but she was enjoying the wine. She surprised Collins by asking for a third glass—something he had never seen her do in the past at dinner.

"I want to do something useful," she announced abruptly. "I am thinking of moving back to New York, permanently, and finding a job."

"A job?"

"A real job. Helping people. Perhaps teaching or working in a hospital. Something worthwhile. I want to do more than play tennis and attend boring cocktail parties like I do in Washington."

"How long have you been considering this?"

"For at least a year. I know what my parents will think. They'll be horrified. They don't want me working, they want me to remarry. It's been long enough, they say, since we lost Brad. Time to find someone suitable."

"Someone suitable. What are those qualifications? Do they have to trace the family line directly back to the Mayflower? Or will arriving in the next two boats of Pilgrims qualify?"

"Dennis," she said. "They're set in their ways. I don't agree with them, you know that, but I am not going to change their minds. I'm doing my best to ignore them."

Collins didn't say what he wanted to, that the one time she had made a choice, it had been for "someone suitable," Taylor Bradford. He was tempted to tell her what Lonnie Marks had said about her never marrying out of her class, but before he could say anything, their waiter arrived with their main course, a lamb fillet with raspberry vinegar, braised chestnuts and green cabbage. Collins was glad he had let François choose their meal.

"What have you been doing with yourself?" Penny asked after the waiter had left.

"As a reader of my columns you should know what I've been doing."

"Surely that doesn't occupy twenty-four hours," she said. "What do you and your friends do when you are not working?"

"Why the sudden curiosity?"

"I don't know. You know I'm curious about your life. I did go to that fight with you, didn't I? I've been wondering what you do when you aren't working. Aren't you quite the man-about-town?"

"Hardly. When I have some free time I try to keep it simple. Catch a ball game. Have some drinks and some laughs with friends from the *Sentinel*. Once in a while I drop by the jazz clubs on 52nd Street."

"It sounds carefree," she said, with a touch of wistfulness. "I envy you."

"Carefree? I'm still coming home to an empty apartment."

She didn't say anything.

"So what are the people like at these boring cocktail parties you attend?" Collins asked. "Do they all work in the government?"

"Many of them do," she said. "That's Washington for you. Unfortunately it attracts a lot of the wrong sort."

"The wrong sort?"

"You know. Small town lawyers and auto dealers who've been elected to Congress and now think they're God's gift to the country."

"That can't describe everyone."

"No, of course not. I think it may be worse with the bureaucrats. All they care about is climbing to the top of State or the War Department, so they spend their time scheming for their next promotion."

"That's not a pretty picture you're painting. Surely there are some honest types wandering around."

"A few. Some of the dollar-a-year men. But they are few and far between. Some of Brad's old friends fit that description. We're all lucky to have them there. Thank God they replaced that horrible man Wallace before the election, because if he had become President when Roosevelt died all of Brad's colleagues, the ones with quality, would have left the government. Truman may be crude, but at least he's not a fanatic."

It didn't sound like the Penny he remembered, but she had been living in Washington, surrounded by her husband's friends and her own conservative family. Collins couldn't expect to hear her sing the praises of the Progressive Party.

"I don't think Wallace is a fanatic. Misguided, perhaps."

"Look at the crowd around him. I'd bet you that the parents of his closest advisors speak Polish or Russian or German." She giggled. "Or worse, Yiddish."

"I know you probably don't realize how ugly that last bit sounded," he said. "It makes you sound like an anti-Semite, and I know you're not."

"Dennis, don't be ridiculous. I'm talking about the radical ideas these people are trying to import. Fellow travelers, isn't that what they are called?"

"I didn't realize you had become so political."

"I haven't. Some of my friends follow these things, and I listen to what they say and I've been learning. They see things much differently than you, Dennis."

"I don't doubt that."

After they had finished their main course, Collins ordered coffee and some chocolate cake, Penny's favorite, for dessert.

"So now what?" Collins asked. "We've missed the Broadway shows, but we could take in a movie."

"Let's go someplace cozy where we can talk some more," she said.

"We could go to the Oak Bar."

"No, I meant someplace really cozy. There will be too many people at the Plaza. Why don't we go to your apartment? It's closer than mine and it fits into my new project of learning more about how you spend your days, and nights."

"Sure," Collins said, again surprised. "We can go there. Shall we walk or take a cab?"

"A cab. I'm feeling lazy from all the good food and the wine."

When they reached his apartment, Collins was thankful that he kept it relatively neat. He hung up their overcoats and draped his suit jacket over the back of a kitchen chair. He poured a glass of wine for

Penny and found a beer in the refrigerator for himself. Penny looked around, taking in his worn down furniture, the few framed photos, the stacks of books and newspapers.

"It hasn't changed much," she observed.

"A few more books, I think."

"You were always a great reader, Dennis."

"Overcompensating for that missed college degree. I figure by now I've read all the books I would have if I had gone to a fancy college. Probably more."

"You don't need to compensate for anything. I don't know anyone as interesting as you. I mean that."

"Thanks." Collins looked around the apartment and decided to take a chance. "I may be interesting, but that doesn't mean I don't get lonely. I'm tired of coming home to this empty place."

"Well, that's one thing I know about," she said. "Loneliness. I think I have become an expert on it."

"It doesn't have to be that way."

"So they say."

Neither of them said anything then. Collins decided he wouldn't push any further, at least for the moment. He figured that he had given her an opening and she hadn't really taken it.

"What sort of music would you like to hear?"

"Something bright."

"No Billie Holiday, then. How about 'Jazz at the Philharmonic'? Charlie Parker and Ella?"

She nodded and Collins put on the record. They sat together on his one sofa and listened for a while, and then she put her hand on his arm. He leaned in and kissed her on the lips. She didn't move away, so he kissed her again. Collins could taste the wine on her lips. They were both more than a little tight.

"That was nice," she said.

"It was."

She kissed him and pulled him closer. Collins really hadn't expected it to go any further, but one thing led to another. They had been lovers before and so it seemed natural when Penny unbuttoned the top buttons of his shirt and ran her hand across his chest.

"Are you sure about this?" he asked. "I don't want you to regret anything."

"Hush," she said. "Let's not talk."

So Collins took her hand and led her into his bedroom. He had imagined her back in his bed for so long, had fantasized about it and had longed for it, that now that it was happening, it didn't seem quite real.

He thought for a moment about Karina. Collins had never been involved with two women at the same time before, and he wasn't about to start. He would have even more reason to break it off with her.

They kissed again, holding each other, and then Penny finished unbuttoning his shirt. She paused to take her strand of pearls off, placing them on top of the night table by his bed, and then switched the overhead lights off. They made love lazily—Penny, giggling and laughing, the wine making her loose and relaxed. She whispered to him how much she had missed him, how good he was, how she had wanted him. After they had both climaxed, he held her close. In the silence that followed, he thought about their painful years apart and how implausible it was for them to be lovers again. He wondered what she was thinking, and then, almost as she had read his mind, she spoke.

"When you held me the other night, when we were dancing, I remembered how sweet it had been," she said. "I wanted you then."

"It was sweet," Collins said. "I have the same memories." Then he said what he had wanted to say all evening. "It can't be like it was last time. I don't think I can handle that. Do you understand? I'd rather end it now, than go through that again."

"I understand. Please be patient with me. I have things I still have to get straight."

"Someone else?"

"Yes. I didn't know how I truly felt about him. I came back to New York to get some distance and to think things through. When you called and asked to see me, I thought, why not? I decided to see you again. A second chance for us."

"Do you know how you feel about him, now?"

"I'm not completely clear about my feelings," she said. "I know it's wrong that I'm not sure and that I'm here with you, but maybe that's the way I'm going to find out. And then I feel guilty, because you deserve a woman who isn't confused. Who is clear about how she feels."

"Isn't that for me to decide?"

"But you deserve someone who can give herself to you without any reservations or hesitancy. Someone who has never hurt you, who starts with a completely clean slate. That would be lovely, wouldn't it?"

"No one ever starts with a clean slate," Collins said. He thought about what Steele had related about Karina and her past. So much for clean slates. "There might not be a shared past, but there's always something, isn't there?"

"I don't want to hurt you, Dennis. That is the last thing in the world I want. So I just don't know what to do."

He was about to respond when the phone rang. He cursed and Penny laughed. "Wonderful timing," she said. "Answer it, Dennis."

Collins picked up the receiver and heard the voice of Morris Rose.

"Hello," Morris said. "Abe? Just wanted to let you know that I'll be in town on Friday."

"This isn't Abe. You have the wrong number."

"Sorry about that," he said and Collins heard the line go dead.

"A wrong number," Penny said. "Wouldn't that figure?"

"I wish that it was a wrong number, and nothing more."

"I don't understand," she said.

"You deserve to know what's happening," he said.

He reached over to his bedside table and switched on his small Philco radio. He found a classical station and turned up the volume on the music, figuring it would mask whatever he said from any microphones in the apartment. She looked at him, puzzled. He pulled her to him on the bed and held her so they were facing each other.

"I haven't been able to talk about this with anyone," he said, lowering his voice. "That was Morris Rose on the phone. He's put me in a difficult place. The security types at the State Department are investigating him. Questions of loyalty. Morris asked me to hold something for him for a few days, some documents, when he went out of town and I said I would. That was a mistake on my part. The FBI is looking for him now and I've come under some unpleasant scrutiny."

"Why did you tell Morris it was a wrong number when he called just now?"

"I'm concerned about who may be listening in. My brother Frank found a microphone here on Sunday. He thinks it was the FBI."

"Dennis, that's terrible. Can't you just tell them where Morris is? He shouldn't have involved you in this."

"I have no idea where he is. Even if I did, I wouldn't tell them. He's no security threat, and I'll be damned if I assist the bastards in their witch hunt."

"What's in the documents you're holding for him?"

"I've told you too much already. I don't want you involved."

"I'm here, in bed with you. I think that counts as involved. Tell me, please."

"Morris gave me some film of State Department memos that exonerate him. Undeveloped film. So I don't really know what's in them."

"Shouldn't you approach someone in authority?" she asked. "Give them the film? Have them handle this?"

"Who? I can't very well go to the very people trying to crucify Morris."

"What about an attorney?"

In Penny's world, Collins knew, that was how you handled trouble. You found an Ivy League lawyer who knew a sympathetic Ivy League judge who would understand the special circumstances and could discreetly make the problem go away. All done smoothly and behind the scenes. There were some problems that couldn't be so easily fixed, Collins thought, and this was one of them.

"That's not going to work. I'm just going to have to wait another couple of days. Then I can return the film canister to Morris and I'm out of the picture. He'll have to face the music himself at that point, not that I don't wish him well."

"And what if you are questioned between now and then?"

"I'll continue to be less than helpful."

"So you have already been questioned?"

"The FBI. And by one CIA official, a man named Steele."

She stirred next to him and sighed. "I see. It sounds serious. What have they asked you about?"

"About Morris. About where he is, and what I know about him. There's not much I can tell him."

"Dennis, you must be very, very careful with these people. You could lose your job. Or worse."

"It will be fine," Collins said. "It will all be over soon. Two days."

"Where is this canister? The one you are holding for Morris?"

"I'll show you," he told her.

Collins went into the kitchen and found the canister in the right coat pocket of his suit jacket, which was hanging on the back of one of the kitchen chairs. He rejoined her in bed and held up the canister so she could see it.

"This is it. I think it's my bad luck charm."

He heard Penny sigh deeply again, her way of signaling disappointment.

"It makes you his accomplice, doesn't it?

"His accomplice? No, it makes me his friend. Morris hasn't done anything wrong."

"You are too trusting."

"I can't change who I am."

"It's too big a risk. You must promise me that you won't do anything that could compromise you further."

"I promise."

Collins rolled away from her and put the film canister onto the night table, next to her pearls. He turned the volume on the music down. When he turned back, she kissed him on the lips, pushing her naked body back against his. Collins didn't need a further invitation and they made love again, slowly, savoring each other. Afterwards, he dozed off with her next to him, their bodies touching comfortably, totally relaxed.

Collins awoke at midnight, when Penny got up from bed. She retrieved her clothing from the floor and went into his bathroom to change. When she returned, she was dressed. Collins could barely make out her face in the dark.

"I have to go," she whispered. "Don't get up."

"You don't need to whisper," Collins said. "Can't you stay? Is something wrong?"

"I'm not feeling too well," she said. "Too much wine. And it's late. I'll have the doorman call me a cab."

"He's gone," Collins said. "He leaves at midnight. Let me get dressed and I'll hail a cab for you."

He threw his clothes on, and they rode down in the elevator together. Penny was silent, and he wondered if she was having second thoughts about the evening. He could see that she was anxious from the way she kept combing her hair with her fingers. He didn't know what to think. At the moment, she clearly didn't want to talk.

On the street, he flagged down a cab. "I'd like to see you tomorrow," he said. "We still have a lot to talk about."

"Call me in the morning," she said and gave him a quick kiss on the lips.

Collins stood and watched her cab speed away. He was unhappy about her sudden departure. It was a strange ending to the evening. Once back in his apartment, he found another beer in the refrigerator and listened to jazz for a while.

He forced himself to get up from the couch so he wouldn't fall asleep in the living room. Just before he climbed into bed, he took off his wristwatch and put it on the top of the night table, next to his radio. That was when he realized that the film canister was missing from the spot where he remembered leaving it.

He went to the kitchen and checked the right pocket of his suit jacket and then the left, thinking that he might have absent-mindedly put the canister back. He turned out the pockets. Nothing. He went back into the bedroom and got down on his hands and knees and checked the floor under the bed. No sign of the canister.

He pulled the sheets off the bed and then checked the floor and under the bed again. No luck.

Could Penny have taken it? She had seen him place the canister on the night table. Why would she take it, though? Did she think that she could protect him in some way? Was that the reason she had left so abruptly? He checked his watch—it was 12:30. He stood there for a moment, not sure what to do. He thought about phoning her but decided instead to go directly to her apartment.

Once there, Collins had to wake up the doorman who had fallen asleep and was resentful that Collins had caught him dozing. When Collins asked him to buzz Mrs. Bradford's apartment the man looked at him blankly and said she wasn't there.

"That can't be," Collins said. "She took a cab home about forty minutes ago. She should have arrived about thirty minutes ago."

"Mrs. Bradford hasn't come in tonight," the doorman said. "Plain and simple."

Collins fought to control his temper. "Are you sure you were awake, then?" he asked. "Maybe you missed her come in."

"I was awake," the man said. "I'm telling you that she isn't here."

"Can you at least buzz her?" he asked.

"Suit yourself." The doorman lifted the intercom receiver to his ear and pushed the button for Penny's apartment. He waited a minute or so and hung up. "No answer," he said. "Like I said. She hasn't returned."

The last thing Collins needed was another confrontation, so he ignored the doorman's undisguised hostility and left the lobby. From the street outside, Collins could see the lights were out in Penny's apartment on the seventh floor. If she hadn't come back to her home, where the hell was she? Where had she gone at one o'clock in the morning? Why had she taken the canister?

It took Collins twenty minutes to find an on-duty cab. When he got back to his apartment he tried dialing Penny's number. It rang through with no answer.

He sat at his kitchen table and drank one beer, going over the events of the evening again and again, and then another before he started feeling drowsy. His bedroom clock showed nearly three o'clock when he finally climbed into bed.

Thursday, September 29

She had only just arrived at her office at the Center when the phone began ringing. She was reluctant to pick it up, fairly sure that it was Morris calling her as he had promised. Finally she reached over and lifted the receiver to her ear.

"How are you?" It was a more confident Morris. He sounded pleased with himself.

"I am fine."

"I'm back in the city now, and I have news," he said. "It doesn't look like I can salvage the situation in Washington, so I'm shifting to Plan B. That means I've had to involve Bob, much as I didn't want to. There was no other way"

"Then he knows about my helping you."

"He does. But I explained that you agreed to help me because of our history together. He understood. He wants you to continue to cooperate with me."

She suddenly felt sick to her stomach. Her worst fears had come true. There was no turning back, now, because it was clear what she would have to do. How could she help Morris if it meant furthering the aims of Moscow Center? She could not do that. And now she had to extricate Dennis from the situation as well.

"Here's what I need you to do," Morris said. "You must bring Dennis, and the item he has been holding for me, to a meeting place tomorrow night. So he knows this is coming from me, tell him that I still have the Babe Herman and I won't trade it, not even for a Jackie Robinson."

"I don't understand."

"Baseball cards. I won't trade my favorite card. He'll understand. Write it down and tell him what I said. Tell him in person, not on the phone."

"Then what?"

"I need the item Denny has been keeping for me," he said. "A film canister. He knows that it contains documents that I need. It's become vital that I quickly retrieve it from him. You could call it my 'Get Out of Jail Free' card."

She understood the reference immediately; the Center had a Monopoly game, donated by a supporter, and Karina had played a few times with other staff members.

Then Morris outlined the details of the meeting. He wanted Dennis and Karina to wait for him at Rockefeller Center, near the Associated Press building. He would walk by carrying a newspaper in his right hand, which would mean that the rendezvous was safe and they had not been followed. If he didn't have the newspaper, or if it wasn't in his right hand, they were to abandon the meeting and instead walk over to Fifth Avenue. They were to head east on 51st Street. Halfway down the block, in front of the side entrance to St. Patrick's Cathedral, a woman wearing a beret would be waiting. Dennis was to pass the canister to her.

"He won't like that," she said.

"Won't he? Are you an expert on Dennis Collins now?" She didn't like the sarcastic way Morris said it.

"He took me to dinner," she explained, stung.

"I see," Morris said. "Is it like that, then?"

"What does that mean?"

"You know full well what I mean. I guess Denny isn't getting anywhere with Penny Bradford. You must be *his* Plan B."

"Whatever I may be to Dennis has nothing to do with you."

"You're right. And I don't care one way or the other if you two are making eyes at each other or screwing like rabbits, as long as you stay on speaking terms through Friday."

"If that's your concern, and you're back in the city now, why don't you have Dennis give you the film today? Why wait?"

"There are arrangements that have to be made."

"Arrangements that Yatov needs to make, no doubt. Or you have to ask his permission. When you came to me last week, you promised that he wouldn't be involved. This just had to do with you—nothing to do with them." She wasn't going to let Morris evade responsibility for what he had done.

"I don't recall promising anything. It's become necessary to involve him. You must know that the stakes are higher now. I need him. And I need your help."

He asked her to repeat the details of the meeting, which she did. He told her tear up any notes she had made, after she had memorized them, and to flush them down the toilet.

"I will see you tomorrow night," he said. "I'm counting on you." Then he hung up the phone.

She found tears coming to her eyes, unbidden. It was ending in the worst possible way.

Her job at the Center had made her even more conscious of her need to find some small way to atone for the past, for the years when she had accepted the privileged life offered by Piotr's family with their connections to the General Government while others had suffered persecution at the hands of Poland's Nazi occupiers. She had a greater debt to pay than the one she owed Morris, and she could not ignore it.

It meant that she could not let Dennis hand over the canister to Morris, even if it meant telling him the truth and losing him. She hated the thought of it, but she couldn't see any other way to keep the film out of the hands of the hard men.

Twenty

Collins woke up to the harsh sound of his wind-up alarm clock ringing. He had set it for six o'clock and he fumbled in the dark to switch off the ringer. He felt lousy. He hadn't slept more than a few hours, and he had the metallic taste of flat beer in his mouth.

He called Penny's apartment after he had shaved and dressed. There was no answer then, nor when he tried thirty minutes later, letting the phone ring repeatedly before giving up. Penny wasn't home, that was clear, and there was no getting around what had happened.

Why had she taken the film canister? He was stumped. It seemed so unlike Penny, so out of character. Did she think she was protecting him by taking it? And where had she gone after she left his apartment?

Collins decided to head to work. He was greeted by a light drizzle and overcast skies when he reached the street, not a promising sign for baseball. He skimmed the papers in the cab on the way to Herald Square and wondered if it was raining in Boston. The Dodgers were running out of time. They needed to complete all of their final four games, and, ideally, they needed to win all four. So did the Yankees. Collins peered out of the cab window trying to gauge whether the sky would clear up and allow an afternoon game at the Stadium.

Collins paged through the *Sentinel*. He was pleased with his column on Josef and Hannah. He thought it captured their shy wonder at being in America, and the contrast between their dark past and the promise of a sunny Saturday at Yankee Stadium. He hoped Karina liked it.

One disturbing United Press story, datelined from Washington, caught his eye. The Loyalty Review Board had announced that more than 100 government employees had been fired "for loyalty reasons" since the program started in March 1947. According to the story, the board had reviewed the records of nearly 10,000 employees and had several hundred still under consideration.

He felt better once he was back in the *Sentinel* newsroom, surrounded by messy desk-tops, cluttered with typewriters, stacks of papers, and empty coffee cups. Since he had arrived much earlier than usual, he got a cup of coffee and finished the papers at his desk.

Joe DiMaggio had taken batting practice at Yankee Stadium, but he looked weak and tentative, according to the beat writers. He only hit one pitch out of the park and told the writers afterwards that he felt like the bat was swinging him. It didn't seem like DiMaggio was going to be strong enough to contribute much to the Yankee cause even if he did return to the line-up before the regular season ended.

Penny had been right about the Humphrey Bogart story. The model, Robin Roberts, was all over the papers, claiming that she had hurt her back when Bogart shoved her to the floor and announcing that she would be pressing charges. The *Mirror* carried photos restaging the end of the El Morocco confrontation, with Roberts lying on the carpet of her hotel room, a pose that conveniently allowed her to display her ample cleavage. Some reporters had journeyed over late in the morning to the St. Regis and interviewed Bogart, still in his pajamas and slippers and wearing a blue bathrobe. He didn't seem too worried about the situation. "Me hit a woman?" he was quoted as saying. "Why, I'm too sweet and chivalrous." His wife, Lauren Bacall, was humming "Some Enchanted Evening," in the background, her own sardonic commentary on the furor.

After Collins finished the papers, he phoned Penny's apartment once more and got no answer. There wasn't much more that he could do, short of returning to her apartment building and waiting for her. So he called Karina at the Hotel Marseilles and, after getting a busy signal, got through on his third try.

"Your column is marvelous," she told him after they had exchanged greetings. "The phone has been ringing all morning because of it, Dennis. We have had several donations on behalf of Josef and Hannah and two families inquiring about adopting them."

"I'm glad to hear that," he said. "We're planning to run a picture of the children at the Stadium."

"Will you be going to the game?"

"Perhaps," he said. "It depends on how the Dodgers play today in Boston."

"Josef is very excited," she said. "He has been asking about it repeatedly. One of our workers here, Chaim Tarasov, will take him and his sister and Mrs. Berliner. Chaim is a Yankee fan."

"Glad that you have it squared away from your end."

"I miss you," she said. "When can I see you?"

"Tonight. Dinner?"

"It can be very hard on a woman," she said. "We are not supposed to call. It is not considered proper. We must wait by the phone for the man to call."

"I called yesterday, didn't I?"

"I need to see you," she said. "There is a matter we must discuss."

"What's that?"

"Let's wait until I see you," she said. "It can wait until then."

"I'd like to talk," Collins said. "That would be good."

They agreed to meet at a small restaurant, the Emerald Lounge, a place near Karina's neighborhood where they could have a few drinks and a light supper. He decided it was better to be in a public place when he ended it, to avoid any ugly scene, although he doubted Karina would make a fuss. After he hung up, one of the copy boys came over to his desk with a message from Colm Higgins. He had the prints ready and Collins could come by and pick them up.

The *Sentinel* darkroom occupied the back third of the Photo Department. When Collins arrived, Colm waved him over to the far side of the office where they couldn't be overhead. He lowered his voice.

"Are you sure that you know what you are doing, Denny?"

"What do you mean?"

"The photos. Did you know what was on them?" Higgins gave him a searching look, clearly disturbed.

"They were memos, right? From the State Department."

"That's right. When I enlarged them, some of them had 'top secret' stamped at the top. I didn't read them, mind you. Soon as I saw what they were, I called upstairs to get you down here."

"It's okay," Collins told him. "These are memos a friend of mine wrote. He's in the government, and he gave me the photos. It's background for a column. You're not going to get in trouble."

"The photos are done and you can take the prints and the developed film," Colm said, his tone flat. "I don't really want to know any more."

Higgins handed him an oversized manila envelope and another small film canister, which Collins immediately pocketed.

"Here's the thing," Colm said. "I've got kids and a wife and I need this job. I can't afford to lose it. And I don't think making prints of secret government documents is a wise thing. If it was anyone other than you, I'd be calling the cops, or the FBI."

"I understand. Trust me that you won't get in any trouble."

"I trust you. It's just that you're not a lawyer. Whether developing that film is legal is what has me worried."

"Well, in point of fact I have the film and the prints, now. And since I'm the only one who knows who developed them, I think you can rest easy."

Collins was embarrassed. He shouldn't have asked Higgins to develop the film. He didn't have the right to involve anyone else. Colm had agreed to develop the microfilm without any idea of what it might contain. Collins apologized again and they shook hands before he left.

He took the manila envelope with photos and borrowed a magnifying glass from one of the darkroom tables. He jammed the magnifying glass in his suit pocket and left, taking the elevator to the ninth floor, where the newspaper had located the credit and accounting department. Collins knew where there was an empty corner office. He was in luck; the door to the office was unlocked. He went inside, closed the door and locked it, and sat down at the empty desk. He turned the desk lamp on and spread the photos on the desktop in front of him.

The first eleven documents were inter-office memoranda to and from Morris. From what Collins could tell they involved a running bureaucratic dispute over the pace of bringing displaced persons to the United States. Most had been written in late 1948 or the first half of 1949. As he read the memoranda, a pattern emerged. An official named Alcorn had argued for a "more orderly process," where the DPs could be carefully screened to prevent "undesirables, criminals and possible subversives" from entering the country. Alcorn conceded that his proposals would slow the pace of resettlement, but argued that the current risks appeared to him to be too high. He also pointed out that the DP program was unpopular with a number of powerful Republicans, including Senator McCarran.

Morris had written several memos in opposition, responding in clear and pointed prose, defending the resettlement program and arguing that current security procedures were more than adequate and that delays and paperwork meant real hardship for the DPs waiting in camps. One passage caught Collins' eye:

It would be more in keeping with our tradition of welcoming those fleeing oppression and persecution. What better contrast to the closed borders of the Communist bloc could there be than such a policy of openness? Whatever security concerns are raised can easily be resolved by the interview of any questionable persons once they have reached the United States.

Reading the memo made Collins proud of Morris. It bore his distinctive blend of idealism and pragmatism. Collins wondered why Morris had photographed the exchange with Alcorn. Was Alcorn one of his adversaries in the State Department? There were three or four additional memos, all written by Morris in 1948, which were stamped "Top Secret" and quoted from extensive conversations that Morris had conducted with Polish, Czech, and Russian officials about the resettlement of displaced persons. He had been exploring these officials'

attitudes towards the resettlement program; apparently there was con-
troversy over some refugees choosing to go to Palestine once they had
left the DP camp instead of immigrating to the United States.

Collins scanned the other memos quickly and could see nothing
that touched on security concerns. Perhaps that was the point? Collins
remembered that Morris had said that he was in trouble for having
conversations with Eastern Bloc diplomats, but the memos demon-
strated how bland and bureaucratic those discussions actually were.
So far, so good, Collins thought. The correspondence appeared to establish that Morris had good reasons for talking with the officialdom
behind the Iron Curtain and their discussions had been routine.

When he turned to the final batch of printed photos Collins
was feeling better about the situation. Morris might have violated internal government regulations by copying the documents, but they
backed up his story. He was no subversive.

It was the first print of that changed everything, that caused
Collins to curse out loud. It, too, carried the "Top Secret" designation, but it was from the Counterintelligence Division of the Federal
Bureau of Investigation. It was dated September 5, 1949 and had been
circulated to J. Edgar Hoover, Clyde Tolleson, and Phillip Andrews
and was titled "Comprehensive List of Government Security Risks."

There was a brief introductory paragraph explaining that the
list had been compiled by the FBI using information from agents'
field investigations, wiretaps, and interviews of informants and defectors. Collins looked over the first page of the document. It had three
columns: an alphabetical list with the name and title of government
employees, a column labeled "Soviet code name," and then, finally, a
"Status" column. Most of the names were middle-level employees of
the State and War Departments, judging from the titles used. Some of
them had code names and some didn't.

He turned to the next print. There, at the top of the photo, was
the information that he had hoped would not be there. Collins looked
at it for a long moment, feeling sick to his stomach. Morris, identified

as a State Department official on the Eastern European desk, was under active investigation. His Soviet code name was "Dodger."

Collins sat there, stunned. He didn't know what to think. There was something about seeing Morris' name on the page that was particularly disturbing. He wanted to believe that it was all some sort of mistake, that Morris had been unfairly named in the document, but the specificity of it, including the code name, made him think otherwise.

Sometimes the small things convince you that you've stumbled on the truth, he thought. It was one small detail—the code name "Dodger"—that gave him a sinking feeling in his stomach. Knowing Morris' sly sense of humor, Collins could see him embracing the code name. Morris would have enjoyed the play on words, the double entendre—he was a Dodger fan but, when it came to his role as an agent, he was also a dodger.

And how could Collins rationalize Morris' possession of the FBI memo? The State Department documents had appeared to demonstrate his innocence, but the FBI list suggested just the opposite. Why would he have photographed it? It wasn't hard to see how valuable the list could be to the Soviets, Collins thought. It would give them the names of every government official the FBI suspected of espionage, and whether or not there was an active investigation underway. That Morris had disappeared so quickly after Miss Shoemaker's arrest, and that the memo specifically listed his name, added to his sinking feeling.

Collins sat there staring at the photos. It didn't look good for Morris. It didn't look good for Collins, then, either.

Collins hadn't deliberately placed himself in jeopardy. It had been a series of steps, a series of small mistakes that had added up. His first mistake had been agreeing to hold the canister for Morris. His second was in not nailing down, from the start, what was really on the film. Now, he told himself, he had made a third mistake. Developing the film and looking at the photos meant that Collins could no longer plead ignorance, or for that matter, innocence.

That meant he couldn't turn the film over to Morris without confronting him about the FBI list. Collins would have to admit to Morris that he had developed the film, but he no longer cared how it looked. If Morris was somehow involved with the Russians, Collins wasn't going to prison for assisting him in stealing government secrets. Once Morris had told Collins the truth, they could figure out what to do next.

Collins took the elevator down to the newsroom. He found a note on his desk asking him to call Mrs. Bradford at her apartment. At least that meant Penny was still in New York.

He decided to stash the developed film and the photos at the *Sentinel*. He remembered there was a small shelf-like space in the back stairwell to the newsroom which would serve his purpose well. Collins glanced around quickly. No one was looking. He went through the door onto the landing, and let it close behind him.

He slid the manila envelope with the prints, and the film canister, onto the shelf-like space above the door. It was hard to see in the dimly-lit stairwell, and Collins was satisfied that the canister and envelope weren't visible.

When he returned to the newsroom no one paid him any attention. He walked over to the side conference room, confident that his brief absence had gone unnoticed. He closed the door to the conference room and phoned Penny at her apartment. Collins found that he was gripping the phone receiver so tightly that his knuckles had turned white. He told himself to relax. When Penny answered, she got straight to the point.

"Are you terribly angry with me?" she asked.

"We need to talk," Collins said. "In person."

"I am sorry, Dennis. Please believe me. I don't know what I was thinking. I acted on impulse. I never should have taken it from your apartment."

"Have you told anyone about this? Have you talked to anyone?"

"No. You have to believe me. No."

"Do you still have the film canister?"

"Of course. Why wouldn't I have it?"

"Can you meet me in thirty minutes?"

"Yes, I can meet you. Where?"

"Somewhere in midtown?"

"The 21 Club?" she asked. "I haven't had lunch."

"Not there," Collins said. "There's no privacy. Why don't we meet at Maison Henri?"

"All right," she said. "Maison Henri. Thirty minutes."

"Bring the canister with you. I need it."

"I'm so sorry," she said. "I was trying to be helpful, Dennis."

Collins cut the conversation short—what he had to say could wait until he could see her in person and read her reactions. He didn't really need her to return the film canister (it was of little value, since it contained undeveloped film, after all), but he wanted Penny to think that he did. What he desperately needed was the truth. Why had she taken it from him? Where had she been all night?

The worst of it was that Collins wasn't sure about Penny, now. Could he trust her? With what he had just learned about Morris, the stakes had been raised even higher. So he was impatient to get to Maison Henri—the sooner he got her answers to his questions, the better.

Twenty-one

This time Caldwell and Leary were waiting for Collins in the *Sentinel*'s front lobby. As Collins stepped out of the elevator, Caldwell quickly approached him. Out of the corner of his eye Collins caught Leary circling behind him—effectively boxing him in. They weren't taking any chances that Collins might bolt past them either to the street or back into the elevator.

Collins came to a dead stop—they hadn't given him much choice in the matter. He gave Caldwell what he hoped passed for a broad smile. He didn't want them to think that he was nervous or rattled.

He was suddenly very conscious that he had just seen stolen FBI top-secret documents, but he also knew it was vital not to show any anxiety in front of the agents. Collins decided to bluff his way past them if he could. He wasn't sure it would work, but it was worth a try and he didn't want to be late to his lunch with Penny.

"I'd love to stop and talk, boys," he said, "but I've got an appointment uptown."

"What happened to your eye?" Caldwell asked. His tone wasn't friendly.

"Ran into a door by accident."

"By accident?" Caldwell smirked, clearly enjoying Collins' misfortune.

"If you'll excuse me," Collins said. "I'm running a bit late."

"This won't take long," Leary said. "As long as you cooperate."

Collins couldn't see him; by design, Leary had stationed himself behind Collins.

"I'd be happy to cooperate," Collins said to Caldwell. "I want to do my duty as a citizen, but I've got a very pretty girl waiting for me and it would be rude to be late."

"Let her wait," Caldwell said.

"That's not very civil. Hasn't anyone told you boys that honey goes further than vinegar?"

"Do you think I care? I'm tired of your mouth. I'm tired of the fucking snow job you've been giving us about your buddy."

"Guess you're out of luck, then," Collins said. "I don't have time for this." He didn't want them to think that he was going to let them push him around.

He had misjudged the situation, because Caldwell grabbed him by the arm and slammed him against the wall next to the elevator. It happened so quickly that Collins didn't have time to defend himself. He felt his ribs twinge with pain.

He was surprised that one of J. Edgar's legendary law school G-men, supposedly always in control, could snap so quickly. Over Caldwell's shoulder Collins could see the startled look on the face of the *Sentinel*'s front lobby attendant, Rudy. Caldwell and Leary must have flashed their badges at him earlier, because he made no move to intervene or call for help. Collins wasn't going to give Caldwell and Leary the opportunity to play the tough guys so he kept his hands at his side

"No need to get rough," Collins said. "I'm cooperating."

"You're cooperating? That's a joke, right? Why is it neither of us feels that you've been square with us? Why do I think that you are fucking with us?"

"Couldn't say." It wasn't a good sign that Caldwell felt free to curse him, Collins thought.

"Then I'll tell you. I think that you've been lying about being in contact with him and about what you know."

"Think what you like."

"I think you're lying about the eye, too," Leary said.

Collins didn't turn around. "I told you. I bumped into a door. It was dark."

Caldwell snorted. "That's believable, Collins. If I had to guess. I'd say it was someone you gave lip to, or some broad's angry husband."

"Since you boys seem to know all about me, why are you wasting time coming by and questioning me? Seems you have all the answers already."

"I don't understand you. Your brother swears that you are a regular guy. He told us that a hundred times yesterday. He said that maybe you're a little confused right now, but that you'll come around in the end and help. He's supposed to be a good cop. But here you are being uncooperative when we just have a few questions we need answered."

"Ask away."

"Any phone calls you want to tell us about?"

"None concerning Morris."

"So where do you think he might be?"

"I have no earthly idea," Collins said. "If he's not in Brooklyn or Washington, your guess is as good as mine."

"What about the photos we showed you?"

"The women without names? I told you that one of them looked familiar but I can't say that I've been able to pin that down. Who it is? Can you give me a name?"

"Which of the women?" Caldwell asked.

"The prettier of the two. I think I may have seen her someplace. But I can't put a name to the face."

"We don't know her name, yet," he said. "We're working on it."

"When you get the name, it may help. It may click for me. You know how it is matching names and faces."

Caldwell had confirmed that the FBI didn't know Karina's name, which meant that Steele had not shared his file on her. Collins knew it was just a matter of time before they learned who she was, but with any luck it wouldn't happen before Friday.

"What about this guy, Steele?" Leary asked. "Have you heard from him again?"

"I thought that you were working together," Collins said, addressing his comment to Caldwell. "Isn't Steele one of the liaisons with the FBI? I assumed that you would be sharing information by now. Leads and clues. That sort of thing."

Caldwell looked as if he'd tasted something sour. "Have you worked out a deal with him? Is that why you're holding out on us? You figure Steele is going to run interference for you, so you don't need to tell us anything?"

"There's nothing to tell."

"There's always something. And Steele has no jurisdiction here, so don't expect he's going to show up on your rainy day and make things right for you. You need to start cooperating with us, here and now."

"I've been trying."

"Try harder."

"Well, I'd be happy to answer any more questions you might have later on, but right now's not a great time, gentlemen. I told you that I'm running late for an appointment."

Caldwell stepped away, clearing his way, and Collins felt a sense of relief—they were going to let him leave.

"Don't think that you're off the hook," Caldwell said. "You're not. If I can prove that you've been lying to us, I'm going to crucify you, Collins. Personally. Being a hot-shot newspaperman won't save you."

"This has been quite instructive," Collins said. He smoothed out the lapels of his suit and straightened his tie. "Can I get a rain check? Continue this later if need be?"

"You can go," Caldwell said. "Don't think we won't be watching. We're betting that you're in over your head, and soon you'll be drowning. But don't look for any breaks then, not when you won't help us now when you have the chance."

"We don't agree on what help is," Collins said. "I won't fabricate things about Morris. That's the kind of help you want from me. I can't give you that."

Before either of them could respond Collins turned and walked toward the front door, giving Rudy a nod as he passed. Collins lengthened his stride, hoping the agents wouldn't follow him out of the *Sentinel* building. He glanced over his shoulder once he reached the street. No sign of Caldwell or Leary behind him. Collins caught the first available Checker cab and told the driver to take him the ten blocks or so to Maison Henri as quickly as possible.

When Collins reached the restaurant, he glanced at his watch. He was running ten minutes late. François met him at the front door and took his overcoat and fedora.

"Bonjour, Dennis," he said, always the affable host. "I have seated the lady already."

Collins thanked him.

"It is good to see both of you again so soon," he said, smiling.

Collins gave him a forced smile in return, not wanting to prolong the conversation. When he reached the entrance to the main dining room, he saw that Penny was already waiting for him at a table. There was a half-empty martini glass on the table in front of her. She looked marvelous, he thought, with a single strand of pearls around her neck complementing the light cream-colored suit she wore.

It was hard, seeing her there so beautiful and poised, remembering that they had made love only hours before, and yet knowing that something had gone terribly wrong between them. She didn't see Collins until he was almost to the table and then, when she looked up, she gave him a shy, nervous smile. Collins seated himself across from her.

"Scotch courage," she said, pointing to her glass. "Would you care to join me? A drink?"

Their waiter appeared and Collins ordered a Manhattan; they sat in silence until he had returned with Collins' drink. Collins tipped his glass to Penny in what he thought was an ironic toast, and drank most of his cocktail in a few swallows, savoring the sudden warmth of the alcohol.

"This is quite embarrassing," she said. "I don't know where to start."

"Why not start at the beginning."

She opened her pocketbook, a small, elegant leather one, and pulled out the aluminum canister. "I guess I wasn't thinking," she said. "You know I took this from you, and I am so embarrassed about it. Please take it back, with my apologies."

Collins accepted the canister from her without comment and tucked it into his left front suit pocket. He didn't say anything, letting the silence grow. He wanted to hear her explanation, unprompted.

"Don't you want to know why I took it?"

"Sure, I'd like an explanation," Collins said. "I'm all ears."

The waiter returned before she could reply and so they ordered. Penny selected a Niçoise salad and Collins asked for a grilled steak with shallots. After the waiter left, there was a long, awkward moment of silence. Penny, usually so calm and assured, seemed flustered, tense; no longer so poised. She played with her napkin nervously, tugging at it with her hands. Collins could see how the muscles around her mouth had tightened. She sighed, and then began speaking.

"Once you explained about the documents, how they were from the State Department, I became quite alarmed, quite worried. I know how things are in Washington now and could see that you were placing yourself in great jeopardy. Holding that film could cost you your job, or worse. I figured that if you didn't have the film in your possession, then you'd be safe. It was just sitting there on the table and I had this sudden thought that I could make everything right." She paused. "You know that I care for you, Dennis. That should have been apparent last night."

"I don't know what to think about last night," Collins said. "We go to bed and the next thing I know you've walked out with the canister."

"I took it to protect you! I have friends in Washington, friends of Secretary Acheson, and I thought that they might be able to help you. I wanted to talk to them before it was too late, before you ever came under suspicion. They know all of the right people, they know how to handle things. But I didn't think that they could help if you were found with those documents."

"I'd be safe if I didn't have them on me? Is that it?"

"That's it."

"What about Morris? What about his chances for exoneration?"

She shook her head from side to side, slowly. "Why should you place yourself in jeopardy for him, Dennis? What has he ever done for you?"

"But I told him that I would hold the film for him. I gave him my word. Didn't you think about what your actions might mean to him?"

"You can be too loyal, Dennis," she said. "I don't see Morris reciprocating that loyalty. What sort of a man drags his friend from childhood down with him? Why is he pulling you into this mess? Something he created himself. And for all you know, he is guilty of something. Have you ever thought of that?"

"Every man for himself? Is that it? Would you let Morris lose his job, let the witch hunters ruin his future, all in the name of protecting me?"

"It was you I was thinking about," she said. "I took it because I was so scared for you. I just wanted to get it out of your apartment."

Collins sat there, wanting to believe her, knowing that even if he did, it didn't excuse her selfishness. She didn't seem to care that Collins had given his word to Morris, and that commitment mattered to him.

"I guess that's the difference between us," Collins said. "I'm loyal to the last. I give my friends every benefit of the doubt. That's what loyalty is about."

The waiter arrived with their food. Collins was sure that he had muttered something in the kitchen about the gauche Americans skipping straight to their main course.

"So you took the canister back to your apartment?" Collins asked. "After you left my place?"

"It was late when I left," she said. "So I went right home. I didn't get much sleep, I can tell you."

Collins sat there, his food untouched. He knew that she had to be lying. He felt that sinking feeling in his stomach return.

"Did you talk to anyone else about this?" he asked.

"Of course not. I told you that on the phone. Not yet. I was going to call friends in Washington, but then I thought better of it. I realized I should call you. I knew I should return this to you, and explain what I had done. To throw myself at your mercy."

"So where were you last night?" Collins asked. "When I realized the canister was gone, I came by your apartment. The doorman said that you hadn't returned."

"He must have been mistaken."

"We buzzed you on the intercom. No answer."

"I went straight to bed. I must have been asleep."

"I called. You didn't answer."

"I said that I went right to bed when I got back," she said, annoyed. "I don't answer the phone once I'm in bed."

"Where did you go, Penny?" Collins asked.

"I didn't go anywhere," she said. "I told you."

She wasn't doing a very convincing job of lying, he thought. He remembered that, in the past, when they were lovers, she had quickly answered his late-night phone calls.

"I don't have witnesses for my whereabouts," she said, adopting a sarcastic tone. It was her preferred defense mechanism, Collins remembered, when she was losing an argument. "I didn't think I would need them."

"Did you go to see another man after you saw me last night?"

"How dare you ask that?"

"You know how jealous I am." Collins paused, studying her. "And you didn't answer my question, did you?"

"It doesn't deserve an answer, but I'll give you one. You're the only man I've screwed this week. Not that it's any of your business."

"You believe that I will forgive you anything, don't you?"

"Of course not."

"You are hiding something from me. And we both know it. I know you were someplace else last night. I know you are lying to me about it."

They sat there in silence for a moment. Collins thought about getting up from the table and leaving, but he wanted to give her another chance to tell him the truth. Penny took a sip of her martini.

"I read your column today," she said. "It was quite touching. The two young children, Josef and Hannah. I found myself wishing I could do something for them. Like the woman that you mentioned in the column, the one who is with the refugee center. Karina Lazda. Was that her name?"

"That's her name."

"What is she like?"

"Why do you ask?"

"Just curious."

"What is Karina like? She's not like the typical girl you meet in New York. It was pretty rough for her during the war. She didn't have it easy. I get the sense she is trying to find her way back to a normal life."

"Is she pretty?"

"She was the dark-haired girl sitting with Lonnie Marks at the Stork Club last Friday."

"I don't think I remember seeing her. Do you find her pretty?"

"In her own way."

"And she's smart."

"Better educated than me, that's for sure," he said. "She speaks three or four languages. Some of that comes from her opera background."

"You almost sound like you are falling for her."

"Who knows? Stranger things have happened." Collins said it deliberately to hurt her, and by the way she flushed it was clear that he had hit the mark.

"Then you should pursue her, and I hope that she is as wonderful as you say. I hope you never accuse her of lying to you."

"Penny, let's not kid each other. You know how I feel about you. You know that if I could make you feel the same way towards me, I would in a heartbeat. But it doesn't matter, not how I feel or how you feel if you can't tell me the simple truth. If last night was a mistake, say so. If there is someone else, say so. Whatever it is, tell me. That's all I want."

"Do you really want that?" she asked. "It sounds marvelous in theory, but most of us don't really want the truth if it is confusing or complicated. Or if it hurts us."

"I want the truth."

"No, you want *your* truth. You want things the way you want them. It all has to be black-and-white for you, except that's not the way things really are."

Collins studied his hands, disappointed in her. There was another long silence. He looked around the room glumly. She played nervously with her pearls. Neither of them wanted to make eye contact. Finally Penny broke the silence.

"Did you see that Humphrey Bogart is ending up in court? Tomorrow, assault charges over those silly toy panda bears."

"I saw it," Collins said. "The papers are having a field day with it."

"People need something to laugh about," she said. "It's so grim otherwise. The Russians and the bomb. The situation in China. Everything is so serious. It wasn't supposed to be like this. Isn't that why we fought the war? So we could all enjoy life again."

"That's what we all thought," he said. "But it didn't work out that way."

Penny didn't say anything. She began toying with her napkin again.

"So where do we go from here?" Collins asked.

"What is it that you want from me?"

Collins cleared his throat. "I would hope that you could figure that one out. I'm confused. You know the saying about not knowing whether you are on foot or horseback? That's how I feel. I don't know what to think."

"I'm sorry about last night."

"Sorry? Not all of it, I hope."

"All of it," she said. "We shouldn't have. I was weak. It was a mistake."

"Did you think so at the time?" Collins asked. He couldn't believe that she was the same woman that he had made love to the night before—she had become a stranger in the few hours that had passed. Her face hardened and she didn't respond. The waiter came over to the table with the check and Collins paid the bill with cash.

"Is there anything more you want to say?" Collins asked. "About what has happened?"

She shook her head. Collins stood up, ready to leave.

"You go ahead," she said. "Don't wait for me. I want to sit here by myself for a little bit."

"Suit yourself," he said.

When Collins stopped at the front of the restaurant for his hat and coat he could hear the muted sound of a radio and the distinctive voice of Red Barber coming from the cloakroom. Hearing Barber's incongruous Mississippi drawl on the Dodgers' broadcasts had always amused Collins—it was a strange choice for an announcer for a Brooklyn baseball team. The radio was tuned to WMGM because the teen-aged hatcheck girl, Michele, who was François' niece, was an ardent Dodgers fan.

Michele had first come to the States when she was ten so her English, although accented, was quite good. She had been introduced to baseball and had fallen in love with the Dodgers, worshipping Jackie Robinson and Pee Wee Reese.

"What's the score?" he asked her as Michele located his hat and coat.

"The Dodgers are winning big," she said. "They're ahead, 8-0."

"What inning?"

"The sixth. Preacher Roe is having a great game against the Braves. They're all hitting, Jackie, Pee Wee, Furillo."

"How about the Cards? Have you heard their score?"

"They're losing! It's swell, isn't it? If the Dodgers win the second game, they're in first place."

She handed Collins his coat and fedora and beamed when he tipped her a dollar.

"There must be a saying in France about not counting your chickens before they hatch," Collins said. "To win the pennant, the Dodgers need to be in first place after all the games have been played."

"There is such a saying: '*Il ne faut pas vendre la peau de l'ours avant de l'avoir tué.*' Don't sell the bearskin before you've killed the bear. So the Dodgers must not sell the bearskin yet."

"Not yet, Michele," Collins told her. "Not quite yet."

Twenty-two

Collins walked the ten or so city blocks back to the *Sentinel* building in a daze, still stunned and confused by what had transpired at lunch with Penny. He couldn't make sense of her behavior. She had to be hiding something, or someone, from him and he was in no mood for mystery. He had enough to worry about already.

When Collins reached the newspaper, he half expected the FBI or Matthew Steele to be waiting for him. To his relief the lobby was empty except for Rudy, the newspaper's sad-eyed attendant.

"Those gents that were here earlier treat you okay?" Rudy asked. "The ones with the badges."

"Not a problem," Collins said. "One of them had a bad temper, that's all."

"What happened to your eye, Mr. Collins? Not from those guys, was it?"

"No, my eye came from somebody else."

"Maybe you should take boxing lessons."

"That's a thought," Collins said. "Or maybe I should learn to duck."

Rudy was still chuckling when Collins got into the elevator. When Collins arrived on the fifth floor, the newsroom was starting to fill up with reporters and editors the way it typically did after lunch.

A subdued Hal Diderick stopped Collins before he could reach his desk.

"The verdict finally came in on Tokyo Rose," he said. "Guilty on one count of treason."

"Only one count? I thought they brought several counts against her."

"They did." Diderick peered at the AP copy in his hand, hunting for the details. "Seven counts. They found her guilty on this one:

'That on a day during October, 1944, the exact date being to the Grand Jurors unknown, said defendant, at Tokyo, Japan, in a broadcasting studio of the Broadcasting Corporation of Japan, did speak into a microphone concerning the loss of ships.' She was gloating about it, apparently."

"It doesn't sound like the prosecution had much of a case, then."

"You could be right. The jury was deadlocked most of the week and the judge finally gave them an Allen talk. You know, where he explains the government has spent a great deal of time and money and he'd appreciate a verdict one way or the other. That seemed to have worked—at least it produced a verdict."

"What do you think her sentence will be?"

"The judge could give her the chair," Diderick said. "It's treason. But I don't think he will, her being a woman and all, and the jury only finding her guilty on the one count. I figure maybe life in prison."

"Would that satisfy you?"

"It isn't a question of me being satisfied. I told you before, I just want to see justice done."

Collins didn't want to debate the Tokyo Rose situation with Diderick so he switched to a safer topic. "The Dodgers still ahead in the first game?"

"They won, 9-2," Diderick said. "I figured that you would be listening to the radio."

"I've been busy."

Diderick gave him a puzzled look. "What's going on? It's not like you to miss the game. At this point in the season?"

"Tell you the truth, Diderick. I'm having a bad week. Girl trouble."

Diderick surveyed him with new interest. In the past, Collins had been fairly close-mouthed about his personal life.

"Sorry to hear that. Anything I can do to help?"

"Afraid not. It's one of those things. Can't say that she picked the best week of the year to act up."

Diderick nodded, but it was clear he wasn't completely comfortable with the direction of the conversation. His constant presence at the *Sentinel* reflected his own unhappy home-life, according to newsroom gossip.

"By the way, the column you wrote today was crackerjack. The Polish DP kids. The boy idolizing Joe DiMaggio. Solid."

"Thanks," Collins said.

When Collins returned to his desk, he found himself brooding about Penny. What was she hiding from him? Why would she lie to him with such a flimsy story? He felt the canister in his suit jacket pocket. Even though it was the replacement can, it made him think of Morris. It was already late Thursday afternoon, and Collins had not been contacted about the hand-off. Had something gone wrong? Had Morris changed his mind?

Collins didn't want to wait any longer, and he decided it was time to force the matter. He left the *Sentinel* and walked over to the drugstore with the pay phone. Once in the telephone booth he placed a long-distance call to Morris' Washington number.

The phone rang ten times, unanswered, and Collins hung up. He didn't know what to think. It could be that Ruth Rose was out shopping or occupied with errands. Or she could be sweating out an FBI interrogation.

There was no point in imagining what was going on in Washington. He tried to think about what he should do next. He slotted a nickel into the phone and called the Hotel Marseilles. Karina wasn't around, according to the woman who answered, and so he left a message reminding her to meet him at the Emerald Lounge at seven o'clock. By then, Collins figured that Morris' contact would have reached him with details of the meeting.

Back at the *Sentinel* he spent the next hour and a half hammering out his Friday column. He wrote about the upcoming weekend and how it looked like it might come down to the last game for both the Dodgers and the Yankees and how in a schedule of 154 games there were so many missed opportunities during the season, blown wins that the managers wished they could have back.

It's no different in the real world, the one you and I live in. That talk you always meant to have with your mother about how much you loved her but never did and then she was gone and it was too late. Or that big sale you almost closed, or the girl you almost asked out, or that chance to go off to college you passed on. It would have been a different life, wouldn't it?

Could have. Would have. Should have. Both the Brooks and the Bombers may end this weekend lamenting one lousy game in April or May, an easy win that slipped away. They may always regret that one lapse.

After he passed his copy to the night desk (Van wasn't back from vacation until Friday), he glanced over at the oversized office clock. It was already past six o'clock, time to leave for dinner with Karina. As he was grabbing his coat from the back of his chair, his phone rang. He hesitated, ready to leave, but then decided to pick it up—it could, after all, be the contact for Morris. But it was a rough male voice and he recognized it was the anonymous caller who had phoned on Monday about Phil Santry and Gentleman Jack O'Reilly.

"Liked the column on Tuesday," he said. "You stirred up things good."

"Who is this?"

"Doesn't matter. What matters is that you stuck it to Santry good. Called him on that joke of a fighter."

"Is that all you called about?"

"Not all. I thought you should know that Santry is telling people that after that column he arranged for you to get a shiner and a new attitude along with it. Says there will be no more such stories about boxing."

"You've heard him say this?"

"Everybody's heard him say it. It's true about the black eye, ain't it?"

"You can tell anyone who asks that I'll write about boxing whenever I please. Tell them that Santry is full of shit."

"They know that already. And the black eye?"

"What about it?"

"Just wondering," he said. "Talk to you again sometime." The man hung up the phone before Collins could respond.

Collins had been so preoccupied with Penny and Morris and the film that he hadn't given the episode at the Trattoria Il Riccio much thought. Collins believed what the caller had told him. It would be just like Santry to brag that he had arranged to have shut up Collins, and Collins' black eye would serve as proof positive of his story.

In the taxi cab on the way to the Emerald Lounge Collins thought more about what the anonymous caller had said. It made him angry. Collins didn't want anyone to believe that he could be scared off a story. Once Collins had the situation with Morris squared away, he would have to confront Santry publicly and then follow up with a tough column on corruption in boxing.

Collins waited for Karina at the Emerald Lounge's polished oak bar with a tall glass of Rheingold beer, foamy and sharp to the taste. He lit up a cigarette and asked the bartender about the second Dodgers-Boston Braves game, and was pleased to hear the Dodgers were winning, 8-0.

"So it looks like they're going to sweep," Collins said. "What about the Cardinals?"

"More good news," the bartender said. "They lost by a bunch to the Pirates, 7-2. Never would have expected that."

"So it looks like the Dodgers will move into first place."

"Who would have thought? Had them left for dead after Sunday."

"Smart money did," Collins said.

Just then Karina arrived, hesitating slightly as she moved into the Emerald Lounge, scanning the room, looking around for Collins. He got up from the bar and went over to meet her. Collins leaned in and kissed her on the cheek and was rewarded with a shy smile. She studied him with her dark brown eyes, hesitant, vulnerable, not quite sure of the reception she was going to get. Or was Collins imagining that? He cursed Steele silently for the doubts about her he had planted so effectively in Collins' mind.

"I was hoping that you would be here first," she said. She brushed a lock of hair back from her face. "I thought about seeing you all day."

"That's nice to hear," Collins said.

They found an open table in the back.

"The Dodgers are winning the second game," Collins told her. "And the Cards are losing."

"This is good?"

"This is very good."

"I am happy for you, then."

"But you don't seem very happy," Collins said. "Let's fix that. How about a drink?"

She nodded; Collins went to the bar and ordered her a Manhattan. The bartender told Collins he'd bring the drink over.

"So what's bothering you?" Collins asked when he returned.

"I will tell you later," she said. "I don't want to spoil dinner."

The bartender arrived at the table with Karina's drink. "Thought you'd want to know," he said. "The game just ended and the Dodgers won, 8-0." His face lit up with a smile. "The craziest thing happened in the fifth, in the last inning. One of the Boston players came out to the on-deck circle with his raincoat on, to show he didn't think they should have been playing in the rain. The umpire threw him out."

"Did you catch his name?" Collins asked.

"I think it was Connie Ryan."

That would figure, Collins thought. Ryan had a reputation as a clubhouse joker. It was a pretty clever stunt, actually. There was no doubt that the league was encouraging the umpiring crew to finish the doubleheader. Once the second game started, they would do everything they possibly could to finish it—they just needed five innings for an official game that would count towards the standings.

"Why did he do this?" Karina asked. "This Connie Ryan."

"Think of it as a work action," Collins said. "The Braves didn't want to play today. They had to be hoping for a rainout. They'd prefer not to play, because they want the money for finishing in fourth place. If the game was rained out, they would clinch fourth."

"I don't think I understand," she said. "I am still learning the game."

"Don't worry," the bartender said. "It's a bit crazy at times. You'll figure it out in time."

After he left, Karina gave Collins a shy smile. "I did not get much done at work today," she said. "We have more arrivals from the camps to prepare for, they are meant to be here in two weeks and I did not make the progress I should have today. It is your fault, Dennis."

"My fault? How is that?"

"I have been preoccupied," she said. "I have been thinking about you. I told you that it was hard to be a woman in these circumstances. It is not considered proper for me to call. I must wait. I cannot say the things I want to. That would be too forward."

"I would like to hear those things," Collins said. "Whatever you want to say."

"Perhaps later. When we know each other better."

"Later, then."

"Are you hungry?" she asked. "I am not. Would you like to come back to my place now? Perhaps we could talk, and if you wish some food, I can cook something."

"I would like that," he said. "There's something we need to talk about."

When they left the Emerald Lounge, he glanced up and down the street. He didn't see anyone watching them but then again, he didn't know whether he would be able to spot professional surveillance.

Collins noticed that her name wasn't on the mailbox for her apartment. Instead, it read: "Lustiger." His first time at her place, still reeling from his beating, he hadn't noticed much, let alone names on mailboxes. Karina saw his glance and explained that she didn't think it was right to change the name. "She is in Europe for the fall, teaching, and I will have to move when she returns."

"She can always forward your mail," Collins said.

"There's no mail to forward."

Collins didn't know what to say, struck by the idea that a woman as beautiful and accomplished as Karina could be so isolated. It made sense, though, he thought, if she had left her life in Europe behind—or if she was under orders not to make close friends.

He hadn't paid much attention to her apartment the first time he had been there. The living room had a nice academic feel to it: a faded Persian rug, bookcases, some framed prints, tasteful wallpaper, and comfortable furniture. He glanced over and saw that there was a pile of what looked like sheet music on the surface of a mahogany desk. There were two or three books stacked there and a small framed photograph of a dark-haired couple, smiling at the camera. Karina saw him glance over the desk.

"The music is mine," she said. "And the books and the photo. Everything else in the apartment belongs to Freda, the woman I am renting from."

"Do you sing from it? The sheet music."

"Sometimes. I am out of practice. And I have been smoking."

"And the photo?"

"My parents. Taken in a happier time in Riga, where I grew up." She paused. "You are such a curious man, Dennis Collins. You ask so many questions."

"I can't help it. It's part of what I do for a living. I ask lots of questions."

"You are not on the job, now." She paused. "Dennis, I have something I must tell you," she said. "Something I should have told you earlier."

"What is that?" He kept his voice level, even though he suspected whatever she had to say wouldn't be a surprise. Steele had made sure of that. Karina could have told him then that she had been Uncle

Joe Stalin's favorite mistress and Collins didn't think he would have blinked. Even so, Collins found that he was tensing.

"I am your messenger," she said. "From Morris."

"You're my messenger? What do you mean?"

"I know that you were informed that you would be contacted today. I am the contact."

Collins kept a puzzled look on his face. He wanted Karina to think it all came as a surprise to him. He waited for her to continue.

"I can tell you where and when to give Morris what you are holding for him. He told me to tell you that he still has the Babe Herman and he won't trade it, not even for a Jackie Robinson."

Collins nodded. The message had to have come directly from Morris. His friend had doggedly refused to sell his Babe Herman card, or trade it, to him. Herman had once been a great power hitter for the Dodgers, but a woeful fielder and baserunner.

"Last Friday Morris asked me to help him," she said. "I know that he is in trouble at work, and that what you are carrying for him, the film, will help him prove that he is innocent."

"Why didn't you tell me from the start that you were his messenger? Why did you hide it from me?"

"It was at Morris' request. He insisted. He wanted us to meet naturally, so anyone watching would not think I was involved. It was to protect us both, you and me."

It made sense for Collins to ask questions, the logical questions someone who was in the dark would pose. "So it wasn't a coincidence that you were at the Stork Club?"

"A coincidence? Morris asked Lonnie to bring me there. I was to be his go-between with you."

"So is Lonnie part of this, too?

She bit her lip. "Lonnie had no idea, Dennis. He thought that he was helping me to get publicity for the Center. Morris told him that I specifically wanted to meet you, so that you would help us with your column."

"And what about us?"

"What do you mean?"

"What's between us. Does that change?"

"Why should that change?" she asked. "I did not plan to become involved with you. That I am helping Morris has nothing to do with the way I feel about you. It is not making this any easier. I can now only hope that you forgive me for deceiving you."

"I don't like being lied to."

"I am sorry."

"You say you know that Morris is innocent of these charges. Are you sure?"

"You are not?"

"I thought I was," Collins said. "I don't know now." He paused, collecting his thoughts. He knew he had to be careful. "I don't mean to say that he is guilty, but I wonder if he has been indiscreet, or careless, in his dealings with the Poles and the Russians. It's why I'll want to talk to him before we meet. Can you arrange that?"

"Arrange what?"

"A phone call from Morris. I want to talk to him. I have some questions I want answered before the meeting."

She considered it for a moment, clearly flustered. "Morris said nothing about phone calls. I do not have a number for him. I have no way of contacting him."

"How does Morris know you gave me the message and that I'm going to show up?"

"I am supposed to come with you. If we fail to show up at the appointed time and place, I'm not sure what Morris will do."

"I don't get any of it. Too much mumbo jumbo."

"Mumbo jumbo? Please, I do not understand."

"Morris is making this too difficult, too mysterious. Where and when do I meet him and give him the film?"

"Tomorrow night," she said. "Ten o'clock. Rockefeller Center. We are to meet him under the clock on West 50th Street across from the promenade, just up the block from the Associated Press building. He will walk by us and then he will quickly double back for the pick-up."

"Wait. Why can't I just meet him in a restaurant? Or a bar? Why all the cloak-and-dagger?"

"If we are being followed it will be very easy to detect outside, in the open. We are to act as if we are on a date, perhaps for a late dinner at the Rainbow Room. If there's someone behind us, trailing us, it becomes very obvious. Morris will have a newspaper in his right hand if all is clear. If he doesn't, then we've been followed and the meeting is off."

"And if that happens? What does he want us to do?"

"We are supposed to leave the area as quickly as possible without raising suspicion. We must walk to Fifth Avenue and cross over to St. Patrick's Cathedral and head east along 51st Street. Halfway down the block, by the side entrance, a woman will approach us and you will pass her the canister."

"No," Collins said. "I'm giving this only to Morris and only after he has answered some of my questions. I'm taking this risk only because it is Morris who asked. I'm not about to hand it over to anyone but him. Who is this woman?"

She shrugged, unsure of the answer. "Another friend of his, I would imagine. He did not say who it might be."

That set Collins back: so besides Ruth and Morris and Karina, yet another person knew about the film canister. So much for Morris keeping it secret. He cursed out loud and Karina asked him what was wrong.

"Half of New York seems to know about this damn meeting." Collins said. "You, this woman, and God knows who else. Morris told me that only Ruth would know about this. So much for keeping it secret."

"I imagine that it could not be helped," she said coldly. "Apparently Morris could not do this without the assistance of others."

"Like I said, so much for secrecy."

"Do you have it with you?" she asked. "The film?"

Collins evaded her question. "What did Morris tell you about the film?"

"That it contained government documents which could clear him of suspicion. Do you have it with you now?"

"No. It's in a safe place."

"There will be no difficulty in acquiring it before the meeting?"

"No difficulty. I just have to stop by where it is hidden and retrieve it."

"May I come with you?"

"I don't think so," Collins said. "That would not be very smart. The safe place is near my office, near Herald Square. There may be government security types around."

"I do not understand."

"You have become quite popular in certain circles, Karina. Because some of these government officials, the ones who are looking for Morris, have shown me your photo. Somehow they have connected you with his disappearance. They're looking for you."

"When did you learn this?" she asked. "Why did you not tell me earlier?"

"Why didn't you tell me the truth about your connection to Morris?"

They looked at each other in shared disappointment. It was, he thought, the classic lover's dismay at discovering the first signs of flaws in the beloved, the initial imperfection, the silence that may mean something more. It was a glum moment; an acknowledgement of their mutual deceptiveness, he knew. They had both been holding back.

She sat on the edge of the couch, facing him, her face visible in the lamplight, suddenly looking tired and worn. She ran her hands through her hair.

"How long have you known?" she asked, now quite subdued. "When did they show you this photo? What did they say about me?"

"What do you think they said?"

"I do not know."

"For starters, they told me that you and Morris had been lovers."

"What else?" she said, her voice now tense. There was no denial, Collins thought. He decided to go further, to see how she would react, to repeat some of the uglier stories Steele had told him.

"They said that he was not the first man you found it convenient to go to bed with. That there had been others in Poland. A Russian officer."

"Do you believe them?" Still no denial. Collins studied her face, looking for signs of shame or fear. She remained calm, drawing upon some inner reserve of strength, not showing whatever anxiety she might be feeling. Then again, some part of her had to know that her past might eventually surface. Perhaps she had been expecting this moment, and was prepared.

"I do not know quite what to believe," he said.

"You are the only man I have slept with since I arrived in America," she said. "I have been here more than a year, and you are the first. Not that it should matter who I have gone to bed with before. But I have had no lovers in America. Not until you."

Collins didn't say anything. He wanted to believe her, but he also knew that she was telling him what he wanted to hear. She probably knew that as well. And it didn't make her past vanish; it didn't wash her clean of what she had done.

"It must not bother you too much," she said. "What these men said. You did not hesitate to sleep with me, did you?"

"You know better. It's a bit confusing, that's all. I don't care about what happened years ago, but I do want to be clear about what is happening with us now. It's a lot to take in at one time."

"What do you want to know? I will tell you everything. Or nothing. Whatever you wish. I will not hide anything from you."

"I'm not sure what I want to know."

"My feelings for you will not change," she said. "No matter what you may think of me."

"I'm struggling with this, Karina. I need to think it through."

"I see," she said. She brushed a stray lock of her hair back from her forehead, and tears welled in her eyes.

He wondered what she was thinking, and he wondered if the tears were real. That was the problem, he thought, once you started doubting, where did you stop?

Their conversation had forced his hand. He had to make a decision, one he had been avoiding since Colm first handed him the prints of Morris' film. He was running out of time. He couldn't give Morris the film on Friday night without an explanation for the FBI memo—a damn convincing explanation, he told himself—and it looked like he might not get one. That Karina was so directly involved complicated matters. Collins knew that he couldn't play Lone Ranger any longer.

"I'm out of cigarettes," Collins said. "I'm going out to buy a pack."

Collins left Karina in her apartment. He walked south until he found a nondescript tavern near Broadway, the only open business in sight. He was in luck; there was a phone booth in the back. The bartender and the scattered patrons congregated on stools at the narrow bar didn't bother to look over when he walked past. He fished in his pocket and found Matthew Steele's card. He slotted a nickel into the pay phone and dialed Steele's number reluctantly, realizing that he was setting an irrevocable course.

Steele picked up after the first ring and Collins knew he had to finish what he had started.

"This is Dennis Collins. We need to talk."

"Do we?"

"Yes, we do. It's about Morris Rose. When can I see you?"

"Is tomorrow soon enough?"

"Can you meet me at the *Sentinel?* Early afternoon? Say, one o'clock.

"Of course."

"In the meantime, if the FBI decides they want to talk to me, officially, perhaps even bring me in, can I have them call you? So you can clear me?"

Steele made him wait. "All right," he said. "If they detain you, give them my card and ask them to phone. Tell them that I am working on an assignment for Carter Clarke and they would be well-advised not to delay contacting me."

"Thanks."

"By the way, I've enjoyed reading your column the last few days. That piece on the displaced children was quite touching. Will they attend the Yankee game on Saturday?"

"They will."

"Good show. Surprised that the boy wanted to see the Yankees. As the consummate embodiment of the underdog, I would have thought the Dodgers might have been more fitting."

"He likes Joe DiMaggio."

"Who doesn't?" Steele laughed. "Even Yankee haters do. The best centerfielder in the game, maybe in the history of the game."

"No argument on that from me." Collins paused, struck by the absurdity of their banter. Perhaps it was Steele's way of trying to make a connection, to win his trust. "I will see you tomorrow, then."

"Wouldn't miss it for the world," Steele said.

After they hung up, Collins lit another cigarette. He took a long drag and exhaled. He toyed with the idea of returning to Karina's apartment and telling her that he would only meet with Morris alone, without her along. He could tell her that he didn't want to put her at any risk. On the other hand, he wanted to know the truth about Karina, and about Morris. He might never learn the truth if he excluded her from the rendezvous. Was she working for the Russians? And was Morris?

He walked back to her building and climbed the stairs to her apartment. When he knocked lightly, Karina opened the door.

"I didn't think you were coming back," she said. "Thank God. You were gone so long that I thought you had left me for good."

"I'm here."

"I do not want to lose you, Dennis."

"You're not going to."

"You are the best thing that has happened to me in the longest time," she said solemnly. "The very best."

"Don't make me out to be better than I am," Collins said. "Things are getting really complicated."

She clung to him, kissing him full on the lips, drawing him towards the bedroom. "Don't say anything more," she said. "When we are here together, it is just us. No one else. Not Morris, or your FBI, or anyone else. Just us."

Part Three

Friday, September 30

She initiated their lovemaking in the early hours. The Upper West Side streets outside Karina's apartment remained peaceful and still, the city not fully astir, the morning rush yet to come, dawn still hours away.

She had kissed him awake.

They were less frantic, their bodies moving together slowly now, enjoying each other with a growing intimacy, delighted by what the luxury of time meant for their lovemaking. She closed her eyes as Dennis kissed her face, her mouth open slightly as she pulled him closer to her and lost herself in passion.

Afterward, he fell back into sleep but she remained awake, lying close next to him so she could feel his skin next to hers. She studied his face, knowing that it was probably the last time they would make love, for she would have to tell him later that day. She was glad that it had been so good.

She left her bed carefully, making sure not to wake Dennis, and found her nightgown in the closet. She put in on, cinching the belt, and went into the kitchen to make herself a cup of tea. She sat at the kitchen table and waited while the water boiled in a small pan. She poured it through a strainer filled with loose bohea tea into her tea mug.

She took a few sips of tea and thought about the day ahead. There was no evading what she had to do. At some point she would have to intervene and stop the hand-off of the film to Morris. That meant telling the truth about Morris, the truth about herself.

From the moment she had met Morris in Straus Park, she had somehow known it was going to end badly. She recognized that Morris was beyond reaching. He believed that his secret work contributed to the advance of history and she couldn't imagine him deviating from the course he had set. Even in the unlikely event that he wanted to, he couldn't. He would be signing his own death warrant if he disobeyed Yatov.

She could only hope that she could make things right before she fled.

She prayed that she would have the courage to do the right thing, the necessary thing. There wasn't much time. She would have to find the right moment to tell Dennis. She could only hope that he would understand. She wasn't certain that he would believe her. It would be her word, that of a relative stranger that he had known only for days, against that of his closest childhood friend, and she knew how far-fetched her story would seem.

Somehow she would convince him. He was a decent man, and she would rely on that decency. He could not help Morris any further because to do so would be to help the monsters in Moscow, men who had the blood of countless innocents on their hands. Once she had the film, she would burn it, to insure that it would never end up in their hands.

She knew that Morris was banking on Dennis' sense of loyalty. Dennis would never want to let a friend down. He wouldn't carefully think through what he was going to do. She knew that he would act impulsively.

She walked back to the bedroom door to catch a glimpse of Dennis, still asleep in her bed, only his tousled dark hair visible above her comforter.

It would not be easy for her. The idea that they might fashion a life together had been wishful thinking on her part, a fantasy, nothing more than what her governess Miss Thatcher would have called a pipe dream.

She could make no mistakes, now. She thought about her preparations for leaving New York. She would call in sick at the Center and waste no time in heading for Grand Central terminal and the first train west. Her initial destination didn't matter, as long as she could put some distance between herself and the city. She would change trains as soon as possible, further obscuring her tracks.

She figured that she would have at least a day's head start. Morris would have to decide whether to stay and give Yatov the bad news, or to make a run for it himself. In any event, she would have some time before they began their search for her. There should be no trail left behind to follow. As long as she cut all of her connections to anyone she knew in New York, there would be no immediate way to trace her.

She was not naïve enough to believe it would end there. They would continue to look for her. She could only hope that Yatov might fall out of favor and be recalled to Moscow Center. Perhaps his successor would be less interested in tracking her down. Yet she could not rely on that; she had to assume that she would have to remain a fugitive.

Dennis stirred in his sleep, moving about. She wondered what he would think about their time together. Would he regret it? Would it seem a strange, random interlude in his life, a bit of craziness before he returned to his regular routine? At least she knew he would not forget her, that she had left her mark on him. It wasn't what she had hoped for, but it was better than nothing.

Twenty-three

They had a light breakfast of scrambled eggs, toast and coffee. Karina cooked for them, humming something melodic—a tune Collins didn't recognize—as she maneuvered the skillet over her small stovetop range. After she had finished cooking, they sat, side-by-side, at a small table in her kitchen to eat. They were a picture of domesticity, he thought.

"I could get used to this," Collins said. "It sure beats breakfast at a diner."

"And if you get used to me, you might grow bored," she said, playfully. "When you know me better. You do not really know me, Dennis."

"Yes, I do," Collins insisted. While in some ways he knew very little about her, he told himself, in other ways he did know the essential things about her. "I know that you have a good heart."

"I am not who you think I am," she said.

"Who are you then?" It seemed an opening, Collins thought, an opportunity for Karina to reveal any connection to the Soviets.

"What they told you. From those files, all those nasty stories. I cannot deny them or that it was me. It was me. You should not be deceived."

"I am not deceived."

"You are a gentle man, a good man. I know. For that very reason, you should not be with me. You deserve a nice girl, an innocent American girl, to have your babies and to adore you and make you happy."

"How about letting me make up my own mind? Maybe I prefer mysterious foreign women. Sopranos with artistic temperaments."

"I am not so mysterious. Or temperamental. I lead a very ordinary life now. I crave that."

"You're still mysterious to me. I need to know you a lot better before you'll ever seem ordinary. I'll have to ask a lot of questions. I told you it's what I do for a living. I can't shut it off."

"What do you want to know?"

"How you got here. What happened after the war." Collins could see her relax, relieved that he was not going to start with difficult questions about her wartime lovers. Collins had a different purpose, of course. He hoped to learn as much as he could about her possible connections with the Soviets. "For instance, when did you first meet Morris?"

"In Poland," she said. "I met him in Warsaw, when he was attached to the American embassy. He had come to tour the refugee camps. Later I became his interpreter."

"And then later you came to America."

"I did," she said. "Morris helped me. He arranged it so I could come and he found me the job with the Center."

"That was generous of him," Collins said, a bit more sharply than he had intended.

She sighed, disappointed in him. "We were lovers. You know that. I do not hide that from you. For a brief time in Poland and then in Austria, we were lovers."

"Did he tell you that he was married?"

"I knew," she said. "I slept with him, knowing that. But he was kind and he was far from home and yes, he protected me. Does this lessen me in your eyes?"

"I don't like the thought of it."

"What bothers you? Is it that he is your friend? Are you disturbed that I slept with your friend? I did not know who you were, then, Dennis. I never imagined that I might be in America. That was a dream, not the reality of my life."

"You should know I am jealous by nature," he said. She was right, Collins admitted to himself. It wasn't a comfortable feeling—and he didn't particularly like the mental picture he could easily conjure up of Karina and Morris joined together. Jealousy was a strange thing.

"There is no need for you to be jealous. What happened with Morris took place in the past. We are friends, now, nothing more. I feel nothing for him."

"Is there anything more that I should know?"

"About my past?" she asked. "It sounds like the FBI has told you what is in their ugly files. Yes, I lived with a Red Army officer in Warsaw. He also protected me. I am not ashamed of that. A woman had to have a protector, then. What more can I say? I will tell you whatever you want to know. Ask me. I am not pure, Dennis, I have done things so that I might survive. But what's done is done. I cannot alter the past."

"As long as you tell me the truth," Collins said. It was an easy thing to say to her—the request all lovers have of their beloved. Tell me what you think. Tell me your heart's desire. Do not deceive me. Collins knew that he could be accused of hypocrisy. He was not telling her all that he knew—a necessary deception in his view, but a deception nonetheless.

"Truth is truth. Shakespeare said that. My English tutor made me memorize that along with other sayings from Shakespeare. I will tell you the truth."

"That's all I ask," Collins said. "So what did you and Morris talk about? When you were lovers? Did you talk about the war? About politics? About the DP program?"

She shrugged. "That is not what I wanted to talk about. I wanted to hear all about New York City. The buildings, the people, the restaurants, the shops. The Statue of Liberty. The Empire State building. And of course, Carnegie Hall. Morris laughed at me, but I think later it was what made him think that I should come to America."

Collins decided to take a different tack. "Did Morris talk about his negotiations with the Polish government? Or the Russians?"

"Never," she said firmly.

Collins was disappointed. He had given her another opening to tell him about her involvement with the Russians. For all her talk of truth, she was not willing to give it to him.

"Morris knew better than to do that. He told me that he had been warned by the State Department security office about any young Polish women he might meet. That they could be working for the secret police. So he did not talk with me about his work."

"Surely he did not suspect you of that. Of working for the secret police, of being a spy."

"He was very careful," she said. "You know Morris. But I was not a spy for anyone. When Sasha left, Morris protected me. But must we keep talking about him? This is tiresome."

"I don't want to be tiresome."

She wasn't going to open up to him, he thought. In a way, Collins couldn't blame her. She had known him for only a few days. How could she take the risk? For all she knew, he might be helping Morris out of more than friendship. Silence was her safest course.

"Now what?" she asked. "What do we do?"

"We meet with Morris tonight and I give him back his film canister. Like I told him I would. That's that."

"And then? What about us?"

"I want to keep seeing you," Collins said, and as he said it, he realized that it was the truth. He was falling for her. It was a chancy thing and it certainly wasn't the smartest play, but he knew he wasn't done with her. He wasn't ready to break it off with her.

"I would like that very much," she said.

As they sat there together finishing their coffee Collins made up his mind about what he was going to do. It had all become very simple. He would go ahead and meet Steele that afternoon. He would trade the film to Steele in exchange for fair treatment for Morris and for Karina. Collins figured that Steele would be Morris' best bet; he would at least consider the evidence before he reached any conclusions. Then Collins would go to the rendezvous at Rockefeller Center with Karina, and he would confront Morris. He would have a chance to learn the truth, then, from both of them.

While he was at it, he would resolve the other complication in his life, the business with Phil Santry. He would see Vandercamp first, and tell him about his past with Santry, and then he would deal with the fight promoter directly. He would also tell Van something about the situation with Morris. His editor deserved to know. Collins couldn't have the *Sentinel* blindsided if the FBI decided to arrest him.

They left the apartment together. Karina agreed to meet him at eight o'clock at the Club Carousel on 52nd Street. They would have a light supper and listen to jazz until it was time to walk over to Rockefeller Center for the meeting with Morris.

After they kissed goodbye, Collins found a newsstand and bought the papers. He needed to make a stop at his apartment before work and he decided to walk the twenty or so city blocks there. He had plenty of time and the weather was inviting, warmer and fair. He tucked the papers under his arm and made good time down Broadway.

When he neared his neighborhood, Collins pulled the brim down on his fedora, hoping it would make it slightly harder to identify him from a distance. He went to the All-American first, where Nicky pulled Collins into an empty booth and gestured at one of the waitresses to bring them coffee. Nicky glanced around nervously before he spoke.

"You're a popular man, Mr. Collins," he said. "Some fellas were here the other day asking about you. Wanted to know when I might expect you to come in."

"What sort of fellows?"

"Police," he said. "They showed me their badges quickly, but I could see that they were federal."

"One tall guy and a younger one a bit shorter? Both with crewcuts?"

"That's them. I told them they could find you at the newspaper, or at the ballpark."

"That's the truth."

"Did they catch up to you?" he asked. "Since I saw them?"

"Not yet," Collins said. He gave Nicky a grin. "Can't hit a moving target, I guess."

The waitress poured their coffee and Collins took a quick sip and glanced over to see Nick examining him.

"Everything okay, Mr. Collins?"

"It is with me, Nicky. How about with your Yankees?"

"Don't get me started. Do you think Mr. DiMaggio will be back? They say he took batting practice again yesterday. That's two days in a row. If he can swing the bat, then he can play, no?"

Collins scratched his chin. "I don't know, Nicky. He's been in the hospital with pneumonia. Someone in the Yankees front office told me that he's lost twenty pounds. I don't know that he can play, or if he can, whether he'll be able to run. Remember, he has to play in the field as well as hit."

"I guess they could pinch hit him."

"They could. But that's just one at bat. They need more from him than that." Collins checked his watch. "I have to go. Thanks for letting me know about the men asking about me. I don't think they'll be around again. The problem they're worried about is being taken care of."

"Sure, Mr. Collins. I'm glad to hear that."

Closer to his apartment, Collins quickly checked both sides of the street, looking for signs of surveillance. It didn't look like anyone was watching the entrance. He pulled his fedora brim down and hurried into the lobby. He stopped at the front desk and was pleased to see that it was Gene, one of the older doormen, who had known him for several years and had always been friendly.

"Anybody asking for me?"

Gene bobbed his head. "Your brother stopped by. I told him that you hadn't been around for a day or so."

"Anyone else?"

He glanced briefly at Collins, avoiding eye contact. "I like you, Mr. Collins, but I know enough to keep my nose out of what ain't my business."

That told Collins what he wanted to know. "Two clean-cut guys come by asking questions? Federal agents?"

Gene stared down at his hands, clearly unwilling to volunteer information directly, but willing to respond indirectly.

"Did they go up to the apartment? Did they ask for a pass key?"

Gene nodded, embarrassed by his own reticence, and then spoke. "Sorry, Mr. Collins. I couldn't really say no."

"No, you did the right thing. I have nothing to hide so, I'm glad you helped them. It's just a misunderstanding."

"I told them you were a regular guy," Gene said. "For what it's worth. That I liked you. That all of us doormen liked you."

"Thanks. Appreciate it. Do me a favor?"

"Sure."

"Buzz me upstairs if they decide to come back. I'm only going to be up there ten minutes."

When Collins checked his apartment he found nothing out of order. There really wasn't anything for the FBI to find. Collins had Morris' film, now developed, securely stashed at the *Sentinel* in the newsroom stairwell.

He took a quick shower and shaved and then packed a few clean shirts and pairs of underwear in his overnight bag. He would leave the bag under his desk at the *Sentinel*. If he needed to lay low for a few days he would at least have a change of clothes.

He found the lobby empty on his way out. He glanced through the papers during his cab ride to the *Sentinel*. The second game of the Dodgers doubleheader in Boston must have been something—apparently the Braves had started a small fire on the top steps of their dugout to "light the way back" for their batters at the end of the game, and to express their disgust at having to play in a downpour. And then there was Connie Ryan's stunt, showing up in the batter's circle wearing a raincoat. It was clear that the umpires had their orders from Ford Frick and the league to get the games in at all costs. The funny thing was that the small group of Braves fans who braved the weather had hooted and jeered their hometown heroes for their reluctance to play. Don Newcombe struck out the side in the fifth and the umpire had called the game then—it had lasted just long enough to be counted as official.

Collins regretted that he couldn't have been there. It must have been a memorable scene: the rain pouring down, the Braves players angry that they had to play under the circumstances and knowing that their fourth-place money was slipping away, the Dodgers wanting to get their five innings in, the umpires caught between the two teams.

Collins pictured Pete Marquis in the press box above Braves field, chewing his gum frantically, agonizing over whether the Brooks were going to get the game in, officially, before nightfall. Collins should have been there.

As the cab neared Herald Square, Collins began to tense up. He did not look forward to his interviews with Peter Vandercamp and Mathew Steele. But he had to see it through. There was no way to know what would happen. He might lose his job. He might lose his oldest friend, and possibly his mysterious new lover. But with any luck he would be able to salvage something for Morris and for Karina. And that meant he would be able to look in the mirror on Saturday morning and believe that Dennis Collins was a half-decent human being.

Twenty-four

When he arrived at the *Sentinel*, Collins went directly to Peter Vandercamp's office. He knew it was going to be an awkward and difficult conversation. While Vandercamp might accept Collins' motives for helping Morris, Collins knew that he would be less sympathetic about his past transgressions with Phil Santry.

Maybe Hal Diderick had it right, Collins thought, that it was harder to put the past behind you than it seemed. In a way, Collins and Morris shared that problem. Morris had his political past dogging him and Collins had his mistakes from his time as a sportswriter at the *Sun*.

Collins could make the argument that most of the New York sportswriters had taken something—money, gifts, favors—whether from fight promoters or ball clubs, and some kept on taking. He had accepted cash from Santry to tout his boxers, but he could rationalize that if those fighters couldn't deliver in the ring, then whatever he wrote in the paper didn't matter. But he had no defense for having bet twice on fights when Santry had hinted at their outcome.

Collins had stopped taking money before he first came to the *Sentinel*, tired of the whole ugly scene, wanting to start fresh. Santry had been nasty about it at first, but Collins had not relented. Now Collins couldn't confront Santry until Vandercamp knew the truth. He couldn't have Van, or the *Sentinel*, caught by surprise if Santry went public about their sordid past.

When Collins rapped lightly on the side of the doorframe of the managing editor's office, Vandercamp waved him over to the worn wooden chair across from his desk. He leaned forward and intently studied Collins' right eye for a long moment.

"I heard that you had quite a shiner," he said. "Very impressive up this close. Was he a counter-puncher?"

"You could say that," Collins said. "But that was Tuesday. Ancient history by now."

"I trust it wasn't fashion models or chorus girls you were scrapping with."

Collins raised his eyebrows. "Not quite. If you wanted to find photos of the guy who clocked me I'd suggest starting with the NYPD rap sheets."

"So what can I do for you, Denny?" he asked.

"Can we have a private chat? It won't take long."

"Technically it's your day off. No column for tomorrow. You could have waited and had this conversation on the clock."

"That's true. But this can't wait. I've got two things I need to talk to you about, Van, that affect me and may affect the newspaper."

"Sounds like something better discussed over a cup of coffee," Vandercamp said. "Let's walk over to that coffee shop near Gimbel's."

They left the *Sentinel* and walked over to the Coffee Spot, where they found an empty corner table. After they had been served their coffee, Vandercamp watched silently as Collins, suddenly clumsy, fumbled with his Chesterfields and Zippo. He was buying time, trying to delay getting to the heart of the matter.

Collins took a few puffs on his cigarette and finally started in, feeling like he was twelve years old in the confessional confessing his impure thoughts to Father O'Hare. "So I have these two things I wanted to get off my chest. The first is a problem with Phil Santry."

Vandercamp nodded. "That's no surprise. You more or less have him headed to Sing Sing. An awfully tough column on Tuesday. I wish I had been there to soften that last bit a tad."

"It's not the column directly. It's what it stirred up from my past, from when I worked for the *Sun* before the war. Santry could say I was a hypocrite when it comes to the topic of corruption."

"Could he?"

"He could claim that he gave me money to tout some of his fighters in the *Sun*. Build them up."

"He *could* claim?"

"I don't think he has the balls to do it, Van. It covers him in mud as much as it does me.

"Is it true?"

"That was eight, ten years ago."

"Is it true?"

"I'm no saint, Van. Never said I was. Yes, it's true. Worse, I bet a few times, on tips from Santry. But I have never taken a dime since I've been at the *Sentinel*. I'd swear to that on a stack of Bibles, because it's true."

"So did you bet against the fighters that he had you touting?"

"Twice. Both times he tipped me that his guy would be taking a dive. I've got no defense for that. Even though I was a kid, I knew better. I was just full of myself."

"We all make mistakes," Vandercamp said. He sighed. "I'm disappointed to hear this. It's sleazy and I wouldn't have expected it from you."

Collins didn't say anything. It hurt to see the look of dismay on Van's face.

"There's another problem you should know about. I guess when it rains, it pours. It's been a bad week. A friend of mine got himself in trouble in Washington. A loyalty investigation at the State Department. And it happens that I'm his closest pal from childhood. The Feds are poking around now and they've been by to talk to me at the newspaper once already. You weren't around that day."

"What's the problem?"

"I think they'll be back to question me more. Hell, they may want to arrest me. Here's the catch. I started out thinking that my friend was as pure as the driven snow. Now I'm worried that he may not be so clean. Not that he's disloyal, but that he may have acted impulsively. The complication is that I've been covering for him. Or at least you could argue that. And I can see how that wouldn't look so good if he has done some stupid things."

"It's not too late to set this right."

"You mean going to the authorities?"

"I do."

Collins shook his head. "I can't do that. It would only make the situation worse, for everyone involved. I just have to hope this works out without any more damage."

Vandercamp looked at Collins doubtfully, exasperated. For Vandercamp, irrationality of any sort was troubling. "I think you are dead wrong. I know a lawyer or two who might be of some assistance. One of them is a Notre Dame grad and knows Clyde Tolleson, Hoover's number two, fairly well."

"I can't," Collins said. "I have to see this through to the end because I think there's a chance I can help set things right. I recognize there may be some fairly nasty consequences, but I don't see any other way."

"That is a shame," Vandercamp said. "I'm afraid that you may become a victim of history, Dennis. This isn't the first time this has happened. Look at Palmer and the Red Scares in the twenties. The Alien and Sedition Acts after our own Revolution when John Adams was throwing newspaper editors in jail. Now we've got our own witch hunt. Good people get hurt, innocent people."

"And some who aren't completely innocent."

"Perhaps so. You know, Marxism is a Christian heresy. Like all heresies it started with some essential truth and then twisted it into something completely different. There has been a long distinguished line of heretics, the Docetists, the Gnostics, the Donatists, the Nestorians. Today it is the Marxists. They mistakenly believe that human sin can be extinguished through the dialectic. Somewhat like Arianism, the potential perfectibility of man."

"My problem isn't heresy," Collins said. "It's the FBI."

"A more serious problem, in practical terms."

"It is. I'm hoping this whole mess can be cleared up by Monday." Collins tried to project a confidence he didn't have.

"By Monday?" Vandercamp gave him a skeptical look.

"That's my hope. At least my involvement in it should be finished."

"Then we shouldn't have much to worry about, should we?"

Collins took another sip of his coffee. He could see why Vandercamp had once been on the path to the priesthood. He had an easy, welcoming manner about him. He made you feel that you could open up to him, could tell him your troubles. "You haven't said anything about Santry," Collins said. "What will happen if he starts screaming that I was on the take, or worse, that I still am?"

"You told me that since you've been at the *Sentinel*, your conduct has been above reproach. I take you at your word."

"Thanks. I appreciate that."

Vandercamp paused, finishing his coffee. "I'm going to have to inform Longworth about this, Denny. Now, before Santry says or does anything. I'm fairly confident that he will agree with me, that for now we should judge you only on your conduct at the *Sentinel*. Longworth may want to talk to you directly about your time at the *Sun*, and he may want your assurances that nothing of this sort has ever happened here."

"I understand."

"If Santry comes forward we'll have to see what he says and then deal with it. My priority will be to protect the *Sentinel*, but I will do my best to see you are treated fairly. I can't promise any more than that. You may be asked to leave the paper."

"I figured that," Collins said.

"For now, we do nothing. We'll wait and see what happens, both with Santry and your situation with the FBI." Vandercamp shook his head. "The smart thing would be for you to keep your distance from Santry and from your friend. Remove yourself from the occasion of sin, as it were. I'd recommend you to take that course of action, but I don't think you would take that advice, would you?"

"No, I don't think I would."

When they returned to the *Sentinel*, Collins was surprised to find Karina waiting there in the far corner of the front lobby. When she saw them, she came across the lobby, quickly taking Collins' left hand in hers. Collins introduced her and, always the courtly gentleman, Vandercamp told her how much he admired what she was doing at the Center. Karina gave him a radiant smile, pleased at the attention.

"I shouldn't have surprised Dennis at work like this," she said. "I should have called him before I came."

"Nonsense," Vandercamp said. "I am sure Dennis is happy to see you." He paused. "You have the most delightful accent. Quite musical."

"Thank you," she said. "I think. I hope it is not hard for you to understand my English."

"On the contrary. Your English is excellent. Where did you learn it?"

"I had a tutor as a child," she said. "She was English and quite precise in her grammar. She was always cross with me."

"She should be commended."

Collins realized again how little he knew about Karina. He had assumed that her family had money, because becoming an opera singer requires years of expensive training, but having an English tutor sounded like a perquisite of the very wealthy.

"Well, I must be getting back to the salt mine," Vandercamp said.

"The salt mine?" she asked, puzzled.

"Ah, yes, that is American slang. It means I have to get back to work."

After Vandercamp disappeared into one of the elevators, Collins pulled Karina aside so he could not be overheard. "This is foolish and very risky. This is the last place on earth you should be. It's very likely that the FBI will be walking in the door at any moment. They know what you look like."

She dropped her head, stung by his reproof. "I wanted to see you. Please don't be angry. I took the rest of the day off from work."

"Is something the matter?"

"I needed to see you. I sat there at my desk, unable to concentrate, and finally decided that I would come here. I felt that I had to see you."

"This isn't a good time. We can talk later, at the Club Carousel, before we go to meet Morris."

"I wanted to talk to you about that. About the meeting."

Collins glanced around the lobby. "He hasn't contacted you, has he? No change in plans?"

"No, no change."

"Then what do we have to talk about? It's very simple, now. We will meet Morris. I give him what I've been holding, and then he uses it to get him out of the fix he is in."

"What about all these people from your government looking for him? Asking questions?"

"What about them? It won't be my problem. Or yours. After tonight it's between them and Morris. I told him that I would hold his film for a week. I gave him my word. So tonight I will fulfill that obligation and I'm done with the whole damn mess. And so are you."

Collins wasn't being completely honest with her. He didn't intend to hand Morris anything at Rockefeller Center. The film would be safely in Steele's hands by then and Collins hoped only to convince Morris to come with him to meet Steele. And Karina? If she was involved, Collins would encourage her to defect, to turn herself in. He was convinced that he could persuade her to do so.

"You are sure of this?" she asked, watching him intently, her brown eyes fixed on his face.

"I'm very sure," Collins said. "You needn't worry. Why don't you go to a museum or take in a film this afternoon? I'll see you at the Club Carousel, like we agreed."

She hesitated. "I do not like waiting."

"I don't like it either, darling." Collins pulled her closer and kissed her quickly on the lips. "I promise that we'll spend some time together soon. Once we have tonight out of the way and the baseball season finishes. Maybe we can get out of town."

"Go some place, you mean?"

"Sure. Maybe to the country. There's a real nice hotel called the Mohonk; it's by a very deep lake. Not too far from the city. We could spend a weekend together there. Would you like that?"

"I would like that. It is a funny name, no? Mohonk?"

He gave her another kiss. "Yes, it is a funny name."

"We must go there," she said. "After this is over." She started to say something more, but changed her mind. "I will see you tonight as we have agreed."

After Karina left, Collins headed downtown to the Five Star Gym, where he figured he would find Phil Santry. It was time to resolve his other outstanding business. And why not? It felt good to take control, he told himself, to confront the ugliness in his life, all in one fell swoop.

After climbing the stairs to the fourth floor of the nondescript warehouse building where Five Star was located, the first person Collins encountered at the entrance to the gym was Moe Monto. Moe squinted at Collins' black eye, but didn't say anything, which Collins appreciated. Monto had been a top-notch cut-man back in the 1920s but now he was too old to handle that responsibility. He loved boxing, so he remained a regular at Five Star, running occasional errands for the trainers, watching the sparring and gossiping with the other old timers. He was definitely a character.

Collins believed that sporting world attracted characters. If you're talented, if you can hit a baseball or run for a touchdown, people look the other way at your eccentricities. You can be a little larger than life, a little crazy. Take Babe Ruth, or for that matter, many of the current Yankees. The *Sentinel*'s Yankees beat writer, Ted Cohn, told Collins that Casey Stengel's toughest job wasn't on the field—it was enforcing the players' curfew. Joe DiMaggio liked to chase chorus girls and most of the rest of the club would burn the candle at both ends if given half a chance.

Johnny Lindell, the big outfielder, was perhaps the biggest tomcat on the Yankees, just as Ellis Kinder was the Red Sox player most likely not to be in his hotel room at curfew. In Kinder's case it didn't seem to make any difference in his on-field performance; there were stories of him closing down a city's bars, finding some female companionship, and showing up at the ballpark just before starting time, smelling of booze. Then he would pitch a masterpiece.

Monto gave him a gap-toothed grin. He was pleased to see Collins. "You here to work out, Denny? Hit the heavy bag?"

"No, Moe, not here for that."

"Haven't seen you down here for months."

"It's baseball season," Collins told him. "Who has the time? I'll be back, though, once it gets cold. You'll see me this winter."

"The legs go when you don't work out," he said. "People think you lose the punch. They think your hands get slow. That's not what happens. What happens is that your legs go weak. When you do get back in the ring your legs are rubbery. And you can't hit hard without power coming from the legs."

"I'm not getting in the ring."

"You never know. You may not be climbing into the ring, but you may need that punching power. Look at that actor. They tried to take his panda bear away from him, but he had punching power."

"Are you talking about Bogart?"

Monto nodded. Collins decided not to point out that Bogart's opponents had been a fashion model and a society girl and that he hadn't actually thrown any punches.

Inside the gym, it smelled of stale sweat, Wintergreen liniment, and cigar smoke. Collins looked around for Santry and located him standing against the far wall, watching two fighters who were taking turns with a heavy bag. Two boxers, lightweights by the looks of them, were sparring in Five Star's one ring, and a few others were jumping rope or working with their trainers. Collins walked over to Santry. The promoter didn't see Collins until he was five feet away. Collins could see him struggling to arrange his features into what would pass for a smile.

"Denny," he said. "Good to see you. What's with the eye? An angry husband catch up with you?"

"You ought to call Arthur Godfrey and ask for a guest spot on his show. You're a real comedian, Phil."

"I try," he said.

"You have a moment?"

"What is this about?"

"Thought we might step out in the hall for a talk. Clear up a misunderstanding."

"Misunderstanding?"

"I'll explain in the hall."

Santry reluctantly followed Collins out of the gym. They were alone in the hallway, the door to the gym closed. Monto had moved inside to watch the sparring practice.

"Listen to me," Collins said. "You better never try to pull a stunt like Tuesday again. Siccing those thugs on me."

"Who says I had anything to do with that?"

"They did."

"Well, sorry about that. They must have heard me talking when I was angry about that shitty column you wrote. They must have gotten carried away. Nothing I told them to do. You know how it is."

"I don't know how it is. And now I hear you're claiming that you've shut me up. Is that so?"

"Who's telling you that?"

"That doesn't matter. Are you telling people that?"

"Don't play high and mighty with me," Santry said. "Unless you want a second black eye."

That's when Collins started abusing him, calling him every curse word he could think of in a loud voice, wanting everyone in the gym to hear him. Santry knew that they could hear Collins, too, and he glowered back at him. Collins was counting on Santry getting angry enough at him to take a swing. Santry did not disappoint him.

When Santry telegraphed his punch, pulling his arm back, Collins ducked and let his blow whistle past. Collins didn't want to hurt his tender right hand, so he hammered Santry in his ample paunch with his left fist as hard as he could. Then he hit Santry a second shot in the gut, just as hard, and Santry crumpled up, bounced against the gym wall, and slid to the floor with a gasp. He curled up, groaning in pain. Collins was tempted to give him a swift shoe in the ribs, so Santry would know what it felt like, but he stopped short of kicking him.

"Get up," Collins said. "Get up. We're not done."

Santry rolled over and sat on the floor, his back to the wall.

"That was for sending your buddies after me."

"I warned you. You had to go and print that shit in the paper."

"I write what I want to."

"You are no cleaner than the rest of us. Remember that."

"Sure, I remember. I was a kid. I took some money to tout some bad fighters. I made a few bets. So what?"

"That wouldn't make you look too good if it came out now," Santry said. "Doesn't quite fit into the picture of the righteous Dennis Collins, the crusading columnist."

"You're not going to do or say anything. You don't want it out in the open any more than I do."

"That depends," he said. "On the corner you back me into."

"Go ahead. It's old news. Ancient history. Do you think anyone's going to care about what happened ten years ago?"

"You care."

"Listen to me. Say whatever you want to whoever you want. Just don't send your goons after me again or I'll be back to give you more of what you just had."

"You arrogant prick," Santry said. "You're no better than any of us. You think that you're a big shot. Let's see how long that lasts."

"Any time you want another beating, call me," Collins said. "Until then, I'd recommend you keep your mouth shut and stay out of my way."

Collins glanced over at the entrance to the gym. Moe Monto and a few of the fighters were there, drawn by the noise of their scuffle. Monto and several of the boxers were wearing grins; Phil Santry wasn't particularly popular at Five Star. Santry got to his feet and staggered into the gym, averting his eyes. He had been humiliated in front of the entire gym, which was exactly what Collins had hoped for. Word would get around.

"I told you," Monto said to Collins. "See how you need punching power? Although you don't need much for a slob like Santry."

"You don't care for Santry?"

"The man's never been in a ring. Not like you, Denny, with the Golden Gloves. Santry manages boxers but he's never thrown a real punch himself. Looks like he can't take one, either." Monto looked him up and down. "You need to come back here, soon. Work the heavy bag, jump rope, get yourself back in shape."

"Sure, Moe."

"Don't 'sure, Moe' me," he said. "Get your ass down here. You been smoking again, Denny. I can smell it on your clothes. You need to cut that out. Bad for your wind."

"You're not the only one who tells me that," Collins said, thinking of Diderick. "But thanks for the advice."

"Punching power," Monto said, his parting words to Collins. "You got to train the legs to have that punching power."

Twenty-five

In a way, it was a relief for Collins to find Matthew Steele calmly sitting in a chair outside the *Sentinel* newsroom a few minutes past their appointed meeting time. Collins was counting on Steele, after all, to keep Morris out of jail and Karina clear of deportation. A lot was riding on their talk, Collins told himself, and he needed to handle matters carefully.

He motioned Steele towards the door of the small conference room. Collins realized that he had been closeted in that cramped room more in the past week than he had in the past two years. As they seated themselves at the table, Steele looked over at the framed front page with the headline about the Japanese surrender.

"Where were you then?" he asked. "When it ended?"

"I was in Hawaii," Collins said. "Rest and relaxation. Hiroshima and Nagasaki came as a surprise. I expected we would invade Kyushu in the fall. Operation Olympic. I was set to return and cover it. How about you?"

"Berlin. What was left of it after our bombing and the Russian assault. Handling some loose ends. I can tell you that we didn't feel like our war had ended. We could see that our adversary had changed, that's all. It was already clear that Ivan was trying to establish his spy networks in our sector. We had to move fast."

"This is awkward," Collins said. "So I'll come right out with it. I have some materials that Morris Rose gave me for safekeeping. Government documents."

"And where do I come in?" Steele asked. He seemed somehow amused by the situation. His attitude irritated Collins.

"I thought that you should have them. Then you could talk to Morris about them and what they mean."

"Talk to Morris Rose about what they mean?"

Collins nodded, glumly. He knew how lame his suggestion sounded once he voiced it, but he kept talking. "I'm hoping Morris can explain himself to you. Keep himself out of jail."

"Where are these documents?"

"I have them. They were on film and now I have photos."

"And what did Rose tell you about the nature of these documents?"

"That they were State Department memos that would prove his innocence. Exonerate him. Keep him from being railroaded by his enemies in the Department. Morris wanted me to hold them in the event that he was arrested. He said that they would clear him."

"And do they?"

Collins figured that Steele knew the answer already. He just wanted to make Collins say out loud that he suspected Morris had been lying.

"I don't know. There are memos that show he had approval for his contact with the Russians and Poles. But there is another document, a confidential list from the FBI. I'm assuming he got it from the Shoemaker girl. It lists suspected agents in the government, along with their code names. On the surface, it appears to incriminate Morris. His name is on the list. I'm troubled that Morris would have the document in his possession."

"I can see why you would be."

"It's not a list that should be circulating. It could tell the Russians what we know about their agents. Morris shouldn't have it. So I'm ready to give it to you. With some conditions."

"Which are?"

"I have to tell Morris about this, that I gave the film to you, so he can explain it to you. I owe him that. His conversation has to be with you, not the FBI."

"Is that all?"

"No," Collins said. "There's also Karina Lazda. That's the other condition. I want your intervention on her behalf, if it turns out she is working for the Russians and is willing to defect. If she is, it's likely that she is being blackmailed into cooperating. I want you to give her a chance to end her association with them."

"And exactly how is that to be accomplished?" Steele contemplated him, making a steeple of his fingers.

"You don't have to do anything. Just be ready if she is willing."

"And why should I do these things?"

Steele's response wasn't what Collins had hoped to hear. "If you agree to my conditions you recover the documents and you get what you wanted, your chance to talk to Morris."

"We will find Morris Rose sooner or later."

"I don't doubt that. But sooner is better than later, isn't it?"

"It is. On the other hand, your negotiating position isn't the strongest. I don't believe that you have many other options. I think we both know that you won't return the film to Morris."

Collins had no ready answer. If Collins wasn't going to give Morris the film, and he wasn't, they both knew that Steele represented his first, last, and only resort.

"That's true," Collins said. "But I can always destroy it. Then you still have to hunt down Morris, and you've lost your evidence."

"I see. Well, the truth is that I would like to talk to Morris. It was prudent that you came to see me. We may be able to quietly repair things. The damage to the State Department, and the danger to you, and to your career."

"To me?" Collins didn't get what Steele was driving at—what danger would he face once Steele had the film? He stared at Steele.

"Yes, to you. I doubt that my good friend Fred Longworth would want to continue your employment at the *Sentinel* if you refused to cooperate with the authorities on a subversion case. Would you, if you were in his shoes?"

Steele's threat didn't rattle Collins. The *Sentinel* wasn't the only newspaper in New York. Collins had no intention of turning the documents and film over to Steele without his conditions being met first.

"I can collect unemployment. Will you meet my terms? For Morris and Karina?"

"There have to be some consequences for what's happened," Steele said. "I don't think a Dutch uncle talk with Morris Rose will be quite enough. I can promise that his initial discussion will be with me. From there, it's up to him. If he agrees to disclose all that he knows, if he is willing to work with us, then we can see about making possible accommodations in his case."

"His case? He hasn't been formally charged with anything."

"Let me explain. I'm sorry to have to tell you this way. It's rather abrupt." He paused. "I have been following your friend's career for several years now. We believe that he has been a Soviet agent since 1939 or 1940, working for the First Directorate, collecting and passing sensitive information from the State Department. His liaison with Miss Shoemaker gave him access to the files of the FBI's Counterintelligence Division. The list of agents was quite a find. I can understand why he would want it back from you."

"I don't believe you."

"In his defense, when Rose first started down this road in 1939 he was motivated by idealism. Your friend saw himself as supporting the one force in the world that appeared willing to resist Hitler and the Nazis. And we were allies with the Kremlin for a time during the war, weren't we?"

"It's a betrayal," Collins said. "Soften it all you want, but that is what you are saying."

"In a way, perhaps. But if you look at it from your friend's perspective, it is a matter of conflicting loyalties. Shifting loyalties. Which one has primacy?"

"I don't believe it," Collins said flatly. "Not Morris."

"I get no pleasure from telling you this," Steele said. "I wish it were not so."

"Do you have any proof of this?"

"Proof?" Steele considered the word for a moment. "I guess that depends on your standard of evidence. Miss Shoemaker's testimony would convince most juries, although I doubt she will ever appear in open court. I can assure you that I would not be wasting my time in

New York if this could be chalked up to a simple misunderstanding. And with all due respect, why did you call me if you truly believe Morris is blameless?"

"It's more complicated than I realized. I just saw the documents for the first time yesterday."

"When are you supposed to return the film?"

"Later tonight."

"I see." He paused, considering something. "What if I asked you to go ahead with the meeting and to return the film to your friend?"

"Why would I do that?"

"It's quite simple, actually. So that we could follow him and see who he gives it to. Those are the chaps we have the deeper interest in, the people behind your friend, the ones running the network."

"So I'm to set him up?" Collins asked. "I'm to hand him the film, knowing that he's going to be compromised and ruined. You want me to play the Judas?"

"You are only doing what he asked," Steele said mildly. "What you would have done if you hadn't looked at the documents and if we had never talked. You are returning what he gave you for safekeeping."

"Out of the question. I'll hand over the film and the developed prints right now to you, but I won't set a trap for Morris like that."

Steele shook his head. "I thought you might be bull-headed about this. Here's my offer. If you pass him the film, I will protect Miss Lazda. She can stay in the country, no fear of deportation, no consequences for whatever mischief she has been up to."

Collins stared at Steele. He was being asked to trade Karina for Morris and he could not do that. He could give Steele the film and keep a clear conscience, but he couldn't set up Morris for the fall. The first course of action gave Morris a fighting chance to recover his reputation; the second condemned him to certain arrest and prosecution, no matter what Steele promised.

"I can't accept your offer."

"You do recognize that you are in possession of classified government documents? That's a crime in of itself."

"I'll take my chances. You'll have a hard time proving anything if the film and prints disappear."

Steele nodded in response. "I see. However, there is one other factor you should consider, one that bears on you personally. When you agreed to help your friend, I'm sure you had no idea of the consequences. Like a stone in a pond, the ripples spread. There's no telling how far. Take Miss Lazda, for example. You never would have met her if you had refused to safeguard Rose's film. There have been other ripples. Imagine my surprise when I received a phone call from Penny Bradford asking if I could help a friend of hers."

"You know Penny?" Collins was stunned to learn that Steele had any connection to her.

"We do both live in Washington. I knew her husband. And her brother-in-law, Porter Bradford, happened to be my roommate at Yale. We served in the OSS together. So it was natural for Mrs. Bradford to turn to me."

"What did she tell you?"

"Enough to confirm that you're in well over your head. So you do need my help, as does Mrs. Bradford. I cannot imagine that you would want her drawn into this mess."

"What the hell does that mean?"

"Certainly you must realize that if you end up under closer government scrutiny, Mrs. Bradford will also face questioning. I know that you told her about the film. She had it in her possession for a period of time, did she not? All of that will need to be explained."

Collins tried to gather his thoughts. Penny must have told Steele about the canister. Had he asked her for the film, and had she refused? Collins saw immediately where Steele was headed. Penny's involvement had been accidental, a function only of her relationship with Collins. She had nothing to do with Morris or the loyalty investigation, but Steele was going to use her anyway.

"You wouldn't drag Penny into this," Collins said. "I can't believe that you're that much of a bastard."

"On the contrary, it's your actions that have entangled her. She had nothing to do with this until you involved her. Rashly, I should add. You didn't have to tell her anything."

Collins questioned whether Steele would really implicate Penny, but he couldn't be sure. There was a calculating hardness under the surface of Steele's polished manners and well-modulated voice. Penny's husband had been in the State Department and it wouldn't take much to make it look as if she and her husband and Morris were all part of a diplomatic spy ring.

"I'm not going to do it," Collins said.

"I cannot protect Mrs. Bradford, then. Or Miss Lazda." Steele spread his hands wide. "It's quite simple. Return the film to Rose as originally planned and there will never be any connection made to Mrs. Bradford. You have my word on that."

"And Karina?"

"As I said, assuming she will cooperate, we can protect her."

"And what happens to Morris?"

"If he is willing to assist us after we make the arrests, he will not be prosecuted."

Collins stared at him, trying to mentally calculate the consequences of agreeing. "I don't know whether to believe you. Can you deliver all this?"

"The Justice Department will grant him immunity if Rose helps us. We want to roll up the rest of the network. He is of less consequence to us."

"This is still hard for me to believe. That Morris would become involved with these people."

"He is only the latest symptom of a much deeper disease." He narrowed his eyes, gazing at Collins with renewed intensity. "So my offer is simple. Deliver the film to him. You do a favor for everyone close to you—Miss Lazda, Mrs. Bradford, even, it could be argued, Morris Rose himself. As long as he cooperates, your friend can stay out of jail."

"I don't know that he will," Collins said. "It's not in his nature."

"Then it will be his choice. You will have done all you could."

For a moment they stared at each other. Steele was offering a way out and Collins had to take it. There wasn't any other acceptable choice. Steele's past friendship and connections with the Bradfords meant that he would be more likely to keep his word and protect Penny. Caldwell and his FBI superiors would not be so accommodating. Accepting Steele's offer also meant safe harbor for Karina, Collins told himself. It would mean a fresh start for her.

Collins couldn't see how he could do any better.

"All right. I'm in."

"Capital. Where is the rendezvous?"

"Tonight at Rockefeller Center. At ten o'clock. Karina will be coming with me."

"Fine. You pass him the film and then be on your way. We'll take it from there."

"What about Karina?"

"What about her?"

"Will you have her arrested tonight? I would like some time to talk to her. Time to persuade her to defect."

"I can give you until Saturday morning."

"And if I can't persuade her?"

"We'll arrest her then. She will be quickly deported. We'll find something in her file, something overlooked by the Immigration authorities."

"That's fair," Collins said.

"Miss Lazda must be quite something. There's always a man ready to act as her protector. You're the latest in that chain."

Collins didn't say anything. He didn't care what Steele thought. All Steele knew about Karina came from her file, and that didn't capture who she really was.

Steele reached across the table to hand Collins a business card. "A different number for you to phone after you've made the hand-off. I'll be on the other end. And it goes without saying that you must continue to act as if you believe Rose is being persecuted, and you're helping him prove his innocence."

"Why didn't he just give the film to the Russians if he is what you say he is? Why bother having me hold it?" It was one of the questions that had been bothering Collins.

"I suspect that he doesn't fully trust them. The film is his bargaining chip. He knows they want it badly and consequently they're more likely to take good care of him."

"What a lousy world you people live in."

"Yet when we make promises, we keep them." Steele rose to his feet. "I must make some arrangements for tonight, so you will have to excuse me."

They shook hands, awkwardly, and Collins waited until the elevator doors had closed on Steele before he went back into the conference room. He found the phone and dialed Penny's apartment. She answered, recognizing his voice immediately.

"Dennis," she said. "I was so hoping that you would call. It was awful the way we left each other yesterday."

"Why didn't you tell me about Matthew Steele?"

"Tell you what?"

"That you knew him. That you called him about the situation with Morris. It's the last thing on earth I would have wanted. You never should have involved him."

"I was only trying to help," she said. "To protect you."

"What did you tell him? It's important that I know."

"Only that Morris Rose had asked you to hold some State Department documents and that I suspected that Morris was taking advantage of your good nature. I hoped Matthew could assist you, Dennis."

Collins noticed that she called Steele by his first name. Steele had not given him the impression that they were that friendly. He wondered what else Steele had neglected to tell him.

"Did you offer him the film? Did you tell him that you had it?"

"Not directly. I told him I could get it for him, but only if you would be protected."

"What did he say?"

"He said that wouldn't work. He said that he was more interested in Rose, and those controlling him, than in simply recovering the film. Matthew wanted me to persuade you to help him in that—in finding those men. I told him no. Afterward I realized I had made a mistake in telling him anything."

"You're telling me the truth?"

There was a long silence. "Yes, it is the truth. Why would I lie to you?"

"Why? Because I've had a week full of deception, from you, from Steele, from Morris. I don't know up from down. All I know is that this whole thing is lousy rotten."

"Can you forgive me?"

"I don't know," Collins said.

"I'm not asking because I believe that it would change anything between us. I just don't want you to think that I would ever try to hurt you."

"It's too late for that."

She didn't say anything for a while. Finally, she spoke again.

"I will be returning to Washington. I wanted you to know that."

"Thanks," Collins said. "That's handy to know."

"I don't deserve your sarcasm."

"You don't? What do you deserve, then?"

Collins didn't get an answer to his question, because Penny Bradford hung up the phone on him. The sad thing was, he thought, that he no longer really cared.

Twenty-six

The Club Carousel was already quite crowded by the time Collins arrived. It was Friday night, after all, and the entire block of 52nd Street between Sixth and Fifth Avenues was jammed with excited club-hoppers and jazz-loving tourists, many of them already tight even though it was early in the evening. The neon signs of the better-known jazz clubs—the Onyx, Club Samoa, 3 Deuces, Tony's, and Club Carousel—bathed the street in bright colors, lending the entire scene a garish carnival atmosphere.

Collins found Karina waiting for him inside the Club Carousel's foyer. She had dressed for an evening out: her hair was pulled back, and she wore a belted dark taupe dress that, along with stylish high heels, showed off her slim figure.

Karina greeted him with a kiss and she took both of his hands in hers for a long moment, never taking her eyes from his face. If she wasn't a woman in love, Collins thought, she was a great actress. He had been eager to see her, even though it had only been a few hours since they had parted at the *Sentinel*.

"You look like a million dollars," he told her.

"It's a new dress," she said. "Do you like it? It was a splurge. Isn't that the word?"

"That's the word. You got your money's worth."

Karina certainly wasn't immune to flattery; she was still beaming when they sat down at a corner table and ordered drinks. A piano, bass, and drums trio was jamming along with a sax player. The group had started with a softer sound but Collins knew that the jazz would get louder as the night wore on. For now, it was still possible to have a conversation without shouting, and without being overheard by the next table. The waitress brought them drinks. Collins lit up, adding his cigarette smoke to the cloud already hanging in the air.

308

"We should celebrate," he said. "Tonight we get rid of the albatross Morris stuck around my neck."

"Albatross? I do not understand."

"It's a figure of speech. It's from a poem by Coleridge, the English poet. A sailor shot a friendly albatross, and his shipmates punished him by making him wear the carcass of the bird around his neck."

"How did the sailor get rid of it?"

"Good question. I don't remember that part of the poem. But I know I'm getting rid of this tonight." Collins produced the aluminum film canister from his jacket, showing it to her quickly, before putting it back in his pocket. Before coming uptown, he had retrieved the developed roll of film from its hiding place in the newsroom stairwell.

He kept the canister with the undeveloped film in his right trouser pocket. Somehow having both canisters made him feel more in control of the situation.

"After this is over," she said, "I want to get to know you better. We will have some time, I hope. To know a person, to know their heart and soul, takes time."

"Not too much time in some cases. You should know me by now. I'm not the deepest guy in the world. I guess you'd say I wear my heart on my sleeve."

"Wearing your heart on your sleeve. That is a strange saying. I would like to know your heart, Dennis. I wish I could this very moment."

"That's asking a lot. How well did you get to know Morris?"

She made a face. "I thought you weren't going to ask me about Morris any longer? Are you still jealous?"

"I'm not jealous. I'm curious."

"Morris does not wear his heart on his sleeve," she said. "I never discovered his heart. I know you better now, after these few days, than I ever knew him. He was careful never to show too much of himself."

"I know him better than you, then, I guess," Collins said. "I have seen him in all sorts of different moods. I remember him at a low point, in March and early April of '39. He was angry with himself for not having traveled to Spain and joined up with the International Brigade."

"To fight against Franco."

"Exactly. He was furious with me because I didn't think it was our fight. It wasn't that I didn't support the Republic in principle. Who wouldn't be sympathetic? But I didn't see it the way Morris did. He would talk about workers coming from all over the world to fight with the loyalists and against the Fascists. I thought we had enough problems here in America without taking on somebody else's fight."

"Why did he not go to Spain, then? If he felt so deeply about it."

"I can't say, exactly. Sometime in the middle of the year his mood changed. He wasn't angry any more. He seemed to have accepted the defeat in Spain. I thought he was over it."

Collins understood it differently, now, because Matthew Steele had filled in the missing pieces of the puzzle for him. Morris must have spied for the Soviets as a substitute for volunteering for the Abraham Lincoln Brigade.

"I have never been political," she said. "Not like Morris. I have always been more interested in music and people. Tell me, is Mrs. Bradford political?"

"Penny Bradford? Why do you ask?"

"When I saw you with her at the Stork Club I wondered what kind of a woman she was. You say that you are not jealous about Morris. I will wear my heart on my sleeve. I am jealous of her."

"You shouldn't be," he said.

"She is very beautiful. Lonnie thought you had been in love with her for many years. I can see why a man would want her. I do not like to think of you with her. Do you blame me for being jealous?"

"No," Collins said, telling the truth. "I don't blame you."

"So I am curious about her, just as you are curious about Morris. Does she like music?"

"She does, but popular music. Not opera, I'm afraid. See, you are very different."

"Does she like baseball?"

"Penny? Baseball? Not particularly. Whenever I would take her to the ballpark she would be more interested in the spectators than the game. She would watch all of the fans, observing them like she was Margaret Mead, an anthropologist in the wilds of Brooklyn."

"Margaret Mead studied the Samoans, did she not?"

"That she did," Collins said. "But I would rather hear about you, Karina, than talk about Margaret Mead or Penny Bradford. Tell me, does coming here and hearing the music make you want to sing, to perform?"

"I will answer, if I may ask one more question."

"Fair enough."

"Do you have room in your heart?"

"I think you already know the answer," he said.

"I want to hear you say it."

"There is room in my heart for you, Karina."

"Then I will gladly answer your question. I love to sing. That is different than performing. I performed because it was a small price to pay to spend my life in the manner I wished."

"Do you want to sing in public again?"

"I am not sure."

"When will I get to hear you sing?"

She gave him a radiant smile. "Are you asking me to sing for you?"

"I am. Not here and now. Maybe when we go to the Mohonk. We'll be by ourselves then."

"The Mohonk," she said and wrinkled her nose. "Not a pretty name."

"It's a pretty place, though. You'll see."

"I will not care. We must stay in our room all weekend and sleep late."

They listened to the jazz for a while and then ordered a simple dinner. Collins had a hamburger and a few draft beers and Karina ate a corned beef sandwich. She talked about her work at the Center, about how excited Josef and Hannah had been at knowing they would be going to Yankee Stadium on Saturday. At 9:45 Collins paid the check and they got their coats and left the club.

They walked east down the block to Fifth Avenue, and then headed south to 50th Street. Collins planned for them to walk through Rockefeller Center and then double back to the rendezvous spot. When they reached the entrance to Rockefeller Center, directly across the street from St. Patrick's Cathedral, they stopped before the massive statue of Atlas holding the world (in the form of an armillary sphere) across his shoulders, bent under the weight. Side-by-side they gazed up at the sculpture.

"When it was first unveiled people thought it looked too much like Mussolini," Collins told her. "Some of the anti-Fascists picketed it."

Karina peered at the statute. "It does look like Mussolini," she said. "Just a little bit."

"So you think Atlas looks Italian? Hell, then it could be Joe DiMaggio or Ezio Pinza."

"You're laughing at me."

"Just a little."

They strolled through the Center and then cut back to 50th Street by the Associated Press building. There, at five minutes before ten, they took up their station under the clock. Collins found his Zippo and lit another Chesterfield. He took a quick puff, before handing it to Karina. Then he lit another for himself.

They didn't have to wait long. At the appointed time Morris Rose came strolling up the street from the west, a minute or so before the hour. He carried a rolled-up newspaper in his right hand, and an umbrella in his left. He walked past them and then about fifty feet or so from where they were standing, he stopped and peered into the windows of a storefront, pretending to be looking at something. A minute later Morris turned and slowly walked back towards them. Collins stepped on his cigarette to extinguish it. His hand strayed to his overcoat pocket where he had moved the film canister.

Morris stopped and greeted them. For a man supposedly on the run, Morris didn't look any worse for the wear, Collins thought. He was well-dressed, as always. Collins noticed that he was wearing expensive leather gloves.

"Hello, Karina," Morris said. Collins watched Karina's face carefully when she responded, but he saw no trace of emotion, nothing to suggest there was anything between them.

"Sorry you've had to deal with Hoover's thugs," Morris said to Collins. "But that's over, now. I should have the situation resolved by early next week. Clean bill of health. Loyal American."

"Glad to hear that."

"Some pennant race, huh?"

"What?"

"The pennant race. The Cards lost today. That puts us up by a game with two to go. The Yanks lost and it looks like they're finished. They would have to sweep the Sox tomorrow and Sunday to win the pennant."

"It is quite a race," Collins said, trying to keep the irritation he felt out of his voice at Morris playing the part of the carefree baseball fan. "I didn't figure that you'd have the time to follow it."

Morris gave a heavy sigh. "Right now I have all the time in the world. I've been staying with a friend and listening to as many of the games as I can. I hope that the Dodgers beat St. Louis. They're a bunch of bigots, you know. Enos Slaughter is the worst. Remember when he spiked Robinson?"

"I remember," Collins said. Slaughter had tried to injure Jackie Robinson when he broke into the league in 1947, deliberately spiking him in a game in St. Louis. Robinson had not retaliated, under orders from Branch Rickey not to respond.

"It turned my stomach when they brought Robinson to Washington this summer to bad mouth Paul Robeson in front of Congress," Morris said. "I had hoped he would stand up to those fascist bullies."

"Robeson was over the line, suggesting that Negroes wouldn't fight for the country if we went to war with the Soviets," Collins said.

"And Robinson's a ballplayer, for Christ's sake, not a politician. What do you expect, Morris?"

"I don't know. I guess I shouldn't expect too much for anyone."

"No," Karina said quickly. She had been silent up to that point, holding tightly onto Collins' arm. "You can be surprised by what people will do."

"Perhaps," Morris said. "But not these days. We Americans are decadent, Karina, can't you see that? The rest of the world can go to hell and we wouldn't care as long as we have our movies and our baseball."

"I am learning about baseball," she said. "Dennis is teaching me."

"I'll bet he is," Morris said and Collins didn't like the way he said it. Judging from her face, Karina didn't either.

"Dennis is a gentleman," she said. "He is all that you said he was."

"I'm his biggest fan. Always have been."

"Can I give you what we came here for?" Collins asked. He was impatient to complete the hand-off.

"Sure. Be my guest."

Collins hesitated and then found himself reaching into his trouser pocket for the canister with the blank roll of film. He realized, at that moment, that he couldn't give Morris the developed roll of film. He wondered how angry Steele would be when he discovered that Collins had not delivered the incriminating film to Morris. Collins would have to find some other way to protect Penny and Karina.

Collins extended his right hand towards Morris, the canister in his palm. "Here. I'm glad to get rid of it."

Before Morris could respond, Karina reached over and pulled Collins' arm away. Collins turned to her in surprise, not quite sure what she was doing.

"Please move away from him, Dennis," she said quietly.

"What did you say?" Collins asked, not quite sure what she meant.

"Move away from me," Morris said. "She has a gun." He said it matter-of-factly, as if he was noting that Karina had a pocketbook, not a pistol, in her right hand. When Collins glanced over he saw that Karina was indeed pointing a gun—with its muzzle directed at Morris. It was a small Colt revolver with a snub-nose barrel. Collins stepped away from Morris, as Karina had directed.

"You cannot give him the film," she said to Collins. "Under no circumstances can he have the film."

Collins carefully held the film canister up so she could see it, and then made a show of slowly putting it back in his pocket. She kept the gun trained on Morris and took her eyes off him for only a moment.

"I've put it away," Collins said. "Can you put the gun down?"

"What is this all about?" Morris asked. "Karina, what are you doing?"

She didn't answer Morris' question. "Do you remember who Morris said he was staying with in New York?" she asked Collins.

"A friend."

"His friend's name is Anatoli Yatov. He is the *rezident* for Moscow Center in New York. The man who gives Morris his orders."

"That's crazy," Morris said.

"It is the truth. If Dennis knew who you were, Morris, and what you really stand for, he would never give you that film. Never."

"She is not well," Morris said to Collins, keeping his voice low. "I think it's the strain of coming here to New York, and the overwork. She has been through too much. She is imagining things."

"I am not imagining who you are. Who you have become. We work for the same master, after all." She turned slightly towards Collins without altering the direction of the gun. "You must believe me, Dennis. I am sorry. I wanted to tell you earlier, but I kept hoping I would not have to. He must not have the film. We cannot let it happen."

Collins didn't know what to say. He was totally unprepared for Karina's sudden disruption of the planned hand-off. For his part, Morris wasn't ready to leave the rendezvous empty-handed. He ignored Karina and spoke to Collins directly.

"Denny, you've known me since we were kids. This is absurd. Do you really think I could be a Russian spy? I don't know what game she is playing. Maybe the FBI is forcing her to do this to keep from being deported. But just listen to her. What she is saying is crazy."

"Then let us take the film to the police," Karina said. "Or to someone you trust, Dennis. Let them develop the film and then decide who is telling the truth."

"I don't want anyone getting shot," Collins said. "Karina, will you let Morris leave here if I promise I won't give him the film until after you and I have talked?"

Collins smiled at her, trying to reassure her, to get her to relax. As tense and jumpy as Karina was, Collins worried that she might shoot Morris by accident. Her finger was still on the trigger. "You can explain all of this to me in a calmer environment."

"Then what?" Morris asked. It was clear that he didn't like Collins' proposed solution. "What about me? I need that film to prove my innocence. I told you that when I gave it to you. That hasn't changed one iota. No doubt she's working for the FBI. She's out to set me up. Can't you see that?"

"We can't resolve this now. Not under these circumstances. Let me hear Karina out. Call me later tonight at my apartment. We'll figure out something in the meantime."

"I need the film."

"Well, I can't give it to you." Collins motioned to Karina with his right hand; she had not wavered—the Colt had remained pointed directly at Morris' midsection. "I don't want to see you shot."

"Are you sleeping with her? Is that it?"

"What does that have to do with anything?"

"Everything. You're taking her side, believing her crazy story." Morris made no effort to hide his anger.

"You're wrong. I'm not taking anyone's side. I just don't want anyone hurt. It's best if you leave now and let me sort this out."

Morris shrugged. "You wouldn't be the first man fooled by her," he said. "Nor, I suspect, the last. It would turn your stomach to know whose beds she has crawled into. But I will let you figure that out for yourself. " He took a step back, his eyes still on Collins. "I will call you later tonight. I'm counting on your help."

Collins nodded, keeping a watchful eye on Karina. She kept the gun pointed at Morris as he retreated. Morris walked slowly up the street towards Fifth Avenue, the rolled-up newspaper now clutched in his left hand. Collins wondered whether it was a signal of some sort. Once he was out of sight, Karina spoke.

"I will take the film, now," she said.

"Are you willing to shoot me if I won't give it to you?"

"I must have the film. It must be destroyed."

"How can I give it to you? After what you just told me? You're one of them."

"One of them?"

"Agents. Operatives. Whatever you call yourself."

"I was. But no longer. Not after tonight. I must destroy the film so that it can never fall into their hands."

"I can't give you the film," Collins said. "But I will listen to your explanation, like I said I would. Where did you get the gun?"

"That is not important. We must leave this place immediately. Yatov will send his men after us when he learns that Morris didn't get the film."

Collins nodded, knowing that he had to follow her lead. They walked rapidly away from Rockefeller Center, moving uptown two blocks and then heading west on 56th Street. Karina kept glancing back over her shoulder. She pulled Collins into a drab coffee shop near Broadway.

"We will wait here," she said. "For a few minutes. I must think."

They sat down in the booth and the lone night-waitress on duty poured their cups of coffee. When Karina tried to spoon some sugar into her coffee, her hands trembled so violently that she spilled some of it on the table. Collins had seen the unsettling effects of adrenaline before on soldiers and cops and firefighters when it set in after the danger had passed. He took both of her hands into his, enveloping them completely in his larger hands, until the shaking stopped. She smiled wanly at him.

"What are you doing?" he asked gently. "What has gotten into you?"

"You must believe me," she said. She pulled her hands away. "Why would I lie to you about this? How could it benefit me?"

"I don't know," Collins said. He wanted to hear more from her. He had to be sure of her reasons for preventing the hand-off to Morris. "Why are you so eager to keep the film from Morris? Are you working for the FBI like he says?"

She shook her head violently. "No. I do this not because I am forced to but because I must. I never expected that I would be granted another chance to set things right, but I have, and I will not squander it." She sighed. "Do you know this Mr. E. B. White?"

"I've read some of his articles," Collins said, not sure what Karina was driving at. E.B. White wrote for the *New Yorker* and had written a best-selling children's book. Collins couldn't see where there would be any connection to the evening's events.

"He is a great writer," she said. She fished in her purse for a moment and found a folded piece of paper. She opened it carefully, almost reverently, and Collins could see there was something written on it. She handed it to him.

"Please read this," she said. "So you will understand why I do this. Why I do what I must, now."

He read it slowly, pausing when he reached the last paragraph:

All dwellers in cities must live with the stubborn fact of annihilation; in New York the fact is somewhat more concentrated because of the concentration of the city itself, and because, of all targets, New York has a certain clear priority. In the mind of whatever perverted dreamer might loose the lightning, New York must hold a steady, irresistible charm.

"I copied this from his book, *Here is New York*, only this week," she said. "When I read this I knew that I could never do what Morris wanted me to. Not when I knew that they now had the atomic bomb. Before that I thought I could. It was not much, was it? A small price to start a new life here. All I had to do was make sure you arrived on time and gave Morris his film. Such a simple thing."

She shifted in her chair. "I bring the writing with me so that I do not weaken. I have loved this city. All the people, living here so happily. How could I participate in any way in its destruction? I agreed to work for them out of selfishness. I never believed, not like Morris. It was only to escape. Now I don't care anymore. They can send me back, but I cannot do what they ask."

Karina had made things immensely more complicated, Collins thought. He would need to talk to Matthew Steele and that meant he would have to tell her some portion of the truth.

"I believe you," he said.

"I wanted to tell you earlier," she said. "I almost did, this morning and when I met you in the lobby at the newspaper. I lost my courage. I thought you would turn away from me once you knew."

"I will not turn away. What is more, I know someone who can help us. I told you that government officials had been asking questions. One of them, who is with our Central Intelligence Agency, approached me earlier this week. He warned me that Morris had been compromised, that he was being controlled by the Russians. He will know what to do."

"Are you also with the CIA?" she asked, suddenly wary. "Do you work for them?"

"No, of course not. I'm a newspaperman, nothing more and nothing less. I've just become entangled in this because of Morris. This man from the CIA told me that you might be involved with the Russians. If you were, I was going to try to persuade you to defect. So he knows about you. I should phone him now so he can arrange a safe place for you."

He could see the hesitation on her face. It was her turn to be surprised and disoriented. Karina had never considered that Collins might have his own secrets, that he might be withholding something from her.

She slowly nodded, accepting the changed reality. "You can call your CIA man from my apartment," she said. "We will be safe there. Yatov and Morris believe that I live at the Hotel Marseilles."

Collins paid the bill and they found a cab to take them uptown to Karina's apartment. They hurried upstairs and Collins called Steele from her phone. Steele answered after the first ring. Collins didn't bother to identify himself—he knew Steele had been expecting his call for quite some time.

"What happened?" Steele asked. "Did Rose take the film?"

"He doesn't have it. Something unexpected happened. Karina Lazda stopped the exchange. She didn't want the Russians to have the film and she felt strongly enough about it that she pulled a gun on us."

"Is that so? She stopped the proceedings?" Steele paused. "What on earth got into her?"

"She won't work for them any longer."

"And she decided that tonight, in the middle of your hand-off? Bad show, that."

"She says she has been under the control of a man named Yatov, and that he has also been the handler for Morris."

"Anatoli Yatov," Steele said. "Quite a nasty individual."

"You'll need to protect her. I'm sure they will come looking for her. Where can we meet you?"

"Slow down. Let me think this through." There was a long pause. "Do you have the film? Or does she?"

"I still have it."

"Very well. How did Morris react when Miss Lazda pulled the gun on him?"

"He was angry, said she was unbalanced. He desperately needs the film, that was very clear."

"And how did you feel? Still fond feelings for Miss Lazda?"

Collins looked over at Karina.

"I'm here in her apartment. Fonder, I guess. She's pretty damn courageous. She wants to make a break, and she didn't want the film in Morris' hands."

"All is not lost," Steele said. "We can perhaps still salvage the situation. Let's make the assumption that Morris will still want to recover the film. He will try to obtain it from you, and you can still give it to him, albeit somewhat reluctantly."

"What about Karina?"

"You can tell Morris that you don't trust her, that her story is too wild. You think she's troubled, unstable. You're ready and willing to give him the film so that he can prove his innocence."

"Will he believe that?"

"It's worth the old college try, isn't it? He'll want to believe it."

"Whether or not he believes me, Karina still needs to be protected."

"I can arrange something for Miss Lazda, but not until tomorrow. Can you stay where you are now, safely?"

"I don't know." Collins turned to Karina, covering the phone mouthpiece with his hand. "Does anyone at the Center know where you live?"

"Only one person, and she is vacationing this week. And Freda, the woman who rented me the apartment, is in France."

"Is she connected to the Russians?"

Karina shook her head. "No. We should be safe here for the time being."

Collins relayed that to Steele, and he agreed that they should stay put. Steele suggested a meeting the next morning at seven in the Carlyle Hotel's coffee shop.

"It's not the sort of spot where Soviet agents are apt to congregate," he said. "I think our little tête-à-tête will be uninterrupted. Tell Miss Lazda not to worry."

Collins thanked Steele and was surprised when he laughed.

"Don't thank me, old chap. I'm only doing my job."

After Collins hung up, Karina crossed the room and hugged him. They didn't let go of each other as they moved into her bedroom. They made love then with an intensity born of the anxiety and fear they were both feeling.

Collins had always thought that danger heightened the desire for sex. Didn't the act serve as an affirmation of life? During the war he had often heard that same theory, or variations of it, from soldiers and Marines as they recounted their conquests. He remembered one Marine sergeant who claimed most Navy nurses were willing bedpartners because of all the death they had to see. They couldn't help but be drawn to the one act, the one affirmation, that somehow canceled out the horror.

There was no holding back with Karina. They clung to each other, defenseless in their nakedness, aware that they had crossed over a threshold. Afterward, they lay together, silent, sharing a cigarette, lost in their own thoughts.

"Dennis," she said. "I wish to say something."

"Say it, then."

"If something should happen, so that we are lost to each other, then you must promise me something."

"Don't talk like that. We're going to get through this just fine."

"I did not expect this to happen," she said. "With you. I had been reconciled to being alone, and then you appeared. I am glad because now there is someone who can keep me somewhere in his heart. There is no one else in the world who can, no one else left for me. Everyone else is gone. So you must promise me this."

"There's no need for that."

"Promise me," she said, fiercely.

"It will all work out."

"Promise that you will keep me in your heart."

"All right. I promise."

"Thank you," she said.

They had finished the last of his Chesterfields. As Collins lay there, he thought about what Morris and the Russians would be doing. They would look for Collins and Karina by stopping at Collins' apartment first, because that was where he had told Morris to call. When they realized Collins wasn't there, most likely they would try the Hotel Marseilles.

He realized that Morris would be clever enough to invent an emergency and get Karina's home address, if it was at all possible. If Karina was wrong, and someone else at the Center knew about the apartment, they weren't safe. Collins cursed out loud at the thought. They couldn't risk staying where they were.

"What is the matter?" she asked.

"I've been a fool," Collins said. "I don't think we are safe, here. Someone at the Center might know that you live here. We can't take the chance. Please, you must get dressed and pack a bag. We'll stay at a hotel tonight."

He got out of bed and pulled his clothes on. "I'll go find a cab," he said. "I may have to walk over to Broadway this time of night. Wait by the mailboxes, in the front foyer. I'll have the cabbie honk the horn."

"Let me come with you."

"Pack," Collins said. "I'll go ahead. Wait for me inside, and stay out of sight."

A block from the apartment, still hunting for a taxi cab, Collins heard what sounded like the cry of a woman in the distance. Then the sound stopped. He turned around, worried, and when he looked back he could see a dark sedan parked in front of Karina's apartment. Collins began sprinting back to her place, and when he was half-a-block away, he saw the sedan's left back door ajar and two men pushing a woman, Karina, into the car.

One of the men slammed the door shut and jumped into the front of the car. Collins was fifty yards away when the vehicle pulled out from the curb and roared away up the street. Collins thought for a moment of running after the car, but then thought better of it. He was outnumbered and the men might be carrying weapons.

Collins realized he should have tried to memorize the license plate number of the sedan, but it had already disappeared into the darkness. He backed away, moving down the street away from her apartment. There might be additional Russians waiting for him inside, and Collins couldn't chance that. He still had the film canister in his suit coat pocket.

He walked briskly away from Karina's street until he found a pay phone in a nearby all-night laundromat and called Steele.

"It's Collins," he began. "Yatov's men took Karina while I was out looking for a taxi. They somehow found out where she lives."

"How many men?"

"I'm not sure. Two men pushed her into a car."

"Where did this happen?"

Collins gave him the address.

"Where are you now?"

"At a pay phone near her place. I'm not going to risk going back to her apartment, or to mine."

"You still have the film?"

"Yes, I have it on me. What do we do now? Call the police?"

"That would accomplish nothing. Needle in a haystack. Why don't you come here? You can stay here with me overnight. It's quite secure here."

"No," Collins said. "I have a place I can go where I'll be safe. Morris will try to contact me once they realize Karina doesn't have the film. He'll call me at the paper in the morning. I'll try trading the film for Karina, then. One for the other."

"I'm sorry, but you may not get the chance. Their discipline is quite severe. Their modus operandi is to liquidate agents who double on them."

Collins felt a sinking feeling in the pit of his stomach. He didn't want to believe what Steele was telling him.

"You think they will kill her? Just like that?"

"We must be realistic. Anatoli Yatov is hardly sentimental, and Miss Lazda has become a liability. He knows that word of her attempted defection won't go over too well with Moscow Center. Better to report that she was quickly eliminated after a thorough interrogation."

His scalp and face began to tingle and Collins recognized the symptoms—he had experienced the same feeling in the Pacific when he came under mortar fire the first time. There was no physical danger, now, only a growing dread about what might have happened to Karina. It was his fault, too, he thought. While they had made love in her bedroom, Yatov and his men had been closing in on them. He cursed his own stupidity and carelessness, placing Karina in harm's way.

"They won't get the film if Karina is killed," Collins said. "I will burn it."

Steele waited before he spoke. Then the words came slowly, reluctantly. "That would be a waste. The film will give us Rose, and Yatov. If you want to avenge Karina, what better way than to shut down their New York operations?"

"God damn you, Steele, we don't know that she's dead. Don't talk about avenging her."

"My apologies. Nevertheless, as long as they take possession of the film, we can arrest them. You will know when Rose calls you for the film; if he is willing to trade, then it's possible that she is alive."

"Possible? If he's trading, she's alive!"

"If Yatov thinks the only way to obtain the film is to give you Karina, he will have Morris agree to a deal whether or not he can follow through on his end."

"Then I'll demand proof. If they want the film, they have to give me Karina first."

"Good luck, then. In any case, call me when you hear from them."

"I will," Collins promised. "I will."

Saturday, October 1

She had tried to resist when they came for her in the vestibule of her apartment, but there were two of them and they were too strong. She never had a chance to reach the revolver, tucked away in her suitcase, left behind when they dragged her to the waiting car. One of them slapped her across the face with the back of his hand when she cried out and she stopped struggling, stunned by the sudden violence.

After they had forced into the sedan, they gagged her and pushed her onto the floor of the sedan. One of them sat in the back seat and kept his foot on her back, pressing it down so that at times it hurt her to breathe. She wondered whether Dennis would realize what had happened. She lay there, helpless, as the car accelerated up the street.

The men spoke to each other briefly in Russian and she thought she heard one say something about returning to the house. They didn't say anything more and all she could hear was the sounds of the passing traffic.

When the car stopped, the two men pulled her out of the car and to her feet. It was too dark for her to see where she was. She was handled roughly by the men as she was brought into a building on the ground floor.

They took her to a small room with a wooden table and two chairs. The only illumination came from a single light bulb. They forced her down into one of the chairs. When she looked up, she found Morris and Anatoli Yatov standing there, waiting. Morris would not look directly at her.

One of the men removed the gag from her mouth. Yatov walked up to her and hit her twice in the face with an open-handed slap. She tasted blood in her mouth and her cheeks stung from the blows. Then he hit her again, just as hard, this time with his fist, catching her on her cheekbone and momentarily rocking her head backward and stunning her. Yatov remained standing over her, glowering at her.

"Where is the film?" he asked.

"I don't have it," she said, still dazed from the punch.

"Who does? Does the newspaperman have it?"

She hesitated and Morris spoke up. "Dennis Collins still must have it," he said. "They are lovers. That gives us leverage. He will trade us the film in exchange for her."

"Do you think so?" she asked Morris. "Now that Dennis knows who you really are? I think not."

"He will. I know him. You don't."

Yatov had been watching the interplay between them. He turned to Morris. "You must make contact with him then and retrieve the film." He glanced over at Karina and grunted slightly. "Whore," he said and spit into her face. Then he turned on his heel and left the room, trailed by the two men.

She was left alone with Morris. He handed her his handkerchief so she could wipe the spittle from her face. "What were you thinking?" he asked. "Have you lost your mind?"

"I could not let you help them," she said. She fought back tears. "Don't you see? They are wolves in human form. All of them. This was my chance for redemption, for atonement. I closed my eyes when I was with Piotr to what was happening in Warsaw. I will not make the same mistake. Don't you see?"

He shook his head. "I don't see. You can waste your life in some stupidly heroic gesture, but you cannot throw mine away. I won't let you. You know what happens if you cross them. Look at Walter Krivitsky and Juliet Poyntz. I have no wish to fall out of a hotel window or have a mysterious heart attack." He grimaced. "You've made a total mess of everything. God help you if Denny doesn't give me the film, because I can't be held responsible for what might happen."

"I hope he refuses," she said. "Whatever it is on that film should be kept from them. You must know that. It's not too late for you to do the right thing."

"The right thing? You don't know what you are talking about. What I am doing is necessary." Morris went to the door. "You will be locked in," he said. "If you make any noise they will come in and hurt you. You don't want that. I will call Dennis at the newspaper in the morning and we'll see if I can repair the damage that you've done."

He shook his head. "It shouldn't have come to this, but you've backed me into a corner. Yatov had already informed his superiors in the First Directorate that I had obtained something of great value. I must deliver it, now."

He ran his right hand through his hair, a nervous gesture she remembered from their time together. His handsome features were drawn and tight.

"If you do this, there is no going back," she said.

"Do you think I don't know that? I've spent the better part of the last week thinking about how to escape from this trap. If there was another way, I would take it. But there isn't and I understand that, now. It's become very simple. There is only one path for me and I will take it."

Morris left the room, closing the door firmly behind him. She heard him turn the key in the lock.

Now that she was alone she felt less sure of herself. She had told Morris that she didn't want Dennis to hand over the film, but she wanted to live. Anatoli Yatov's anger had terrified her; she knew that she could expect no mercy from him or his men. Even if Morris was willing to intervene on her behalf, she could see that he had little, if any, influence on Yatov.

She told herself that she should not feel guilty about wanting to live. She had tried her best and she had failed. It was that simple. What more could she do? Now she only wanted to salvage what she could: a chance to fashion a quiet life with Dennis. Perhaps that was selfish, but Morris was right, the time for heroic gestures was over.

She found herself crying. She blinked back the tears and closed her eyes and pictured Dennis, with his slightly crooked smile, and the way he looked at her before he kissed her. She longed for his presence.

She wished he was there, whispering something reassuring to her. Just thinking about him comforted her.

She knew that the course of anyone's life could not be predicted, nor directed. She had learned that. There was nothing to do now but to accept what might happen in the hours ahead. She tried to think of what the future could be with Dennis. As long as she could hold onto that idea, she had hope. There had to be a reason why they had been brought together. Was it fate, or destiny, or whatever name people gave to the mysterious force that animated things? She didn't know.

She feared that she didn't deserve him, but she would cling to him for as long as she could. What else could a woman in love do?

Why hadn't she said something to him earlier? She had been ready to, in the lobby of the newspaper, but something held her back at the last moment. If only she had been stronger then, or when they were together alone in her apartment, it might have all turned out differently, for the better. They wouldn't have gone to meet with Morris, and Dennis would have found a way to protect her from Yatov. But she hadn't, and now she would face the consequences of her weakness.

Twenty-seven

In the hours that followed Karina's abduction, Collins realized how powerless he was. He had no idea where she had been taken. All he had was the film. He would have to wait for Morris to contact him, and hope that the Russians didn't deal with Karina as Steele thought they might.

He needed a place where he could think things through and catch some sleep. He took a cab down to Herald Square and walked over to Killeen's on West 35th Street, where he figured he could go to ground. Anyone looking for Collins would be more likely to start at the Stork Club or 21 and then maybe try Bleeck's or Gough's, known watering-holes for reporters and editors, but not Killeen's, which didn't attract a newspaper crowd.

He decided that he would wait until the *Sentinel*'s night crew had completely cleared out and then he would go to the newspaper and catch some sleep in one of the newsroom's empty offices. In the meantime, Killeen's would be his sanctuary—if a shabby beer-and-shot place was worthy of such a designation.

Once there, Collins sat at a table in the back where he could see the front door. He kept his back slightly turned away from the bar to signal that he wasn't looking for companionship or conversation. He nursed a warm beer, trying to sort things out. Someone had put Frank Sinatra's version of "All the Things You Are." Collins remembered when Tommy Dorsey first recorded it, back in 1940, but that seemed ages ago, now, ancient history, before Pearl Harbor, in a more innocent time.

Collins drank his beer slowly. He couldn't afford to be hung over or sloppy in the morning, when he figured Morris would try to contact him. At 2 AM, he decided it was time to finish the night at the *Sentinel*. He walked through the darkened and near-empty streets at a rapid pace and arrived in the *Sentinel* newsroom in less than five minutes. Collins knew there was only one late watch editor on Saturday duty, a young guy named Farkas, who must have stepped out for coffee, because the room was deserted.

Collins tried sleeping in Peter Vandercamp's office, on his short couch, but he didn't have much luck. He was still tense from the evening's events. He found himself picturing Karina's face as they sat in the coffee shop and she told him her reasons for taking her life in her hands. She had hungered for redemption, he thought, and resisting Anatoli Yatov and Morris must have seemed like a good place to start. This was America, after all, the place where everyone started over. Why not Karina? Why not get it right this time?

He went to the men's room and washed his face and hands, staring at his image in the large mirror over the sink. His face had a strange half-raccoon-like look with his black eye now fading into a greenish-gray. At least his rib wasn't aching, he told himself.

Collins wandered back into the newsroom and sat down at his desk and tried to write his Sunday column. Anything to keep his mind occupied. At six o'clock, when some of the dayside crew straggled in, he sent one of the copy boys out to get the early papers. He sat near the back of the room, away from the entrance, where he could exit down the back stairway if need be. He scanned the *Times*, *Herald Tribune* and *Daily News*, looking for any crime stories, shootings or stabbings that involved young women. Nothing. It didn't mean that Karina was alive, he knew, but it gave him hope somehow, nonetheless.

The front pages of all of the papers carried bad news. The national steel strike had started as 500,000 steelworkers walked off the job. The Chinese Communists had named Mao Tse-tung the leader of the new People's Republic of China.

The tabloids were crowded with details of the "battle of El Morocco" court case. They all carried photos of Bogart, surrounded by fans, and of the model, Robin Roberts, dressed in a velvet suit with rabbit trim, in front of the Mid-Manhattan Court. In the end, Bogart had walked free, with the magistrate concluding that he had acted in self-defense.

The sports pages were filled with speculation about the weekend series for the Dodgers and the Yanks. The Brooks were in great shape—a full game lead over the Cards. A confident Burt Shotton had talked to the beat writers just before the Dodgers took a late train to Philadelphia on Friday night. It was a completely different story in the Yankees clubhouse after their loss to the Athletics. Casey Stengel was putting up a brave front, but the players were down and appeared whipped. They knew they had to beat Boston twice to win the pennant. A loss would end their season. According to the papers Joe DiMaggio had worked out again at the Stadium and Stengel said he hoped to play him on Saturday.

The phone on Collins desk rang, drawing him away from the sports pages. He picked it up on the second ring.

"Hey, Denny."

Collins knew immediately it was Morris. "What the hell is going on?" he asked.

"You tell me. I tried you repeatedly at your place last night. The phone just kept ringing."

"I was out," Collins said. He wondered for a moment what would have happened if Morris had reached him at home. Would his friend have tipped off Yatov that Collins was there? Would they have come for him? Collins found it surprisingly easy to suspect the worst.

"I hope you don't believe any of Karina's crazy talk," Morris said. He sounded calm. It was as if they were discussing some trivial personal quarrel and Morris was trying to set things right. "Someone from the government must be threatening to deport her unless she lies about me. That's the only explanation that makes sense."

Morris had used the present tense in describing Karina, which gave Collins sudden hope. "Do you have her?"

"Do I have her? What do you mean?"

"Karina was taken from her apartment last night. Forced into a car. I am assuming that it was on the orders of your friend Anatoli Yatov."

Morris didn't respond. Collins waited, letting the silence grow. Finally, Morris spoke. "Look, I'm in a bad place, Denny. I was supposed to have the film. A lot depends on that. You have to help me out."

"What about Karina?" He was intent on making Morris answer the question.

"This is an open telephone line. Anybody could be listening."

"We'll have to take that chance, then. Is she still alive? Do they have her?" Morris had to recognize that he couldn't bluff Collins. Any trust he had in his friend was long gone.

"I need the film. It's even more important that I get it back."

"You haven't answered me about Karina. If you want the film, then you have to tell me about her."

"If I could satisfy your curiosity about that matter, could we arrange for another hand-off?"

"I want her freed."

"Is that what you want?" Morris didn't sound happy at the idea of Collins making demands. Collins didn't care. He held the proverbial hole card—no Karina, no film—and he was determined to play it.

"It's become very simple, actually. I have something that you want. You can't get it until I get what I want."

Morris sighed. Collins could picture him frowning, his handsome face creasing around the eyes. "What happened last night was a horrible mistake. I can't believe that Karina reacted the way she did. Now I have to have the film."

"Then we trade for it. It's your choice. I don't know why the damn film is so valuable, and I don't want to know, but I want Karina released."

Collins remembered how Steele had counseled him on Friday not to resist handing the canister over to Morris. Now Collins couldn't surrender the film without Morris convincing him that Karina would be freed. He could see the irony in the turn-about, but he just couldn't appreciate it with so much at stake.

"There's nothing on the film that can hurt anybody," Morris said. "It's paperwork, stupid bureaucratic paperwork. Somebody on this side thinks it's important. One bunch of bureaucrats concerned about another bunch of bureaucrats. It's no different the world over, but the rest of us have to play their games."

"It should be worth Karina to them. And I'll need to talk to her on the phone before any trade."

"I see," Morris said. "Look, I can't make that decision by myself. I will have to call you back."

After hanging up, Collins exhaled slowly, his spirits suddenly lifted. It seemed clear that Karina was alive. He had to hope that Yatov would be willing to exchange her for the film. Collins didn't want to get ahead of himself, but things were looking better.

The phone rang. He jumped, startled, and picked up the receiver.

"What did he say?" Collins immediately asked.

"Dennis?" It wasn't Morris, it was Peter Vandercamp.

Collins wanted to curse: Van was calling at the worst time possible.

"Hello, Van," he said. "Sorry, thought it someone else."

"Are you going to Philly today?" Vandercamp asked. "For the game?"

"I can't," Collins said. "I'm working on something else." He would have to get Vandercamp off the phone as quickly as he could. He didn't want Morris to encounter a busy signal.

"Then we need to talk," Vandercamp said. "Can you see me first thing when I come in?"

"Can it wait until tomorrow?"

"I'm afraid not."

"When will you be here, then?"

"The regular time. Can you wait for me?"

"Sure," Collins said.

Then the phone sat silent on his desk for an interminable, grim hour. Collins worked on his Sunday column, trying hard to focus, but glancing over at the phone every other sentence, willing it to ring. Finally, while Collins was still on his first page of copy, it rang and Collins picked it up before the second ring.

"I have your answer," Morris said.

"What is it?"

"The trade is acceptable, but only after I have the film back. She will be released an hour later."

"That won't do. We make the exchange at the same time. Karina comes with you to the hand-off. I give you the film only after she is with me."

"I'm not completely surprised. I told Bob that you wouldn't go for the first idea."

"I won't. I don't trust him, whether his name is Bob or Anatoli." Collins didn't need to say that he didn't trust Morris either.

"Okay, we'll do it your way, then. Karina comes with me to the rendezvous. I turn her over and you give me the film. That's the deal."

"The Russians will agree to this?"

"Yes."

"I have your word on that?"

"You have my word."

"Why, Morris?" Collins asked. "Why did you have me hold the film? Why did you involve me?"

"Simple. There was no one else I could trust. You might not believe this, but I was ready to end my association with Bob. The departmental memos on the film showed that I hadn't done anything wrong in my dealings overseas. I had a fighting chance at keeping my job."

"What good are the memos to you now? You're not going to clear yourself with them."

There was another long pause, and then Morris spoke again. "There is something else on the film. Information I can trade. An insurance policy, you could say."

"I can't believe you're doing this. How can you?"

"How can I? How can I not? 'Their open eyes could see no other way.' Have you ever read that poem, Denny? I had my eyes opened when Franco marched into Barcelona and butchered the last of the Republicans and the so-called democracies did nothing to stop it. After that I could see no other way. Why did I agree to help the only people in the world willing to fight Franco and Hitler and the other dictators? The only force for the rights of the working class, for the Negroes, for the downtrodden and forgotten. Is that your question?"

"That's not my question. I'm not questioning your desire for justice. I'm wondering why this is the way you chose. Why would you ever consent to spy for them?"

"It wasn't like that at all." There was no apology in Morris' voice.

"It wasn't? That's the way it looks to me. Passing information to the Soviets? That isn't a betrayal?"

"They were our allies," Morris said. "All through the war. We were happy with our Russian comrades when they stopped Hitler at Stalingrad and decimated his army in Belorussia. We didn't object, or question anyone's politics, when millions of Russians were fighting and dying to stop the Nazis. But the minute the right-wingers in Congress decide they need a new enemy, then it becomes subversion, treason, to keep helping."

"Can you hear yourself? You have all these elaborate justifications for doing something that you know is wrong. But I'm not going to argue with you. We've talked long enough. There's one last condition. I need to talk to Karina on the phone. I need that before I agree."

"Fine," he said. "We anticipated that. She will call you later. Stay at your desk. We make the exchange tonight. Remember where we went the night before you shipped out to the Pacific? The last place? Meet me there at nine o'clock. You must come alone. No police. No FBI."

Collins knew immediately the spot where Morris wanted to rendezvous. They had spent that last night before Collins shipped off to the Pacific drinking in a series of bars, and they ended up on the

Lower East Side, by the Al Smith housing project, sitting on a bench near the Brooklyn Bridge. It had been just the two of them. It was ideal for Morris' purposes—relatively deserted, with open sight lines where he could see anyone coming or going. And it was dark there, with few streetlights.

"I'll be there," Collins said. "You have to come alone. Just you and Karina. Yatov and his men can't be there."

"They won't. Just me."

Collins marveled at how fluently Morris lied. There was no way Yatov would let him meet Collins without some of his men around. How long had Morris been lying like that, he wondered? When he first started doing the bidding of the Russians? When was that? 1939? 1940? When you had lied for that long you became good at it, Collins thought, or maybe lying became so much a part of you, that you didn't think twice about it.

"Frank will be coming with me, Morris."

"Bob's not going to like that."

"That's tough. I need some sort of protection against a fast one, and Frank is it."

"Suit yourself. But Frank comes as your brother, not as a New York cop."

Before Collins could respond, the line went dead.

He stayed at his desk. He wouldn't leave until the call from Karina came. He had tried not to think about her too much, but she had been there, in the background, the entire time. And now he had hope. Morris had confirmed that she was alive and Yatov was willing to trade her.

Collins found himself praying, silently asking God to protect Karina from harm, promising that if Karina was spared he wouldn't squander their second chance. He felt better when he finished.

The phone rang. Collins answered, giving his name.

"Dennis," she began. "This is Karina."

"Are you all right?" Collins could feel his heart racing. He gripped the phone tightly.

"I am all right."

"Is anyone listening?"

"I am here," a deep male voice answered. His Slavic accent was noticeable. "I am sharing this call with Miss Lazda. You understand, no doubt."

"Listen to me, then," Collins said. "You don't get what you want without her release. She must be handed over to me tonight, unharmed. I will live up to my end of the bargain, if you live up to yours."

"We will do as we have promised," the voice said. "But there must be no interference from the authorities."

"No interference. Tell Morris I will be there tonight, just as we agreed. I'll hold up my end of the bargain. Karina, don't worry. I am doing the right thing for us. Trust me."

"Tonight, then," the voice said, and then there was a click and the line again went dead.

Twenty-eight

Collins must have downed at least four cups of bitter city room coffee, trying to stay wide awake for the rest of the morning. At least the coffee was hot. The caffeine kept him relatively alert but it gave him a bad case of the jitters.

He found himself wandering around the newsroom, nervous and distracted, not able to sit down and concentrate. Collins tried to think about anything other than the rendezvous and Morris and Karina, but he kept coming back to it in his imagination, again and again.

"Denny, interested in a story on the DPs?" It was Hal Diderick clutching a roll of yellow teletype paper. He stopped Collins in mid-stride with his question.

"What sort of story?"

"It's from United Press in Washington. The American Legion is demanding that the Senate delay the DP Bill. That's the one that would let another 134,000 refugees come here. The VFW is against it as well. They're arguing that Senator McCarran is in Europe and the Senate shouldn't move on it until he gets back."

"Because they want McCarran back to lead the fight against the bill."

Diderick nodded. "Exactly. They're saying that it's an open door for subversives, and that the DPs will take jobs from Americans."

"Why don't they dynamite the Statue of Liberty while they're at it? No more 'give me your tired and poor.'"

"I figured you wouldn't like it, Denny."

"I don't. Especially after seeing the people up at the Hotel Marseilles. All they want is a chance to start over and live in peace. After what they've been through, they deserve that chance."

"You must be a do-gooder. The head of the American Legion says that it is only do-gooders who want more DPs."

"Can I have that copy?" Collins asked. "Maybe I can write a column about it later next week, after the baseball quiets down."

Diderick nodded and handed the roll of paper to Collins, who folded the copy and tucked it under his souvenir snow dome paperweight from the World's Fair on his desk. The snowflakes were still falling onto the miniature Trylon and Perisphere inside the dome moments later when Peter Vandercamp arrived at his customary Saturday time. Collins followed Van to his office.

You look like hell," he said to Collins. "Burning the candle at both ends?"

"Didn't get much sleep. I'm going to write two alternative columns today. You can run the one if the Dodgers win, the other if they lose."

Van checked his watch. "Are you planning to go out to the Stadium with those DP children?"

"No, I'm not. I'm in a real jam. I have to stay here, in the city."

"What sort of a jam?" Vandercamp gave him a hard, searching look. "Something new, or more of what you told me about yesterday?"

"What we talked about yesterday. The political trouble. I'd imagine that the FBI is looking for me, but there's something I have to do first before I can talk to them. I'm not going to say anything more because I don't want you put in a difficult situation if they question you about me."

"It's that serious? You expect the FBI here at the *Sentinel?*"

"I'm hoping and praying that it won't come to that."

Vandercamp cleared his throat. "I talked to Frederick Longworth about the Santry thing," he said. "That's why we needed to talk this morning. He wasn't happy, as you can imagine."

Collins didn't say anything in response.

"But," Vandercamp said, "he appreciates your contribution to the paper and he accepted my argument that you hadn't done anything at the *Sentinel* that would cause us to question your integrity."

"I really appreciate this."

"It would be a loss to the *Sentinel*, if you had to step aside. You have a gift for this work. Some people do, some don't. It's not just the writing. It's more than that. It's finding the story and bringing it to the reader in a way that speaks to them. As good as a novelist as John O'Hara is, I didn't think he was much of a newspaperman. You are."

"Thanks."

"So we wait and see whether Santry comes forward. We'll deal with that if and when it happens."

"I appreciate what you've done for me, Van. I truly do."

Vandercamp cleared his throat, ready to move on to another topic. "The young lady I met yesterday. Is she somehow mixed up in this loyalty investigation business?"

Collins reluctantly nodded. There was no point in deceiving Van about Karina's involvement.

"I was afraid of that."

"It will all work out," Collins told him, with a confidence he didn't really feel. "It will be fine."

Once back at his typewriter, he finished his Sunday column. Considering the distractions of the past twenty hours, it wasn't half bad. He walked it over to Vandercamp's office and his editor invited him to sit for a moment.

"The publisher called a few minutes ago. His Saturday plans changed because there's no Yale-Fordham football game today. Canceled because a few of the Yale players have been diagnosed with polio. They're lucky, mild cases, no paralysis. That gave Longworth some time to rethink your situation. He wants you to take an immediate vacation."

"Now? The weekend before the World Series starts? That's nuts."

"That's what I told him. More diplomatically."

"And what did he say?"

"He was uncharacteristically direct. He still wanted you to take some time off. I pointed out that it would hurt us to lose our lead columnist on the weekend that the Dodgers were scratching for a pennant. And I reminded him that we had agreed that we wouldn't take any action on the Santry matter until it became public."

"What did he say to that?"

"He said it wasn't Santry that had him concerned. He said he has heard that you have political troubles and that it might spill over into the paper in some way. I asked him how he knew about it, and he evaded the question."

Collins understood immediately. Vandercamp deserved as much of the truth as Collins could give him. "Longworth has friends in Washington who know about my friend's loyalty investigation. He must be worried that I'm going to write something they won't like."

"I see," Vandercamp said. "Well, I salvaged the situation as best as I could. I promised that I would talk to you and that there would be nothing political in your columns, just baseball."

"And Longworth agreed to it?"

"Grudgingly. You will write about baseball. Period."

The phone rang. Vandercamp picked it up on the second ring.

"I see," he said, frowning. "Thanks for the heads up, Rudy."

He looked over at Collins and grimaced. "The FBI is here. I asked Rudy to alert me this morning if we had any unusual visitors."

Vandercamp rose to his feet and Collins followed suit.

"They're taking the elevator up to the fifth floor as we speak." He glanced at his watch. "I would like to be able to tell them that they just missed you."

"Thanks, Van."

"May God bless you and keep you, young man."

Collins moved through the newsroom quickly, trying not to appear in too much of a rush. He turned the corner by the wire room and headed for the back exit. Collins galloped down the dark stairwell, two steps at a time. He reached at the lobby level in a few minutes and then was out the door and into the afternoon sunlight of 39th Street.

He walked back over to Killeen's. There weren't many customers, and his entrance attracted no interest. The regulars were talking about the Yankees-Red Sox game.

This time the rendezvous was going to be different, he told himself. He was going to be prepared; if he didn't get Karina, Morris wouldn't get the film. The bitter irony, of course, was that Morris would be immeasurably better off without the film. He and Yatov were frantic to get their hands on the very documents which would provide Steele with proof of their complicity in espionage. But then again, a trap needed the right bait.

He slipped into the phone booth in the back of the bar, fed it a nickel, and called the number Steele had given him. Steele answered on the first ring. "It's on," Collins told him. "Morris called me and wants the film. And Karina is alive."

"I am glad to hear that. Our Russian friends must be quite anxious. I would not be surprised in the least if that is your friend's only bargaining chip with them. It ensures his safe passage, now."

"His safe passage?"

"They are no doubt arranging to exfiltrate Rose."

"What does that mean?"

"Once he has delivered the list, Yatov will try to spirit him out of the country. Across the border to Canada or Mexico, and then on to Russia. Or perhaps they plan to use one of the freighters leaving New York. There are numerous escape routes."

"Morris told me he had wanted to break it off with the Russians. That when he gave me the film he was hoping to convince the investigators that he was clean—he was going to use the memos as evidence of that."

"Perhaps. But he was covering his bet with that FBI Counterintelligence list. He needed Moscow Center to know he had something of significant value."

"I think he wanted out. I think he would have quit if he could."

"Think what you like. When are you passing him the film?"

"I have the new drop-off time and place," Collins said. "It's set for tonight. I am trading the film for Karina, one-for-one."

"Splendid," Steele said. "This may work out to our advantage after all. Trading for the girl helps establish your motive for handing over the film. They won't be overly suspicious if they think you are a moonstruck lover. You couldn't have planned it any better."

"Sorry if I'm not overjoyed about that. They still have Karina. I'll rest a lot easier once she's been released. So you know—after what happened last night I'm not concerned about Morris. My conscience won't bother me. As far as I am concerned, he deserves whatever he gets."

"I wouldn't be too hard on him. He is hardly acting on his own, now. Yatov is calling the shots."

"Does that make it any better? Not in my mind."

"Few, if any of us, determine our own destiny. Rose isn't unique in having lost control over his immediate future."

The same thing could be said about him, Collins thought, and perhaps Steele wanted him to make that connection. Wasn't Steele calling the shots for him, now?

"You haven't asked me where and when," Collins said. "The time and place for the hand-off."

"Who set the location?"

"Morris did. But I had conditions that he accepted. He doesn't get the film until Karina is physically with me, and he has to come alone to the rendezvous."

"Where will this take place? And when?"

"Near the Brooklyn Bridge. At South Street and the river, near the Al Smith housing project. Nine o'clock."

"In the shadow of the Brooklyn Bridge. Has Morris been reading poems by Hart Crane?"

"Nothing poetic. It's wide open there and you can see anyone coming from a long way away. The traffic keeps moving. Morris picked a place where he can exit quickly."

"It doesn't matter. We will have it covered. We'll move in after the hand-off."

"It's crucial that your men aren't seen. One of the Russians—I think it was Yatov—threatened me about not involving the authorities."

"Yatov? You talked directly to Yatov?" Collins could hear the surprise in Steele's voice.

"I think so. I insisted on talking to Karina, so I could be sure that she was alive. He came on the line."

"Well done," Steele said. "It was clever to ask to speak to her. As for tonight, don't worry about my men. They are professionals and they won't be seen. You don't have to do anything heroic—just give him the film. We'll do the rest." He paused. "One last thing. I would appreciate it if you phoned me after the drop. I will be waiting."

"You won't be there?"

"Lord, no. I'm hardly fit now for the field. A bit long in the tooth for adventures like this."

After they hung up Collins called the *Sentinel* and asked for Peter Vandercamp. He didn't identify himself—he couldn't be sure that the *Sentinel*'s phone lines were clean—but he knew that Van would recognize his voice.

"I'm looking for Denny Collins," Collins said when his editor picked up the phone.

"He's not here," Vandercamp said.

"Where do you think I could find him?"

"Seems as though you'll have to get in line. Several interested parties were just looking for him. They were quite angry that he wasn't around. They said they were considering a warrant. I wouldn't be surprised if they have stationed someone to watch the entrance to the *Sentinel*."

"Okay," Collins said. "Could you give Denny a message when you see him?"

"Sure."

"Tell him that all's well that ends well."

"I will tell him that," Vandercamp said. "And pray that it proves true."

Twenty-nine

Collins finished the afternoon at Killeen's, occupying a booth in the back where he could monitor the front door and where he would be left alone. The bartenders must have wondered what had gone wrong in his life, Collins thought, because he had spent more time in their lousy bar in the last twenty-four hours than he had in the past year.

He needed the time, though. It was crucial that he think through that night's exchange. There was no margin for error. If the hand-off of the film to Morris was botched it could prove disastrous for Karina. While Alfred Hitchcock's regular-guy heroes in movies like *The 39 Steps* always figured out how to triumph over the foreign spies, Collins was painfully aware that he wasn't playing a part in a movie. Things could very easily end badly.

The Yankees-Red Sox game was playing on the television set above the bar. Collins wondered how little Josef and Hannah were finding their first baseball game. Collins thought about Karina, about how quickly they had fallen for each other. He now believed that that her feelings for him were authentic, not something she had been ordered to feign by the Russians. And since she had pulled the gun on Morris, Collins told himself, Karina had freed herself from their control.

He found it hard to concentrate. He had learned in the Pacific, on Okinawa, that the worst time came before action, the waiting and the imagining in the hours before things happened. He remembered what his friend Charlie Adair had told him about fear.

"We're all scared of combat," Adair said. "Anyone who says he isn't is lying. You're out in the open and you are being shot at, shelled, strafed. The natural thing is to run as fast as you can, as far as you can, to get away from the danger. So what do you do? The only way you can function is if you've been trained to do something, anything that will focus you on an idea other than whether you are about to be killed yourself. Firing your rifle at the enemy. Moving forward. Anything concrete."

Collins would have to improvise at the exchange if it didn't go as he had planned. What if Yatov and his men tried to take the film from Collins without releasing Karina? No matter what Morris had promised, he was no longer in control of the situation.

Collins had gone back-and-forth about involving his brother, but the more he thought about, the more he realized that he didn't want to risk the meeting without back-up. Collins moved to the back of Killeen's and slid into the phone booth.

Frank answered on the first ring and didn't hesitate when Collins asked him if he could help with a last-minute problem. He asked Frank to meet him at 8:15, at the Stork Club.

Collins somehow managed to kill the time until eight o'clock, and then took a cab uptown. Normally he would have walked but he wanted to get there quickly. His brother was already standing outside the club, talking with one of the bouncers, when Collins arrived. They moved away from the entrance and stood together on the sidewalk in front of a haberdashery storefront.

"So what is it?" Frank asked. "More problems with Santry and his friends?"

Collins shook his head. "I fixed that. It's Morris. You were right about him. It's all gone bad."

He quickly told Frank the truth about the past week, knowing how outlandish his story sounded. He wouldn't have believed it himself if he hadn't lived through it. He explained the aborted hand-off at Rockefeller Center, and the deal he had worked out to exchange the film for Karina, and how Steele's men would arrest Morris and the Russians on the other side of the trade. When Collins finished, his brother shook his head.

"You poor bastard," he said. "You've really been left holding the bag."

"That doesn't matter, now. I need you there for the exchange tonight in case of any bully boy tactics. If it goes smoothly, we let Morris take the film. Steele handles the rest."

"Did Steele clear this with the FBI?"

Collins considered the question for a long moment. "I don't think so. Steele seems to operate independently."

"That makes this even riskier. Are you sure about this? You're prepared to burn Morris?"

"You're changing your tune. I thought you detested Morris."

"I do, and I'd burn him in a second. But he's your friend, from way back."

"I want Karina freed," Collins said. "Even if giving up Morris is the price. So I don't really have any choice."

"So what's she like?"

"Karina?" Collins paused, wondering what to say. "I like what I know of her. She's had it rough, but it hasn't made her hard or cynical. There's a spark there between us, has been from the start. I never imagined that I could fall for someone so fast. It's only been a few days."

"That's more than long enough."

"In some ways it is. In others, it's not. She's got a past, not a very savory one. There's that to consider."

His brother shrugged, always practical. "What do you care? What does she do for you now? Can you see a future with her? That's what matters."

"I think so, but I'm not sure."

"Do you love her?"

"Maybe," Collins said, surprising himself. "Not the way it was with Penny, but maybe. It's one thing to fall hard for a girl, and another to truly love them."

"That's progress. You're talking about Penny in the past tense. I think you deserve a woman who doesn't keep you guessing. You owe it to yourself to figure out whether this one is the right one."

"I'll worry about that after we have her back."

"Where's the meet?" his brother asked. "How soon?"

"Near the Al Smith project, at nine."

"Clever."

"We can grab a taxi in front of the Stork," Collins said. "If you're okay with this, with riding shotgun for me."

"Isn't that what a big brother is for?"

They spent the cab ride downtown in silence, each lost in thought. The cabbie dropped them off in front of City Hall, and they went from there on foot. After they had walked a block, his brother stopped and pulled Collins into a nearby doorway, into the shadows. There were no signs of anyone following them; the neighborhood, filled with government workers and Federal Courthouse employees by day, was deserted at night.

Collins checked his watch when they reached the corner of South Street and Pearl. It was 8:50—they had ten minutes until the rendezvous. To their immediate south the Brooklyn Bridge loomed in the dark, the sound of the crossing cars, trucks and buses creating a man-made surf in the distance. There wasn't much traffic in the immediate neighborhood.

The sudden blast of a horn from a tugboat on the East River seemed somehow reassuring to Collins. He accepted one of his brother's Chesterfields, enjoying the feel of the smoke in his mouth and throat. Collins remembered when he and Morris had last been on that corner: the night before Collins left for the Pacific. Penny stayed in Washington with her parents—to avoid a sloppy goodbye, she had said—so Collins had slept alone on his last night in New York.

Collins remembered talking with Morris about the changes the war had made in the country—the shared sacrifices, the clear sense of purpose, the feeling of unity—and how the returning veterans might further alter things for the better when they returned. They were both tight from a night of drinking.

"When the war ends we can get back to work," Morris said. "The real work that we never completed."

"I'll settle with finishing off Hitler and Tojo. First things first."

"I want more. All that the New Deal was supposed to give us. So the war is more than just beating the Nazis."

Collins didn't argue with him, hoping only to return in one piece from covering the war. That would be a good enough start.

At one minute before the hour, a figure appeared in the distance, moving towards Collins and his brother. Once he came closer, Collins could see it was Morris, wearing a stylish topcoat against the evening chill. Collins stepped out into the circle of light cast by the overhead street lamp so Morris, and whoever else was observing, could see him clearly. His brother remained behind him in the shadows. Morris stopped a few feet from him and nodded.

"Where is Karina?" Collins asked curtly, dispensing with any greeting. "I told you that she had to be here."

"She is here. Behind that building to the south. Waiting with Bob."

"The deal was just you and Karina."

Morris shrugged. "That was one of Bob's conditions, that he witness the exchange. You're not the only one with conditions." He peered into the dark behind Collins. "I see Frank came along."

"Just being prudent," Collins said. "You know my brother. He's going to make sure that this stays on the up-and-up. So let's get it over with."

"As long as your brother keeps his distance. Do you have my film?"

"I do."

"Okay, then, here's how it works. When I raise my hand in the air, Bob will send Karina. When she reaches us, you hand me the film. The two of you stand here, in the light, while I leave. As long as I am not stopped on my way back to my colleagues, you and Karina will come to no harm."

"What the hell does that mean?"

"Another one of Bob's conditions. One of his men with a high-powered rifle is somewhere out there watching us. The Red Army developed some fairly skilled snipers at Stalingrad. A necessity, since

Roosevelt and Churchill left them to fight off Paulus and the Sixth Army by themselves."

"Always the victims, are they? The Poles and the Finns might argue with that."

Morris coughed again, exasperated, and then wiped his mouth with a handkerchief.

"Can't shake free of that catechism, can you, Denny? The world was so simple back on Warren Street. But it isn't that way, at all. It's not the Yankees and the Dodgers, and the loser gets to try again next season. Can't you see that the big money boys will stop at nothing to destroy the Soviet Union? That's why the War Department has plans to use atomic bombs on the major population centers in the Soviet Union. Did you know that?"

"Come on. There's a world of difference between Harry Truman and Stalin."

"If we had fought the Nazis street-by-street in New York and Washington and we'd been pushed back to St. Louis, and if we had lost a third of our people, then Truman would be more like Stalin. Hard times make hard men." Morris paused. "There's no point in arguing. But you should know that I do regret involving you. It was a mistake and I'm sorry for it."

He checked his watch and then carefully raised his hand in the air, the signal to Yatov, wherever he was watching and waiting. Collins peered into the distant shadows, trying to see Karina. Slowly a figure emerged from the darkness, walking slowly towards them. As they watched her approach, it was if Morris suddenly flipped a switch and became the smart, likeable kid from Brooklyn—the smart aleck who could make you laugh.

"So, Denny," he said. "What are the latest odds on the Dodgers winning the pennant?"

Collins ignored him. He glanced over at Karina, who now was only ten feet away. As she moved into the light Collins could see large bruises on the side of her face, the marks of a beating, and he cursed. Collins shouldn't have been surprised, but he found himself filled with a sudden cold anger. Karina passed by Morris, ignoring him, and walked unsteadily towards Collins. When she reached him, she collapsed into his arms. He could feel her entire body shaking. "Thank you," she whispered.

Collins pulled away from her, gently, so he could study her face. She tried to smile. He touched her left cheek, gently, and she winced.

"You're safe now," he told her.

"The film, please," Morris said. "Pass it to me slowly."

"How could you let them beat her?" Collins asked. "What have you become?"

"The film. We have a deal. It's not the time or place to debate comparative morality."

"How do you know it's the correct film? How do you know I haven't switched it?"

"Because I know you are smarter than that." He looked at his watch again, clearly on some sort of timetable. "There could be severe consequences if you tried a stunt like that. How long do you think either of you would last if you crossed them?"

Collins dipped his hand into his right jacket pocket for the canister with the developed images. He didn't hesitate; he would leave the blank film in his trouser pocket.

He turned to Morris and reached out with the canister in his free hand, making sure it was visible. Then he dropped it onto the street; the canister bouncing once and then rolling a few feet away from them. Morris did not react to the calculated insult. He calmly walked over to the canister, reaching down and picking it up from the pavement, and carefully placing it in his pocket.

"I had the film developed," Collins told him. "I know the truth."

To his surprise, Morris reached out to shake hands. Collins kept his arms around Karina, giving Morris a hard, unforgiving, stare. This time, Morris recoiled slightly.

"I guess it'd be foolish not to think there might be hard feelings," Morris said. "Believe it or not, I wish you both whatever happiness you can find." He turned on his heel, and began the walk back to his handlers. It would be a rude awakening for him, Collins thought, when Steele's men closed in.

He wondered what Morris would think when they arrested him. Would he recognize that Collins had handed the film over to him knowing full well the consequences? That Morris might spend the next ten or fifteen years of his life in a federal penitentiary? As long as Karina was free, Collins didn't care.

His next thought was to get Karina somewhere safe. Morris had started walking into the shadows to the southeast.

"You gave them the film," Karina whispered to Collins. "I am so sorry. I wanted to keep it from them."

"Trust me, it won't help them."

Collins guided her toward the sidewalk. When she saw his brother, who was standing twenty feet away from them, outside the circle of light that the streetlamps made, she flinched and reflexively pulled back.

"No, don't worry," Collins said. "He's my brother."

He could see that Frank had his hand in the pocket of his suit jacket—a hand on his revolver—as he watched Morris retreat. Collins had seen his look of dark, primal hatred before on the faces of soldiers and Marines in the Pacific. Collins knew that his brother would have killed Morris on the spot if he could have, with no regrets.

"Dennis, they will never let me go," Karina said.

"But they already have," he said, gesturing to his brother and the safety of the shadows, a few steps away.

She was about to say something more to Collins when he heard a sound, like a muffled car backfiring, followed by a sickening thud and a sudden gasp from Karina. She slipped from his grasp and fell to the pavement. Before Collins could react, he had been tackled to the ground, knocking the breath out of him. It was his brother, now lying on the pavement next to Collins.

"Stay down." Then, more quietly, directed to Collins. "That was a rifle shot. I think the girl's been hit."

Collins fought for air. His bruised ribs ached. He lifted his head high enough to see Karina, a few yards away. She sprawled on the pavement awkwardly, like an abandoned rag doll, not moving, her body limp. He could see something shining on the pavement next to her head and neck in the light from the street lamp. He realized then that it was blood, trickling from a wound in her head.

"Karina," he called over to her. "Karina, are you all right?"

There was no answer. He peered to his right. Frank had his revolver out and was slowly crawling on his hands and knees back towards the shadows. Collins could feel himself going numb, the feeling he had first experienced on Saipan, the sensation he got when horrible things were happening and he couldn't control them. Part of him knew then that she was dead, but somehow Collins believed that if he could get to her side, he could change that. All he wanted was to reach her, to touch her, to tell her that it was going to be all right.

"I'm going to help her," Collins said.

"Stay put," his brother said. "It's not safe."

Collins didn't say anything. He began crawling on the pavement toward Karina, back into the full light, working his way back to her slowly, hoping not to attract the attention of the gunman out there in the dark. There had been no movement or sound from her. His heart pounded violently, and the sweat ran down his chest. He moved slowly toward her, trying to stay as low to the ground as he could, the gravel on the pavement digging painfully into his knees.

Once at her side, he gently touched her arm, then tried tugging at it. Karina didn't respond. He pulled on her arm, harder, but again she did not move. His heart kept racing, the adrenaline rushing through his body.

"Karina," he whispered. "It's Dennis. It will be all right. I promise it will be all right."

Except she didn't answer Collins, and then he knew that she never would. It didn't make any sense, he thought. They had the film. Why shoot her? Hadn't he made his own bargain with God, that he wouldn't squander a second chance? He called over to his brother to tell him that Karina wasn't responding.

"Keep down, damn it," Frank said. "Don't give them a target. Crawl out of the light."

Collins did what he was told, inching his way on the ground, away from Karina's body, away from the light of the streetlamps, feeling naked and vulnerable and ashamed that he wanted to live. It made Collins think again of the Pacific, and the unrelenting fear that came when you were caught out in the open, the fear that made some men crack. But there were no shots, just the sound of traffic and the noises of the river.

Then Collins was out of the light and he crawled faster into the welcoming safety of the dark. He didn't stand up until he reached the fence that surrounded the Al Smith apartments, where the trees blocked out most of the light from the streetlamps and the shadows offered deep sanctuary. His brother joined him a moment later.

"You okay?"

"She's gone," Collins said. "She hasn't moved."

"There's nothing we can do for her."

"There was no point to it, Frank. We lived up to our side of the deal. They had the film."

"I never had a chance to return fire. That shot came out of nowhere."

"Karina said they would never let her go," Collins said. "That's the last thing she said."

"Morris didn't try to warn you?"

"He could not have known."

Frank glanced back over at Karina's lifeless body, and then looked at Collins, his eyes fierce with anger. "It really doesn't matter what he knew, or what he wanted. He is in too deep, an accessory to murder now. Remember what I said before. A dog can't have two homes."

Thirty

His brother handled everything after that. He had to, because Collins was of little use to anyone, still stunned by what had happened, numbed by the shock of it. Frank gently placed his overcoat over the top half of Karina's body, covering the horrible head wound, and then forced Collins to walk over to a nearby green wooden park bench and sit down. Then his brother went inside the apartment complex to call the police.

Collins didn't have to wait for very long before Frank returned and a squad car from the 11th Precinct appeared; the NYPD headquarters was situated only blocks away. Collins noticed that Frank had pinned his police badge to the lapel of his coat and the polished shield caught the reflected light of the streetlamp.

His brother spoke in a hushed voice to the two uniformed policemen in the car, explaining the situation. Collins heard him say "an FBI matter" and then "keep a lid on." An ambulance arrived a few minutes later, rolling quietly to a stop. The attendants put Karina's limp body on a stretcher and loaded it in the back of the ambulance.

Collins and Frank rode in the back seat of the squad car as it followed the ambulance uptown to Bellevue Hospital. There, it was only a formality for a doctor to meet the ambulance and pronounce Karina dead. Hospital attendants wheeled her body into the side door; she would be taken directly to the morgue, Collins knew, and tried to put that scene out of his mind. Collins gave the cops from the squad car what information he could: Karina's name, where she worked, the address of her apartment.

"Any next of kin?" one of them asked. "We should inform them."

"No family here," Collins said. "She was a refugee."

Collins realized that he had never talked with Karina about her family. There hadn't been time for that, to indulge in the explorations of the past that lovers so enjoyed. Her past would always remain a mystery.

"So what is your relation to her?"

That was when Frank took the cops aside and had another long talk with them and Collins saw that they stopped writing in their notebooks. They stayed away from Collins after that. After his brother had finished with them, he came over and sat across from Collins. Neither of them spoke and Collins knew Frank was waiting for him to break the silence.

That was when they both saw the FBI agents Caldwell and Leary advancing down the hallway toward them. Before Collins could say anything, Frank explained that he had asked the police dispatcher to call the federal agents with a message about what had happened.

"They're going to be involved in this," his brother said. "Better to get it over with now."

Frank intercepted the agents before they could talk to Collins. Collins couldn't make out clearly what his brother was saying, but he heard him mention Karina and Steele. Then Frank stepped aside and Caldwell came over to stand in front of Collins. Leary stayed slightly behind him. His brother followed Caldwell and stood by Collins' side.

Caldwell gave Collins a disgusted look. "You stupid bastard," he said. "Look at what you have done."

"That's enough," Frank said.

Caldwell ignored him. "Your brother needs to hear this. This wouldn't have happened if he had talked to us when it could have mattered. He kept us in the dark. And now there's a dead girl, and Rose has walked away."

Collins reached in his coat pocket and found Steele's business card. He handed it to Caldwell. "Call him," Collins said. "I was doing what he asked. He can explain."

Caldwell took the card and looked at it, his face darkening. "We'll see," he said.

Then he said something to Leary and the younger man nodded. Caldwell left and they spent an awkward five minutes, Leary glaring at Collins while he continued to chain-smoke, watching the smoke float to the ceiling. His brother stood next to him, returning Leary's hostile stare with his own.

When Caldwell returned from the call his face was set and hard.

"Steele wants to see you," he said scornfully, looking at Collins. "In an hour. At the Stork Club." It was clear what he thought of Steele, of Collins, and of their meeting place. Why Caldwell's open contempt bothered Collins, Collins couldn't explain, but he felt compelled to explain.

"They're planning to arrest Morris," Collins said. "He has top secret documents, on film, with him. That was Steele's idea."

Caldwell glared at him. "You really are a stupid shit, aren't you?"

"What are you saying? Steele's men should be arresting Morris and the Russians as we speak."

"He didn't say anything about that," Caldwell said. "I couldn't tell you what Steele is planning to do. It's no longer an FBI counterespionage case. We are not to pursue Rose, or the Russian station chief. That's direct from Steele. He's got the Army, CIA, and FBI all in concert on this. No New York FBI office involvement. That comes from the very top, so I guess it means that Hoover agreed to this."

"You are cut out of this?" Frank asked, incredulous at the thought.

"I wasn't given a choice," Caldwell said.

"What the hell is going on, then?" Frank asked.

"I'll tell you what I think. Steele and his OSS asshole buddies have some clever cloak-and-dagger plan involving Rose. They're going to keep everyone else in the dark about what it is."

"Well, I'm going to find out what the hell is going on," Collins said.

"Fat chance," Caldwell said. "He's been using you all along. He knew from the start that you could get him close to Rose. You did that. I don't think you'll get the time of day from him now."

Collins didn't say anything. Some of Caldwell's anger had to come from being removed from the case, he told himself. Steele and the Washington FBI would get the credit when Morris and the Russians were arrested, not Caldwell and the New York field office. Collins could care less about their petty little bureaucratic turf battles. What mattered to him now was to hear from Steele that Karina's sacrifice had led to the destruction of the Soviet espionage network in the city. That's what Karina would have wanted.

In the cab on the way to the Stork Club, Frank left Collins alone to his own thoughts. Collins felt tired and disoriented. What had happened at the rendezvous still seemed like a bad dream: the political argument with Morris, Karina crossing the street to reach Collins, the sudden deep report of a rifle being fired, and her sickening collapse to the ground. His hand went into his coat pocket, where the film canister had been. Its absence meant that all of it had happened.

At the Stork Club door, Al waved Collins and Frank inside the gold chain, past a long line of hopefuls waiting to get into the nightclub.

"They both lost," Al said. "How do you figure that?"

Collins looked at him blankly.

"The Dodgers and the Cards. They both lost."

When Collins didn't respond, his brother spoke up. "Denny's had a tough night, Al. He's a bit under the weather."

"Sorry," Collins said to the doorman. "I guess I have a lot on my mind."

"At least the Yanks won," Al said.

"So we go to the last day," Frank said. "One hell of a season."

They paused when they reached the maitre d's station. Collins looked around for Gregory, but he must have been occupied elsewhere. When he scanned the dining room he quickly spotted Matthew Steele seated at a corner table facing the entrance to the Cub Room. Steele was wearing a dark suit and a light-gray bow tie. Collins could clearly see Steele's face but couldn't see the face of his companion at the table, a stylishly dressed blonde woman. Frank volunteered to wait at the bar while Collins talked with Steele.

Steele noticed Collins when he was halfway to the table, and he raised his hand in greeting. That was when Collins first saw the face of the woman sitting across from Steele and realized it was Penny Bradford. He came to a dead stop, stunned by finding her there.

"This is awkward," Steele said. "I hadn't expected you to arrive this quickly." He turned to Penny and said something in a low voice Collins couldn't make out. Collins didn't believe Steele for a moment—Penny's presence at his table had been deliberately staged. There was no mistake about that, Collins thought, but what was the connection and why did Steele want her there?

"Penny, my dear, if you would excuse us for a few minutes."

"No," she said, glancing over at Collins and then back to Steele. "I wish to stay."

"That would be particularly awkward," he said. "Quite."

"Then let it be particularly awkward," she said.

Penny did not look directly at Collins again. It didn't matter: Collins had already seen the interplay between them, the unspoken intimacy, as strange and unlikely as it might be.

"I didn't know that you two were such good friends," Collins said. "You make quite the pair."

Penny finally looked at him in response to the barb, but it was Steele who responded. He motioned for Collins to sit in one of the open chairs at the table. Collins sat down slowly, his eyes on Penny the entire time.

"Penny's late husband was a friend," Steele said. "With Taylor's passing, Penny and I were thrown together in Washington, and it's fair to say that we've grown quite fond of each other."

"You neglected to mention that to me yesterday," Collins said. "When you suggested that Penny might end up under suspicion if I didn't do what you asked."

"Is that so?" Steele said. "I think that perhaps you jumped to premature conclusions there. It was your future on the line, not hers, and I think I made that rather clear."

"Were you part of this from the beginning?" Collins asked Penny. She looked down at her hands resting on the table. "Did he ask you to spy on me? To find out what you could about Morris?"

Steele spoke before Penny could respond. "She had nothing to do with it until you dragged her into it."

Penny remained silent. She had retreated into herself; her face, a mask. Collins couldn't tell what she was thinking, but he couldn't let it go.

"You didn't answer me," he said to her. "I want to hear it from you."

"I was not spying for him," she said, coldly.

"We do have matters to discuss," Steele said. "So if that has satisfied your curiosity, I am sure Penny would be willing to excuse us for ten minutes."

"I will go," Penny said. "But after you are done, I wish to talk to Dennis myself. Alone."

Steele nodded. "Fair enough," he said. "We shan't be too long."

The men rose to their feet and they both watched in silence as Penny left, disappearing into the Cub Room. Collins took Penny's vacated seat, his back to the entrance, so that he could directly face Steele. Steele remained calm, unruffled by Collins' obvious hostility. Collins wondered what it would take to rattle Steele, to disturb his arrogant composure.

"Shall we get you a drink?" Steele asked. "You prefer beer, don't you?"

He finished his martini and signaled a waiter.

"Don't bother," Collins said. "This won't take long. You know from Caldwell that we made the drop of the film. Did he tell you about Karina?"

"He did. I am sorry."

"Yatov is a monster. To order that."

"It was a simple matter of self-preservation. It may not make you feel any better, but Yatov had no choice. He had to clean up his mistakes. No ammunition for any detractors in Moscow. In the end, it was either Karina's life or his own."

Collins stared at Steele, fascinated yet repelled, by the man's chilling detachment. He could have been relating the strategy of a colleague on the back nine of a tough golf course for all the emotion he brought to describing Yatov's dilemma. Collins had seen it before, in general staff officers, when the boxes and pins denoting Marine units on the map at headquarters became no more than the building blocks of their battle plan, not living, breathing, dying men with families and futures and souls. Steele was no different.

Collins started again. "How soon do you arrest Morris and Yatov and the others?"

Steele waved his hand. "Let's not get ahead of ourselves."

"I understand you've asked the FBI to back off. Are your men in the field ready to move in and make the arrests? Yatov and his men are guilty of more than spying, now. They're murderers as well. I think you could charge Morris as an accessory if you wanted to. That might make him more cooperative."

The waiter returned with a fresh drink. Steele raised the new glass to his lips and sipped it carefully. "I'm sorry. There has been a change in plans."

"What do you mean?"

"It isn't the right time to force the issue."

"What does that mean?" Collins could feel his anger rising at Steele's evasiveness.

"The latest developments have altered things."

"The latest developments? A Soviet agent killed Karina in cold blood tonight. Shot her down on a New York City street. What are you waiting for? You need to arrest him and the others now. Morris has the film, remember? I gave him the film, like you told me to. They are going to make a run for it, I'm sure."

"That would not serve our purposes at the moment," Steele said. "I am sorry about Miss Lazda. I believe I said that already."

"What are you saying?" Collins couldn't believe what he was hearing. "Why would you wait to move in? Are you going to let Morris pass along that list of names to the Russians? Are you going to allow it to reach Moscow?" Collins brought himself under control. He fought the temptation to reach across the table and grab Steele by his freshly starched white shirt. Steele must have sensed it, for he moved back in his chair, putting more distance between them.

"I'm sorry. I must ask you to keep your voice down."

"You're sorry? You told me you were going to arrest Morris and the Russians after I passed him the film."

"I know what I told you. It's more complicated than that."

"More complicated?"

"I will explain this to you, under the condition that you keep your voice down. I will also remind you that I can still have you arrested. And your brother. On federal charges."

"You bastard."

Collins fought back his rage. He ached to smash Steele in the face; instead, he clenched his fists and tried to control his anger. Steele lowered his voice, forcing Collins to lean forward to hear him. "We wanted him to steal the list of agents, you see. We fed it to him through Miss Shoemaker. Then we wanted Morris and by extension, Yatov and Moscow Center, to believe that we were moving heaven and earth to recover the list. Hence all the pressure on you, all the time signaling to Morris that he had something we greatly prized. After all that effort, it would be counterproductive to stop him now."

"Why?" Collins was confused, and then he remembered Caldwell's open disgust with the situation; he must have realized that Steele was letting Morris escape. "Why would you let him go? Why?"

"For a number of excellent reasons. Morris brings our list to Moscow Center. It includes nearly all of their agents in the government. This will cause a flurry of activity as they will move to salvage the most important of their clandestine assets. The lesser lights will be left in place, sacrificed like pawns in a chess game. The Russians will assume that we will have them arrested or fired."

"I don't understand? Why tip your hand?"

"Suffice it to say that we kept a few things to ourselves. The list Morris has stolen is our list, vetted, approved, containing only the specific names we want passed. We are withholding other names. This will obscure what we have learned over the past four years from the cable traffic from Moscow Center to New York and Washington."

"The cable traffic? Isn't that coded?"

Steele stirred his drink with his swizzle stick and didn't reply, but his faint, satisfied smile told Collins all he needed to know.

"So you have broken their code," Collins said. Steele, the cryptologist, must be particularly proud of that accomplishment, he thought. It must have given him an incredible sense of power, an almost God-like omniscience, to know what his adversary was thinking, in advance. "You must know who they are from the cables. I still don't understand. Why would you leave their agents in place?"

"The object of the game is not to eliminate all of the Soviet cells in our government. A scorched earth policy would be a grave mistake. They must believe that we are blind to their remaining agents. First, we had to convince them that Morris Rose had stolen something from us of great value. That is why we pursued him, questioned his wife and friends, and why I made that clumsy attempt to have him come in for a chat. Of course we didn't want to catch him. In the end, I spent a considerable amount of time convincing the FBI that they needed to stand down. It has worked. We can now begin to feed Moscow Center disinformation through a few of the surviving agents that *we* control."

"You've done all this to send them bad intelligence?"

"Precisely. With some good scraps of information here and there, to disguise what we are doing and who we control."

Steele adjusted his bow tie and glanced over Collins' right shoulder. Collins resisted the urge to turn around; he figured Steele was keeping an eye on the entrance to the Cub Room, watching for Penny's return. Collins wasn't ready to give up. He would keep at

Steele until Penny returned, hoping that Steele might say something that Collins could use against him.

"And who gives you the authority to play God? What about justice for Karina Lazda? Was she just expendable? Where's the justice in that?"

"Justice?" Steele paused for a moment, considering his response. "What on earth do you think is justice? Is it holding trials? Or sensational Congressional hearings? Telling the entire world about our failures? I think not."

"That's a minority view in Washington. Isn't the idea to expose the secret Communists? Isn't that the reason for the witch hunts?"

"No doubt. Which is all the more reason for discretion. The President and his closest advisors have proven that they can't keep a secret. The White House is a sieve when it comes to sensitive intelligence. And the Veldeans in Congress are no better. They would reveal our sources and means without hesitation to score political points."

"If this ever comes out, that you allowed Morris Rose to escape, it will look like you're on the side of the Russians."

"Might as well be hanged for a sheep as a lamb. I will take that calculated risk." Steele studied Collins for a long moment. "The story of what has happened tonight will never see the light of day. Certainly not in your newspaper, or any other paper. And you would be well-advised to keep your own mouth shut."

"Or what?"

"I can have you arrested. Here and now, if need be, along with your brother. Do you want his life ruined as well? If that is not enough to silence you, remember that you have no proof, no evidence. Who will listen to you? Certainly no one in an official capacity. I can make sure of that. And to what end? Morris Rose will be long gone by then. And somehow I don't think you could bring yourself to go to the witch hunters, as you call them. Could you?"

Collins knew Steele was right. Collins couldn't, and wouldn't, even if it was the best way to strike back at Steele. There were still thousands of innocent people who would be hurt by any validation of the idea of a Red conspiracy in the government. He couldn't go public. He realized something else. Collins couldn't very well reveal that the FBI list was a plant, for that knowledge would only help those who had killed Karina. He was sure Steele had already calculated that.

"So now what?" Collins asked.

"Now? No more theatrics. No, from here on, life returns to the routine. You go back to covering the Dodgers. Your friend is exfiltrated to Russia where, if he is lucky, his reward will be a job at Moscow State University teaching English to the spoiled sons and daughters of Party members. If he should fall out of favor, he will disappear into one of Uncle Joe's Siberian camps, where his life expectancy will be six months."

"And what happens in Washington?"

"We watch and wait and see if the Russians will take the bait."

Collins didn't see Penny arrive—he realized she was back only when Steele stood up. Collins rose to his feet and relinquished the chair to her. She and Steele exchanged glances. Collins wondered what that meant. Had they talked about what Steele would tell him?

"I'd like to speak to Dennis for a moment, now," she said to Steele. "Alone."

"If that is what you want," Steele said. "I will return in ten minutes." He glanced at his watch and then rose to his feet and walked away.

"I have some things I have to tell you," she said.

"It's a bit late for that."

"I don't want to have a horrid scene here," she said. "I want you to understand."

"How thoughtful."

"It's not what you think."

"It isn't? It seems damn familiar, being played for a fool."

Collins saw tears form in her eyes. It meant that at least he had reached her, hurt her, and that, he had to admit, was exactly what he wanted. For a long moment they stared at each other, neither wanting to speak. He wondered what Penny saw in Steele. That was partially a mystery, but not completely. Steele had a hardness and a ruthlessness about him, a certainty, that Collins knew Penny would find appealing. Moreover, he was, by her parents' criteria, suitable, a man from her own world.

She blinked back her tears. "It'd be lovely to think that we could have lasted, Dennis, but you know in your heart that it wouldn't work. I guess that I was trying to find something that could never be. You were right, the past should remain the past."

"Is this what you wanted to tell me?"

"No, I wanted to apologize. For everything. For how I've treated you. I so wish that I could have made you happy. I wish I could have loved you back the way you love me. But I can't. I'm just not made for that."

"I believe that now," Collins said. "I never thought I would, but I believe that now."

"I'm sorry," she said. "I truly am."

"So you took the film canister on your own? It was your own idea?"

She nodded glumly.

"Did you go to Steele with it that night? When you weren't at your apartment?"

"Yes. You see, I couldn't tell you the truth. I was returning to Washington on Monday when Matthew called and stopped me. He knew that I had seen you here in New York. He told me about you and Morris and the girl. And then when you showed me the film canister, I thought I could help you. So I took it."

"And what happened when you brought it to Steele?"

"He told me that I had to return it to you. He was adamant about that. He said that it was the only way that they could trap Morris. He promised me that you would be protected."

"What did you tell him about us?"

"That we had been lovers once. He understood. He didn't judge me. That is one of his best qualities. You should know that we had seen each other off and on in Washington, Dennis, but when I came to New York we were not together. It was coincidence that you were connected to Morris and I was connected to you. And to Matthew."

"What did he tell you about Karina?"

"That she was working for the Soviets. Not that she was a professional spy, more a case of being blackmailed into it. He believed that she had seduced you and he wasn't unhappy with that. He thought that she was working under orders to do so and there was some link with Morris. When he told me, I was jealous. It surprised me. I don't think I have been jealous like that since I was seventeen."

"She was killed tonight," Collins said. "Murdered in cold blood. Executed by the Russians."

"I am sorry." She bowed her head. He wondered if Steele had already told her.

"There is hope from the sea, but none from the grave."

"Pardon me. I don't understand."

"Something my father used to say. One of our primitive tribal sayings. But it applies now for Karina, and I guess for me, too."

"I'm sorry."

"Why don't you ask your close friend Matthew about it? He is letting her killers go free so he can keep playing his cloak-and-dagger games. She was deemed expendable. So tell me: how can he live with himself?"

"Matthew is doing what he thinks is right. Protecting the country."

"Forgive me. I didn't know that he had the authority to decide who lives and dies."

"I don't want a scene," she said. "Please, let's not have a scene."

"I wouldn't waste the breath."

Collins stood up, ready to leave. He glanced away from her, knowing that he would never see her again, and that what had been love would turn to bitterness, if not hatred. What other resolution could there be? She knew it, too.

"Is this the way we say goodbye?" she asked.

"As good a way as any. I can find my own way out."

He walked across the room, back towards the bar. Steele saw that he was leaving and moved to slip past him but Collins reached out and grabbed his shirtfront. Frank appeared from the end of the bar and moved closer, waiting to see what would happen.

"Listen to me," Collins said to Steele, tightening his grip on the bunched cloth.

"I'm listening."

"I don't want you to ever forget what I am saying. Her blood is on your hands. I hope you burn in hell for it."

Steele didn't say anything. Collins released his shirtfront and stepped around him. He and Frank walked out of the Stork Club together. Collins pulled his brother over to the same spot where they had started the evening, and then he told him that Steele had let Morris escape.

"That bastard. How can he justify that?"

"Because Morris is just a pawn in the game. Steele wanted the Russians to have the documents." Collins paused. "I'm afraid Caldwell was right. There's some stupid master plan behind this, some elaborate scheme to fool the Soviets."

"And Penny?" Frank asked. "What was she doing there? How does she fit into all this?"

"It's an accident that she got involved," Collins said. "One of those coincidences you wouldn't believe if it didn't happen to be true. She was in the wrong place at the wrong time. And she became another pawn. Like me."

Now Collins better understood the sequence of events over the past week. When Penny offered Steele the film canister, he must have been taken aback. It was crucial that Morris recover the film with its carefully prepared list of agents and pass it on to the Soviets. Then, just when it looked like Morris was going to take the bait, Karina had intervened.

Steele must have sweated that one out, Collins thought. If Yatov had not been willing to trade Karina, or if he had already killed her, Steele would have been left with nothing. Yet in the end, Steele could not have scripted it any better. Karina's impulsive derailing of the first hand-off must have convinced the Soviets of the value of Morris' stolen list. That Collins was willing to trade the film only for her freedom had served to further validate its worth.

"I'm sorry," Frank said. "Bad luck all around. So what do we do?"

"Nothing. There's nothing we can do. Unless you want to end up in federal custody, not that it would accomplish anything. The killers are long gone by now. At least I told Steele what I think of him, and Penny knows, too."

His brother put his hand on Collins' arm. "You're staying at my place tonight," he said. "On the couch."

"That's not necessary." Collins stepped back.

"It is. I don't want anyone tidying things up tonight by removing you from the picture. They may be watching your apartment."

Collins shook his head. "No, it's over. Morris is gone. Karina is gone. Why bother with me, now? Not the Soviets, not the FBI. Not anyone. I'm going to have to go back to my life sometime. It might as well start now."

"I think that's a mistake."

"I'm not going to argue with you," Collins said. "I'm going to go home and get some sleep and then catch the train to Philly in the morning so I can cover the last game of the season. With any luck I'll see the Dodgers win the pennant."

"Are you sure you want to do that? After what happened tonight? Maybe you should take it easy."

Collins met his gaze. "I need to do something, Frank. If I sit at home I'll go stir crazy. I need to get my mind off all of this. I'll go to the ballgame and write my Monday column from there."

"This wasn't your fault, you know. You did everything you could. You can't blame yourself for what happened to the girl."

Collins exhaled slowly. His brother had reminded him of an unmet obligation. "I need one more favor," he told him.

"Just say it," he said. "It's done."

"Can you go to the Hotel Marseilles in the morning and tell them about Karina? Make certain that she is taken care of? The arrangements?"

"Sure. I'll make certain it's done right."

"Thanks. I don't think I could face that."

"Hey, Denny," his brother said. "Life carries on. It's a hard thing to say to you, now, but it's true."

"You're right," he said. Collins knew better, but he wasn't going to argue the point. "Life carries on."

Epilogue

And life carried on.

On Sunday morning Collins took the train from Penn Station to Philadelphia to cover the final game of the season for the Dodgers. He read the papers on the way. There was nothing in them about Karina. Her death passed unnoticed, just one of the thousands of anonymous New Yorkers who died every day of the year and whose names never made it into the newspapers.

The *Sentinel* carried a nice photo of Josef and Hannah sitting in their seats at the Yankees game with a brief headline: "First Baseball Game for DP Kids." Josef wore a broad smile; Hannah clung to a gray-haired older woman with glasses, Mrs. Berliner. Karina would have liked the photograph. The Yankees won, with Joe DiMaggio playing the hero's role. Buried in the back pages of the *Sentinel* was a small item—classic Diderick—noting that the American embassy in India had dispatched a plane to Tibet to pick up Lowell Thomas.

Once he reached Shibe Park, Collins lost himself in the familiar details of the game, the green field spread out below him, the Dodgers making history, winning over the Phillies in ten innings, 9-7, with Jack Banta shutting down the Phils in relief and being carried off the field by his teammates after the final out. Back in the Bronx, the Yankees also waited until the last moment to defeat the Boston Red Sox and capture the American League flag, so it meant a Subway Series. Collins wrote his column and then took the late train home to New York.

On Monday he returned to his routine at the *Sentinel.* That afternoon they held a hasty service of remembrance for Karina Lazda at the Hotel Marseilles. Frank had to tell him about it later, because Collins couldn't bear to go. They buried her in the Evergreens Cemetery in Brooklyn, in a donated plot.

In the days that followed, the city stirred with excitement over the Subway Series. Humphrey Bogart and Lauren Bacall came to watch the first game at Yankee Stadium, along with 66,000 other fans. Collins was in the press box along with Pete Marquis and the heavyweights of the New York sports writing fraternity—Red Smith, Grantland Rice, Arthur Dailey, Jimmy Cannon.

The opener was decided on one pitch. Don Newcombe started on the mound for the Brooks and he had a marvelous day, showing power and control, striking out eleven batters through eight innings. His Yankee counterpart, Allie Reynolds, had matched him almost pitch-for-pitch, with nine strikeouts.

It was still a scoreless game in the bottom of the ninth. Against the first Yankee batter, Tommy Henrich, Newcombe left the ball up on the third pitch and Henrich hammered it into the right field stands. One bad pitch and the Yankees had won, 1-0. The casual fans didn't care for a low-scoring game. Commenting on the lack of offense, Red Smith cracked afterward that Bogie and Bacall had put on more spectacular battles in El Morocco by themselves.

Game Two caused the sportswriters to start calling it the Shut-out Series, because Preacher Roe shut out the Yanks, 1-0, making judicious use of a pitch he called a forkball but everyone else (except the umpires) recognized as a spitter.

The Series turned on Friday's Game Three, played at Ebbets Field. With the game tied, 1-1, in the ninth inning Long John Mize hit a line drive that reached the right field screen and brought in two runs and drove Ralph Branca from the game. In the end, the Yankees won 4-3 and then went on to win the Series in five games.

The Series ended eight days after Morris Rose vanished from New York. Word of his disappearance never found its way into the newspapers. Nor did the Soviets trot him out for a show press conference in Moscow, the way they did with some defectors. It was as if the earth had opened and swallowed him up whole.

And life carried on.

The weekend after the Series finished, Collins commenced a month-long vacation from the *Sentinel*. He wasn't given a choice in the matter. Longworth had insisted that Collins make himself scarce for thirty days. So Collins flew out to California and looked up his Marine buddy, Charlie Adair. He tried not to think ahead, or behind, and he let the days slip by. He went swimming in the Pacific and ate halibut with fisherman's sauce at the Tadich Grill in San Francisco. He drove down the coast to San Luis Obispo and Santa Barbara, the old Spanish mission towns, and didn't do much except sit in the sun and drink beer.

When he flew back to New York it was cold and gray and winter had arrived in Manhattan. Macy's and Gimbel's had holiday displays in their windows and shoppers in heavy wool coats filled Herald Square. At the *Sentinel*, they were calling him "Hollywood Collins" behind his back with a rumor circulating he had failed in a bid to become a screenwriter with one of the big movie studios.

In one of his first columns after his return he wrote with some sadness about how Jake LaMotta would never fight a rematch with Marcel Cerdan. The French boxer was killed in October when his plane crashed over the Azores en route to New York, where Cerdan had planned to hear his lover Edith Piaf sing at the Versailles.

Weeks later, in early December, Gentleman Jack O'Reilly was knocked out by a journeyman heavyweight, a Canadian stiff who apparently didn't realize he was supposed to make the Gentleman look good. Phil Santry's hopes for a title bout ended when his fighter hit the Garden canvas in the second round and didn't get up.

Santry had remained silent about the past. Collins didn't know precisely why—perhaps he had been bluffing all along with his threat to go public—but Collins figured they were even.

A few days before Christmas a letter postmarked in Mexico City reached Collins at the *Sentinel*. There was no return address. Inside the envelope Collins found a Babe Herman baseball card and a small folded-over piece of paper. On the paper was written: *Maybe next year. Keep this. You always wanted it.*

Wherever he was, Morris had been able to follow the World Series, to know that the Dodgers had lost again. Perhaps the Babe Herman card had traveled to Mexico in a diplomatic pouch before being mailed to Collins. It made Collins wonder if Morris had been given access to the New York newspapers in Moscow. As grim as it must be to live in that frigid and unfriendly city, far from home, it had to be worse to pick up the paper and read the ball scores and know that you could never come back, never see a real baseball game again, never see your friends and family.

In early January, the *Washington Star* carried a story in its society pages announcing the engagement of Mr. Matthew Steele and Mrs. Virginia Allen Bradford. Their marriage was set for June in the National Cathedral. Collins called his brother and he came by that day after work and they went to Killeen's and closed the place. Frank's comment was that they deserved each other. Collins didn't say anything. He was out of words.

Later in the month Alger Hiss was convicted of perjury in his retrial in federal court in New York. The jury didn't believe him when Hiss denied having spied for the Soviets. Collins didn't cover the trial, and he didn't write about it. He didn't believe Hiss, either.

And life carried on.

It had begun to snow lightly on the February day that Collins picked to travel over to the Evergreens Cemetery in Brooklyn where they had buried Karina. He paid the taxi driver and got out at the front gate. The place was empty, at least of the living. It wasn't ideal weather for visitors.

He got lost trying to find the correct plot. It took him almost thirty minutes of wandering around to find her gravestone, a gray-marble marker flat to the ground etched with her name in capital letters, KARINA LAZDA, and the years, 1920-1949.

Collins stood over the plot for the longest time, getting colder and colder, thinking about Karina. The snow grew heavier. He remembered the look on her face the first time they had made love. He thought about her lying on the pavement on Pearl Street, her life draining out of her, and how unfair it all was and about how little he actually knew about her, and yet how it seemed that they had lived a lifetime together in that September week.

He had promised Karina that he would keep her in his heart. He realized now that it wasn't a promise he could break, even if he had wanted to. It was cold comfort, but he hadn't lost her completely; he brought her with him, etched in his memories, wherever he went.

Standing there, Collins watched the snow accumulate, watched it fall softly and silently, covering her stone marker with a thin white blanket. He brushed the snow from the surface twice. Then he let it gather, and when he couldn't see her name any longer, he figured that it was time to go.

Author's Note

In 1946, after years of effort, U.S. Army Signal Intelligence Service cryptographers cracked the Soviet Union's diplomatic code. This top secret program, dubbed Venona, deciphered cables between Moscow and its diplomats and intelligence agents in New York and Washington.

Those cables contained the code names for more than 300 Americans in the State Department, the War Department, the Justice Department, the Treasury Department, and the Office of Strategic Services (the precursor to the Central Intelligence Agency) who had spied for the Soviets.

"No modern government was more thoroughly penetrated," the CIA's Hayden B. Peake later remarked. Venona cables proved instrumental in identifying Alger Hiss, Julius Rosenberg, Harry Dexter White, and other underground Soviet agents. In 1949 William Weisband, a Russian-born naturalized American citizen secretly working for Moscow (code name "Link"), disclosed the nature of Venona to the Soviets, prompting them to quickly alter their diplomatic code.

Not until 1995 were the Venona materials finally made public. What if they had been released earlier, perhaps even in the 1950s? In his book *Reds,* Ted Morgan has argued that a timely release of Venona "would have nipped McCarthyism in the bud, for the true facts about real spies would have made wild accusations about imaginary spies irrelevant." It's possible that American history might have taken a different course.

To better understand Soviet spycraft in the United States, I turned to the scholarship of John Earl Haynes, Harvey Klehr, Alexander Vassiliev, Steve Usdin, Ron Radosh, and Allen Weinstein. I also relied on *The Spy and His Masters: A Short Course in the Secret War* by Christopher Felix, a brief but fascinating insider's consideration of

Cold War espionage that I stumbled across in a Dublin bookstore many years ago. Any errors in fact or interpretation about the history of the period are mine alone.

Finally, *Herald Square*'s portrayal of New York City in the late 1940s was profoundly informed by discussions over the years with my father, Stephen C. Flanders. We talked about his experiences as a newspaperman in post-war New York and what it was like to be a returning veteran in that vibrant metropolis. It is my hope that I have, in turn, captured some of the spirit of that time in the pages of this novel.

About the Author

Jefferson Flanders has been a sportswriter, columnist, editor, and publishing executive. His parents met in the newsroom of the *New York Herald Tribune* in the late 1940s.

Made in the USA
Middletown, DE
10 August 2015